THE
KING
OF THE
IRONWOOD

THE
KING
OF THE
IRONWOOD

by

KIRSTY INIC

The King of the Ironwood
Copyright © 2023 by Kirsty Inic

First edition: October 2023

Paperback ISBN: 9780645167818
EPUB ISBN: 9780645167825

With special thanks to:
Editor; Chloe Hodge
Cover artist; Sara Oliver Design
Formatting; Susanna Kanto
Illustration; Tess Pollard

Want to stay in touch? Find me at:
www.kirstyinic.com
Instagram: @kirsty_inic
Facebook: Kirsty Inic Author
TikTok: @kirsty_inic

For my husband. Thank you will never be enough. I love you.

One

Theo's face swam before me, the darkness surrounding us disfiguring his features and billowing around him like a thick black cloak. I could still make out his toothy smile through the undulating shadow. It was the same grin that pulled at the scar on his cheek and crinkled the spattering of freckles across his nose. I couldn't believe he was standing in front of me. My heart beat fast in my chest as our eyes locked over the space between us. Dense fog swept over the deadened grass, the heavy cloud clinging to my skin. Somewhere amongst the darkness, the low caw of a night bird bristled the hairs on my neck. It wasn't safe in the woods at night. As I took a tentative step forward, Theo mimicked my movements—each step bringing us closer together until we stood only an arms-length apart. My fingers trembled as I tried to take his hand in my own—to feel the reassuring squeeze he would always give me—but something was wrong. Shifting my gaze to where I knew his hand should be, my stomach turned to stone at the set of long claws gleaming in its place. My eyes darted back to Theo's face, the colour quickly draining from my cheeks. His blue eyes, which once looked upon me with love and kindness, were replaced with giant red orbs brimming with hatred. The creature—who took on Theo's face—let out a menacing growl, making the shadows ripple around us. My chin trembled as a taloned hand arced towards me in a long, sweeping movement before a scream tore through me.

I blinked back the tears brimming my eyes and wiped a trembling hand over my sweat-slicked forehead. Unable to focus on any specific details, my room swam around me until my mind adjusted to being snapped out of the vision. I inhaled deeply through my nose, relishing in the smoky scent emitting from the fireplace, before letting my breath out slowly with a small sigh. Theo had been with me, but it wasn't *my* Theo. It wasn't my friend who had sacrificed himself to prevent me being pulled through a portal and suffering a deadly fate. It wasn't my Theo who had risked everything to help me rescue my mother from King Elias. He'd been a monster. A monster with the same eyes I had glimpsed amongst the shadows in the Ironwood. The ones that plagued my nightmares ever since my encounter with Elias. Heat cascaded over my chest and neck, my hands fumbling with the cotton bedsheets as I tried desperately to untangle them from my legs. The fire's usually calming warmth now felt stifling. As I swung my legs over the side of the mattress, the book I'd been reading tumbled to the stone floor, landing with a small thud by the side of my four-poster bed. For a few seconds, I stared down at the golden tree embossed on the cover before finally bending down to retrieve it. My hand lingered a few inches above the brown leather cover, apprehension gnawing at my insides. *Would touching it again cause another vision?* I'd been flicking through the fragile pages when the vision came on with blinding intensity. While the visions themselves didn't bother me, it was the uncertainty that stayed with me for days after. The constant battle of determining if they would one day come to fruition like Hazel believed, or if the sight was simply nonsense like the elders continued to tell me. The visions left me feeling light-headed and nauseous for hours. I honestly didn't know what to believe. There was very little written about the magic of visions, but until I could figure out if they meant anything, I would continue to heed them with caution. Especially when they spoke of my loved ones.

With a resounding sigh, I plucked the book from the floor, and my fingers tingled with the remnants of the book's magic. Ever since King Elias pulled Theo through the portal, I'd been constantly leafing through Althea's book. As she was the Wise Witch who had predicted the prophecy about my uniting the Kingdom of Ellesmere and overthrowing the cruel king, I'd hoped that her book would contain the key to finally putting a stop to his reign. That it would contain even a hint of a clue to how I could rescue my friend. From the moment Theo's fingers had slipped from my grasp, my heart had ached with the apprehension that I may never see him again. And, with each passing day that brought no new leads as to how to get Theo back, the ache that stemmed from the broken pieces of my heart only grew. There was nothing I wanted more than to have Theo home, where he belonged. My eyes had trawled through every page, clinging to each word as if it was a lifeline preventing me from breaking into a million pieces. Flicking through the pages again, I stopped at the section reciting the prophecy. I ran a finger over the looping letters, Althea's messy scrawl covering every inch of space, remembering what the prophecy spoke of—only the spirit witch would have the power to defeat King Elias. Turning the page—careful not to tear the thin paper—my hand brushed between the book's inner seam where a thin rip ran the length of the binding. I'd come across the missing page in the early days of Theo's disappearance. Immediately, my mind had conjured up all the possibilities of why someone would remove it. Did it hold the key to fulfilling the prophecy? Was it even important that the page was missing? It had been torn so close to the spine it was almost invisible, yet the paper was rough beneath my touch. Whoever removed it had been extremely careful to prevent anyone from noticing it was missing. *Who could have taken it?* My mind reeled with the many possibilities. I only hoped it wasn't the other person the prophecy spoke about. Shaking my head to clear the erratic thoughts clouding my mind, I placed Althea's book on the nightstand. My fingers lingered momentarily on the soft leather before I pulled them back. Stretching my aching muscles, I padded across the stone floor to the large window by the end of the bed. Early morning light bathed the room in silvery hues as I pushed aside the sheer curtains. Stars still glistened against the blanket of deep blue, winking prettily as they shone down upon the grounds of Ellesmere Castle. Sprawling green hills as far as the eye could see and garden beds filled to bursting with varieties of sweet-scented flowers were only a few of the beautiful features that made the kingdom so mesmerising. Even in the eerie light of early morning it still took my breath away. A faint golden glow peeked over the tops of the Ironwood Mountains as I stared at the horizon, signalling dawn would soon be approaching. A cool breeze made the white curtains flutter lazily, the scent of dew-soaked grass filling the room. Goosebumps prickled my exposed skin, making me shiver, but I embraced the coolness. The warm nights of Mabon had long since passed, leaving room for the cold tendrils of Samhain to creep into every crevice of the castle.

Lately, I found myself out amongst the grounds more often. Despite the crispness of the air, the gardens brought me a sense of peace—something I couldn't find within the stone walls of the castle. It still didn't feel real to me that this beautiful place was my home. I had only resided in Ellesmere for just over a month, but it felt more like my home than Pryhollow ever had. I *belonged* in Ellesmere. Somewhere I could be my true self. I still thought of my first home every now and then. It was usually when I suffered a gruelling day at the hands of the elders, or when my visions plagued my mind with darkness. I would often think of my mother's apothecary; the cosiness of the parlour as a warm fire blazed in the fireplace, and the smell of freshly cut herbs being bottled into jars. Mostly, I thought of Maeve. One of my mother's oldest friends, she had been the grandmother I'd never had. She had been a part of my life since I was a child and, as the weeks slowly rolled over, my heart ached to see her again. I missed her desperately.

Despite the sun inching its way over the peaks of the Ironwood Mountains, bathing the Kingdom of Ellesmere in a golden glow, whisps of shadow continued to hover above the Ironwood. A chill that had nothing to do with the cold stiffened my spine. I watched the shadows swirl above the precise place the ash tree resided. A week had passed since Alpheus came bearing the terrifying news of the growing darkness spotted amongst the murky trees of the dreaded Ironwood, which meant Theo had been stuck there for two weeks. A fortnight had passed since my friend's capture, and we were no closer to finding a way to rescue him. Gnawing at my bottom lip, I continued to watch the darkening shadow float in the air like a growing storm cloud. Its presence was a constant reminder of what awaited Ellesmere should I fail in fulfilling the prophecy. Rubbing a hand over the back of my neck, I turned from the window, not wanting to look at the growing shadows any longer. My eyes itched with the need for sleep, but my mind was too preoccupied to drift off into a dreamless slumber. My fingertips tingled with the need to use my magic and I longed to release some of the anxious tension that had tightened my chest over the last few days. Throwing on a pair of dark pants, I threaded a leather belt around my waist, securing the silver buckle tightly, and pulled on a blue sweater. I ran my fingers through my unruly curls, attempting to tame them slightly before giving up and pulling my hair into a messy top knot. A long ornate mirror hung on the wall opposite my bed and, giving myself a once over, I let out a long sigh. Deep, dark circles sat under my hazel eyes, making me look even more tired than I felt. My cheeks lacked their usual rosy complexion and my lips were chapped from my constant biting at them—a habit I recently picked up when the stress of current events weighed down on me. Turning my back on my reflection, I pulled open the heavy wooden door, hoping to find some peace in the castle grounds.

The hallways were blissfully quiet at this time of the morning. The castle's patrons remained in their beds, lost in dreams or nightmares of their own. I enjoyed the early start. It was the only time in my day when I could escape the whispers, side-glances, and the watchful eyes of the elders. A time I could escape my responsibilities of being the spirit witch and Ellesmere's next queen and just enjoy being the old Braelyn. The Braelyn who got into mischief with Maeve while my mother pretended not to notice. The girl who could spend time with Theo at the Forest Festival and enjoy the freedom of not having to worry about my actions affecting anyone other than myself. These were the memories I focused on when my duties became too much and when the pressure of the prophecy became so overwhelming it felt like I couldn't breathe. I missed the simplicity of being a witch without the prophecy and the weight of a kingdom hanging over my head.

As I walked down the north wing staircase, the sound of my boots on the stones echoed around the empty stairwell. Coloured tapestries depicting great battles long passed lined the walls, but despite their thick woven fabric, they did little to keep out the chill. Reaching the grand staircase, dawn light streamed through the large intricate window, bathing the foyer in beautiful pink and orange hues. Incorporating all elements, the window's silver design came together in a perfect circle, symbolising the spirit witch. Each time I looked at it, my chest would tighten and my hands would tingle—the reality of my imminent future was a reminder everywhere, and it weighed heavy on my shoulders. Continuing past the foyer, the large double doors leading to the front gardens loomed in front of me. Pushing on the wood with both hands, the heavy oak door groaned in protest, the sound echoing around the vast space. Scrunching my nose at the sharp squeal of the hinges, I hurried through the open door. The sound would have surely woken someone, and I wasn't ready to deal with Mrs Boswell, my lady's maid, just yet. Closing the door with a resounding *thunk*, I hurried down the steep front steps to the expansive gardens below. The moment my boots stepped onto the lush grass, it was like the world around me stilled. The silence of dawn settled over me, calming the jittery feeling rippling through me. The soft golden light warmed my face and, despite the terrifying events of the morning, I smiled. My mind felt calmer than it had in days.

It was only a short walk to the gardens where most of my magic training took place. Since Theo's capture, the elders had deemed it necessary for me to learn how to properly wield my spirit magic. It hadn't taken long for rumours to spread around the castle of the magic I used to rescue my mother, and while some people believed me to be a hero, most of Ellesmere's citizens thought I was reckless. It was said recklessness that the elders were concerned about. The magic of spirit wielders was connected to our emotions and, when in control, we were like any other witch or warlock. Lose that control and we could very well set the world alight. Many witches and warlocks were dispatched to assist in my magic training, but there were only two people I trusted enough to guide me. The elders had eventually allowed Grey Bishop and Verena Porter to reside in the castle as my instructors. My estranged grandmother, Hazel, had introduced me to both when I first learned of the prophecy. They were two of the most talented elemental wielders in Ellesmere and had both become my most trusted friends. As far as the elements were concerned though, they were complete opposites. Verena's fire magic burned as brightly as her red hair—her flames often dancing around her like a phoenix mid-flight. Grey, on the other hand, was calm, his water magic bright and crisp like the first fall of winter. Together, their magic was a beautiful and deadly combination. Grey and Verena had been instrumental in teaching me how to wield my water and fire magic back at Hazel's cottage, and under their watchful gaze, I had managed to gain more control of my power.

Rounding the trees blocking the training area from the rest of the garden, my eyes widened at the lonesome figure sitting on the dew-specked grass. I hadn't expected anyone else to be out here this early. His back was turned towards me, his blue shirt spotted with morning condensation.

"Grey." My voice sounded loud against the quietness of the morning.

Turning his head, Grey smiled back at me. His mousy-brown hair fell over his forehead, shielding his deep honey eyes from the growing morning light. If he was surprised to see me, he didn't show it. Instead, he waved, gesturing me over to where he sat. Sitting beside him, I crossed my legs underneath me, the dampness of the ground seeping through my pants, making me shudder against the cold. Grey sat with his elbows resting on his knees, and I glimpsed the faint twisting blue lines covering his bare arms. He'd been out here using magic. Clearly, I wasn't the only one who struggled to sleep these days.

After Theo was taken and Grey had been dispatched to the castle, he'd made his intentions clear of helping with Theo's rescue. Whatever we needed, no matter how dangerous, he would help. It was at the end of a very gruelling magic lesson that Grey had eventually confided in me about his reason why. He cared deeply for Theo—and not just in the way I cared for him. When he spoke of Theo, his eyes would sparkle and turn distant, a smile tugging at one corner of his mouth as though recalling a long lost memory of the two of them together. I'd remembered the way Grey's gaze had lingered on Theo's face the night of the Forest Festival and the spark that seemed to charge the air around them as they spoke. The way Grey had leaned closer to Theo's touch, his face lighting up as he whispered to him. Grey's love for Theo was evident, but there was no mistaking the sadness that constantly lined his face the longer we went without answers. I wouldn't rest until they were reunited. Until *all* of us were reunited.

"You're up early," Grey said softly. His eyes never left the hills.

"I've been up for hours. And, it appears, so have you." I pointed to the pale blue marks lining his forearms, and he chuckled softly.

"I struggle to sleep these days. Every time I close my eyes, images of Th—" His voice cracked at the beginning of Theo's name before it trailed off. He hung his head between his hands, his eyes downcast.

My heart ached for him. I missed my friend more than anything, but the pain Grey must feel was unfathomable. The thought of having the one person who truly understands you being taken away so suddenly sent a chill over my skin.

"We're going to find him, Grey. I promise. I won't rest until Theo is back with us." Taking his hand in my own, I gave it a tight squeeze, trying to put as much reassurance in this one small gesture as possible.

Finally, Grey looked at me. The sadness brimming his rich golden eyes made my own tingle with unshed tears.

"I know," he whispered into the air between us, before giving my hand one last squeeze. Getting to his feet, Grey held out his arm for me to take and pulled me up.

"I'm guessing you didn't come out here to simply ask how I was," he said, tucking his hands into his pockets. The blue tinge still visible above his black pants.

"No," I replied. "I actually came out here for some peace. Being out in the open is the only place I find comfort these days."

Turning my head to take in the view of the hills, I closed my eyes and breathed deeply. Dawn was well and truly behind us. Sunlight reached over the Ironwood Mountains, sweeping over the grounds and awakening the kingdom. The sweet smell of grass and pine tickled my nose; a scent I'd come to associate with Ellesmere. Imagining the tension in my shoulders drifting away as if it was a leaf on the breeze, my muscles relaxed, but it wasn't enough to put my mind at ease. When I opened my eyes, Grey had turned his face back to the scenic view, but his eyes soon settled back on me.

"I'm always here for you, Grey," I added.

"I know," he whispered. He kicked the damp ground, the toe of his boot worrying at a tuft of grass. "Have you found anything?"

My stomach lurched. Every day, Grey asked me if we'd made any progress with Theo's disappearance, and every day my heart would thud loudly in my chest, my pulse like rapid fire beneath my skin when I would tell him, "*No.*"

Today was no different.

He gave me a small smile and nodded once. A few seconds passed, neither of us wanting to puncture the solitude that settled between us. Eventually, Grey broke the silence.

"Should we get a quick lesson in before Mrs Boswell comes to steal you away for the day?"

The thought of my lady's maid bustling down through the dirt to chastise me for being out on the grounds—rather than making myself presentable for the day—made a laugh bubble up inside me. She was a nice enough woman, but the permanent scowl on her face was enough to send anyone running for the Ironwood.

"Better late than never, but perhaps you should hold off on using any magic until you've been to see my mother."

Grey looked down at his hands, the blue streaks twisting over his arms now more prominent. Without the healing elixir to cure him, he was at risk. Magic always had consequences. With every flourish of our element, our soul suffered, the magic drawing from our essence and marking our skin. If left untreated, it could be fatal.

"Okay, deal," he said. "Now, let's begin."

A small smirk fluttered across my face as I took a few short steps backwards. My hands hung by my sides, the tingling already growing more intense with each of my footfalls. Small snowflakes rained down around us, and Grey's smile intensified into a grin. With a click of my fingers, a ball of water appeared from thin air and floated above my outstretched hand. The cool breeze caressed my face, loosening stray pieces of hair from my bun. Grey watched me carefully, eyes narrowed in the direction of the rippling orb. Magic bubbled up inside me, reacting to the anger and frustration that had built within over the last few days. The tingling in my fingers grew with sharp intensity before I released my magic in a blinding show of strength.

Two

The watery orb in my hand solidified to ice and, with a quick flick of my wrist, it flew towards the trees before shattering against the bark into thousands of tiny shards. Thick grey mist swept across the grass, consuming everything in its path. It swarmed around Grey's feet, enveloping them in an undulating cloud before continuing down the steep slope of the hills. My heart beat a fast rhythm in my chest as an internal flame ignited beneath my skin. Earth magic blossomed beneath my fingertips, pulling the creeping vines from the trees. They snaked along the ground, encircling me in their strong embrace. Lightning followed, lacing through my fingers with white-hot intensity. It struck the ground with a resounding crack, raising the small hairs along my arms. Grey nodded his approval, his golden eyes assessing me closely. A satisfied smile pulled at the corner of my mouth and, wanting to impress him further, I conjured more magic. With a sharp click of my fingers, deadly blue flames flickered to life. They sparked against the electricity still curling around my wrist, the crackling pop sending a thrill over my heated skin. Calling to the elements, magic ignited in my heart, my body tingling with the adrenaline of wielding it. The world around me was illuminated in golden hues, yet the more I conjured, the more I craved, until a darkness spurred to life deep within me. The once calming flow of my magic increased to something more sinister, the air around us growing heavy with each beckoning call. Smoky tendrils of dark magic tinged the edges of my vision. They mixed with the potency of my fire magic, turning the edges of my flame a deep ebony. The magic flowing through my veins intensified. I relished in the feel of its power—the strength it made me feel when I reached out to it and the satisfaction that I had somehow been able to wield it. What would happen if I tried to conjure more? My heart beat faster at the prospect, my fingers twitching at the promise. Grey stood about ten paces away from me, his hands crossed tightly over his chest. A small frown pulled at his thin brows as he watched my movements and a small voice in the back of my mind warned me to be careful. "*The darkness beckons,*" it said. "*Tread carefully.*"

I needed to stop.

Reining in my magic before the darkness could take hold, the mist surrounding us slowly receded, disappearing until it was like it had never been. With one last resounding crack, the lightning painting my fingers a silvery blue sparked once more before disappearing into the air around us. My darkening flame fizzled like a snuffed candle, the erratic tingling in my fingertips the only indication of my magic use.

Grey walked towards me, a quizzical look lighting his eyes. "Well, the strength of your magic has definitely grown over the last week, but for a moment there, it felt like you were holding something back." He raised a questioning brow in my direction.

Grey's knowledge of magic and how to wield it was one of the things I admired most about him. He was never quick to judge if something took me longer to learn, and he was as patient as he was kind. On the other hand, it meant very little escaped his assessing gaze.

Averting my eyes, I toyed with the hem of my sweater, contemplating whether to tell him of the darkness lingering within my grasp.

"Brae," he continued, "if something's wrong, you can talk to me."

A weak smile tugged at the corner of my mouth. *Could I?*

I thought about my lessons back at Hazel's cottage. I'd always managed to have great strength when wielding earth, air, and water magic, but fire had been a different story. It was erratic and dangerous. Each time I conjured it, I would struggle to contain it, but ever since my encounter with the ash tree, conjuring all elements hadn't felt at all hard. King Elias had noticed the dark magic lingering inside me and had taunted me with it when I'd rescued my mother, but now it felt different. The more magic I summoned and the stronger I felt, the more potent this dark magic became. While part of me tried to lock it away, a bigger part craved the power I felt when summoning it.

This, above all else, is what terrified me.

Grey's eyes searched my face in the hopes of discovering my secret. Picking at the chinks in my armour until he would eventually find the wound festering inside. Something seemed to dawn in his knowing gaze. He opened his mouth, but before he could utter a word, the sharp crack of a broken branch pulled our attention towards the thick line of trees. A tall figure picked its way through the pines' lower branches before a familiar face emerged into the sun's golden rays.

"I thought I might find you out here, sweetheart." A small smirk pulled up the corner of Julien's mouth, and my breath hitched in my throat.

He'd been away from Ellesmere Castle for a few days, venturing back to the Ironwood Village to check on his apothecary and bring back stock for my mother to use in her potions and salves. Since Theo's capture, we'd spent almost every waking minute together, pouring over books in the castle library in the hopes of finding a way to stop King Elias. The time he'd spent away had been the longest we'd gone without seeing each other. Now that he stood in front of me, my legs felt like dead weights tethered to the ground.

Julien's deep brown eyes found mine across the field, his smile deepening to reveal a small dimple on his cheek. I wanted to run to him, to feel the warmth of his arms encircled around my waist, but with Grey's watchful eye not too far away, I stood my ground, merely staring as his muscled form grew closer with every beat of his heavy black boots.

"Julien, it's good to have you home," Grey said, puncturing the silence and clapping him on the back.

Julien smiled warmly at him, his brown eyes creasing at the sides. "Your mother sends her regards, and Gillie misses you."

At the mention of his family, Grey's shoulders drooped. He had left his mother and younger sister back at the Ironwood Village so he could assist in finding Theo and teach me in the meantime. I knew the empty feeling Grey felt at being separated from his family and I hoped to reunite them one day.

"Gillie also said, and I quote, 'Tell Braelyn she better be taking care of my brother or else.'" Julien had come to a stop a mere arms-length away from me. All I needed to do was reach out, but my hand trembled. The thought of finally feeling the warmth of his skin sent my stomach into a flutter.

Since our brief kiss before my mother's rescue, Julien and I hadn't spoken of what that moment had meant to us. We'd lapsed into a comfortable relationship that, for the moment, seemed to revolve solely around Theo's capture and our attempts to save him. While this didn't bother me, I couldn't deny how my feelings towards Julien had only grown in the time we'd spent together since. I also couldn't help wondering if Julien perhaps felt the same fluttering in his stomach that seemed to affect me any time he was near.

Grey's light laugh echoed around us, pulling me from my thoughts. I recalled the sweet brown-haired girl I'd protected against King Elias's guards. She had been kind, like her brother, and a small smile pulled at my lips as I imagined her telling Julien to pass on her protective message.

"So, how's the magic training going? Learnt any new tricks yet?" Julien raised a brow, his lips quirked up at the corner in a lopsided smile.

Taking a small step forward, I tilted my head up and stared through my thick lashes into Julien's dark eyes. His inner fire glistened in their depths, sending my heart into a frenzied pitter-patter, but he never took his eyes off mine.

"How about I show you?" My voice was light and teasing, which only caused Julien's gaze to turn molten.

I took a few steps away from him and flicked my eyes to Grey, whose eyebrow quirked up as he tried to keep the smile off his face. Julien shrugged off his black coat, tossing it to the side where it landed in a heap on the grass. He rolled his shirt sleeves up to his elbows, exposing his muscled forearms. Something stirred deep in my belly, but I pushed the feeling aside, focusing solely on my magic and definitely *not* how the action of Julien raking a hand through his curled hair sent my pulse racing.

"Okay, Braelyn. Let's see what you've got." Julien's voice echoed around me, a teasing smirk picking up the corner of his mouth.

Heat flushed my skin as flames flickered to life in my palms. They danced in the cool breeze with bright intensity, waiting for my command. Julien mimicked my movements, bright orange flames licking up his forearms. He winked playfully at me, and a smile lit up my face. I'd missed him these last few days.

"Don't go easy on me," I shouted towards him, my voice carrying on the light breeze. My fire magic grew more potent with each second that ticked by.

"I wouldn't dare," he replied before sending a torrent of blazing flames in my direction.

Our fiery battle didn't last long. Julien was unable to keep up with the intensity of my magic. Dark red lines marked his tanned forearms as he wiped the sweat from his forehead. That's not to say he'd gone easy on me. Scorch marks lined the grass where he'd sent a searing line of flames snaking along the ground in my direction. I'd deflected them easily enough, my water magic dousing the flames before they were able to do any real damage. I had retaliated with a barrage of fire, each flickering ball radiating enough heat to devour a small field. Julien managed to sidestep the first few before once again conjuring his own flame. The wall of fire absorbed the remainder of my magic, each ball consumed by the heat permeating from his natural ability to wield even the deadliest of flames. Small embers still burned amongst the charred grass and, stomping them out with my foot, I bent down to inspect the damage. Taking a deep breath, I brushed my hand over the dead grass, manifesting my earth magic. Fresh seedlings sprouted from the soot and ash until any evidence of Julien's fire had disappeared beneath fresh greenery.

It was late morning by now, and I was surprised no one had come to look for me. Maybe Mrs Boswell, in her haste to organise the rest of the castle staff, had forgotten to fetch me. I scoffed at my wishful thinking. Mrs Boswell ran a tight ship, and it was more likely she was running about the castle in the hopes of finding me. Only my mother, the elders, and my friends knew of my training sessions. The elders had thought it best no one else know of the spirit witch's concerns with magic and, honestly, I preferred it this way. The last thing I needed while learning to master my magic was an audience. Besides, Mrs Boswell would never freely admit she had misplaced the spirit witch. It would tarnish her reputation. She organised every aspect of my day, from waking me in the morning and selecting my clothing, to ferrying me between my lessons with each of the elders. Since arriving at the castle, the elders had taken up residence in the throne room, acting as my advisors until I was ready to be crowned queen at the end of the Samhain Festival in a few weeks' time. They oversaw the running of the kingdom and taught me valuable lessons to prepare me for ruling. Mrs Boswell coached me on etiquette, how to read the language of old, and the proper way to speak like the queen I was born to be. She had been in the employ of my father and grandfather for years and it was her job to make sure I was ready to ascend the throne when the time came. So, if she hadn't found me yet, it appeared I was off the hook for as long as I could avoid her.

"Should we head to the library, Braelyn, to see if we can find anything new?" Julien looked at me expectantly, before turning his gaze to Grey. "You're welcome too, Grey. The more eyes the better."

"Anything to keep me out of the war path that is Mrs Boswell," I replied.

I could imagine her pinched lips and deep scowl as if she was standing in front of me, her hands on her plump hips as she tried to tell me how I needed to be more responsible.

"Grey, are you up for it?" I asked, my voice soft.

The pained look on Grey's face was answer enough. With each dead end, he only grew more distant from our sessions at the library. He'd told us it was too difficult to continue searching without finding the answers needed to bring Theo home.

Placing a tender hand on Grey's shoulder, I tried to give him a reassuring smile, but it was hard to comfort him when the same thoughts often plagued my mind. Despite countless hours of searching, we were still yet to find a solution, but I wouldn't stop. Not until I found a way to bring Theo home and put a stop to Elias.

"It's okay, Grey. We'll let you know if we find anything."

Grey gave me a weak smile before he turned on his heel, making his way back up through the trees towards the castle, his hands stuffed in his pockets. My chest tightened once again. The anxiety I'd managed to dispel earlier this morning returned with full force. My hand worried at my wool sweater, my fingers kneading at the ache beneath my ribs.

"He's still taking it pretty hard, isn't he?"

"Wouldn't you?" I replied, looking up at Julien's face.

He smiled sadly, but there was a hardness in the set of his jaw that hadn't been there a moment ago. "The difference with me, Braelyn, is I would see the world burn before I let anything happen to you."

Three

The library was in the south wing. It was seldom used by any of the occupants residing at Ellesmere Castle, which meant it was the perfect spot to escape the watchful gaze of the elders and Mrs Boswell. Julien promised to meet me at our usual place as soon as he'd been tended to by my mother. At the end of our training session, his arms had been covered up to the elbows in deep red marks. My hands remained clear—the one upside to being a spirit wielder. I was able to conjure more magic than other witches and warlocks at any given time while still resisting the pull on my soul. Still, even as the spirit witch, I had limitations. The more potent the magic, the more exhausted I became. From experience, using too much wasn't something I intended on doing again. Memories of the night we rescued my mother often hovered in the back of my mind—the heaviness of my limbs, the sharp ringing in my ears, the weariness that seemed to seep into my bones at having conjured too much. These thoughts teetered on the edge of my mind each time I summoned my spirit magic. It would take an immense amount of power for me to stop Elias and I only hoped I'd be strong enough to wield it.

Castle residents intent on reaching their destinations bustled around me as I climbed the south staircase. The witch who assisted Mrs Boswell bustled out of the door leading to the kitchens, a steaming basket clutched beneath her arm. In my haste to get out into the fresh air, I'd skipped breakfast, and the sweet smell of fresh bread wafting up the stairs did little to soothe the sharp pang in my stomach. As I moved away from the delicious scent, a witch—who looked to be about my age—knocked into my shoulder, her eyes widening.

"Apologies, my queen," she mumbled and, with a quick curtsey, she hurried off in the opposite direction. Her head was bowed over a bunch of scrolls I was almost certain came from the elders' chamber.

The new title was something I still couldn't get used to. No matter how many people called me their queen, I didn't feel it was a station I was entirely ready for—or had earned, for that matter. Mrs Boswell assured me that with time and after more lessons with the elders and herself, I would feel more at ease when the time came to take my rightful place on the throne. I wasn't so sure. But these were the cards the elements had dealt me and I would make sure the outcome tipped in my favour.

The noise of the castle fell away as I continued up the winding stairs to the library. Being amongst the thousands of books was one of few instances I enjoyed being stuck within the castle's walls, but each time the doors came into view, my hands trembled. The prospect of coming across yet another dead end loomed like a dark cloud in the depths of my mind. Today was no different. As the heavy wooden doors became visible, my hands twitched. Fear clawed at the back of my throat, choking off the slow, easy breaths I practised when the anxiety became too overwhelming. My thoughts moved to Theo—to the torture he must be enduring at the hands of the former king. At the hands of *my* negligence. Were they starving him? Hurting him? These questions plagued my mind constantly. A constant barrage of pain I endured every day. I knew they wouldn't stop until Theo was safe. The anxiety I'd experienced all my life had only worsened at Theo's disappearance. Now, there lay the weight of constant blame I felt for not being able to save him sooner. I leant against the wall, the chill from the stones seeping through my sweater and sending a cold rush over my skin. My breath hitched at the stark temperature change, but it was enough to pull my attention from the anxious beast clawing to be released. Inhaling through my nose, I let the breath out slowly, counting to five before opening my eyes again. The dark oak doors waited patiently before me and, as I pushed myself away from the wall, the tightness in my chest became more bearable. Opening the door, the hinges groaned under the weight of the wood, making the noise echo through the vacant hall. My eyes lingered on the staircase in the hopes Julien would come traipsing up any second, but it remained empty. I let out a heavy sigh before lowering my gaze and stepping through the doors.

The room still felt cool and, with a quick snap of my fingers, a spark ignited in my palm, sending a warm thrill up my arm. After lighting a few of the sconces by the door, the large room became bathed in beautiful hues of oranges and reds, the warm light deepening the dark grain of the mahogany shelves. The weight I seemed to carry on my shoulders slackened as the sweet, musky smell of ink and paper wafted up my nose. A smile tugged at the corner of my mouth. It was a smell I would never grow tired of. Books had been my greatest companions growing up. Living in a town filled with superstitious people made for a lonely time. So, after school, I would rush home to immerse myself in the stories of brave heroes and heroines. Sitting for hours in the small parlour at the back of our apothecary, I would pour over the words that would set my soul alight. Now, being the heroine of my own story, the worlds I'd found comfort in felt too real.

Keeping my flame alight, I made my way through the tight, twisting shelves towards the back of the library. Some of these books hadn't been opened in years and a thick coating of dust layered the untouched spines. When I stepped around a rickety bookshelf, the space instantly grew brighter. The sun's tendrils reached lazily through the windowpanes, making the large bay window glisten like hundreds of sparkling diamonds. My hand tingled with the absence of magic as I extinguished my flame, but I pushed the feeling aside and plucked a book off the closest shelf. Julien and I had poured over countless books about magic, potions, and weapons, all in the hopes of finding something, *anything*, that would bring us closer to stopping Elias and destroying the circulum—the taloned tipped ring he used to siphon the magic of others. Each time it resulted in slammed books and often several unsavoury words from Julien. Each time it became more disheartening. Pulling over the rolling ladder, I climbed the metal rungs and pulled out a rather dusty book from halfway up the shelf. The dust billowed around me in a musky cloud and a loud sneeze nearly sent me careening to the stone floor below.

Death by book. Wouldn't that be a headline.

Tucking the heavy tome under my arm, I descended the ladder one rung at a time before jumping down the last few steps, landing with a thud on the hard ground as the impact reverberated through my legs. Usually, I would curl up on the soft cushions by the window and lose myself in the words of each book piled up beside me. I was too fidgety to relax today, so I pulled one of the rickety chairs out from underneath the table, cringing as the legs screeched along the stone floor. Taking a seat on the hard wooden chair, I stared down at the cover, settling into the library's usual blanket of silence. I began sifting through the text, hoping something would jump out at me. Time seemed to move at a snail's pace with each flick of the page, but as I continued to read another chapter, a growing irritation began to build inside me.

Nothing. There was nothing.

Roughly turning yet another useless page, a faint tapping in-between one of the shelves caught my attention. Spinning around to face the darkness between the bookcases, I gnawed on the inside of my cheek, my eyes roaming the long, dimly lit aisles. The shadows moved like a silent stream, sending a cold chill tingling over my skin. The tapping grew louder and I clicked my middle finger against my thumb, conjuring a small fire in the hopes the extra light would calm my nerves. Flickering like a candle flame, my fire magic grew with the fear blossoming in the pit of my stomach. As quickly as it came, the tapping stopped. The air around me felt charged with the angst sending my pulse racing beneath my skin.

A light touch on my shoulder was my undoing. The flame in my hand faltered as a small squeak sputtered from my lips.

"By the elements, Braelyn, it's me," Julien said, his hands gripping the tops of my arms. He eyed me like I might break apart if he let me go.

Swallowing hard, I reined in my magic. My heart thundered against my ribs and my veins pulsed with static energy.

"Why would you sneak up on me like that?" I shouted, my voice sounding high-pitched and shrill. My fingers trembled as they swiped at the trickle of sweat beading along my forehead.

"I'm sorry," he replied quickly, brushing a soothing thumb over my cheek. "But you knew I was meeting you here. I thought you would have heard me."

He shrugged off his coat before taking a seat next to me.

Logically, he was right, but my vision from this morning had my nerves running wild. The shadows of the bookshelves hadn't helped. I gave him a brief smile before shifting my gaze, knowing my face had a knack for bearing all my secrets. But, of course, Julien's assessing eyes were too quick. Taking my chin softly between his fingers, he tilted my head back to face him. His dark eyes searched my own for the secret that had plagued me all morning.

"What is it, sweetheart? I know that look." Julien's tone was soft and my heart constricted at the concern lacing his words.

"It's nothing," I whispered, trying and failing to keep my voice steady.

Julien's grip on my chin tightened the tiniest amount, preventing me from turning my head.

"Tell me the truth," he breathed out.

It's not that I didn't want to tell him what had happened this morning—every fibre in my body urged me to blurt out everything—but I had hoped to understand it better before telling anyone. Sighing, I filled him in on the visions I'd been having each time I touched Althea's book and of the missing page I'd come across. Julien listened carefully and without interruption, his brow furrowed in concentration as I told him everything. By the time I finished, my chest felt lighter for it.

After a moment of silence, Julien got to his feet and paced along the window, his arms folded across his broad chest. His shirt sleeves were still folded up, the sun-kissed skin no longer riddled with red marks.

"Do you think this has something to do with what Elias has planned for Ellesmere?" I asked, my hands worrying at the book's pages.

"It's hard to say. As only spirit wielders can see visions, there's very little known about them and the part they play in magic. If only we could find another spirit wielder and figure out what this all means."

"Well, Elias put a stop to that, didn't he?"

My hands flicked idly at the corner of the page, the paper soft beneath my fingertips. As I toyed with the fraying edges, a few sentences jumped out at me. I was vaguely aware of Julien talking to me, but his voice fell away as I concentrated on reading the words.

Darkness plagued the world, growing stronger with each piece of magic Lilith obtained. And so, she was burnt at the stake. The first and only witch put to death by the magic she so willingly conjured.

I scanned the passage three times to make sure I'd read it correctly. It was as if a candle had been lit, clearing the fog clouding the depths of my mind. All this time, we'd been searching the library for the wrong answer in the right place.

"Braelyn, are you listening to me?" Julien's voice washed over me, his face pinched in concern as he looked between me and the open book on the table.

"I found the answer," I whispered, a smile pulling at the corners of my mouth.

"What do you mean?" Julien stood beside me, peering over my shoulder at the page.

"All this time we've been searching these books for the answer to stop Elias, but it's not these pages that hold the key." Thrusting the book towards Julien, I pointed to the sentences that finally gave me hope—a feeling I had begun to think would never come.

"By the elements, Braelyn. Tell me again exactly what Alpheus told you the night he came to see you."

My brow furrowed as I tried to recall word-for-word what Alpheus had said. The jackalope had been instrumental in helping us find our way out of the ash tree clearing not so long ago. Without him, we would have never made it to the castle to save my mother in time.

"He told me that evil was growing in the Ironwood and that, if it was released, it would wreak havoc on Ellesmere."

Ever since Alpheus spoke these words to me, I'd been wondering what it was that Elias could possibly do to cause so much destruction. My mind had immediately conjured up the vision I'd endured at the Forest Festival—of the terrifying creatures I'd seen attack the Ironwood Village—but they couldn't be what Elias wanted. After Alpheus left me that night, I came to the library and searched through hundreds of books in the hopes of finding an image of the creatures from my vision. After hours of searching, I had finally found it. The creatures I'd seen were called monstrum. They were evil beings created from necromancy and dark magic. Once summoned, they would kill and maim until the witch or warlock responsible for their creation told them to stop—or their blackened heart was destroyed. Even if Elias had resorted to necromancy, creating these creatures would take time and that was something he did not have. The longer he waited, the more powerful my magic would become. He wouldn't let that happen. I was Elias's biggest threat and he wouldn't risk giving me time to grow stronger. No, he was planning on unleashing something else and, if my assumptions were correct, it would result in the end of Ellesmere.

"Julien, what if the evil Alpheus spoke of isn't a creature of Elias's making, but one that already existed and required a great amount of power to summon?"

Julien had begun pacing again and my watchful gaze followed him carefully as his bushy brows continued to dip lower over his eyes. "You don't think he means to unleash…" Julien's voiced trailed off, the tension in his arms the only tell-tale sign of his childhood fear bristling his usual stoic facade.

"I think he plans to put his fascination with dark magic to great use and practice what he learnt from one of the greatest dark witches of our time."

My mind recalled the story Elias had told me on the night he'd taken Theo. He'd spoken of his fascination with the dark witch's grimoire and how he'd deemed it a gift from the elements that he was destined for greater things. Slowly, my mind began to piece everything together. Julien stopped his pacing and turned to face me, his eyes widening as a spark of realisation finally settled over him.

"You think he's going to use The Book of Lilith to summon dark magic?" Despite his faltering earlier, Julien's voice now held a note of steely vehemence. "Do you think it could hold the key to stopping him?"

The grimoire Elias stole from my mother to complete the circulum must hold some crucial information these books didn't. Gnawing on my lip, I tried to connect all the pieces together—Alpheus's warning, my vision of Theo's red eyes and taloned fingers, and the information I'd found in the book. It could only mean one thing.

"I think it could give us the answers to stopping him, but I also think it will tell us what sort of evil Elias plans to unleash."

Taking a deep breath, I turned my eyes back to Julien. He watched me closely, his hands resting flat on the tabletop as he leant towards me with rapt attention. My stomach rolled at the thought of what could happen should Elias succeed, but what troubled me more is the fear I knew Julien would feel once I told him.

"I think he's going to try and unleash the Wraiths of Umbra."

Four

Julien's shoulders tensed at my words, his childhood fear of seeing the Wraiths of Umbra in the basement of his apothecary rising to the surface. He'd spoken of this only once, but I recalled the look of terror on his face when he'd told me and Theo in the grimy tunnels beneath Ellesmere Castle. My throat tightened as guilt rolled in the depths of my belly. This was my fault. If I'd never come to Ellesmere, Theo would be safe and Julien wouldn't have to face the creatures he feared. These thoughts had plagued my waking mind since the day King Elias fled, pushing through the barrier I tried to maintain. Each false lead and dead end we reached only made the tightness in my chest worse. If it wasn't for me, none of this would be happening.

Julien's dark eyes studied me closely, a knowing look sparking in their depths. He came over to where I sat at the head of the small table, pulling out the chair next to me. Leaning forward, he placed one hand on the back of my chair before turning it around, so my eyes met his over the small, empty space between us. My heart fluttered wildly, his heady scent of smoke and fire filling the air around me.

"I know that look, Braelyn, and you aren't to blame for any of this." Reaching out, he tucked a stray piece of hair behind my ear, his fingers lightly brushing my cheek, making my skin tingle with warmth.

"How is it not my fault, Julien? If I never stepped through the portal all those weeks ago, Theo would be safe and—"

"Braelyn, listen to me." Julien's words cut me off before I could finish. "Whether you'd come to Ellesmere or not, King Elias would still have found a way to destroy us all. But, at least with you here, we actually stand a chance of defeating him."

Julien's dark eyes pleaded with me to understand, but despite the truth behind his words, regret at not being able to stop Elias when I'd had the chance knotted my stomach.

Julien's hand lingered on my cheek and his thumb traced soothing circles over my skin. Closing my eyes, I tried to let his words comfort me and ease the slow ache that had begun to tighten my muscles. Slowly, he moved his hand to settle at the base of my neck. Heat blossomed over my cheeks as he pulled me closer, our foreheads pressed lightly together.

"What if I'm not capable of stopping him?" I whispered.

When telling Julien about the visions and Alpheus's warning, I'd left out the feelings I'd been experiencing when using my magic. Telling him would only cause him to worry and we had more pressing matters to focus on.

"Braelyn, when the time comes, I know you will do what needs to be done."

I opened my eyes, finding Julien's were still closed, his brows slightly pinched together in the middle and his dark lashes brushing the tops of his cheekbones. Reaching a tentative hand up, I covered his large hand with my own, giving it a tight squeeze. A small smile pulled at the corner of his mouth, revealing the small dimple I loved. My legs brushed his as I shuffled closer and, finally, Julien's eyes found mine. I leaned forward, our lips only inches apart. Heat radiated off his skin, setting mine alight. His hand tightened on my neck as the other one came to rest just above my knee. The subtle caress of magic flickered inside my chest, sending tingles over my skin as my emotions intertwined with my spirit magic. Julien closed the distance between us. His lips brushed mine in the softest of touches before a loud bang startled us apart. Goosebumps covered my arms, my body feeling like it had been doused in icy water, but as we jumped up and searched for the source of the noise, a small laugh sounded from behind me.

"It was just the book you were reading." Spinning around, Julien bent to pick up the large tome which had fallen to the floor. "You must have knocked it off the table."

We stood much further apart now, but my fingers longed to touch him, to once again feel the warmth of his skin against mine. We hadn't spoken much about what existed between us, but in the weeks since Theo's capture, it seemed the affection we felt for each other was only growing stronger. Or so I hoped.

Placing the heavy book back on the table, Julien raked a hand through his tousled curls. The sun's rays made the golden flecks in his dark eyes glisten like melted honey and my stomach fluttered as the longing I felt to be close to him was reflected at me.

"We should probably start searching for the grimoire." My voice trembled, our eyes never straying from each other.

Julien simply nodded his head once in agreement. "I think I know where we can start."

He held out his hand to me. I expected him to lead me back out through the library's front doors, but instead he walked in the opposite direction. We wove through the bookshelves in comfortable silence, our footfalls the only sound echoing around the once-quiet space. My mind whirred with the promise of finding the answers we needed until Julien pulled up short at a large tapestry, jolting me back to reality. The woven artwork was nothing like the tapestries hanging in the halls above us. The fabric was almost the same colour as the stone wall it hung on and the image depicted nothing more than an array of green, yellow, and brown patterns.

My brow furrowed. "It's... lovely?" I said, confusion tingeing my voice.

Julien chuckled softly, his lips quirking in a playful smile. Gripping one edge of the bland tapestry, he pulled it aside to reveal a door. My eyes widened in surprise. It was made of the same dark oak of the doors in the rest of the castle, but where the others were polished and shiny, this one was rough and unkempt. We had spent so much time in the library, but in all my wanderings through the packed shelves, I'd never given the tapestry a second glance.

"Where does this lead?" I asked, a little stunned, my mind still trying to work out how Julien had found the hidden door.

Julien winked at me. "I'll show you."

The hinges groaned in protest as he pushed on the copper handle and I found myself staring into a dark, narrow hallway. Cool air leaked out from the shadows, making me retreat back a step with a small shiver. From the unlit sconces and the damp air, the passage looked like it hadn't been used in years. Julien took a tentative step forward. The moment he passed over the threshold, his hand tight around mine, the bones in my fingers cracked under the pressure of his grip. Lifting my left hand, I clicked my fingers together, producing a small flame that flickered against the cold air. Holding my palm towards the ceiling, my flame grew to the size of a small apple. Heat flooded through my veins, transforming the narrow confines into a comfortable temperature. I cupped my hand around the flame, illuminating the path in front of us in an orange glow.

"Not bad," Julien said with a teasing smile, but I could hear the apprehension lacing his words. "You might just make a decent fire witch after all."

"Well, my teacher's pretty good, so I shouldn't expect anything less than perfection." I puffed out my chest, feigning cockiness.

"Only 'pretty good', is she?" Julien feigned shock. "I'll have to let Verena know she might need me to take over your lessons. Teach you how to wield the powerful fire magic." Julien gave me a playful nudge, but his words made my chest constrict.

The memory of this morning's lesson still lingered in the forefront of my mind. The lure of the darkness. We walked single file down the hallway, my small flame lighting the way. Our footfalls stirred up the thin layer of dust coating the floor, each step creating small tornados of dirt to billow around our ankles. Cobwebs covered most of the walls and ceilings, the small black spiders scurrying away from the fire each time the light moved over their fine, silvery webs. Coming to the end of the hall, another door like the one we entered through appeared out of the darkness. With a small shove, the door opened onto a large circular room cloaked in a cool blue light; the sun had not yet reached this side of the castle. Still holding on to Julien's hand, I followed him over the threshold into what appeared to be someone's study. A large, gilded desk stood in the middle of the room, taking up an obnoxiously large portion of the small space. I ran my hand along the gold detailing, noting papers littering almost every inch of the surface of the desk. Most were written in the language of old, though I couldn't decipher the scribbled words. A feather quill lay forgotten by a stack of old yellowed parchment—the ink staining the silver tip a deep blue. Picking up a book, I leafed through its pages, not knowing what I was looking for.

"It's King Elias's study," Julien said, his voice breaking the silence.

I ran my hands over the chair tucked behind the desk, my fingers tightening around the soft leather. This was where Elias planned all the evil he bestowed upon Ellesmere. On the people I loved. He would have poured over the contents of The Book of Lilith here, plotting his revenge on all who stood against him.

"How did you find this?" I asked quietly.

Julien shrugged, a mischievous smile playing on his lips. "Well, while you were in your meetings and lessons with the elders, I took it upon myself to do a little exploring."

I chuckled at his nonchalant demeanour. "Ever the adventurer," I murmured back to him.

In one of the rare moments of peace I had between magic training and meetings with the elders, Julien had told me of his love for adventure. It hadn't surprised me in the slightest, considering one of our earlier encounters had been after he'd spent the night traipsing through the Ironwood looking for ingredients for his apothecary.

"What's life without adventure?" he whispered in my ear as he moved to my side.

I smiled and turned my attention to the small arched window behind the king's desk. It looked out far beyond the castle grounds, towards the ash tree nestled deep in the centre of the Ironwood. Grey plumes of smoke rose from between the trees like a menacing storm as they gathered presumably where the ash tree stood. I wrapped my arms around my waist, gnawing at my lip. Julien placed a comforting arm around my shoulders and I sank into his warm embrace.

"I know that's where he's hiding, Julien. Where he has Theo." My voice came out low and even.

The muscles in my shoulders tensed as the anger I'd felt since Theo's capture unfurled inside me like the wings of a woken dragon. Magic ignited along my fingertips, the grimy glass reflecting the sharp silver-blue icicles spreading over the stone window ledge. Despite knowing deep down that the ash tree had to be where Elias lingered, we couldn't go there without a plan. We'd be walking straight into a trap with no escape. We needed to know what Elias was planning and I could only hope The Book of Lilith would help. Turning me away from the window, Julien placed both hands on either side of my face, forcing my gaze away from the darkening sky.

"We will save him, Braelyn. I swore I would help bring Theo back— and I will—but first we need to find that grimoire. It's the only way to get one step ahead of him."

Julien's dark eyes slowly helped calm the storm that had been growing within me since the moment Theo disappeared through Morrigan's portal.

Taking a deep breath, I relaxed my magic. The time would come when Elias would feel the full force of it, but for now, all we could do was focus on finding the book.

"So, where do we even begin to look?" I moved away from the window, trying to put the ash tree out of my mind, instead focusing on the tall bookshelf that wrapped around the length of the wall adjacent to the desk.

There was no order to the books stacked on the wooden shelves. Some stood vertical, the spines in pristine condition, while others looked as if they'd been shoved on the shelf in a hurry, the pages creased from carelessness. My eyes darted back to Julien.

His gaze narrowed on the shelves, his dark brows raised in curious contemplation. "Well, I'm guessing he wouldn't have kept it in plain sight," Julien said. "So maybe we start looking at the books concealed by the others."

"That could take hours. Time isn't exactly on our side." Gnawing at my bottom lip, I studied the shelves in the hopes it might jump out at me. *If I was a grimoire, where would I hide?* Tilting my head as if looking at them from a different angle might help, a thought materialised in the back of my mind. "Julien, is it possible for books to have magical properties?" From the corner of my eye, I could see his face turn in my direction, but my focus stayed on the towering shelves in front of me.

He nodded before saying, "It's what makes them so sought after by other magical beings. Why do you ask?"

"It's just, when I came across Althea's book, I felt the presence of magic within its pages—like a magical residue. Do you think, maybe, it's the same with The Book of Lilith?"

Julien folded his arms over his chest, the muscles straining as he raised a questioning brow. "It might be possible. How did it feel the last time?"

I shrugged once. "I'm not really sure. I was rummaging through some old books when I found Althea's journal and felt an overwhelming surge of magic."

Stepping over to the hundreds of books lining the shelves, I placed a shaking hand on the rickety shelf. There were so many of them squeezed into the small space that the wood looked as if it would snap under the weight. I ran my eyes along the line of coloured spines and reached a tentative hand towards a book on the far left. My fingers traced the cracked spine, feeling the fractures and dips in the deep brown leather.

"So, what makes you think King Elias wants to release the Wraiths of Umbra and not some other evil creature?" Julien's soft voice broke the quiet, his words raspy with apprehension.

I knew he would be feeling daunted at the prospect of coming face-to-face with the monsters from his nightmares.

As I walked along the shelf, I continued to trace my fingers gently along the spines, waiting for the magic to call out to me. Nothing happened.

"It's just a hunch, really," I said at last. "When Alpheus told me about the darkness growing in the Ironwood, I thought he was speaking about Elias. That maybe he was still siphoning magic from others and growing stronger. But now, after reading that sentence in the library book today and seeing the shadows grow over the ash tree, I'm starting to think maybe it was the Wraiths of Umbra he was after all along."

"That's a very big hunch, Braelyn," Julien said sceptically.

I glanced over to see him leaning against the large desk. His eyes were downcast, but despite not being able to see his expression, I knew his words were more hopeful than disbelieving. He shuffled his feet against the stone floor, avoiding my gaze.

"I know. It's just... things are starting to add up. Elias creating the portal, his search for the book and taking the power of other elemental wielders. I'm starting to wonder if this was all for him to gain enough power to open a portal to the Underworld. Alpheus said darkness is growing in the Ironwood. How much darker can you get than an army of wraiths hellbent on destroying the world?"

Julien rubbed a large hand over his face. The exhaustion of travelling to the Ironwood Village was finally taking its toll on him.

"I won't deny that your theory makes a lot of sense, Braelyn. I just hope you're wrong." His voice echoed the tiredness rimming his eyes a deep purple.

Turning my attention back to the mounds of books, I checked shelf by shelf, carefully running my fingertips along every spine and touching every page. As the morning ticked away and the sun inched its warm tendrils further into the study, my heart only grew heavier. No magic seemed to show itself. Pulling my hand away with a frustrated sigh, I stretched my fingers, opening and closing them quickly before returning to the books in front of me. My head throbbed with the promise of an oncoming headache and, squeezing my eyes shut, I tried to relax my deepening frown. Inhaling through my nose, I held my breath for a few seconds, letting the pressure build in my chest before releasing it slowly. When I opened my eyes, sunlight sparkled in my vision before my gaze settled on a large cloth-bound book at the edge of the middle shelf. It was leaning slightly to one side—its pages yellowed from the sun. As the tips of my fingers brushed the faded pages, a weak tingling sensation washed over me with the promise of magic. It was the same feeling I'd experienced when picking up Althea's book at the Forest Festival, only this time, rather than being overwhelming in its intensity, it was slow and sluggish. My head snapped around to where Julien leaned back in the chair, his feet now propped up on the desk, a slow smile building on his face.

"You found it. Are you sure this is the right one?" He looked at me expectantly, his dark brows disappearing into his hairline.

"I don't know," I replied earnestly. "It's different to how I remember it, but it's the only book I touched that my magic reacted to." I ran my hand over the soft cover and felt the tell-tale signs of magic bubble up once more inside me.

"What's it supposed to look like?" Julien asked as he stepped around the ornate desk to stand beside me.

My mind shifted back to when I'd first found The Book of Lilith in the parlour of my mother's apothecary. It was a small, black leather book with delicate pages. The book I held in my hands now was a large crimson tome with a cloth cover. Brushing a hand over it, my fingers tingled excitedly as magic buzzed like static in my veins. This book definitely had magical properties, but it couldn't be the dark witch's grimoire. Julien leaned forward to examine the cover as I set it down.

"I remember it being much smaller, and it was bound in leather, not cloth."

I flipped open the front cover to the title page, which read *A History of Necromancy*. It was written in long, looping letters—the author's name disfigured by an ink smudge. Lifting the corner of the page, I went to flip through the rest of the book, hoping to gain some insight as to why my magic had singled out this tome. When I tried to lift the thick pages, they wouldn't budge. It was like something had sealed the book shut. Julien's face hovered over my shoulder, his warm breath tickling my neck. Suddenly aware of how close he stood to me, a warm blush coloured my cheeks, and I shuffled aside to create more distance between us. Now was not the time for my brain to addle at the fact his hand lingered near the curve of my hip. As I placed *A History of Necromancy* on the desk, the tingling in my fingers immediately subsided.

Mimicking my earlier movements, Julien ran a hand over the cloth cover, his eyes growing wider the longer he stared at the book. My hands itched to hold it again, but I refrained from the temptation.

"By the elements," he blurted out, causing me to jump. "I think I've figured it out." Julien picked up the large book, turning it over in his hands as if it weighed no more than a piece of parchment. He studied every inch of it, his brow creasing the longer he looked at it. "I never thought I would see magic like this." Julien's voice was softer now, but there was something beneath his words that sparked my curiosity.

"See magic like what?" I asked, my body perking up at the awe in his voice.

The necromancy book appeared no different to all the others that sat on the shelf, but I couldn't deny there was something intriguing about how this book reacted to my magic.

Julien lifted it from the desk, the pages barely rustling as he tried to pry the book open. "Many years ago, there were tales of the qui decepitor, I believe you know of them." His eyes flashed with amusement and a hint of a smile flickered at the corner of his mouth.

The name Victoria had given me when I first arrived in Ellesmere still cropped up every now and again. *Qui decepitor*, the ancient word for deceiver—the one who showed up unexpectedly and tricked others into divulging the whereabouts of their grimoires and other prized possessions. The witches and warlocks of Ellesmere were a superstitious bunch, and it wasn't uncommon to hear the occasional whisper of qui decepitor when I walked throughout the halls. It never bothered me, but to know the rumours still filtered through the castle weeks after my arrival spoke volumes of how superstition played a huge part in the daily life of many within the kingdom. I narrowed my eyes in Julien's direction until his face lost some of its humour and he returned to a more serious tone.

Clearing his throat, he continued, "Well, around one hundred years ago, witches and warlocks were terrified that the qui deceptor would steal their grimoires and gain all the secrets to their magic." Julien handed me the book and immediately my magic began to bristle. "So, in order to protect their secrets, they used sanguis magicae to bind their grimoires shut so that in the event of it being stolen, the qui deceptor couldn't open it."

"What is *sanguis magicae*?" I asked eagerly. I'd never heard of the term before. I knew magicae referred to 'magic' in the language of old, but the other word eluded me.

"Sanguis magicae means blood magic, Braelyn."

My eyes widened. Blood magic was a form of dark magic, and not something a witch or warlock used lightly, if at all. This magic was dangerous, and very few of our kind were ever able to redeem themselves after using too much of it.

Despite the feeling in the pit of my stomach that told me I already knew the answer, I asked the question anyway. "Julien, is there a way Elias could have used blood magic to seal The Book of Lilith inside this one somehow?"

Julien leant back on the desk and folded his arms across his chest, the corded muscles of his forearms tensing as he contemplated my question.

"I mean, with King Elias anything is possible. But it's not that simple, Braelyn." He ran a hand through his dishevelled hair again, making it stand on end. The bags under his eyes were growing deeper as the day wore on. I knew he needed rest, but if we could find out if Elias had hidden the book in here it would make rescuing Theo so much easier. We would know what we were up against and could form a plan of how to get him back. My heart softened as Julien stifled a long yawn.

"What would we need to do?" I asked softly, trying to conceal the urgency in my wavering voice.

Julien let out a long sigh. "In order to break the binding magic, a witch or warlock with the same element must conjure the dark magic used to seal it."

The answer had already materialised in my mind, but I needed to be sure. "How do I open the book?"

A sombre look appeared on Julien's face, dulling his usually bright eyes.

"With blood."

Five

With the creation of the circulum, Elias had forcibly siphoned the magic of hundreds of elemental wielders in the hopes of turning himself into a spirit warlock. He'd succeeded. By capturing my mother and discovering the whereabouts of The Book of Lilith, Elias had been able to create the circulum and use its power. He'd hunted down every spirit wielder to eradicate any witch or warlock powerful enough to challenge him. I was the only one left. Which meant as the last remaining spirit witch, it was my blood that could break the spell separating us from the one chance we had at saving Theo. Magic bristled beneath my fingers, calling out to me, but it wasn't the calm flow of spirt magic. The darkness lingering in the deepest parts of me beckoned to be released. It clawed at the invisible restraints I'd put up and my stomach churned at the thought of what could happen should I wield it.

"Braelyn, this is powerful magic. Are you sure you want to go through with this?" Julien's brows pinched together, a small frown forming between his eyes. "Blood magic is not something you want to be messing around with. It's extremely risky."

A lump formed in my throat. My fingers tapped nervously against the book clutched in my hand. "What are the risks?" I asked, ignoring the anguish rolling in my stomach.

Julien rubbed a hand over the back of his neck, his jaw clenched and eyes distant. "Braelyn..."

"Tell me, Julien."

With a resounding sigh, he said, "Using blood magic goes against the balance we create with the elements. When we wield our gifted element, it weighs on our soul and, in turn, we draw on the energies of other less potent witchcrafts to heal us."

"Like potion making and botany," I cut in.

Julien nodded. "Exactly. When we use dark magic, however, it doesn't just weigh on our soul, Braelyn, it takes hold of it. It goes against nature's balance. When a regular elemental wielder submits to the pull of dark magic, it eventually kills us, rotting away every good part of us. Spirit wielders, on the other hand, can control the darkness and wield it like any element. But the more they use, the more they crave. It eventually becomes too much for them to resist and they resort to only using dark magic. Blood magic is usually just the beginning."

"How do you know so much about this?" I asked softly.

Julien spoke of blood magic like he had used it, but from what he'd said about the repercussions of its use, he would have succumbed to its hold. Something must have happened for him to understand it as well as he did. A deep frown was etched into his forehead, his eyes downcast as he stared at the stone floor.

"If I tell you, Braelyn, I don't know what you'll think of me."

Reaching out a trembling hand, I covered Julien's where it gripped the edge of the desk, his knuckles white with the tension cording his words. His eyes found mine and my chest constricted at the unease reflected at me.

"It was my father," he said blankly. "He used blood magic."

"But I thought—"

"That he died in the royal war? He did. But before this, he'd begun using blood magic to seal our grimoire. He'd thought because he was trusted by Elias, other witches and warlocks would want to know the secrets of our magic. He was an arrogant fool and he was killed in the war before the darkness was ever able to take hold of him."

Hazel had told me of Julien's family ties to Elias, but I'd never held it against him. He'd been a child when the war had begun, and I didn't think it fair that others still held him responsible for his family's mistakes. But Julien carried his family's treachery like it was his own burden to bear. My grip on his hand tightened, anger flaring in the pit of my stomach and flooding my body with heat. Elias would pay, not only for what he'd done to countless innocent lives, but to Julien, Theo, and my mother. Julien stepped closer to me, cupping my face in one of his warm hands.

"Elias has taken so much from me," he said softly. "And, believe me, no one more than I dreams of the day where he will cower at my vengeance, but not at the expense of you wielding such a deadly magic."

I leant into his touch as his thumb traced soothing lines from my chin to my cheekbone. The tenderness of the strokes eased the frantic beats of my angered heart.

"Are you sure about this, sweetheart?"

My teeth worried at my bottom lip as my head went to war with my heart. But it was a useless fight. I'd already made the decision.

"It's the only way to get the book, Julien. I have to."

Despite the curt nod he gave me, Julien's brows remained low. The same concern in the pits of his fiery eyes churned in the pit of my stomach. He made his way around the back of the desk and pulled out a long, silver letter opener from beneath a stack of parchment. The sharp tip glinted at me with a menacing wink, making my hands turn clammy. I knew what came next.

"Okay, now you need to do exactly as I say," Julien told me as he came back around the desk, the letter opener in his hand like a dagger pulled from its scabbard.

My stomach quivered as a sense of unease spread over me. It had taken weeks to master the power of being a spirit witch and now I was about to use some of the darkest magic known to our kind. This witchcraft required a power even more potent than spirit magic. Just thinking of the repercussions of using it made my legs tremble, yet the tendrils of dark magic I'd buried deep within me reached out like beckoning fingers. A small part of me craved to feel that power again, which only made the apprehension gnawing at my insides worsen. Julien watched me closely, assessing my face for the slightest sign I'd changed my mind. He wouldn't find it. I would endure whatever I must to have my friend back where he belonged. Pursing my lips, I gave Julien a curt nod before holding out my palm towards the stone ceiling. With a deep sigh, he stepped towards me and placed the tip of the letter opener along my palm.

"This may sting a little," he said in a strained voice as he pressed the tip of the blade into the skin below my thumb.

I flinched, the sharp sting of the blade cutting into my flesh. In a quick movement, Julien sliced down towards my wrist. Blood began to slowly pool in my hand, filling the room with a metallic odour. My head spun, but Julien's warm touch on my arm kept me centred. His natural scent of smoke and fire burnt through the tangy smell of blood, allowing me to focus on his instructions.

"Okay, Braelyn, in order to break the bind, you'll need to squeeze a few drops of your blood onto the cover and repeat the words '*aperi magicam tibi iubeo*'."

"What does that mean?"

Julien ran a rough thumb across my cheekbone, sending goosebumps prickling over my skin. "It means, 'I command thee to open thy magic to me'. Now, you need to pronounce it exactly as I said it. Are you ready?"

Too nervous to respond, I simply nodded and turned my attention to the book balanced on my other palm. Squeezing my hand into a fist, my pulse beat a heavy rhythm beneath my fingers, the blood throbbing. With a trembling hand, I held it over the book's cover and gently began to unclench my fist, saying aloud the words Julien spoke to me.

"Aperi magicam tibi iubeo."

We watched with bated breath as my blood dripped over the ink, seeping into the fine fibres invisible to the naked eye. At first, nothing happened. We studied the book, not daring to blink in case we missed a vital piece of information, but it remained unchanged. The only difference was the darkened cloth from where the few spots of my blood disfigured the title. I glanced sidelong at Julien, who was frowning down at the book as if his uneasy glare would help speed up the process. My heart sank into the pit of my stomach at the thought of failing yet again, but as we stared at the drying blood, trying to ease the sense of hopelessness settling over us, something began to change. My fingers tingled with overwhelming intensity. The blood spattered on the cover began to undulate beneath the fibres of the cloth, curling and twisting until they formed into a blood-red crescent moon. My pulse pounded in my ears, drowning out all other sound. I was aware of Julien's hands cupping my face, but his mouth moved silently, his words lost amongst the noise in my head. The shadows clinging to the corners of the room shifted as if they had a mind of their own. Their dark tendrils stretched out towards me, urging me to use a magic I so desperately wanted to conceal. The cut along my palm burned like someone had taken a fire poker and stabbed it into the middle of my hand. Tearing my gaze from Julien's worried expression, my eyes finally settled on *A History of Necromancy* still balanced on my outstretched hand. The pages that were sealed shut now ruffled, as if a wind had somehow broken through the closed window. They flicked open with rapid intensity while the pain searing through my veins reached a crescendo. My scream broke the deafening silence and the book tumbled to the floor. Julien's arms wrapped around my waist, stopping me from crumpling to the ground and, as quickly as the pain came, it was gone. The heat turning my blood molten receded and the magic that set my hands on fire was extinguished. The shadows receded back to the deepest, darkest corners of the room, no longer pulling me into their murky embrace. Wiping a shaking hand over my sweaty brow, I sank into Julien's arms, feeling the knowing pull of exhaustion against my heavy limbs. Too scared to see what expression lined Julien's face, I turned my attention to the discarded book. It had landed open on the plush patterned rug, but that's not what surprised me. Nestled in a hollow within its pages, sat The Book of Lilith.

Six

The incantation worked. My mind spun with what this could mean for Theo's rescue. We were the closest we had ever been and, with The Book of Lilith, we now had a chance of finding a way to stop Elias's plan to release the Wraiths of Umbra and finally bring Theo home. I bit back the laugh threatening to burst from my chest and let a wide grin spread across my face. Julien stiffened beside me, his grip on my waist tightening as he pulled me close to him and placed a soft kiss on the top of my head.

"You did it," he said, returning my smile, his eyes crinkling at the sides.

I gave Julien's hand a reassuring squeeze, and he loosened his arms from around my waist, taking a step backwards. The Book of Lilith still sat snugly within *A History of Necromancy*, in its perfect hiding place. I reached out a shaking hand, my mind whirring with the possibilities of what could happen should I touch it. *Would I be thrust into another vision? Would the dark magic bristling beneath my skin finally emerge in full force?* The moment my hand connected with the worn leather cover, my fingers tingled with a magic so intense my breath caught in my throat. My knees trembled and my head clouded over with a thick fog. Squeezing my eyes shut, I welcomed the knowing pain of a vision; The Book of Lilith clearly possessing the same magic Althea's journal contained. My head throbbed as the magic thrumming in my veins began to dissipate. Muffled voices echoed somewhere in the distance. When I opened my eyes, I tried to locate the source of the sound. Instead of the cool stone walls of Elias's study, I found myself amongst the overarching trees of the Ironwood. My stomach churned as I spun in a violent circle, the wall of tightly packed trees looming above me in a blur. Sucking in a deep breath, I tried to contain my fear. Memories of death and decay swam behind my eyes as I desperately tried to blink away the images of barghests, gremlins, and dark magic—all of which I'd encountered on my initial journey to the castle.

I *hated* this place.

I placed a trembling hand over my erratic heart, taking in a few deep breaths and counting each inhalation. *One, two, three.* With each count the tension slowly eased from my shoulders. Once my pulse returned to a normal rhythm, my eyes flitted to the dense trees, seeking comfort in the knowledge I was well hidden. Slim, leafless branches encroached on me in every direction, their tall, lifeless trunks reaching towards the canopies in the hopes of finding the light they so desperately needed. Dense thickets of the trees ran far into the shadows to my left, so there was no telling where in the Ironwood my vision had brought me. I picked my way through the trees, desperate to find a path, when the slow tingling in my fingers turned static. Unease settled over me, sending a cool chill down my spine. When I turned on the spot and noticed a break in the overcrowded trees, I realised where I was with sickening clarity. I'd forgotten just how menacing the ash tree looked. The monstrous roots twisted into one mangled trunk, tangling into the canopy that stretched high above, each creak of the ash tree's branches a nasty reminder of the power I'd harnessed amongst its presence. Nothing had changed in this clearing since my last visit but, unlike the first time, I wasn't alone. A figure materialised from the gaping hole created between the two gnarled roots. Leaves crunched softly beneath my boots as I edged closer to the trees bordering the clearing, trying to get a better look at the lone figure. Every fibre in my body told me who it was, but I needed to see him with my own eyes. Skirting around a large tree root, a loud crack pierced the air, my boot snapping a long-dead stick beneath the underbrush. My blood ran cold and I cursed myself for being so heavy-footed, but whoever lingered in the clearing appeared unfazed by my presence. Crouching behind one of the larger trees on the edge of the clearing, I placed a gentle hand on the deadened bark to balance myself. The uneven forest floor proved more difficult to traverse the closer I ventured towards the ash tree. The magic that once sputtered to life beneath my touch was now absent, and my heart ached as an overwhelming sadness tightened my lungs. Whatever dark magic was being conjured here was drawing on the life force of everything around it, sucking the magic dry until, soon, there would be none left. Peering around the rough bark, I was met with a familiar pair of obsidian eyes. Elias stood a few paces away, his gaze transfixed on the space between the ash tree's curving trunks. With his hands resting lightly behind his back, he appeared so at ease it was almost like the tree held him in some sort of a trance. Despite Elias being oblivious to my presence, my heart still thundered wildly in my chest. Being this close to him, I wanted nothing more than to put an end to his cruelty—to unleash the growing storm building inside me. My hands tingled violently, and I curled my fingers into fists, letting the magic surge to the surface. A fire burned hot beneath my skin, but as I unfurled my hands and conjured my deadly flame—beckoning it forward to carve a path towards Elias—nothing happened. Magic bristled against my skin, but my ability to conjure it was non-existent. My body burned with the need to unleash the building magic, but no matter how hard I tried to summon the elements, my magic wouldn't react. Agitation tightened my jaw, making my teeth ache under the pressure, but as the static feeling began to subside, my annoyance slowly turned to unease, my gaze pulled towards movement in the centre of the clearing. King Elias stepped back from the ash tree, a wide smile breaking the smooth lines of his face. Slowly, dark shadows seeped from the twisted branches and Elias's obsidian eyes gleamed with elation. Moving around the large trunk to get a better view, I slowly edged away from the safety of the trees and stepped closer to the front of the clearing. It was the perfect vantage point. My eyes roamed the space, searching for any sign of Theo, but he was nowhere to be seen. The hair on the back of my neck stood on end, a cold sweat breaking out across my forehead.

Had Elias killed Theo? Had he siphoned his magic and disposed of his body somewhere in the Ironwood?

Fear tightened my shoulders and hardened my stomach. No. It had to be a trick. I still didn't fully understand the magic associated with visions, but I had to believe the reason Theo wasn't here was because I was being shown another vital piece of information. Theo had to be alive.

Elias's movements were now in my direct line of sight. He walked slowly around the ash tree, his eyes never straying from it. Reaching out a steady hand, he rested his palm on the rough bark where the two large trunks crossed paths. Keeping his hand in place, Elias thrust his free one into the pocket of his tunic and pulled out a small vial. His fingers wrapped around the glass protectively, preventing me from seeing the contents. He popped the tiny cork from the top with a quick flick of his thumb and tipped the vial. Crimson liquid dripped down to his feet, his other hand still firmly planted on the intersected trunks. He closed his eyes, muttering something under his breath. I strained to hear the words, but his voice was lost to the wind before it reached me. The moment his mouth stopped moving, the tall trees around us groaned in warning. Their deadened trunks were proof the ash tree could suck the life from anything in its path. The breeze increased, whistling through the tightly-knit tree branches and tousling my hair around my face. The faint smell of burning wood drifted through the clearing and, despite the dire situation, it seemed to have a calming effect on my jittery nerves. Unable to turn away, I watched with wide eyes as the bark of the ash tree began to splinter and crack beneath King Elias's touch. Even with the chaos erupting around him, his watchful gaze never faltered. The gap between the ash tree's trunks swirled with thick, dark shadows before a crimson light burst through the shade, illuminating the clearing in a blood-red glow. My brain urged me to run, but my feet were rooted to the leafy ground as if the trees surrounding me kept me captive. A high-pitched screech tore through the cool night air, and I threw my hands over my ears to block out the ear-splitting sound. Large, dark shapes began gushing from the hole in the ash tree, shrieking as they unfurled long wings made of shadow and billowed from the dark depths of some unknown place. Red eyes gleamed at me in the moonlight, one of the creatures passing so close to my hiding spot I could smell the fire and brimstone that clung to its form. My throat constricted with a scream that never came, the intensity of my fear leaving me voiceless. So, this indeed was his plan. King Elias would release the Wraiths of Umbra, and the ash tree was the key. One Wraith hovered in front of me for mere seconds before a soundless command seemingly pulled its gaze and called it back. My breath shook and my heart pounded loudly in my ears. Fixing my gaze on the king, his face beamed with an ear-splitting grin as he watched the monsters he'd conjured circle the clearing in a growing black mass. For a split second, the face that lingered on my hiding spot looked like my father. Or how he might have looked upon me had King Elias let him live all those years ago. Unshed tears stung my eyes, but I was forced to push the thought aside as the clearing was plunged into an eerie silence. The wraiths circled above the ash tree, their presence throwing us into even darker shadow. King Elias turned his attention back to the giant tree, his hands turning over one another as the grin he'd worn flattened into a thin line. My eyes darted between him and the ash tree. *What else was he waiting for?* Seconds turned to minutes, the silence almost suffocating. My mind whirred with all the possibilities of what Elias could be waiting for when a movement between the trees pulled me from my thoughts. A gnarled hand protruded from the hole, tipped with claws so long they put the barghest's to shame. The fine hairs at the base of my neck lifted as a cold chill ran down my spine. It wasn't only the wraiths he wanted to unleash.

The woman stepped from the shadows, her face half concealed in the low light. Elias dropped to his knees, bending his head in a deep bow at the woman's feet. White-blonde hair fell in front of her face as she tilted her head towards him.

Elias's voice was muffled as he spoke, but there was no mistaking the title that tumbled from his lips. "My queen."

A thread of memory tugged at the back of my mind. '*Your father found me with The Book of Lilith once—the grimoire written by one of the greatest dark witches of this century.*'

My mind raced, searching for answers just out of reach. I couldn't help but recall the story about the dark witch who had been burnt at the stake more than one hundred years ago. She had suffered a terrible fate for summoning the Wraiths of Umbra... could this be the same witch Elias had spoken of?

The woman quickly disregarded him, instead turning her head in my direction. The sight of her face made me cup my hands to my mouth, stifling the scream threatening to tear me apart. Half of her profile was that of a beautiful woman—high cheekbones, full lips, and arched brows—but the other half was ravaged. In place of her skin lay nothing but bone, her skull a stark contrast to the beauty on the other side. Her ruby eyes locked with mine, and a sinister smile spread across her beautiful lips. That face looked so familiar—there was no mistaking which bloodline this witch had once belonged to. The resemblance between Victoria and the witch before me was uncanny.

As if sensing my unease, a melodious laugh echoed around the clearing as the woman walked towards me with an air of grace.

"I have been keeping a watchful eye on you, Braelyn." Her words were cold but not unkind, yet it was her use of my name that caught me off guard.

How did she know who I was?

She tilted her head in my direction, and I continued to watch her with narrowed eyes.

"Who are you?" I shot back.

Even as I asked the question, I already knew the answer. I could feel the power of the ash tree's magic combining with my own, giving me the strength to confront the witch in front of me.

She let out a sharp cackle that cracked like a strike of lightning. "You already know the answer to that question, Braelyn."

My breath caught in my throat as magic ignited in my veins.

"Lilith," I replied, my voice coming stronger than I anticipated.

Searing heat flooded through me before a cold chill stiffened my spine. The trees bent and twisted in the wind that whirled around the clearing, as if readying themselves for a fight. Lilith halted before me, that cruel smile disfiguring her face even further. I readied myself for a fight to the death, distracted only by a murmuring in the back of my mind that pulled at my subconscious. The deep voice I'd come to know so well called my name over and over, desperately searching for me in a place he couldn't follow. It sounded soft at first, then slowly grew to a crescendo, holding with the howl of the wind. Lilith's smile never faltered and, gliding closer to me, she placed her mouth beside my ear.

"I will be seeing you soon, Braelyn."

Her cool breath tickled the hairs on my neck, making them stand on end. With one last glance at Lilith's face, everything around me went black.

Seven

My head throbbed so hard I thought it might crack as the urge to vomit roiled in my stomach. The Ironwood dissolved into little more than memory as I threw my eyes open. My back was pressed into the cold stone floor of the king's small study at Ellesmere Castle. Julien's brows drew together as he hovered over me, creasing further as he helped me into a sitting position. I rubbed a clammy hand over my face, my head still pounding in time with my rapid heartbeat.

"Are you okay, Braelyn? You had me worried for a second." He shuffled closer, his arm resting on his knee as he knelt beside me. Taking my chin gently between his steady fingers, he tilted my head towards him, searching my face, assessing that I was truly okay.

"Yes." I exhaled heavily. "But let's just say the Wraiths of Umbra aren't the only things King Elias plans to unleash on Ellesmere."

Julien's frown deepened the longer he contemplated my words. In the last few weeks, I had never experienced a vision quite like this one. It felt real. In every other, no one had been able to interact with me the way Lilith had. My pulse quickened at the thought of what this could mean, my head still pounding with the remnants of the vision's magic. *Had Elias already succeeded in summoning Lilith? Were the shadows above the Ironwood the beginning of her resurrection?* My mind whirred with what I could do to stop it—them. The hatchings of a plan begun to form in my head, but before I could set things in motion, there was someone I needed to speak to.

As I rose to my feet, I flinched as my palm touched the cool stones, forgetting about the cut on my hand. The bleeding had mostly subsided, but tiny droplets still emerged each time I flexed my fingers.

"Here, allow me." Julien glanced about the small study for something to wrap my bleeding palm with, but there was nothing but parchment, books, and the odd pot of ink.

Holding my injured hand gently in one of his, he pulled at the bottom of his shirt and ripped a length of fabric away like it was no more than paper, revealing a small section of his tanned stomach. My cheeks blazed a bright crimson, but if Julien noticed, he was kind enough to keep it to himself. He wrapped the length of fabric around my palm a few times before fixing the ends in a small knot.

"Thank you," I murmured.

Turning my hand over in his, he brought it up to his lips and placed a small kiss at the base of my wrist. Sparks ignited at my fingertips, making me jump back from him. My entire body burned with heat as a hot flush crept up my chest. *Damn this spirit magic.*

Julien raised a thick brow at me, his eyes glittering mischievously at the flush moving over my collarbones and up my neck.

"So, are you going to tell me what monsters the cruel king is planning to unleash on us?" He let go of my hand and crossed his arms, waiting for me to reveal what I'd seen in my vision.

Taking a deep breath, I chose my words carefully, knowing Julien wouldn't like what I had planned next. "Yes, but first there's someone we need to pay a visit to."

While we walked through the castle, I told Julien everything. He listened in quiet concentration, but when the witch's name left my lips, he stopped in his tracks.

"There is no way Elias can unleash Lilith, Braelyn. Are you sure that's who you saw?" Julien kept his voice low, but it didn't stop the stares we were getting from the castle's tenants walking by.

We were huddled on the small landing above the foyer of the castle—a stark contrast to the dark, quiet space I'd walked through earlier this morning. The iron sconces had been lit and the large chandelier hanging above had been decorated with hundreds of flickering candles. The faint aroma of roasting meat and baked potatoes wafted from the kitchens, making the foyer smell divine. Witches and warlocks bustled around us frantically, amid prepping the castle for a grand ball happening in a few days' time. The ball gave the elders the opportunity to showcase me to the rest of Ellesmere as their future queen, and it was all anybody could talk about. All the most notable magical beings would attend, and the whole castle was buzzing with excitement at the prospect of seeing elves and dwarves in the halls of the castle again.

A young witch, no older than me, hurried past us pushing a cart stacked with floral china. The plates tinkled as she quickly walked by, shooting a small smile in Julien's direction before disappearing around a corner. My stomach hardened at her brazen actions. It wasn't unusual for Julien to catch the eye of many of the girls living within the castle, but it still set my teeth on edge when they did it so boldly in front of me. Julien appeared none the wiser. He watched an old wizard using air magic to hang a garland of greenery along the banister of the stairs. I shook my head at the absurdity of my thoughts. With everything going on, it was irrational of me to be bothered by something so trivial.

Turning back to Julien, I replied, "She spoke her name to me. She was as real as you are right now." My voice shook slightly, and I watched as the serious look on Julien's face softened at the edge of panic lacing my words. His eyes no longer burned brightly as they had before, but instead turned dark like the shadows shrouding the Ironwood.

"I believe you, sweetheart. It's just..." His voice trailed off and he ran a hand through his thick hair—a movement I now recognised as a nervous trait. "Lilith was burnt at the stake almost one hundred years ago. It would take some form of necromancy to bring her back from the dead. This is one of the most potent forms of dark magic. You can't get much darker, really."

King Elias's voice echoed in my mind. '*The greatest dark witch of this century.*' Lilith was one of the most powerful witches known throughout Ellesmere's history. The true creator of the circulum, she had continuously craved more power than she already possessed. After raising the Wraiths of Umbra, Lilith had unleashed a terrible war on Ellesmere and all who refused her the power she deemed she deserved. Defeated by the Great King, she was eventually burnt at the stake for her treachery and thereafter became a warning to witches and warlocks everywhere of what would happen should they ever succumb to dark magic. The story terrified me—spoke to me in ways I didn't truly understand. There was a dark side to my magic and, every so often, it rattled the cages I'd pushed it behind. The power showed itself the first time I laid eyes on the ash tree, then again the night we broke into Ellesmere Castle to rescue my mother. I swore after those instances I would lock that power away, but only this morning that same darkness clawed to be released. In my vision of Lilith, it reared its face again. I was constantly torn between my hatred for the darkness and a longing of how I craved to wield it. Spirit wielders teetered on the edge of light and dark magic. It was what terrified me above all else, given my power. Julien's eyes were filled with concern as they searched mine for reassurance, but it was something I couldn't give him.

I cleared my throat, wanting to think of anything but the darkness I'd shut away.

"I know the story, Julien, but I'm telling you, Lilith was there in the Ironwood, and I'm sure I know someone who can confirm the truth."

Pulling Julien towards the left set of stairs, I led him down the small corridor towards the dungeons and to the one person who I hoped could give us answers.

Eight

"You can't be serious, Braelyn!" Julien spat at me.

I recoiled from his words. I'd known he wouldn't agree with my actions, but the vehemence in his voice pierced me like a knife to the heart. His outward reaction was precisely the reason I hadn't outrightly told him *who* we were going to see. A small part of me knew he wouldn't understand.

"We don't have a choice," I retorted. "We need clarification that what I'd seen in my vision was part of King Elias's plan. Victoria is the only one who can give us that."

Julien's nostrils flared, his shoulders rippling with the same anger hardening his gaze. His silence was suffocating as we descended the stone stairway towards the dungeons, and in contrast, our footfalls echoed loudly against the cold stone walls. The air was much cooler in this part of the castle, making goosebumps rise on my exposed skin. I hadn't been down here in some time, and the memories that flashed in my mind were unwelcome. The sight of Balor, the tall, muscled elvish prince, and Lorcan, the mighty dwarven weapon forger—both beaten and bloodied—still haunted my dreams. Squeezing my eyes shut for a few moments, I pushed the memories aside, focusing on the real reason we'd ventured down here. Lit sconces lined the walls, their burning flames giving us enough light to see by, but doing little to ward off the chill. Venturing toward the middle of the room, I stopped at one of the cells. The light was too dim to see all the way inside, but I knew whose presence lingered behind the bars.

"Well, well, well. To what do I owe the pleasure of this visit, qui decepitor?" Victoria's voice dripped with sarcasm as she sauntered over to the iron bars that separated us.

Her once pristine blonde hair was now slick with grime from being holed up in the dungeons. King Elias had abandoned her the night he took Theo. Despite her heinous acts, she'd been treated fairly, but her refusal to accept even a morsel of food now showed in the way her clothes hung limp on her already slim frame. Imprisoned for being one of his most loyal followers, Victoria had refused to provide any information on the king's whereabouts. She remained loyal to her so-called king and his cause, opting to remain in the dungeons with Julien's brother Sebastien.

Another set of hands grasped the bars in the cell next to Victoria's, his knuckles white under the sheer pressure of his grip.

"Brother, how nice of you to come and visit." Sebastien's deep voice echoed around the dungeon, his words dripping with the same hatred that made the muscles in Julien's forearms turn rigid. Julien's lip curled as he kept his gaze fixed on the wall above Victoria's cell, refusing to give his brother the satisfaction of riling him.

"Nice to see you too, Victoria," I replied with a slight smile. She raised one of her perfect eyebrows. Even malnourished and dirty, she still had an air of beauty. "What do you know of King Elias's plans to raise Lilith from the dead?" I kept my eyes locked on her and, despite all her efforts to keep her face neutral, a flicker of hope touched her icy eyes. It was all I needed to confirm my vision was true.

"How do you know this?" she said through gritted teeth.

Her once smug face was now a portrait of anger, her brows drawn low over her eyes, the muscles in her neck straining. A low animal-like snarl sounded from Sebastien's cell, but I ignored him, instead focusing on pulling more information from Victoria.

"I have my ways," I replied calmly. "But what I would like to know is how you're related to her."

The stone room fell into absolute silence.

It may as well have been just Victoria and me down here. Her blue eyes grew wide as she stared at me—her chest rising and falling rapidly.

Julien made a small noise behind me, and I turned my head to see a look of utter confusion written across his face. I spun back to Victoria, noting her narrowed eyes as she tried to figure out how I'd pieced it all together.

"I know she's related to you, Victoria," I continued. "I could see the resemblance in her face."

Victoria let out a small bark of laughter. "Is that so?"

Sebastien's dirty face appeared in the light of the fiery sconces, his lips pulled back in a menacing smirk. "You are clutching at straws, qui decepitor. There are only a select number of people who know of King Elias's plan and we would never divulge the information you seek."

It was going to take more than us feigning our way through knowing Elias's plan. If we wanted the knowledge she held, I would need to touch on the one thing she craved above all else. Julien took a step towards his brother, his nostrils flaring and his fists clenched tight by his sides. He made to shield me from Sebastien's cruel retorts, but I placed a hand on his chest, stopping him from going any further. Julien's dark eyes burned into his brother's, but Sebastien's smirk only widened.

"I can see your new pet has you trained well, Brother."

Julien's muscles stiffened beneath my touch, his eyes flashing with a deadly blaze that burned beneath his skin.

"Speak of her again and I won't hesitate to kill you where you stand." Julien's voice was venomous.

Sebastien leant forward, the iron bars casting sharp shadows over his face. "Tell me, was she worth forsaking the only family you have left?"

Julien lunged at him, the muscles in his arms rigid as he collided with the bars, the only obstacle separating him from his brother. Sebastien tried to step out of the way but his reflexes were slow. Julien gripped the collar of his shirt in a fisted hand, the other one at his throat, cutting off his air supply. My eyes widened and I could suddenly see the dangerous side to Julien everyone warned me about. I could see the unpredictable wildfire that simmered beneath the surface of his handsome exterior. But it was this danger that lured me in, that under his charming cockiness there was someone fierce ready to fight for me. I took a small step forward, my hand wrapping around the curve of his bicep, the muscles easing slightly beneath my touch.

Julien eased his fingers from his brother's throat, curling them into a fist as he continued to watch him with narrowed eyes. Sebastien sagged against the iron bars, sucking in the stale air as he tried to draw in enough oxygen to satiate the rage curling his lip. Julien inhaled deeply before his face carefully regained its composure. Feeling like he was no longer going to set the dungeon ablaze, my gaze drifted back to my target.

"There's no point trying to hide it from us, Victoria. I've seen Lilith. Once he's summoned her, Elias will leave you here to rot. He doesn't care about you."

Guilt tightened my throat, but I managed to keep my voice steady even as the hurt cut across Victoria's features. She shrunk back from the bars, her eyes darting between Julien and myself as if assessing my honesty. Her vulnerability lasted only a second before her face slipped back into its usual mask of composure.

"I know that's not true," she spat back. "Our king needs me. He told me so."

"Victoria," Sebastien said through clenched teeth. "Say no more."

My heart was beating so loud, I was surprised no one could hear it. We were so close to cracking the stony facade she put up, and I knew the words that would unravel her.

"He doesn't need you anymore, Victoria. Why would he need a useless air witch when he has the most powerful dark witch by his side?"

It did the trick. Her face turned ashen, my words piercing through her defences and striking at her weakness—her desperation for power and her need to belong somewhere.

"Victoria, listen to me. She's taunting you. Don't let her deceive you." Sebastien's deep voice punctured the silence, but I could hear the desperate plea hidden beneath his words.

She stared at Julien and me, her eyes glazing. After a second, her eyes locked on my own, anger burning in their icy depths. Her lips curled back in a snarl as she launched herself towards the bars, rattling them like a caged animal.

"There is no way you could have seen her, Braelyn, because we hold the key to bringing her back."

With a quick flick of her finger, she gestured between the two of us.

Only the blood pounding in my ears drowned out her deranged laughter. My back hit the cold stone of the dungeon wall as I took several steps back, but I barely felt the sharp jolt of pain. Victoria and Sebastien posed an even larger threat than before. If what she said was true and she was one half of the key to summoning Lilith, we could no longer leave her down here. The elders believed the prison was enough to contain both Victoria and Sebastien—the heavy iron preventing them from conjuring any magic—but with this new information coming to light, the castle was under threat of attack. We needed to remove any possibility of them being reunited with Elias. A ruler from one of my books would have executed them on the spot to save their kingdom, but was that the type of tyrant ruler I wanted to be? Could I condemn two people to death purely out of fear? Julien hovered beside me, trying to mentally slot the puzzle pieces together, but I'd already figured it out. My heart beat rapidly in my chest as the threads of a plan looped together in my mind. I knew exactly how we would get Theo back and stop Elias from waging war on Ellesmere. The only flaw in my plan was that I would need to put a small amount of trust in someone who believed me to be a deceiver.

Julien threw open my bedroom door, the wood crashing against the stone wall as he stormed over to the open window, his back rigid and shoulders tense. He gripped the window ledge in a fiery grasp, the flames dangerously close to the sheer curtains. I closed the door with a quiet click, not wanting anyone to overhear our heated conversation. When I turned around, Julien was already facing me, his hands balled into fists at his sides.

"How could you even think of trusting that witch?" he spat at me through clenched teeth. Anger rippled off him in waves, and I flinched back from the harshness of his tone.

"We have no choice, Julien. She confirmed the truth of my vision. If putting myself in danger helps get Theo back, I'll do it." I squared my shoulders against the dark glare he shot in my direction. "Besides, we won't be alone."

"She tried to kill you, Braelyn. More than once. How can you trust a word that comes out of her mouth?" He leant back on the windowsill, his fingers flexing by his sides.

"I can't trust her, but I trust you, Grey, and Verena. This is the only way we can get Theo back. I need you to believe in me, Julien. Please." My voice shook, betraying the anguish in my heart.

Julien's hands relaxed, his eyes staring unseeing at his boots. From the look on his face, he knew there would be no changing my mind. He ran a hand through his hair and released a low sigh. Closing the short distance between us, I took Julien's face in my hands. His cheeks were rough with a few days' growth, but his skin felt warm beneath my fingers. I stood on my tiptoes so our eyes were almost at the same height. I needed him more than anything now. For weeks, Julien had been the person holding the pieces of my broken heart together. He soothed the guilty ache in my chest and gave me the strength I needed to continue moving forward no matter how hopeless it seemed. I couldn't do this without him.

"You are the only thing I believe in, Braelyn," he replied, his voice firm.

Bringing his face forward a few inches, he rested his forehead on my own. I closed my eyes for a moment, relishing in the closeness. When I opened them, I found his dark eyes searching my face. I'd never been very good at keeping my feelings hidden, but no matter how hard he tried to convince me otherwise, my mind was made up. Letting out a small sigh, he placed his hands over mine—pulling them away from his face and holding them between us.

"So, what's our next move?" A small smile tipped up the corner of Julien's mouth, but the hint of a frown still lined his forehead. I knew he would never completely trust a plan that involved someone whose hatred of me was so deeply entrenched in her person, but he trusted me and, for now, that was enough.

A smile tipped up the corner of my mouth. "We organise reinforcements."

Nine

Julien had made his feelings towards the elders known to me many times and, despite his belief I was making the wrong decision, my conscious told me I needed to tell them of Elias's plans. It wasn't just about protecting the people I loved. We also needed to be prepared should I fail.

The hairs on the back of my neck prickled as the dark wooden doors to the throne room appeared in front of us. Even though it had been weeks since our fight against Elias, I still hated this part of the castle. Every inch of the throne room had been fixed and redecorated but, to me, it was still the same scene of destruction. The place my friend had disappeared. Pushing the memories from my mind, I squared my shoulders and crossed the threshold. We were welcomed with a wall of heat—someone had been in early this morning to light the three large fireplaces—and the flames crackled softly in the grates, making the whole room feel stifling. Dozens of gilded candelabras lined the outskirts of the room, the subtle scent of honey hovering in the air. Where Elias's ornate golden throne once sat, a long wooden table covered in parchment, ink pots, and quills now took its place. It ran the length of the far wall. The Elders of Ellesmere sat behind it, two witches and warlocks currently deep in conversation and none the wiser to our entrance. Julien cleared his throat lightly to get their attention. Immediately, four pairs of eyes filled with wisdom and knowledge beyond their years turned in our direction.

"Miss Grey, given you failed to show up for your earlier lesson, we weren't expecting to see you today."

The Elder Helene rose, her hands resting on the wooden tabletop. She appeared to have been rifling through numerous scrolls before we interrupted them, but despite her slightly disapproving tone, she smiled down at us. Helene was the youngest of the four elders and, in my opinion, the kindest. She was the epitome of elegance and grace, her slim build often swathed in the finest silks and fabrics her title afforded her. But, whilst the other three kept mostly to their chambers or the throne room, Helene would often be seen around the castle grounds assisting the staff.

I felt a twinge of guilt at my absence from this morning's lesson and knew Mrs Boswell would be giving me an earful when she found me, but in the scheme of things, it was of little importance.

"We're sorry to interrupt, Elder Helene, and I apologise for my tardiness, but we have some news."

With this admission, the other three elders turned their heavy stares towards us. Beside me, Julien shifted from one foot to the other—his dislike towards the elders evident in the set of his shoulders—but I maintained my rigid stance, eyes never straying from Helene.

"Well, speak up, Miss Grey. What is it you need to tell us?" Helene's voice was not unkind, but it held the authority her title afforded.

Swallowing the lump that had formed in my throat, I squared my shoulders and tried to make my voice sound stronger than I felt. The elders had a way of making me feel like I was being scrutinised beneath their gaze. It was an uneasy sensation that made my knees tremble and a thin sheen of sweat to break out on my upper lip.

"I've recently learned that King Elias plans to raise the dark witch Lilith from the dead. Once he does, he will attack Ellesmere."

Helene's golden eyes widened as she turned to the other elders who were murmuring quietly between themselves. I chanced a quick glance at Julien, but his face appeared as if carved from stone. He didn't return my gaze, instead studying the elders with a wary detachment, but his hand brushed mine softly, giving me the reassurance I needed.

"How did you come by this information, Miss Grey?" the Elder Silas asked.

He was by far the oldest, with black hair dotted with flecks of grey and light blue eyes rimmed with deep wrinkles. Despite his age, he was a powerful warlock.

Julien finally turned to me, his eyes burning into my own, imploring me not to tell them, but I had no choice. My fate was tied to the four people in front of me, and if I ever wanted them to trust me, I needed to do my queenly duties to not only protect my loved ones, but my kingdom as well.

"I had a vision of Elias's plans. I watched the entire thing unfold before my eyes."

Helene's dark brows disappeared into her unruly hair. "You saw this, Braelyn?"

I nodded once. Julien's face was hidden from view, but his rigid stance and clenched fists conveyed his feelings loudly enough. He wasn't happy with my decision.

"Mr Thorne," Silas said. "You do not look pleased that Miss Grey is divulging this information to us."

Julien cleared his throat. "No, Elder Silas, I'm not."

Silas raised his bushy grey brows, a small smile touching his full lips. "And why is that Mr Thorne?"

"Because I believe this gift puts Braelyn in great danger. She is already wanted by King Elias for being a spirit witch. Her visions only make her more of a target."

Silas inclined his head in Julien's direction. "Thank you for your honesty, Mr Thorne." He turned his head in my direction. "Now, Miss Grey, what is it that you're asking of us?"

"To allow us to meet Elias head on. To infiltrate his hideout in the Ironwood and put a stop to him."

The elders watched me in quiet contemplation. Silas's hands were steepled beneath his chin, his face expressionless. Helene wrapped a dark curl around her finger, golden eyes flicking between me and the other elders. Aramis, the other warlock elder, leaned back in his chair, arms folded across his chest as he eyed me with great curiosity.

My hands were slick with sweat and weakly tingling, making my fingers twitch in anticipation.

"While we appreciate your candour, Miss Grey, surely you must know our answer."

My head spun as Silas's words fractured any hope I'd had. My mouth hung open, disbelief silencing the many retorts dancing on my tongue. Julien snorted loudly beside me, his stiff demeanour making him look like a soldier called to attention.

"If I may, Elder Silas, maybe we shouldn't be so quick to dismiss the girl's revelations."

My eyes snapped to Aramis. Like Helene, he was the younger of the two warlocks. Standing a head taller than the other elders, he looked dapper in a rich, blood-red tunic, his chestnut hair tied back from his face, accentuating his chiselled jaw. He watched me closely, his grey eyes flicking between me and Julien. He stood from his chair at the end of the table, arms tucked loosely behind his back.

"What is it you are trying to say, Aramis?" Silas said. "That we should allow Miss Grey to take Ellesmere guards and rush into a fight she cannot win?" While his voice wasn't harsh, it dripped with a warning that made me take a small step back.

Aramis simply shrugged and turned towards the other elders.

"All I'm saying is maybe we should heed Miss Grey's warning. King Elias grows stronger every minute he is still out there. If we prepare and send—"

Silas held up a hand, cutting Aramis off mid-sentence. My stomach turned leaden as he glanced towards the two witches, who inclined their heads in a single nod.

Silas cleared his throat. "While I appreciate your honesty, Elder Aramis, we will not send a parade of witches and warlocks into the depths of the Ironwood to be slaughtered by the cruel king and his followers. It is a foolish plan, to say the least."

Helene's eyes darted between the two warlocks. It was only fleeting, but I swore they narrowed as they landed on Aramis.

"Elder Silas," Aramis began, "please reconsider your—"

The icy stare Silas shot in Aramis's direction cut his sentence short again, but this time he remained silent.

Whilst each elder reigned over Ellesmere in my stead, Silas and Magdalena were the wisest and by far the most powerful out of the four. They would hear what Aramis and Helene had to say, but ultimately the final decision was theirs alone.

My heart sunk into the pit of my stomach. They refused to act. With all my training and teachings, I had believed the elders would finally

KIRSTY INIC

see me as somewhat of an equal, but they still looked at me like I was a child. But that wasn't true. I was the spirit witch and the future Queen of Ellesmere, and I vowed I would do whatever it took to protect my home and the people I loved. Tapping my fingers against my thigh to release my pent-up frustration, my hands began to prickle with magic.

"How can you sit there and do nothing?" I said in a strained voice. "If Elias isn't stopped, he will unleash a deadly army on Ellesmere, and we will be too weak to do a damn thing." My voice rose a few octaves. Magic coursed through me, powerful and unstoppable, but I refrained from letting it overwhelm me.

"Miss Grey, you cannot possibly believe we would let you chase after a deranged warlock to stop something that may not even come to fruition," Silas said, raising his brows. "Visions aren't the most reliable source of magic. You of all people should know this."

Magic history was the only lesson I had with Elder Silas. Being the oldest and wisest of the elders, he'd taken it upon himself to educate me about the types of magic conjured by our kind—visions being one of them. Not always reliable, a vision could change depending on the seer's decisions and how they interpreted the information shown to them.

"And what about Theodore Edwards, Elder Silas? Do you plan on sending anyone to rescue him from the clutches of this deranged warlock?" Julien spat out.

"What has happened to Mr Edwards is tragic, but we will not send an army of witches, warlocks, not to mention the only known spirit witch, to their deaths just to save a warlock who disobeyed our orders in the first place, Mr Thorne. She is not strong enough yet." Silas pointed a long, shaking finger at me. "The only way to protect you is to keep you safe behind the walls of the castle. We will post more guards on the perimeter, but our outer wall is impenetrable."

It was the final straw to release the anger that had been building over the last few weeks. They were words that had been whispered throughout the castle since King Elias fled. *Not strong enough. Not capable enough to use spirit magic.* But neither the elders nor the gossipmongers of the castle knew the determination tightening my muscles and stiffening my spine. When the time came, I would be more than capable of wielding my magic like a sword to save the people I cared about. My lips pressed into a thin line as an intense focus narrowed my vision.

59

"How will extra guards help us stop Elias?" I seethed, my voice rising. Magic sparked at my fingertips, darkness tingeing the edges of my vision. The more I let my anger and frustration grow, the more the dark magic reacted to my call. It slithered through my veins like a slow-acting poison, the shadows in the deepest corners of the room begging to be called upon. Julien's fingers brushed the top of my hand in the softest of touches, the sensation snapping me out of the intense darkness that clouded my mind. I shifted my gaze to Julien, noticing the way his eyes flicked down to my hands. A faint black mist hovered around my outstretched fingers. My shoulders tightened, my body feeling frozen to the spot. In the midst of my rage, I hadn't felt myself conjuring dark magic. Reining in my emotions, I breathed deeply through my nose, letting the sweet scents of the honeyed candles ease the tension in my muscles. The elders eyed me closely, their gaze moving to my flickering fingers. Silas's nostrils flared, his chest rising and falling rapidly with each breath. Helene's eyes seemed to burn like melted gold, but there was a hint of a smirk lifting her full, dark lips. Aramis sat at the end of the table, his arms crossed over his chest as he studied me with a raised brow. My skin bristled at their judgement. No one questioned the elders' decision, but I didn't care. Not when I knew they were making a terrible mistake.

"We have one of the finest armies in Ellesmere, Miss Grey, and they will defend this kingdom until their dying breath if they must. By posting extra guards on the wall, we will have a better chance at knowing when, or even if, Elias will attack." Magdalena stared down her long nose at me, nostrils flared, her half-moon glasses resting on the very tip. A vein in the side of her neck pulsed in time with the flickering anger in her one good eye. The other was milky white with blindness. "You think by questioning our authority you will get us to change our mind? All it shows is how much you have to learn, child."

Her good eye flicked to the other elders, whose grim faces were stony. Helene and Silas inclined their heads once again. Aramis was the only one whose eyes stayed fixed in my direction, his steepled hands covering the hint of a smirk.

"So, you won't heed our warning then?" I said coldly.

"Enough!" Elder Magdalena replied, her lips flattening into a thin line as she dismissed us with a lazy flick of her hand. "We stand by our decision."

I stood my ground, wanting nothing more than to argue against their verdict, but Julien gripped my hand and, with a gentle tug, pulled me towards the double doors. We walked in silence, my blood boiling. When we were a few metres from the throne room, Julien pulled me into a small alcove hidden behind a hanging wall tapestry. My temper was beginning to settle, but my heart still beat a heavy rhythm beneath my blue sweater.

"I don't know why I even bothered to tell them. I should have listened to you. They don't care about anything but their paperwork and meetings. King Elias could attack the castle and they would stand behind the stone walls and watch it crumble." My voice came out shaky with the angry, unshed tears threatening to spill over my cheeks.

How could they treat my friend with such dismissal? How could they be the ones to uphold the law in the kingdom but let Elias continue his tyrannical actions? It made no sense to me, but if they weren't going to protect the kingdom, I would.

"It's okay, sweetheart. It's in your nature to take the righteous path first, but we don't need them. We'll think of something and we'll come up with another plan." Julien brushed a thumb over my hand, and I let one heavy, angry tear fall over my cheek. It was the only one I would allow.

"I'm tired of doing the right thing, Julien."

Brushing the tear from my face, I tilted my head up so our eyes locked across the small space between us. Leaning forward, Julien tucked a stray curl behind my ear, letting his fingertips trace a soft line down to my jaw. He cupped my cheek, making my breath hitch in my throat. Even in the dim light, his eyes seemed to sparkle with excitement.

"So, Braelyn Grey, what's the plan? I know that look in your eyes, and you aren't going to stop just because the elders told you to." He raised a questioning brow at me, and I couldn't help the smile that pulled up the corner of my lips.

"You know me too well, Julien Thorne. We leave in two days."

Ten

The plans had been set. We would wait until the ball commenced in two days' time. It would be too risky to leave any sooner. My encounter with the elders had only made them watch me closer, and we couldn't risk them stopping me from leaving. So, we would make them believe I'd listened to their warning and only escape the castle once all the formalities of the ball were complete. Everyone would be too full of food and good cider to notice us sneaking off... or so we hoped.

After evading Mrs Boswell's tail for a whole day, she'd become even more overbearing in her attempts to keep me close. She woke me at sunrise and escorted me to my lessons with the elders, arriving just before it finished to then take me to the training area to start my magic practice. Any hope I'd had that she would leave me alone with Grey and Verena was quashed when she pulled out a needle and began darning a pair of socks. Every now and again she would glance up at our progress with a nod of approval, only to turn back to her work. It was infuriating. While I quite liked Mrs Boswell, her constant lingering only made me more agitated.

"She's relentless, isn't she?" Verena whispered in my ear as we practised sparring with fire.

Verena's hands sparked with each jab she sent in my direction. While none of our punches landed, she said it was a good way to learn to conjure magic without relying on the use of space for large hand movements. It also worked well for us to talk without being overheard.

"You have no idea," I murmured back. My hands mimicked her movements, sending a steady stream of flames in Verena's direction.

She dodged each one with the ease and grace of someone who had been practising the art of fighting for years. She was a force to be reckoned with and, even in the last few days, my fire magic bristled with renewed vigour from simply being around her. Grey watched us from the sidelines, his mood visibly improved since we'd told him of our plans. As predicted, Grey had no issues with my proposal. I would create a distraction to pull Elias's gaze while the others snuck into his camp to free Theo. Verena had her doubts, but in the end she'd agreed to come along if only to keep an eye on Elias and make sure we stayed out of harm's way.

"So, I'm guessing you haven't been able to finalise the last few pieces of the plan yet?" Verena's eyes subtly shifted over to where Mrs Boswell was making steady work on darning her socks.

Her deft fingers worked the needle and thread quickly through the fabric, no doubt her air magic aiding her in speed. It wouldn't be long until she finished, and I'd be whisked off to the next thing she had arranged for me to do.

"You guess correctly. All I need is to visit the apothecary and grab a few things for the journey, but I'm starting to wonder if I'll be left alone long enough to go down there."

Grey made his way over to us, his back turned in Mrs Boswell's direction, allowing us a moment of privacy.

"Could Julien not go down and get what we need?" His voice was soft as he toyed with a small silver coin, flipping it between his fingers. A gift Julien had brought back for him from Gillie.

"It would be the more logical thing to do, Brae," Verena replied.

It made sense. With Mrs Boswell's constant gaze focused on my every movement, it would be near impossible for me to get down to the apothecary unseen. But, aside from wanting to actively contribute to the preparations of our plan, I desperately needed to see my mother. She had spent the last few days in the apothecary, stocking her shelves and making sure she had everything in her arsenal for the many witches, warlocks, dwarves, and elves who would be attending the ball. '*You can never be too prepared,*' she'd told me over breakfast yesterday before rushing off again. Since her rescue, my mother had taken it upon herself to work in the castle's apothecary and assist in healing those who lived here. It was where she felt most comfortable, and she was good at what she did, but it left very little time for me to speak with her privately.

"Magic practice is over, Miss Grey." Mrs Boswell's voice broke my train of thought. She watched us with wary scepticism, her hands placed firmly on her hips.

Looking back to Verena and Grey, I gave them a quick smile. "I'll get to the apothecary," I whispered, before following Mrs Boswell back through the trees and up towards the castle.

The chance to visit my mother came the morning of the ball. Like clockwork, Mrs Boswell bustled into my room at sunrise, pulling the sheer curtains aside and bathing my room in buttery light. The chilly air of Samhain caressed my skin, making me shiver as I dressed behind the changing screen. When I emerged a few moments later in a pair of trousers and a cream sweater, Mrs Boswell clucked loudly, abandoning all attempts to hide her disapproval of my refusal to wear a dress like the rest of the witches in the castle. After sitting in front of the ornate mirror, Mrs Boswell ran a brush through my curls before plaiting my hair down my back and securing the end with a blue-grey ribbon.

"Just lovely," she said with an approving nod.

I smiled kindly, but remained silent. My mood was as stormy as the grey clouds dotting the sky, and anything I said would surely be taken out of context.

"Now, my attentions will be required elsewhere today, Miss Grey. With the ball mere hours away, there is much to do, so Miss Rigby will be attending to you today."

My mood picked up at her words. While I had no idea who Miss Rigby was, she would surely be a lot easier to avoid than Mrs Boswell.

"I'll be back in moment, Miss Grey." She bustled towards the door, closing it firmly behind her.

The tell-tale click of the lock sounded seconds after she took her leave. I waited a few minutes to allow her time to get down the hallway and out of sight before picking up a long hair pin from the table by the mirror and rushing to the door. I had minimal time before Mrs Boswell returned with Miss Rigby, so I needed to make this quick. Placing the hairpin in the lock, I moved it around slowly, trying to listen for the click. Julien had shown me how to do this. He'd told me every great explorer should know how to pick a lock in case of capture. My gut told me he'd learned it to get himself into trouble rather than out of it, but I had watched him intently as he showed me and found I was quite good at it. My chest rose and fell rapidly, my heart rate quickening the longer it took me to crack the lock. After what felt like a very long few seconds, it finally clicked quietly. A wide grin spread across my face.

"May the elements bless you, Julien Thorne," I whispered against the door.

Pushing it open just enough for me to see into the hallway, I glanced around the empty space, letting out a shaky breath upon seeing no guards posted by my door. *Thank the elements.* The elders had insisted on having someone stationed by my door at night, no doubt to prevent me from sneaking off. This morning, however, the chair remained empty, the guard most likely on their way for their shift patrolling the wall. I stepped into the hallway and made a dash for the stairs, hoping Mrs Boswell and Miss Rigby wouldn't walk into me. Luck seemed to be on my side. I reached the landing above the foyer, the castle below bustling with activity. Earth wielders were busy conjuring floral wreaths and garlands, and a group of air witches hung them about the grand staircase with expert precision. A fire warlock dashed around to the sconces lining the wall by the entrance, lighting each one before moving on to the next room. Everyone was so preoccupied with their own tasks, no one bothered to look in my direction. Weaving through the many witches and warlocks, I made my way to the corridor leading to the apothecary. Compared to the busy foyer, this part of the castle was blissfully quiet. I settled into the silence, enjoying the quiet solitude as I rounded the corner.

The door to the apothecary was propped open. I paused just shy of the landing, lingering on the last step as my hands trembled. My main reason for coming here was to obtain herbs for our journey, but a small part of me wanted to divulge everything to my mother. To admit my fears, my doubts, and have her tell me everything would be okay. But I couldn't. It was better for her not to know. Pushing the door open the rest of the way, I stepped into the small room and found my mother's back to me. She faced the large storage cabinets, her head bent over the bench as she worked the large mortar and pestle. Her hands moved deftly as she added herbs and oils to whatever mixture she was preparing. I cleared my throat so as not to startle her and she spun around, a smile lighting her beautiful face.

"Braelyn, what a pleasant surprise." Wiping her hands on the apron tied about her waist, her black dress swished around her ankles as she wrapped me in a tight hug. She smelt of rosemary and lavender oil. A smell I would only ever associate with her.

"What are you doing here?" she asked.

Holding me at arms-length, her smile faltered as eyes so like my own searched my face—extracting all my secrets before I could tell her myself. I tried to turn my face away from her assessing gaze, but her long fingers tilted my chin until our eyes met. It only made it harder to hide from her.

She let out a long sigh, her lips pursing the same way Hazel's did when my grandmother disapproved of something. "You're going after Theo, even though the elders forbade it."

I shifted my gaze, not wanting to see the disapproval and instead focusing on the herbs hanging above the square table.

"I have to," I replied gently.

"Braelyn, have you thought this through? What you're doing will have severe repercussions. Not to mention the countless dangers you would be putting yourself in." My mother's voice was soft, but it held a sharpness she used when trying to make me see reason.

"I don't have to think it through. The elders aren't willing to do what needs to be done to rescue Theo and protect the kingdom, so I will. It's my fault Theo was captured in the first place, and I won't leave him behind."

"It's not your fault, Brae. Theo knew of the dangers when he made his choice. You can't blame yourself for that." Her voice softened further, helping to soothe the guilty ache that had grown steadily in my chest since Theo disappeared. I turned my eyes back to my mother, who watched me carefully, the green specks in her hazel eyes glistening like broken sea glass in the dim light.

"I understand," I whispered back, "but this is my burden to bear and only I can make it right."

My mother's chin dropped to her chest. She let out a deep sigh, scrubbing her hands against the square apron secured around her small frame.

"Are you going to try and stop me?" I asked quietly, not sure if knowing her answer would make it any easier.

She took one of my hands, her calloused fingers rough after years of grinding herbs. She gifted me a small smile. "No, Brae. I'm not going to stop you. But it doesn't mean I agree with what you're doing."

Turning back to the cabinets, she walked slowly along the bench and pulled several vials from the shelves. I recognised the old, yellowed labels from Julien's apothecary. A jar of moon water, sparkling like stars on a clear night; a bottle of healing elixir, the contents a light rose colour from the pink salt used to brew it; then two long vials laid on their sides. The first one contained sanitatem—the healing poultice—useful for preventing infections. The other was convaluisset—the recovery elixir—a foul-tasting potion that had once helped me recover from exhaustion brought on by excessive magic use. I watched her hands adeptly mix the potions we needed for our journey, reminding me of the hours the two of us spent in her parlour. Those were simpler times that seemed so long ago now. My mother continued pulling strips of fabric, oils, and salves from the many draws built into the cabinet. Lastly, she reached up and cut a few stems of the dried herbs hanging above us. The subtle aroma of lavender, chamomile, and sage floated through the room, mixing with the fire's woody scent. It was cosy and warm and reminded me of the parlour in our apothecary in Pryhollow. It was no wonder my mother loved it here. Wrapping the herbs in twine, she folded everything into a length of brown cloth.

"Just a few essentials. In case you or Julien get hurt. I'm assuming he's going with you?" A knowing glint appeared in her eyes and a warm blush crept up my neck. I had only told my mother a few things regarding my relationship with Julien, but something told me she knew more than she let on.

"Please be careful, Brae," she whispered as she pulled me in for another hug. "Your duty might lie with protecting the kingdom, but my duty will always lie in protecting you."

My heart ached at the amount of love my mother poured into her words. She had devoted her life to keeping me safe, and I hated being the cause of her worry. But, if I could stop Elias, she would no longer have cause for concern and we would be able to live out our life peacefully at Ellesmere castle.

"Always," I whispered back before pulling away. "You'll come and help me get ready for the ball, won't you?"

She smiled lovingly at me. "Of course."

The rest of the day consisted of trying to avoid Miss Rigby—which was hard considering I'd never seen her before—and squeezing in a last-minute magic session with Verena. Much to Grey and Julien's annoyance, they had been roped into assisting in the set-up of the Grand Hall.

My chest rose and fell rapidly as I dodged another stream of fire from Verena's flaming hands. Sweat dampened her bright red hair, her arms lined with crimson from the consequences of her magic use.

"We should probably head back up to the castle now, Brae," Verena called out.

The sun had begun to sink below the horizon, turning the sky a deep shade of purple. Not even my sweater could keep the chill from my skin as the shadows around us lengthened, reaching towards us like thin, spindly fingers.

"You're probably right." I sent one final blast of flames in Verena's direction, trying to catch her off guard.

She simply caught the scalding flames between her hands before extinguishing it with a small click of her fingers.

"You're getting much stronger," she said while retrieving her orange coat from the damp ground and throwing it around her shoulders.

"I feel stronger," I replied, my chest swelling with pride over Verena's compliment. I flexed my fingers, smiling as a few flickers of lightning continued to curl through them.

We walked side-by-side up the steep gardens, watching the last-minute preparations for the ball take place. A few earth wielders were still fiddling with the flowers by the entrance, and a stack of ornate chairs floated in front of us as we ascended the front steps. As we came to a stop just inside the foyer, Verena pulled me into a corner, away from prying eyes.

"What's wrong?" I asked, my smile faltering at the look of concern on her face.

Verena glanced around the busy foyer. "Brae, are you sure you want to go ahead with this plan of yours?"

"We don't have a choice, Verena. It's not foolproof but it's the only way we can get Theo back." My brow furrowed. "I thought you were okay with the plan?"

Verena shook her head. "I said I would come along to make sure Elias behaved himself, not that I was okay with it."

I placed a hand on her arm and gave it a reassuring squeeze. "It'll be okay, Verena. Everything will be fine."

She turned her golden gaze back to me and let out a small sigh.

"Okay, Brae, but if he does one thing that puts us in danger, it'll be the last thing he does on this earth." With a flick of her ruby hair, she turned her back on me and pranced up the stairs towards the bedchambers, her hips swaying saucily until she was out of sight.

ffff

I made my way back to my bedroom to find it buzzing with half a dozen witches already waiting for me. My mother floated gracefully around the room, instructing everyone on what they needed to do, but there was one person I did not expect to see. Maeve sat in the large, embroidered chair by the window, her long legs thrown over one of the chair's gold arms. Her eyes found me across the room and a bright smile spread over her face. Returning her smile, I crossed the space and embraced her in a long hug. Maeve's chest reverberated with a small chuckle before she stepped up and held me at arms-length.

"Let me get a good look at you, pet." Still beaming, Maeve looked me up and down, her green eyes raking over every inch of me as if trying to take mental pictures to take back to Pryhollow. "Well, haven't you grown into a stunning witch these last few weeks?"

My cheeks warmed at her compliment. She hadn't changed in the weeks I'd been gone. Her long grey hair fell in a tangled mess over her bony shoulders, her face shining with the heat lingering in the room.

"What are you doing here? I didn't expect to see you."

Maeve's eyes widened. "Blimey, pet, you didn't honestly think I would miss a ball held in your name, did you?" Giving me a playful shove, she took a seat back on the chair by the window.

Almost immediately, an elderly witch took me by the arm and steered me towards the large bathroom. A bath had been drawn for me in the gold-and-white clawfoot tub, steam filling the small space and making me feel overly warm beneath my sweater. Discarding my clothes, I put a tentative hand to the water, testing the temperature. It was perfect. I sighed with contentment as I stepped into the porcelain tub, the warm water soothing the tension in my muscles. Numerous herbs floated delicately on the surface, giving off scents of lavender, chamomile, and rose. Allowing the heady scent to envelop me for a moment, I closed my eyes and enjoyed the weightless feel of the water. In a matter of hours, we would be on our way to rescuing Theo. This relaxation would be traded for action, so despite the elderly witch's stern words commanding me to get out, I enjoyed a few extra minutes of the water's warm embrace.

"Braelyn, if you don't get out now, you're going to send Mrs Boswell into a flurry." My mother's soft voice brought me back to the present.

Opening my eyes and taking one last deep inhalation of the bath's beautiful aroma, I stepped into the soft towel my mother held open for me. She steered me over to the stool in front of the dressing table where Mrs Boswell waited. A terse look glinted in her eyes and she clicked her tongue like an old mother hen before setting to work. Pulling a brush through my unruly curls, she arranged my hair into a knot at the base of my neck, securing small pieces with glittering hairpins. She let a few loose curls fall around my face in elegant waves. Next, she pulled out a few tubes of rouge-coloured lipsticks and held them up to my face. Tutting to herself, she eventually settled on a dusty pink and brushed the sweet-scented stick over my lips. Lastly, she pinched at my cheeks, making them appear rosier than usual. My mother blocked my view from the mirror, but as she moved to my left, I caught a glimpse of myself. I hardly recognised the girl looking back at me. My cheeks were a rose-coloured pink and the faint shimmer of lipstick made my lips appear full. Mrs Boswell had even managed to tame my curls for the night.

"Thank you, Mrs Boswell," I said, my voice catching at the last moment.

She nodded once, her cheeks reddening at my compliment and her face softening.

My mother smiled lovingly at me. "It's time for your dress."

A small tawny-haired witch stepped from behind a folded screen, a dress the colour of lavender draped over her thin arms. She passed it to my mother with a small, shy smile.

"It arrived from Mrs Bishop's shop just this morning."

Grey's mother owned the local dressmakers. She had gone to so much effort to create a garment for me to wear tonight. If we made it back from our journey, I would need to thank her for her generosity.

I didn't look at my reflection as I changed until my mother had secured the small button at the base of my neck. Closing my eyes and taking a small breath, I turned my gaze to the mirror, my eyes widening at the reflection staring back at me. Purple-grey leaves wrapped around my arms and chest, shimmering brightly in the firelight. The intricate pattern cascaded down one side of my body, the other side coming to a stop at my waist. The softest lavender silk made up the skirts of the dress, which hugged the curves of my hips before falling loosely to the ground around my feet. It was the most beautiful dress I'd ever worn.

"You look like a true queen," my mother whispered, cupping my cheek softly in her hand.

I smiled at her, not knowing if the nerves rolling in my stomach would allow me to speak. For the first time since the prophecy had been foretold, I felt like the queen I was born to be.

Eleven

Entering the grand hall was like being transported into a different world. The large doors stood open, allowing the beautiful, lilting elvish music to float out and pull you into the space beyond. Garlands of greenery dotted with spring flowers of every colour hung from the chandeliers, their floral scents of jasmine, gardenia, and honeysuckle settling in the air. If I closed my eyes, I could almost imagine being back in Hazel's garden. My grandmother was knowingly absent from tonight's festivities, having declined her invitation weeks ago, my mother explaining she'd never liked big events. Green foliage wrapped around the balustrades of the balconies above, while tiny fairy lights twinkled like golden stars between their leaves. Candles flickered romantically in tall candelabras, casting a wonderful warm glow amongst the room. It truly was a magnificent sight.

It seemed every witch and warlock from the kingdom had turned out for the event. Dressed in their very best, witches swathed in every colour and warlocks cloaked in their finest robes filled the large room. My mother walked beside me, her face glowing with warmth. Her long, dark hair was worn out and cascaded down her back in a shimmering sheet. She had discarded her usual preference for black, instead looking resplendent in a deep silver-grey dress with a sweeping neckline. A long silver chain was secured around her elegant neck, a small pendant dangling from the end. I recognised it as the one Hazel had been wearing the night I'd met her and wondered if she had sent it to my mother to wear tonight. Everyone's eyes were trained in our direction, and I was grateful for her comforting presence next to me. As we weaved through the guests in attendance, many stopped me to congratulate my newly found queendom.

"So lovely," a witch in bright pink whispered to her friend as they walked past.

"Just delightful, she is. Had the pleasure of talking..." Another voice trailed off as a warlock bragged to his friends of our supposed conversation.

"So wonderful to see Prince Evander's descendant on the throne," said a warlock dressed in robes of starlight silver. The mention of my father's name made my heart flutter, and my mother went rigid beside me. I wondered if this was the reason she spent so much time in the apothecary, her heart unable to bear the constant mention of my father. The warlock grasped my hand, shaking it profusely before his bearded friend launched into a detailed conversation about his travels to the castle.

While I shook everyone's hand and smiled politely, there was only one person I wanted to find. My mother stuck close to my side, introducing me to some of the witches and warlocks she tended to at the castle's apothecary. While talking to my mother's friendly patients, I was aware of someone watching me from the corner of the room. Balor stood by the entryway, his arm linked with an older elf who was draped in a long, billowing cloak made of forest leaves and bird feathers. His pearlescent skin shimmered like moonstone in the firelight, his long antlers rivalling that of Balor's. They wore the same arrogant expression, their eyes flicking to the witches and warlocks crowding before them with haughty derision. The older elf could have only been the King of Silvae, Balor's father. The elven prince inclined his head in my direction and I returned a quivering smile as my eyes shifted to the spot where one of his antlers had been hacked away, used in the creation of the circulum. Balor raised a hand to his head, smoothing his silver hair over the vacant spot, his face a mask of indifference. The king of the elves piqued my curiosity, but my eyes continued to roam the hall in search of the man I most wanted to see.

I almost didn't recognise him.

Julien stood at the other end of the ballroom, his usual dark jeans and t-shirt replaced with black pressed trousers and a matching jacket. He'd even managed to brush his tousled hair. He was speaking animatedly to someone I immediately recognised as Lorcan Lightbeard—the joyous dwarf we'd rescued from the castle dungeons after Elias had fled. Lorcan was first to spot me. He bowed deeply upon my arrival, making Julien turn on the spot.

"Braelyn, you are wonderful to behold, my dear." Lorcan grasped my hand in his large one and brushed a soft kiss across my knuckles, making me blush at his formality.

"Thank you, Lorcan. I'm so pleased to see you."

He beamed with happiness before excusing himself and rushing off to speak to another dwarf who watched us closely with hooded eyes. His watchful gaze made me shift uncomfortably, but it didn't last long, Lorcan pulling his attention elsewhere.

Julien still hadn't said a word since I arrived. Now, standing closer to him, I was taken aback by just how handsome he looked. A charcoal vest was fitted perfectly against his chest, a white cravat poking from the top. The torso of his jacket was adorned with a brilliant red embroidery in the shape of tiny flames that cascaded down the sides of his jacket.

"Someone brushes up nicely," I said, trying to break the awkward silence that had settled between us.

Julien took a step closer to me, reaching out a hand to gently brush aside one of my curls. "Braelyn, I..." His brown gaze explored every inch of me. Clearing his throat, his dark eyes settled back on my face, a soft look in his eyes.

"Braelyn, I have no words."

My heart fluttered like tiny bird wings against my ribs as Julien held out a hand to me, bowing slightly at the waist.

"Would you like to dance?" he asked, stepping back just enough for me to look up into his face.

"I'm not very good at this type of dancing," I replied, gesturing around to everyone's slow, melodic movements on the dancefloor.

"Do you trust me?" he whispered beside my ear before giving me a warm smile. He backed away, his hand held out towards me.

"Always," I replied, feeling my cheeks warm with my response.

Julien's eyes glistened as I placed my hand in his, the hundreds of candles making the amber flecks burn like gold. He pulled me towards the large group of people who twisted and twirled to the soft, whimsical music. There was only one elf playing and his long, elegant fingers brushed the piano keys so lightly it seemed like he barely touched them. His dark-blue skin glittered with hundreds of golden specks, each one glinting in the candlelight the more he swayed to the music. I recognised him as the elf who played at the Forest Festival over a month ago. Sensing my gaze, he turned in my direction, his fingers never faltering on the piano keys. The moment our eyes met, he placed a large hand over his heart, bowing his head slightly. I was taken aback by his gesture and, not knowing how to respond, I offered him a small smile.

"It seems I'm not the only one whose attention you've captured tonight."

I followed Julien's gaze, noting the many occupants spinning close to get a better look at their future queen. Beaming faces stared at us from every direction, making me feel even more self-conscious. Julien pulled me close, my chest grazing his as he wrapped one arm around my waist. His broad form blocked most of the onlookers' awed expressions, helping to ease the anxious feeling in the pit of my stomach. Gently lifting my hand, he laced his calloused fingers through my own and slowly led me around the dancefloor. Julien's steps never faltered, each footfall carefully placed and in time with the soulful music. After a while, I forgot about the stares and lost myself to his touch. Julien's thumb traced small circles over my hand, the rhythm following the tune of the melody. Each step brought his body closer to mine, causing magic to bristle beneath my skin. My cheeks flushed and I heard Julien's deep chuckle reverberate through me. Tightening his arm around my waist, he pulled my body so close I could feel the warmth of his skin through the thin fabric of my dress. He leant forward, his lips brushing my ear.

"You're breathtaking, Braelyn, especially when you blush like that." He stroked the back of his hand softly down my cheek, making my face smoulder.

My stomach fluttered wildly and my skin burned where his palm rested at the small of my back. He studied my face with such intensity, my fingers sparked with electricity. My heart hammered so hard, my emotions entwined with my magic and set my soul ablaze. Trailing my hand over his shoulder, I ran my fingers down the sleeve of his jacket to squeeze his forearm tightly. Julien's gaze settled on my lips and I tilted my head forward, my breath hitching. Our lips were inches apart when a sharp trill made me jolt away. The music had quietened almost entirely, and a soft clinking sounded from the back of the hall. With the music dimmed, Julien stopped our movements. Placing a finger under my chin, he brought my attention to his face again and gave me one of his lopsided smiles. The heat from our near kiss still hung in the air, but the electricity tingling my fingers had dulled to a low thrum.

"Are you sure you're ready for this, sweetheart?"

I took a deep, steadying breath, calming the magic shivering nervously in my veins. "As ready as I'll ever be."

Julien took my hand in his and walked me towards the large dais running the length of the back wall. The elders stood at the top, adorned in dresses and suits relating to their element. Helene looked striking in a bright emerald dress that flowed down past her ankles, the colour complementing her beautiful, bronzed skin. Silas wore a sky-blue suit, making the brightness of his blue eyes sparkle like diamonds. Magdalena stood at the top of the stairs adorned in a silver-grey dress that rippled like a stormy sky. And lastly, Aramis sat on a seat towards the back of the dais, dressed perfectly in deep-red tunic and black trousers. He leaned against the plush chair, one of his long legs crossed over the other. Upon seeing me glance in his direction, he nodded once before standing and taking up residence with the other elders at the front of the stage. A small smile tipped up the corner of his mouth. Of all the elders, he was the most puzzling. I still couldn't understand why he'd taken my side at our meeting, but there was something about him that made me wary of his actions. Julien released his grip on my hand, nudging me gently to make my way up the small set of wooden steps. A hush fell over the ballroom as all eyes fell on me. I spotted a few of the elves amongst the sea of witches and warlocks, their magical appearance striking amongst the differing colours of the elements. A few dwarves stood at the foot of the dais, their long, thick hair pulled back in braids. Instead of traditional dress, they wore their battle armour with pride.

The dwarf Lorcan was speaking to earlier watched me closely. Standing taller than the other dwarves around him, his dark hair was pulled back into a thick ponytail at the base of his neck and secured with an engraved copper fastening. His leather tunic was emblazoned with dwarf-ish runes, an intricate pin fastened to his broad chest.

Magdalena cleared her throat. "We, the Elders of Ellesmere, stand before you to present your next Queen of Ellesmere. Braelyn Grey. Spirit Witch."

Applause broke out through the ballroom as Helene stepped forward and tucked my hand tightly in the crook of her elbow. Hundreds of faces smiled up at me, but some stood out from the others. My mother's hazel eyes glistened with unshed tears as she smiled lovingly at me from just below. Maeve stood by her side, dressed in simple blue pants and a blazer. She clapped along with the other occupants, her face creased in an ear-splitting smile. Only a few metres from them Grey and Verena beamed up at me, their chests puffed out proudly. Like Julien, Grey wore a simple black suit adorned with light blue embroidery befitting his water element. The pattern looped and twisted over the lapels of his jacket in an arrangement of waves. Verena's dress was a stark contrast. Wearing a deep orange silk slip, it accentuated every part of her body. Her red hair fell in waves over one shoulder, complementing her look.

Gazing out at the crowd of people, my heart ached at the one missing face. Theo's absence tonight had slowly turned my stomach to stone. He was never far from my thoughts these days, and I longed to exit the stage so we could put our plan into motion. The noise in the ballroom continued to rise, but it did little to hide the loud scream that echoed around the stone walls. It pierced the growing commotion, drawing everyone's attention to the middle of the hall. As the crowd parted, I had the perfect view of what had caused the disruption. One of Ellesmere's guards lay on his back; a large bloody gash sweeping across his torso. People cried out in horror at the gruesome wound, but I already knew the creature responsible for this type of damage. We were running out of time. We couldn't wait for the formalities to be over.

We needed to leave now.

Twelve

T he large arched windows overlooking the grand hall shattered, glass raining down on the people below as a snarl tore through the air. Dozens of monstrum descended on the room, their deafening screeches drowning out the terrified screams echoing around the hall. The monsters from my nightmares poured into the building, their twisted wooden limbs creaking with each movement. Ellesmere guards darted through the doors, their hands already alight with magic. Flashes of red and blue coloured my vision as fire and water wielders tried to hold off the barrage of creatures still streaming through the windows. Two monstrum circled towards a group of elves, the creatures' obsidian eyes glinting with malice as they stalked them. One monstrum lashed out with razor-sharp claws. A few of the elves managed to dart out of the way, but one wasn't so lucky. Her screams split the air as the creature's claws slashed over her back, blood dripping from the tips. Running down the wooden steps, I met Julien at the foot of the dais, his arm snaking around my waist protectively. A few dwarf warriors ran past us, their iron forged weapons raised and ready to taste blood. They hacked at the closest monstrum, the creature lashing out with frenzied movements, but the dwarves' skill rivalled that of the Ellesmere guards, and they managed to take it down without injury.

"We need to leave," Julien said hurriedly, his dark eyes wide and alert.

"We need to help everyone," I yelled, straining my voice above the terrified cries filling the room.

I pulled against Julien, desperately trying to free myself, but it only made him tighten his hold. He spun around to face me, his hands gripping my shoulders, the tightness of his grip making me wince.

"Braelyn, if we don't leave now the castle will be put on lockdown and we'll have no chance of getting to Theo. It's now or never."

He was right. My head screamed at me to go with him, but my conscience urged me to fight. It was my duty as the future queen of Ellesmere to protect my people, and how could I do that if I fled?

How could you do that if you were dead? argued the little voice in the back of my mind. They were right. As I shook my head to clear my thoughts, Julien took my hand and pulled me to the edge of the hall. He pushed through the frightened crowd of fleeing people desperate to find their loved ones, and Verena and Grey found us a few seconds later.

"What the hell are those things?" I heard Grey yell over the screams, but there was no time to reply.

My stomach constricted as three monstrum leered before us. I stared at the large ram skulls perched atop their shoulders and the jaws pulled back in a snarl. Magic pulsed through my body, reacting to my fear. Julien and Verena's hands lit up the space around us, their flames flickering menacingly as the creatures stalked us. Grey's water magic hovered in front of him, the icy daggers aimed directly at the monstrums' chests. The creatures let out an eerie growl and, after swallowing the bile rising in my throat, I let my magic loose. Thick, heavy clouds rose in front of us, my air magic creating a protective barrier and the distraction we needed. With a flick of his wrist, Julien sent a ball of fire careening into the monstrum closest to him. The creature howled as its tree-like limbs erupted in flames. Verena and Grey took down the last two before Grey grabbed my wrist and pulled me across the dance floor. The stones were slick with blood, my delicate heels slipping more than once. Grey kept a firm hold of my arm, his grip never faltering. We skidded to a halt on the other side of the room, discord continuing to unfold behind us. Grey hunched over, his hands on his knees as he tried to catch his breath. The energy erupting around the grand hall was chaotic. Magic rippled through the air, everyone doing their best to fight against the advancing monstrum.

"What are we doing, Julien? I thought you said we were getting out of here?" Turning back to the pandemonium, my eyes searched the crowd, needing to locate my mother. I couldn't leave without knowing she was safe. But no matter how hard I searched the sea of faces, I couldn't find her amongst the turmoil unfolding around the hall.

"We are, I just need to find the... Yes! Got it."

My head snapped back to Julien's wide smile. His hand rested on a small rectangle of stone slightly darker than the rest. Grey and Verena looked between each other, their wrinkled brows reflecting my own confusion at Julien's sudden burst of excitement.

"Julien, what are you..." My voice trailed off, eyes growing wide as part of the stone wall swung inwards to reveal a dark passageway.

"Come on," he shouted, gesturing for us to move.

Grey and Verena hurried through the door, but again, I searched the crowd for the one person I needed to see. After a few long, drawn-out seconds, my eyes settled on her face. The elders and my mother hurried between the injured littering the floor. She was talking animatedly to Helene, her words lost amongst the shrieks and screams. When she looked up and found me, a sad smile touched her lips before she motioned with her hand for me to go. My lip quivered, tears stinging my eyes. I didn't even get the chance to say a proper goodbye, but I couldn't dwell on it. This was our only chance. Tearing my gaze away from the bloodied ballroom, I slid my fingers through Julien's and let him pull me through the doorway, throwing my world into darkness.

Julien and Grey pushed the door closed, their shoulders thrust up against the stone, sealing us off from the chaos. Verena clicked her fingers together, a tiny flame igniting above her hand.

"Where does this lead?" I whispered.

"It's a secret passageway that leads to the dungeons. It was built in case the royal family needed to escape the castle should it ever be overrun. Pretty useful in my opinion." Julien shrugged one shoulder, giving me a cheeky smirk.

"So, what's the plan now?" Verena asked quietly, concern lining her face. "There could be more of those creatures around the castle. We may walk straight into the jaws of the enemy."

Grey's brow was furrowed in concentration, his eyes flicking around the small, dank passageway as if trying to sift through his thoughts.

Julien ran a hand through his hair before his gaze found mine in the dim light. My mind worked through all the scenarios that could play out, but none of them seemed like a logical solution to our problem.

"We'll need to risk it," Julien said. "If there are more out there, we can lose them in the Ironwood."

He led the way through the dark corridor, lit only by Verena's flame. The stones were damp and a constant trickle of water ran in small rivulets along the cool rocks. The stale, musty smell of mould wafted around us the deeper we ventured into the castle, the stench making me cough and gag more than once. As we rounded a sharp corner, a bright glow finally illuminated the path before us. The staircase leading to the dungeons twisted down to the right and I breathed a sigh of relief, knowing we'd come out at the right spot. The lit sconces lining the wall flickered in friendly welcome, their warmth wrapping around me like a blanket. We descended into the belly of Ellesmere Castle. No guards awaited us—just as I'd hoped—all too busy with the madness still transpiring floors above us.

"Back so soon, Braelyn?" Victoria's crisp voice echoed through the dungeons, her face just visible behind the iron bars. "It sounds like quite a party up there." Her smirk made my blood boil.

"Ignore her, Brae," Verena said calmly.

Julien threw me a pack he'd cleverly concealed in a hole in the wall. Earlier this morning, he'd ventured down here to hide our belongings in the off-chance we needed to make a quick getaway. I'd never been more thankful for his foresight.

"Everyone needs to change quickly," Julien told us.

"The man with a plan, are we?" Sebastien said with a harsh bark of laughter. "It won't protect you, Brother, we heard the creatures hunting you."

Julien ignored his brother, but his agitation was evident in the way his shoulders tensed and his lips pressed into a thin line. Julien shrugged off his jacket and began to unbutton the silver fastenings on his vest. Grey and Verena stripped off their garments, not caring about changing out in the open. I had no intentions of doing the same. As I moved discreetly towards an empty cell, Julien reached out and grabbed my arm, his fingers wrapping around my wrist.

"Where are you going?" he asked, his other hand pausing over the top buttons of his shirt. He had already removed his vest and his white shirt was untucked from his trousers.

"You might all be happy to change here, but I need some privacy," I replied, my eyes shifting to the empty cell next to Victoria.

"Oh, sorry. Just with everything going on..." Julien's voice trailed off. I could just make out the slight blush colouring his cheeks in the warm lighting.

I smiled back at him. "I won't be long."

Concealed in the dark cell, I discarded my beautiful dress in exchange for the clothes Julien had stolen from the armoury. The dark trousers felt rough against my skin after wearing my silk dress for the last few hours. Tucking in the white shirt, I picked up the brown leather armour and was shocked at how light it felt. It had been crafted by the dwarves in the Ironwood Mountains and could withstand blows from both magic and weapons. I pulled it over my head and nodded. It was enough to protect my chest and shoulders. It was a little tight as I secured the clasps beneath my armpits, but I felt more at ease with its protection. I stuffed my feet into my black leather boots before casting one last look at my dress. It seemed silly to be sad about parting with something so trivial, but it had been the first time in weeks that I felt somewhat normal. With one last longing look, I picked it up off the cot and handed it to Julien as I joined the others. He stuffed our discarded formal attire into the same hole he'd hidden our packs in before covering it over with a stone.

"Okay, there's only one thing left to do." My gaze shifted to Victoria's cell.

Julien stared at me with wide eyes. "You can't be serious."

"We don't have a choice," I said, stepping closer to him so Victoria and Sebastien couldn't overhear our conversation. Verena and Grey stared between us, their eyes narrowed and lips pursed. "Elias knows she's here and if Victoria is part of the key to summoning Lilith, we can't risk him finding her. At least if we take her with us, we can keep an eye on her."

"Brae's right," Grey said. "It's safer to bring her with us. We would control the narrative then."

Julien let out a frustrated huff. "Fine. What about him?" He gestured to Sebastien with a quick nod of his head.

"He's the lesser of two evils, Julien." I looked over to where Sebastien still leaned against the iron bars, his arms crossed over his chest in a gesture that looked so much like his brother it almost took my breath away. "He stays here."

Victoria stared at us, a small smirk lifting one side of her mouth, but before Julien was able to take a step towards her, a noise from the staircase made us spin in a flurry of magic. Elemental magic ignited from each of our raised hands. Julien and Verena's were ablaze with fire, while Grey's were an icy blue and covered in tiny, needle-like icicles. My hands crackled with lightning, splintering menacingly as it formed around my fingers. But as the person came into view, I sagged in relief, immediately extinguishing my magic. Maeve stood framed in the dungeon archway, her thick curly hair standing up at all angles. Her face was pinched in a frown, eyes searching the room before finally landing on me.

She let out a small, exasperated sigh. "Oh, thank the elements I found you, pet. Your mother told me you might be down here." Rushing over to me, she pulled me tight to her chest before holding me at arms-length.

"Maeve, what are you—"

She held up a finger to her lips, pulling me away from the others to a quiet corner sheathed in darkness.

"Brae, there isn't much time, and I can't say this in front of certain people." Her eyes shifted to Victoria and Sebastien's cell before settling back on me. "Once you leave Ellesmere Castle, you can't come back."

My eyes grew wide as a deep cold began to settle in my bones. "I don't... what are you—"

"Brae, listen to me, the elders are never going to understand the real threat that King Elias poses. They are so set in their belief that history would never repeat itself, they couldn't begin to comprehend what is coming. Trust me when I say you need to gather reinforcements. Something dangerous is coming, and we all need to be ready when it does."

Maeve's beautiful green eyes bore into me with such ferocity I had to turn my gaze away. Her hands bit into the tops of my arm. Confusion clouded my mind as I tried to decipher the meaning behind her words, but despite knowing the dangers that could occur, I couldn't understand why Maeve was telling me these things. What was I supposed to do? Shaking me to refocus my attention, Maeve looked at me, her eyes imploring.

"I need you to trust me, Brae. Please."

My heart beat wildly as I stared back into the face of the woman who had helped raise me, but despite my confusion, I nodded. I trusted

Maeve with my life. If she was telling me to stay away, there was a good reason behind it.

"Okay, Maeve," I replied. "Where do I go?"

A noise sounded above, making me startle. Taking one of her hands from my shoulders, she thrust it into the pocket of her deep blue trousers. I'd never seen Maeve so elegantly dressed before tonight—she radiated natural beauty. She placed something soft in the palm of my hand before pulling me in for one last hug.

"What I've just given you holds my instructions. Show it only to those you trust."

Tears welled behind my eyes. "Will I see you again?"

She touched a soft hand to my cheek. "I hope so, pet. Now go."

Her hands fell from my arms, the absence of her touch sitting heavy on my chest.

"Goodbye," I whispered as I watched Maeve's shape disappear into the shadows of the dungeon.

When she moved into the firelight once more, her face was illuminated in an orange glow. A small smile pulled at her lips, but it was the wink—that same playful wink which had eased my nerves at my induction ceremony—that blurred my vision and opened the flood gates. Tears trailed silently down my cheeks. I hoped we would see each other again.

Julien had already released Victoria from her cell and was waiting for me at the base of the stairs leading to the castle grounds. He'd bound her hands before her with iron manacles, preventing her from conjuring any magic.

"What a touching moment, qui decipitor. Too bad you won't be alive long enough to see her again."

I bit back my retort, knowing there was no time to waste on Victoria's words. It was time to go.

❦

Getting out of the dungeons was easy. The narrow corridor led us all the way up to the wooden door Julien, Theo, and I had used to break into the castle only a few weeks prior. But as we came to a halt at the entryway, we reached the place where so many things could go wrong.

I spotted no guards patrolling directly outside the door, thanks to the small slit I peered through. The elders had diverted most guards to the attack on the grand hall. It was standard protocol to protect the weakest spot, but it left the rest of the castle exposed. My lessons with Magdalena taught me about our defensive strategies, and when she told me of this one, I was sceptical. But as I turned my gaze skyward, I noted Ellesmere guards patrolling the castle wall. If we were quiet enough, we could probably sneak over to the tunnel unnoticed, but it wouldn't help us once we got to the other side. The exposed clearing between the castle wall and the Ironwood would be where we needed coverage.

"What do you see, Brae?" Verena's whispered voice sounded somewhere behind me.

"There are guards on patrol at the wall," I replied, my voice soft.

"We'll need a way to divert their attention if we want to slip by with no one sounding an alarm," Verena said.

"You've done this once before, qui decepitor, you could certainly do it again." Victoria's voice dripped with sarcasm, bringing back some of the memories I'd buried in a locked chest in the back of my mind. "If I recall correctly, you did some serious damage with your magic that night."

Remembering back to the night we broke into the castle, my mind conjured up the images of the guards I'd slain in order for us to rescue my mother. I had never meant to hurt anyone, but the magic that rushed through my veins that night had felt like it had a mind of its own. Bile rose in my throat, leaving a bitter taste in my mouth. Their tortured screams still haunted me.

"Brae, don't listen to her! You did what you needed to do to save your mother." Verena's soft voice wrapped around me, pulling me back towards the light.

She was right. Those men had worked for King Elias. If I hadn't stopped them, they would have gladly handed me over to the king to siphon my magic, or worse.

"What if we just knocked them out? It would give us enough time to get through the tunnel and into the shadows of the Ironwood before they would wake," Grey said, his fingers once again flipping the silver coin.

I shook my head. "If Elias sends more monstrum to attack the castle, we will need all the guards we have."

I sifted through the possibilities, my mind slowly piecing together a quickly hatched plan. It wasn't foolproof, but if it worked, we would reach the Ironwood without being seen.

"I've got an idea," I whispered. My voice sounded a lot stronger than I felt. "We'll need to be quick to get across to the tunnel."

"And once we're on the other side?" Julien asked, eyebrow raised in question.

"We'll use magic to conceal us."

"As good a plan as any," Grey said.

"All right. Verena, keep watch from the door and wait for my signal to come out."

"Be careful," Julien whispered from the back of our group. He'd insisted on keeping a watchful eye on Victoria, not trusting her to oblige.

"Always am," I replied with a wink.

I caught Julien's smirk and the shake of his head before I slipped through the door and into the cover of darkness.

Thirteen

O ut in the cool night air, I was grateful for the olive-green jacket that went with my ensemble. Like the rest of my outfit, it was made from soft, light wool that was warm and easy to move in. The season of Samhain was fast approaching and, with it, the first winds of winter. A cool breeze bit at my cheeks and I buried my face in the collar of my jacket to keep warm. Sticking to the shadows along the outskirts of the castle, I stopped a few paces away from the dungeon door, looking up and down the courtyard. It was empty. The guards patrolling the wall had their backs turned to me, no doubt searching the Ironwood for any signs of another attack. The two closest to us were huddled together, hands turning over each other as they tried to keep warm. A small orange glow emanated from one of the warlocks' hands. Guards were stationed at equal intervals, their stance rigid and ready for anything. From our position, it was only a few metres to the tunnel. If we were quick and silent, we would make it unseen. When I rapped my knuckles once on the wooden door, Verena's golden eye peered through the crack. I gave her a quick nod and she opened the door, allowing the rest of our troupe to flood out into the silver light of the full moon. Julien and Victoria were the last to exit, and I couldn't help but feel like something had happened in the small amount of time I'd been outside. Julien wore a stony expression—his dark eyes narrowing in Victoria's direction. A cruel smirk spread across her face the longer she watched me. Ignoring her smugness, I took his hand in mine, feeling the muscles in his arm loosen slightly at my touch.

"Did something happen?" I whispered, close to his ear.

Julien smiled, but a small sigh escaped his lips before it was lost on the wind. If I hadn't been standing so close to him, I might have missed it. "It's nothing, Braelyn. Just Victoria being her usual cruel self."

I studied his face carefully, his deep brown eyes almost black in the shadows. His brow creased slightly in the middle, reflecting the concern that began to settle in my stomach. I bit the inside of my lip, then nodded once. I wasn't sure what had passed between them in the corridor, but I knew for a fact that, whatever it was, it couldn't be good. Clearing my throat, I walked to the head of our group and studied the faces of my friends as they stared back at me, waiting for my next instruction. In a matter of hours, I'd gone from a nervous soon-to-be queen to the head of a small band of soldiers. This journey had so much riding on it and it wasn't just Theo's life hanging in the balance, it was all of Ellesmere. Taking a steadying breath, I squared my shoulders. I was ready. Ready to save Theo and finally put an end to Elias.

"Let's do this," I said. A small grin spread over my face, but it did little to stop the nerves rolling in my belly.

My friends returned encouraging smiles, their faces bright in the moonlight. We turned our backs on Ellesmere Castle and ventured into the tunnel's depths. The stagnant smell of dirty water and mould wafted up my nose, making my stomach churn. Memories from our first journey flooded my mind and fear clawed its way up my throat as I wondered what awaited us on the other side. Julien's lips were pinched, tightening the longer he stared down the length of the tunnel. His shoulders were rigid, no doubt recalling the fear he'd suffered from his claustrophobia.

"Well, this should be fun," Verena said somewhere behind me.

"Let's just get this over with," Julien growled, pushing Victoria deeper into the tunnel without waiting for anyone to follow.

His muscled form was swallowed by the encroaching darkness and, with one last breath of fresh air, I followed behind him, hoping he would be okay until we got to the other side.

Once in the tunnel, Julien refused to stop and it seemed everyone was happy to comply. The muscles in his shoulders were pulled tight, as if all his strength was being used to prevent himself crumbling to the damp ground. I longed to reach out and ease the tightness that corded the muscles in his neck, but I refrained. The others didn't know about his fear of dark spaces and it wasn't something I wanted Victoria to know. Her cruelty knew no bounds, and she would only use it to torment him.

The stench in the tunnel was so pungent, I longed to be amongst the trees in the Ironwood—a notion I never thought I would hope for. As we continued to wade through the mud and water lining the walls and floor, the silver light of the moon suddenly loomed ahead of us. I could almost feel the tension ease from everyone's shoulders as we stepped out into the fresh, clean air—gulping it in as we kept our backs pressed against the wall.

"I hope I never have to set foot in that disgusting hole again," Victoria said.

She tried unsuccessfully to brush the grime from her trousers, but Julien's grip on her arm was too tight for her to move. She grumbled as much when I came to stand by Julien's side.

"Are you okay?" I asked quietly.

I knew his fear of confined spaces had taken its toll on him the first time we'd entered the tunnel and I needed to know he wasn't going through that again. The image of Julien huddled against the wall, his eyes closed and brows pinched in terror was something I would never forget.

"I'm fine, sweetheart." With his free hand, he brushed along my arm, his warm fingers lingering a little longer than usual. Goosebumps that had nothing to do with the crisp air prickled over my skin.

Somewhere behind me, Verena cleared her throat with a small cough, breaking the trance between us.

Julien turned his eyes away from me, blinking a few times as if to clear his thoughts. "We should get moving. Braelyn, what's the plan?"

I smiled and clicked my fingers, a dark cloud permeating the air in front of me. Julien raised a questioning brow, the corner of his lip pulled up in a lopsided smile. Bringing my hands together, I summoned as much air magic as possible, drawing it into my hands to create a dense, dark cloud. Magic rippled beneath my skin, the call of the darkness like a gentle hum in the back of my mind. I pushed it aside, focusing all my efforts into containing my magic just in my hands. Victoria scoffed, her manacled wrists twitching ever so slightly as she watched me call on her element.

"Everyone move closer to me," I whispered.

Grey and Verena stepped to my right side, while Julien pulled Victoria in closer and came to stand behind me, his body only inches from mine. The dark cloud grew as I lifted my hands from my sides, the shadows spreading until we were concealed in the cool misty air of the cloud cover.

"Impressive, Brae," Grey whispered to my right, and I could hear the pride strengthening his words.

"Together," I replied, my eyes focused on the tree line metres ahead.

We moved in unison, stepping out into the open clearing with nothing but my air magic concealing us. It provided us with enough cover to blend in perfectly with the heavy shadows. My heart pounded in my ears as we reached the halfway point. One slip and the guards would spot us. We didn't stop until we reached the shadowed edge of the Ironwood where everyone took a moment to catch their breath. The dark clouds began to recede as I curled in my fingers, causing the mist to fade into the shadows of the Ironwood. Verena and Grey passed a waterskin between themselves, offering it to Julien who declined with a quick wave of his hand. He stared into the vast expanse of trees before us, seemingly lost in thought, but I knew better. He would be searching the woods, keeping a watchful eye for any sinister creatures lurking in the shadows. He knew the Ironwood well, as did I. Nothing was ever as it seemed here. A faint rustle through the underbrush to my left caught everyone's attention, shifting their gaze to where Julien still glared into the shadows. It sounded loud against the quiet night. Verena's hands emitted orange-red sparks as she drew on her magic, but a tiny pull in my mind alerted me it was no foe.

"It's okay," I said. "It's only Alpheus."

It was like saying his name aloud had conjured him before us. The jackalope appeared in a sliver of moonlight, long antlers glinting menacingly.

"Is that a... a..." Grey's voice shook as he watched Alpheus stop in front of me.

His kind, owl-like eyes watched Verena and Grey closely, as if he was assessing their worthiness. I stifled a chuckle as I watched the two of them try to make sense of the incredible creature standing before them. To all who lived in Ellesmere, the jackalopes were a superstition, little more than a story parents told to children. But to me, Alpheus was one of my dearest friends.

"Verena, Grey, I'd like to introduce you to Alpheus. Our distraction."

On cue, Alpheus tipped his head in a small bow of acknowledgement. After Julien had left my room on the day we'd been to see Victoria, through the connection in our mind, I'd reached out to Alpheus to ask for his help once again. As much as I wanted to be the one to help, I knew my presence in the clearing would only hinder our chances of getting Theo out safely, so I told him of our need for a distraction—something that would pull the eyes of Elias's guards away from our attempts to free Theo. He'd obliged willingly. Verena and Grey continued to stare at the jackalope with wide eyes and open mouths. I could only imagine how years of superstition were preventing them from believing what they were seeing.

"*It always fascinates me watching your kind see one of us for the first time,*" Alpheus's light voice sounded in my mind. His almond eyes shifted between Grey and Verena with the utmost curiosity.

"Alpheus." Julien's smiling face appeared beside me. He bent down to lay a hand between Alpheus's antlers, a touch of affection between old friends.

I often wondered what would have become of us and Ellesmere had Alpheus not appeared that day by the ash tree. *Would we have eventually found our way out of the clearing? Would we have ever made it to my mother in time?* These questions often plagued my mind in the early hours when nightmares had woken me from a fitful sleep. But, deep in the pit of my stomach, I knew. I'd seen the consequences of my failure in the visions that Althea's journal and The Book of Lilith provided. We couldn't fail. *I* couldn't fail. A warm touch jolted me out of my thoughts and I looked up to find Julien's steady hands grasping my arms firmly. I let out a shaky breath, my racing heart slowly returning to its normal rhythm.

"Braelyn, are you all right?" Julien's brow creased in concern, his dark eyes searching my face to check I was okay.

His hands dropped to my own, and his thumb traced soothing circles on the base of my wrist.

"I'm fine. Just... a lot of memories linger in the shadows here."

He laced his fingers between my own and gave my hand a reassuring squeeze. But it wasn't only the memories that plagued me. Maeve's note was a heavy weight in my pocket and her words echoed through my mind. She spoke of these dangers like they were certain. She told me history would repeat itself. Did she know of Elias's plan to summon Lilith from the Underworld? Could the reinforcements she spoke of be mending the feud between the dwarves of the Ironwood Mountains and the elves of Silvae?

"*My friend.*" Alpheus's voice sounded in my mind, jolting me from my thoughts. "*We must be on our way. We have lingered too long here.*"

Giving Julien's hand a quick squeeze, I let it fall between us. It was time to rescue Theo, fulfil the prophecy, and put an end to Elias's vindictive games.

"*Lead the way, Alpheus,*" I said with a brave smile, praying to the elements that no dangers would befall us.

We followed our good luck charm into the belly of the beast.

⟨⟨⟨⟨⟨

After a few hours of walking, my feet were beginning to throb painfully in my boots. The moon sat high in the sky, the silvery light barely bright enough to reveal the path Alpheus led us on. With Samhain soon approaching, the ground was littered with pine needles and leaves which crunched noisily under my boots. The trees creaked and groaned in the cool breeze, whispering amongst each other. My eyes darted in every direction, searching the shadows for dangers I knew lingered just out of sight. My constant probing of the darkness caused a permanent frown to etch itself into my forehead. I hated how on edge the Ironwood made me feel, but I had every reason to be cautious. These woods had a mind of their own.

Alpheus came to an abrupt stop, forcing me to sidestep to avoid crushing his tail beneath my boot. Grey and Verena's reflexes weren't as quick. They bumped into my back, almost sending me face-first into the thick blanket of leaves covering the ground. Both murmured a quick apology, but my attention was already back on Alpheus.

"*Is there something wrong?*" I asked him.

His ears twitched slightly, pricking up at any rustle or creak, listening for something our ears couldn't hear.

"The woods are too quiet. Something is lurking amongst the shadows, but what it is, I do not know."

My magic hummed to life at Alpheus's warning, making my fingers tingle. Power buzzed within my veins and unfurled within my chest. Small flickers of fire curled around my fingers and raised the tiny hairs on my arms, but Alpheus's soothing voice calmed my storm.

"*It is okay, my friend. Contain your magic. It is not needed yet.*" Alpheus gave one last glance around the Ironwood before leading us onwards. "*Come, there is somewhere we can rest a while before we reach the place you seek.*"

We arrived at a small crop of trees a short while later, which proved to be an excellent spot to rest our weary feet. The tall pines had grown in what appeared to be a crescent moon shape, standing so close together you could barely see between the trunks to the other side. While we were still exposed from the front, we were perfectly hidden from behind which, according to Julien, was an advantage.

"We'll rest here for a little while before we start moving again," I told everyone before dropping my leather satchel beside a fallen pine tree and stretching out my aching back. Each muscle was stiff and sore from the hike.

Julien checked Victoria's shackles to ensure they were secure. With her hands tightly bound by iron, her magic was no use to her, but it seemed Julien was taking no chances. Gripping Victoria's shoulder, he moved her to sit on the fallen pine tree.

"Easy there, Julien," Victoria crooned, then smirked in my direction. "No need to be so rough."

Julien's posture stiffened, his hands curling into tight fists. An animalistic growl sounded low in his throat before he turned on his heel and stalked off. Bitterness burned through me, my clenched jaw aching from the pressure.

"I'll watch over her," Grey said to no one in particular.

He took a seat beside her, shooting a quick glance between Julien and me. After a moment's deliberation, he turned back to face Victoria, but every now and again, his eyes would shift to the silver coin he flipped between his long fingers. I wondered why he toyed with the small trinket so much. The closer we got to Theo, the more Grey retreated into himself. It made me wonder if the fears that hardened my stomach also played on Grey's mind. Verena stretched herself out on the ground, her face turned to the canopy above. She smiled softly and closed her eyes, lacing her hands together and resting them on her chest. I wished it were that easy for me to relax. Magic made my fingers tingle violently. I stuffed them in my armpits, trying to ease the pressure still building along my shoulders. The ash tree was close, and knowing there was so much riding on the next part of our journey was causing my magic to jump erratically beneath my skin.

Julien stood to the side, his back turned to the alcove of trees. The muscles in his shoulders were tight and his hands were stuffed into the pockets of his coat. I ventured over to him, observing the tension in his jaw.

"Penny for your thoughts?" I asked, my voice soft as I tried to coax out whatever had made the fierce anger inside him rush to the surface.

Julien ran a hand through his hair and took a deep breath. The muscles in his jaw relaxed only slightly as he turned to face me.

"It's nothing, Braelyn."

I knew better. Getting Julien to talk about his feelings was like trying to extract poison from a barghest bite—slow and dangerous.

"What happened between you and Victoria?" I asked, not sure I truly wanted to know the answer.

My hands fiddled with the hem of my coat, folding and unfolding the fabric with anxious fingers. Julien let out a long sigh and ran another hand through his hair, keeping his eyes ahead as he spoke.

"It was just before you came to Ellesmere," he replied, his voice low. "It was coming up to the eve of my mother's passing and Victoria and I had been spending a lot of time together."

The jealous monster residing in the very depths of my heart reared its ugly head. I knew Julien had a life before I came to Ellesmere, but to know something had existed between him and Victoria—someone who hated me so intently—made my stomach twist.

"I ended it before things got too serious, but she never seemed to move on. Then when you came along..." Julien's voice trailed off, and he finally turned to me. "She just knows how to get under my skin. Every time I must see her, I'm reminded of the person I was when I was with her. A person so full of darkness and hatred, worthy of the whispers and rumours people spoke about me."

He searched my face, his dark eyes drinking in all my features. The distance that had settled around us began to close. Whatever feelings existed between Julien and me bound us together in a way I would never truly understand. But I desperately wanted to. Reaching up, I cupped his face in my hand, the coarse stubble coating his cheeks rough against my palm. Julien's eyes burned deep and dark before he pulled me close, the warmth of his body easing the tightness in my chest. He lifted his hand to my face, brushing his thumb over my bottom lip before trailing it down my chin. My body flooded with heat, my cheeks blazing a deep crimson. Conscious of Grey, Verena, and Victoria only a few paces away, I tried to pull away from him, but he only held me closer. His arm snaked around my waist, pulling me to his chest. The air around us was charged, burning with electric heat. Julien slowly eased his arm from around me, my skin tingling as cool air settled on the place it had rested. Leaning back a little, he searched my face once more.

"What's wrong? he asked, seeing the small frown pulling at my brow.

I wrapped my arms around my mid-section, trying to hold in some of the heat from his touch.

"I've dreamed of being in this exact moment for so long, but now we're here, I can't help but think of all the ways this rescue could go wrong."

Despite the unease churning in my stomach, my voice came out steady. My eyes roamed the encroaching darkness as if I might be able to pull the dangers forward with my gaze alone. It was almost dusk and soon we would need to ready ourselves to infiltrate Elias's camp. Our plan wasn't bad, but it still held so many risks, especially now Victoria was here.

"Braelyn, I promised I would do anything to help you bring Theo back, and I meant every word. You're not alone in this, sweetheart. And besides, we have a badass spirit witch on our side. It's got to count for something, right?"

With a quick smile, he retreated to our friends, who were preparing to walk into the clutches of our enemy. To *save* our friend. And while my heart still felt heavy with worry, I couldn't help but hold on to the small flicker of determination that clawed its way to the surface. Julien was right. I was a badass spirit witch and, by the elements, I was done with Elias's continued cruelty. Taking a deep breath, I let myself feel the magic I had tried so desperately to suppress since my last encounter with the ash tree. If we were going to pull this off, I would need to call on all of my magic—even the parts that lingered in the shadows, waiting for the chance to be unleashed.

Fourteen

Safely concealed amongst the twisted tree trunks, we were able to see into most of Elias's camp, but not all. Parts of the clearing were shrouded in darkness and, with the heavy cover of trees in front of us, it was difficult to get a perfect view. A large, cream-coloured tent had been pitched in one corner of the clearing, no doubt where Elias was hiding himself. Dozens of his followers milled about the clearing, their voices carrying on the breeze as they walked the outskirts, eyes trained on the forest around them. They no longer donned their traditional iron armour, likely due to arrogance at having no enemies amongst the Ironwood. All the better for us. Their simple pants and tunics would not protect against our magic should we need it.

Cool wisps of night air tickled the exposed parts of my skin, sending small shivers down the length of my spine. Pulling my coat tighter around me, I breathed a puff of warm air into my cupped hands, hoping this small action would help keep the chill away, even if only for a moment. Now that we had arrived at the outskirts of Elias's hideout, my nerves had begun to get the better of me. Verena had left to scout the rest of the camp—the first part of our plan set in motion. We had no idea what might await us on the other side of the ash tree and, before sending Alpheus into the clutches of our enemy, I had to know what we were up against. My stomach fluttered nervously as I shot a quick glance to Julien and Grey and took in their worried expressions. Verena hadn't been gone long, but we were all anxious for her return. We only had one chance to rescue Theo. The longer we remained by the clearing, the higher the risk of being caught. Once Elias knew we were here, it would only be a matter of seconds until he set his guards on us—or worse, the evil creatures I knew would be hiding not far from here. We needed to have the element of surprise. Only then would it give Grey the time he needed to free Theo.

I peered between the mangled branches, trying to find where Theo might be held. Had Elias tethered him to a tree? Was he in the tent, bound and gagged? My heart constricted each time I spotted blond hair or a freckled face, only to realise it was just another of the king's men. Sighing heavily, I turned my attention to the ash tree. Its long-lifeless branches stretched seemingly endlessly into the night sky, disappearing into the canopy above. The gentle hum of dark magic called out to me from the gaping hole that pierced the middle of the ash tree's trunk— coaxing me forward like a beckoning hand. I remembered the way I'd felt the last time I used magic here. Effortlessly powerful. My palms tingled with the promise of wielding that power again, but despite my growing desires, I tore my gaze away from the tree. Instantly, the tingling in my palms began to subside and my eyes became more focused. I needed to be careful. We couldn't afford for me to lose control of my magic. Not yet. A soft rustle to my right startled me from my thoughts, but a second later, Verena's red hair appeared through the shadows. Her nose and cheeks were painted a light pink, chilled from the cold air.

"We have a problem," she said.

"What did you see?" Grey asked, taking the words from my mouth.

Verena moved in the direction she'd just come from, beckoning us to follow her with a quick incline of her head. We moved in single file behind her, conscious of avoiding the sharp snap of a twig and alerting the guards to our whereabouts. Grey walked in front of me, his head bent against the low hanging branches. Julien and Victoria brought up the rear. Every few seconds I would hear him grunt in frustration as she tried to pull away from his tight grip. Her hands were still manacled in front of her, but we'd decided to use a strip of fabric my mother had provided to cover her mouth, preventing her from calling out and giving away our position. We hadn't moved far from where we'd been standing, still safely concealed amongst the trees when my stomach lurched at the sight before us. A large cage sat behind one of the ash tree's twisted roots and, through the thick bars, I could just make out the features of Theo's face. Grey gasped somewhere behind me, his line of sight on par with my own. Julien growled low in his throat, his hands curling into tight fists at his sides. My heart thundered so loud I was surprised none of the guards nearby heard.

"It's made of iron," Verena whispered. "I overheard a guard bragging to his friends about how it was his idea."

My worst fears were coming true. I knew attempting to get Theo back would be difficult, but this presented an entirely different set of problems. Witches and warlocks were some of the most powerful magical beings in all of Ellesmere, but even our magic had limits. It was no match for iron-made weapons or traps. Forged by the dwarves in the depths of the Ironwood Mountains, iron held its own set of magical properties and had been a deterrent to witches and warlocks for centuries.

"By the elements, Brae." Grey's voice shook with unshed tears. "How are we going to rescue him now?"

Blood pounded in my ears and my hands shook with a wave of overwhelming anger that threatened to bring me to my knees. Theo's kind face had been beaten bloody, no doubt by the hands of some or all of King Elias's men. Even from this distance, there was no mistaking the spread of dark purple bruises mixed with the yellow green of old ones. Fresh blood trickled from an open gash above his eyebrow, blood matting in his dirty hair.

"Braelyn, what do you want to do?" Julien pressed.

It took all my energy to pull my eyes from Theo and focus on Julien's face. Even in the cover of darkness, I could see the white-hot anger in the set of his jaw. A fire burned behind his dark eyes as my own magic clawed to be released. This wasn't over yet.

I reached a trembling hand into my hair, still fastened in a knot at my neck. Pulling one of the hair pins free, I handed it to Julien, whose frown shifted into a wide smile. The sharp pin glinted in the small slivers of moonlight. Alpheus could still provide the distraction we needed to get Theo free, only now, it would be Julien, not Grey, who would be the one to release Theo from his iron prison.

"Do you think you could pick the lock quickly enough to avoid being seen?"

Julien quirked a brow as he plucked the pin from my fingers, turning it over in his hand.

"No problem, sweetheart." He gave me a quick wink before turning on his heel and disappearing into the darkness.

It wasn't exactly what I'd planned, but the situation called for a change. We waited in silence for Julien to reach the other side of the clearing. Once in position, he'd conjure a small flame just bright enough to signal he was ready before extinguishing it, then Alpheus would make his move. The minutes ticked over slowly and I gnawed at my nails, my eyes never straying from the spot between the trees where Julien's flame should appear. After a lengthy wait, a tiny orange glint blossomed in the darkness. It disappeared as quickly as it came. A shaky laugh escaped my lips, my shoulders slumping forward in relief.

"Okay, Alpheus, you're up."

He inclined his head in understanding before darting to the left and disappearing between the trees.

"Do you think this is going to work, Brae?" Verena said behind me, her face hovering over my shoulder.

"Yes," I replied, wringing my hands together. "It has to."

We didn't need to wait long before we saw Alpheus dart from the shadows. He skirted the trees lining the clearing, his fur a caramel blur amongst the muddy browns and deep greens of the underbrush. A handful of guards milling about a small fire turned their heads in his direction as they warmed themselves by the fire's glow. Their mouths moved, but I was too far away to hear what they were saying. Again, Alpheus flitted through the trees, pulling the guards' attention. A few of Elias's men called to others across the clearing, and a group of them moved to the spot where Alpheus had disappeared. I turned my gaze back to Theo, whose nose was pressed to the bars as he tried to see what had pulled so many guards away from their post. A second passed and Julien darted from the shadows, his body bent low to avoid being seen. Theo stumbled back as he reached the bars, his eyes growing wide as

Julien inclined his head in our direction. My heart felt like it was lodged in my throat, its fast rhythm pounding against my ribs as I watched Julien pick the lock. My teeth worried at my lip, eyes darting to where Alpheus still held the guards' attention. They watched the shadowed trees with rapt attention, fire and lightning sparking in the night air as they searched for the jackalope's whereabouts. Alpheus appeared just to the right of their search party, his almond eyes glinting in the warm light of the campfire. He raised one of his back legs before letting it slam against the dirt, the ground shuddering beneath our feet. Dozens of eyes turned in his direction, but as he made to escape back into the cover of darkness, a stream of fire shot from a witch's hands, aimed directly at Alpheus's side. My breath caught in my throat, a low cry squeezing from my tightening chest. He managed to dart out of the way, but not before the flames singed the fur on his left side. The jackalope staggered, but he managed to disappear back into the shadows, his light voice echoing in my mind.

"*The cruel king,*" was all I heard before the tether connecting us closed.

Fifteen

My head snapped to the tent in the corner of the clearing where Elias stood in the opening, illuminated by the golden glow of a lantern. He looked almost ethereal in the warm light with his white tunic billowing in the wind. Too preoccupied with making sure Alpheus, Julien, and Theo escaped unscathed, I hadn't initially seen him emerge from his quarters. He watched the guards through narrowed eyes before his gaze settled on the iron cage. A chill settled over me, my stomach turning to lead. Theo mouthed something to Julien, who shot to his feet, his hands still desperately trying to pick the lock.

Elias's face flushed a deep crimson, a smirk pulling up the corners of his mouth. A dozen guards surged toward the cage, just as Julien managed to swing the door open.

"They need to get out of there," Grey said through clenched teeth, his face ashen as he stared at Theo's small form.

Theo stumbled as he clung to the bars, fighting to be free of his iron prison. His white t-shirt was stained brown, and his cream-coloured trousers hung low over his bony hips. He'd suffered greatly in his time here. My fingers pried at the laces on my chest armour, fumbling to loosen the ties to ease the guilt constricting my chest. Julien tossed Theo's arm over his shoulders, trying to support his weight. He took one step towards the tree line, Theo's feet dragging along ground, when both stilled, seemingly frozen in time.

"Braelyn." Verena nodded in Elias's direction.

The circulum glinted in the firelight as Elias curled his fingers towards himself. The air in the clearing shifted and my legs turned to stone. I watched with wide eyes as Julien and Theo turned mid-air, as if held with invisible strings.

"We need to do something," Grey urged, his hands shimmering a brilliant blue as he struggled to contain his magic.

"It needs to be me," I said quickly. "I'm the only one he'd be willing to speak to."

"What are you going to do, Brae? You can't hand yourself over to him. He'll kill you." Verena gripped the top of my arm, her hold deceptively strong. I could just make out her face in the dark, her lips pressed into a thin line and her brow creased in concern.

"I'm not going to do that, but we can give Elias what he wants," I said between clenched teeth. "One life for the others."

Verena let go of my arm, her face falling as she turned to Victoria. "Brae, I don't know if this is a good idea."

"If it's between her, Julien, and Theo, I'll take the chance, Verena. I refuse to leave them behind. Please trust me."

Grey hurled Victoria to her feet. She'd been sitting amongst the leaf litter, still bound and gagged. He pushed her forward and she stumbled over her feet. No longer needing her quiet, I removed the gag. To my surprise, she was frowning.

"You're being stupid, qui decepitor. Do you really think King Elias is going to let you just walk out of here?"

Her voice held a softness I hadn't heard before. Now that we were in the presence of her king, I expected her to be elated—thrilled to be reunited with him so she could fulfil what she believed to be her destiny. Instead, it seemed she was having a change of heart. Could I sacrifice Victoria if she no longer wanted to side with Elias? I had no choice. If it was between her and my friends, I would gladly hand her over. Ignoring her words, I pushed her towards a small break in the twisted trees and thanked the elements for the decaying leaves silencing our footfalls. If my plan was to work, we needed the element of surprise. It was only a short distance from where we'd been hidden to the edge of the clearing and, despite the coolness of the night, I felt too hot beneath my coat. My heart seemed to beat in time with my heavy steps, each one seeming to echo in my chest. I tried to calm the magic bristling more violently with every step closer to the ash tree, but the steady hum of magic lingered around me like an unwanted guest. Powerful and dangerous. I stared at the lifeless branches as we neared the edge of the clearing, noting how death and decay had spread further since I'd last been here. The ash tree pulled on the life force of everything surrounding it. If Elias was successful with his plans, there would be nothing left of the Ironwood. As if sensing our arrival, a sharp squeal pulled my attention towards the canopy. My eyes searched the shadows for whatever had made the noise. For a moment, I could've sworn something was perched high up in one of the trees, but when I blinked, it was gone.

Turning back to Victoria, I gave her my most sincere smile. "Are you ready to be reunited with your king?"

She snickered in response, but her usual icy glare was distant. I pushed her through the opening of the clearing and immediately became aware of two things. One, an ever increasing group of the king's followers stood either side of the ash tree, their lips pulled back in vicious toothy smirks. And two, Theo and Julien were being held by not only Elias, but Sebastien. So, I had been right. Elias had infiltrated the castle to free his two most dutiful followers. The king stood in front of the ash tree, his onyx eyes gleaming in the firelight, a knife held firmly to Theo's throat. Sebastien held an arm around Julien's neck, too, a dagger pressed over his heart.

"Hello, my dear niece." Elias smirked at me, his long fingers tightening on Theo's shoulder. "What an unexpected surprise."

The hand holding the knife remained steady as Elias pushed Theo forward with a quick nudge of his leg. Filled with tears, Theo's eyes never left my own.

"Brae."

Theo's voice was a broken whisper and it shattered my heart into a million tiny pieces. He looked weak. Exhausted. Dark circles shadowed eyes that once glistened a bright blue. Now, they were dark and desperate. My hand twitched at my side, the magic within reacting to the rage unfurling in my chest. Elias would pay for what he'd done.

"Braelyn, you shouldn't have come," Julien managed to bark out before Sebastien silenced him, tightening his arm about his throat.

My hand twitched as Sebastien's lips curved into a cruel smile. Side by side, the two brothers no longer looked alike. Where Julien was broad with muscles cording his arms, Sebastien was leaner and taller. Their bronzed complexion and dark eyes was as far as the resemblance stretched. Clasping Victoria's arm tightly, I turned my attention back to the king.

"I believe I have something precious of yours," I replied to Elias, my words spitting like venom from a serpent.

I shoved Victoria forward and her eyes widened slightly at Theo's appearance. If I didn't know any better, she looked almost sad for him. That gaze soon turned to King Elias, though, and her face softened into adoration.

"My king," she said breathlessly, before inclining her head forward.

"Ah, Victoria. How wonderful it is to see you again. I was sorry to leave you behind in my dash to escape." To my surprise, he almost sounded sincere. "But, Miss Grey, as much as I missed the loyalty Victoria showed me, I cannot fathom why you'd think I would trade her for the two warlocks I possess?"

A blank look appeared on the king's face. A face that, at times, looked so much like my father's I had to remind myself he was no longer here. That it was by the king's hand he had died all those years ago. My mind clouded with confusion as he stared at me. Did he not know Victoria was part of the key to releasing Lilith? If not, I had the upper hand. I held all the cards and, by the elements, I would have him at my mercy. As I opened my mouth to speak, something Helene had taught me in one of our lessons stopped my thoughts in their tracks. For centuries, kings and queens were often blackmailed into giving others what they wanted, so it was in our best interests to feign ignorance. To not let the other person see they held something of great value to us. My gut told me Elias was playing the game, but I needed to be sure.

"My apologies, Elias, but I was under the impression you knew exactly who Victoria Belfour was when you brought her into your employment."

His smirk faltered at the lack of title, but it only lasted a second before his porcelain face shifted back into its usual stoic facade. I shook my head, feigning ignorance.

Elias looked between me and Victoria with an unreadable expression on his face. His onyx eyes narrowed as I watched him consider his next move.

I sniggered. "I believe you once told me you take the time to acquaint yourself with all peoples within your kingdom. Or is this no longer your kingdom?"

I thought back on the day I'd rescued my mother. Elias had made such a show of knowing so much about Theo and Julien's past, and I was astounded he wouldn't take the same interest in his followers. My mouth quirked up at the corner, the hint of a smile touching my lips. He knew exactly who Victoria was, but he was testing me as I was testing him. Heat flooded Elias's cheeks and anger seemed to roll off him in waves. His hand tightened around the knife held at Theo's throat.

"You have grown bold over these last few weeks, Miss Grey." His voice snapped on the last word. "I see those crones have been teaching you well. What is it you want?"

All manner of the once cunning King of Ellesmere dissolved into nothing but hatred towards me and the information I possessed. If I could keep this up long enough, maybe I could get us out of here without bloodshed. And yet... despite having the upper hand, my palms grew sweaty. Magic buzzed like static beneath my skin, growing more potent and powerful the longer I remained close to the ash tree.

"I want a trade," I said, a little too quickly. "Victoria for Theo and Julien. A more than fair exchange in my opinion."

Elias narrowed his eyes at me. "And why should I give them up, Miss Grey, when you have so kindly brought both of the remaining pieces to me?" A flicker of satisfaction lightened Elias's dark eyes.

My mind whirred as I recalled the small vial Elias had been holding in my vision, the dark liquid oozing over the roots of the ash tree. Victoria was right. We did hold the key to summoning Lilith, only, 'key' was a polite term for coining what really unlocked the spell Elias needed: our blood. Part of me had hoped Victoria was only lying to get what she wanted when she'd first mentioned the key in her cell, but as Elias's elation soon disappeared, his regal expression back in place, I knew better. While I would have traded anything to get Theo and Julien back, a small part of me worried about the look that had appeared behind Elias's eyes. Unease gnawed at the back of my mind about what would happen if I failed the next part of my quest. To stop my hand from trembling, I shoved it deep into my jacket pocket, and my fingers found the crumpled note Maeve had given me earlier.

I lifted my chin. "At the moment, I hold both keys to Lilith's release, and you hold none." My hand trembled ever so slightly as I waited with bated breath for him to deliberate on what he'd heard.

Elias's smile widened into a malicious grin. "I clearly hold all the power here, Miss Grey. You are outnumbered." He waved around at his band of loyal followers. Each one stood at the ready, their hands bright with shimmering displays of blue, red, and green.

"If you don't let them go," I said slowly, "I will kill Victoria where she stands."

Thick vines curled around Victoria's feet as I raised my hand. They snaked over her body, wrapping around her arms and cutting off the air in her throat. She thrashed against their hold, but they tightened ever harder. "Would it not be prudent for you to have at least one of your keys?"

Elias's skin turned a mottled red. His hand tightened over the knife's hilt, his knuckles turning white beneath the pressure. I could sense the rage bubbling beneath the calm exterior, his vanity fractured over the fact I'd beaten him at his own game.

"So, are we in agreement?" I continued, my eyes never leaving Elias's face. "Victoria for Theo and Julien?"

After what seemed like an eternity of waiting, he smiled maliciously at me. His face contorted once more into the cruel king I'd met mere weeks ago.

"We are, dear niece. The useless warlock and the traitor for Miss Belfour."

Elias removed the knife from Theo's throat and took him by the arm, forcing him to move forward while using Theo as a human shield as he did. With a quick incline of his head, he gestured for Sebastien to do the same. I dropped my raised hand and let the vines encircling Victoria uncurl, then pushed her forward.

The entire clearing had gone deathly quiet. Even the wind seemed to hold its breath in the wake of our exchange. As Theo and Julien crossed the short distance towards me, I loosened my grip on Victoria's arm and we backed away from the line of Elias's followers. I didn't dare take my eyes off the king until we were safely tucked between the trees of the Ironwood. Elias watched me through narrowed eyes as a burly guard with cropped dark hair appeared at his side. The tension in the clearing was palpable, settling over us like a thick blanket. The longer it took for us to reach the edge of the clearing, the heavier it became. My hand gripped Theo's frail wrist so tightly, I swore the bones cracked beneath my fingers. Julien stood in front of us, his arms thrown out protectively. Elias mouthed something to the guard next to him, his obsidian eyes still watching us. Magic bristled the hairs on the back of my neck, my fingers tingling violently as I eyed the approaching guards. The darkness I tried so desperately to conceal beat heavily against its cage, the ash tree's magic beckoning it from the shadows. Victoria's pallid face stared at our retreating forms. There was no way Elias would let us walk out of the clearing alive, but if it was a fight he wanted, it was a fight he'd get. I just hoped Verena and Grey were ready.

Sixteen

Guards descended upon us from every corner of the clearing, their shouts and battle cries echoing around the previously quiet space. I tried desperately to pull Theo towards the safety of the Ironwood. Julien's hands were alight with magic as he sent a barrage of flames raining down on the guards closest to us. If we could just escape the clearing, we could lose them amongst the tangled roots and never-ending wall of trees. We only had to make it to the edge of the woods, but Theo was far too weak. His feet could barely carry him forward a few steps, let alone the many we would need to outrun Elias's men. I stopped abruptly as two guards blocked our path, my plan shattering. They were wide as they were tall, their shirts pulled tight across broad, muscled chests. Worse still, they were no longer the only ones surrounding us. The rest of Elias's followers had formed a circle around Theo, Julien, and me—caging us in and cutting off any chance of fleeing. It reminded me of battles the elders often quoted when they taught me about Ellesmere's history. Stories of great witches and warlocks who battled until their magic was no more, the conqueror revelling in the spoils of war. Only we weren't the victors. My heart beat a steady rhythm despite being outnumbered twenty to one.

"What's the plan, Braelyn?" Julien asked, his hands still engulfed in flames. He eyed the burly guards, watching their movements like a predator eyeing its prey. A small smirk tipped up the corner of his mouth in my favourite lopsided smile. "Are we going to fight them all?"

"We need to hold them off until Verena and Grey can help us get to the tree line."

Any response he might have had was drowned out as the magic inside me began to rush to the surface. Heat flushed my chilled skin as my eyes hardened with icy resolve. The trees circling us groaned in response to my growing magic, answering my beckoning call with creaking shouts of their own. The air around the clearing picked up its pace, weaving through the trees with the ease of a fast-running stream. I smiled around at the sneering guards.

"So, who wants to go first?"

A shout to my left caught my attention. I span on the spot, facing off a tall guard as she rushed towards me, her light brown hair billowing behind her. Giant tree roots erupted from the ground, twisting their way towards me like enormous wooden hounds hunting a rabbit. I pushed Theo behind me and conjured the flames smouldering beneath my skin. They caught alight in the palm of my hands, hot and dangerous. Despite my previous hesitations to wield my fire magic, it now reacted to my every command. Gone was the panic and unease that usually coursed through me, replaced with confidence and a burning need to control it. Flames enveloped my clenched fists as I waited for the perfect moment to strike. The earth witch's magic barrelled towards me, unrelenting and never slowing. Theo tensed behind me, but before the possessed roots were able to reach us, I finally released my magic. Flames burst from my palms, unfurling like a phoenix's wings as they engulfed the guard's earth magic in a fiery display. Heat licked up those vines, but despite the inferno, the earth witch gritted her teeth and stood her ground. She was strong. I could feel the force of her magic trying to break through the fiery snare mine had entangled hers with, but her unwavering strength was no use against my inferno. Flames snaked around the roots, capturing them in a fiery grasp, deadly in their bite. The strong tree roots groaned beneath the heat until fire consumed every inch of the dry, cracking bark. After only minutes, the earth witch drew back, burnt from the flames that had put a stop to her magic. Her lips rolled back in a fierce snarl, her green eyes narrowed at me, pure hatred glittering in their depths.

Two short, muscled guards rushed towards us, their eyes staring at my flaming hands. Never stopping, they called out to their magic and the air around the clearing shifted as gale-force winds swirled, angled in our direction. Julien blocked an onslaught of icy daggers, their sharp tips evaporating against the fiery wall he'd raised around us. It wasn't enough to stop the piercing cold air from caressing my exposed skin with a silent touch of icy death. It loosened the hair around my face, making it whip across my cheeks. Theo's teeth chattered behind me as the icy air closed in. My lips trembled as my fingers began to go numb, the chilling bite of air making them feel frozen to the bone. The second warlock sniggered at our discomfort, his hands sparking ferociously— white-blue lightning weaving through his stumpy fingers. He turned his head to Elias, who stood with his arms behind his back, watching the commotion unfold. A wicked smile spread slowly over his face, malice glinting in his blackened eyes.

"Bring her to me, dead or alive, just don't spill a drop of her blood."

The burly air warlock fixed his grey-blue gaze on me again. "Your time is up, little spirit witch."

I could just make out his words over the rush of the wind, but that was the least of my worries. As the guard's hands began to clench into fists, I felt the wind around me shift, seeming to suck all oxygen out of the vortex we stood in. My breaths came in ragged gasps, constricting my chest with each shallow inhale. I heard Theo try to suck in what little air was left, his breathing growing shallow as his bony chest heaved with each gasp. Julien coughed beside me, his once flaming hands now extinguished and grasping his throat.

"He's sucking..." Julien took a small breath, his eyes bulging. "Out all..." Another breath. "The air."

I shook my head, trying to clear the fog clouding my mind. My chest ached and I struggled to concentrate or summon any type of magic. Shouts and jeers penetrated the ringing in my ears as Elias's guards encouraged the warlock to continue his assault. Black spotted my vision, threatening to swallow me whole. I cast my gaze over to Theo, his frail hands clawing at his chest, each breath growing shallower. His eyes found mine and my heart almost exploded with the pain I saw behind them. My muscles contracted with the effort it took to raise my hands in front of me—a last ditch effort to save us—but before I had the chance to summon an ounce of magic, a flicker of red darted from the trees and flames erupted in front of me. The sheer force of Verena's flames knocked the air warlock off his feet, breaking the link to his magic. Air rushed over me and I greedily gulped down a lungsful of fresh, cool air. The fog clouding my head began to clear and, with my vision returning to normal, I rushed to Theo's side. At some point in the last few seconds, he'd collapsed behind me. His eyes were closed, but his chest rose and fell with each raspy breath he took. Satisfied he'd be okay, I turned back to the unfolding chaos and found Verena. She nodded in my direction, her golden eyes ablaze with the fire burning up her arms. Julien and Grey were scattered throughout the clearing, fending off the onslaught of guards now raining down upon us. The fire still smouldered in a dark crimson line before me, the smell of smoke and burnt leaves making me cough, my lungs still paining me to breathe. Squinting through the thick smoke and bursts of magic, I tried to locate Elias and Sebastien, but it was a useless endeavour. The chaos around us made it impossible to decipher their faces from the other guards advancing from every direction, but I knew Elias would be watching.

Grey's water magic glistened as he summoned a shower of icy thorns, and a group of warlocks screamed as they rained down from above, the tips flashing like tiny dagger tips, piercing their skin with sharp intent. Julien and Verena stood back-to-back, their fire magic taking down all in their path, but even with the help of my friends, Elias's followers were too many.

My palms tingled violently and I focused all my energy on the soft caress of magic brushing against my skin, but I knew what I really needed. The dark magic I'd tried so hard to keep hidden tempted the tips of my fingers. It called out to me like a siren's song, alluring and desperately trying to pull me under. My knees trembled, knocking together as if they would give way at any minute. So close to the power of the ash tree, the darkness felt all consuming as it twisted through my veins and curled around my heart. It taunted me as I watched my friends slowly lose the fight they had fought so hard to win. The mist cloaking the clearing shifted and, through the dense clouds, I finally found Elias's face. He watched the disarray with pleasure, his chest puffed out with the proud look of a king who didn't know loss. My lips curled back and I bared my teeth as anger ignited the flame in my chest. Dark tendrils reached out to me like a beckoning hand, pulling me towards the power I knew lingered in the shadows. My chest ached in protest as I inhaled deeply, but I pushed the feeling aside and called out to the dark power I'd tried so hard to suppress since my first encounter with the ash tree. A power so bewitching, it rushed through me, igniting every inch of my skin. The darkness surged to the surface, overwhelming in its intensity, but I welcomed every inch of it. The hair on the back of my neck prickled, but for the first time since welcoming the dark magic inside of me, I was no longer afraid. I called out to my spirit magic, and it answered with a fierceness I never knew I was capable of. My fingers curled and uncurled by my sides as the shadows around us began to shift. Dark fog rolled through the clearing like a growing storm cloud. It shifted over the ground, growing denser and darker with each call of my deadly witchcraft. Briefly, the world felt like it stopped. Every witch and warlock's gaze fell on the cascading shadows billowing into the clearing. The weight of everyone's stares threatened to crush me, but I took no notice. Instead, I focused on the shadows I'd conjured from the darkest depths of the Ironwood. Somewhere to my left, a fire warlock bellowed something to his comrades before rushing at me with hands full of flames. After a second, the rest of Elias's guards followed, their shouts ravenous as they ran towards me with murderous intent. Curling my fingers into fists, the shadows followed my command, shifting along the ground and devouring everything in their path. Screams filled the air, my magic consuming the guards in a blanket of darkness. I let the anger that had filled me over the last few weeks grow until I thought my chest would explode beneath the pressure. Elias's gaze found mine over the deadly shadows, his head tilted to the side, his eyes full of curiosity. I made to step in his direction when the toe of my boot hit something hard. My gaze flicked to Theo's limp form before it landed back on Elias, a smirk splitting his somewhat handsome face. He knew I wouldn't leave Theo unprotected. He raised a hand in farewell, the circulum glinting in the last remnants of light before he slithered from my reach, a handful of followers by his side. A scream tore through me at seeing his escape and, with one last show of strength, I opened my clenched hands and watched as the shadows I'd conjured pulled the guards back into the darkness of the Ironwood. Their cries were lost on the wind.

My head pounded in time with my throbbing pulse as I let the darkness fade. When it was gone, I saw bodies littering the forest floor, their eyes open and unstaring at the twisted canopy above. Evidence of our magic use was burnt into the leaf litter on the ground, small spot fires still smouldering under the dried leaves. Wisps of shadow still clung to the outskirts of the clearing, waiting for my next command. With a small flick of my wrist, they receded, the dark magic within quieting after its feast. I bit my lip, worrying what my friends' reactions might be. Up until now, I had tried to keep my darkness controlled, but seeing them near death had broken the tight restraints holding it in place. There was no knowing the repercussions I would face for summoning such magic, but I would gratefully endure them if it meant my friends were safe. Theo began to stir at my feet and Grey rushed to his side, hands fluttering around his face. Julien and Verena stood over them and I could feel their heated gaze warming my body. Finally, I made myself look at them. Verena's eyes were narrowed, her arms crossed tightly over her chest and an unreadable expression on her face.

"Braelyn," Julien said quietly.

His usual sun-kissed skin looked pale, but it was his inability to look me in the eye that threatened to bring me to my knees. I'd never seen him look at me with such apprehension. A low sob broke free of my chest and, in a few long strides, Julien was at my side. All remnants of his previous expression were gone, but it still burned behind my closed eyes. I wouldn't forget it.

"What happened, Braelyn?" His voice was low and soothing, brushing my sweat-soaked hair from my forehead.

I tried to let the calm of his voice wash away the tension in my shoulders and slow the racing of my heart, but I couldn't. A cold shiver ran down my spine as I stared out at the carnage I'd created. The faces of the deceased guards imprinted on my mind.

The rest of my friends now crowded around me, their concerned faces swimming beneath the unshed tears I refused to let fall. Too close. They were all so close, I couldn't breathe. I clawed at my leather armour, trying to pull the laces free to ease the pressure tightening my lungs.

"How did she..."

"I've never seen her use magic like that before."

Their voices sounded like I was listening to them underwater. Distant and too far for me to reach. Concern laced their words the longer they speculated on the type of magic I'd summoned. The lingering remnants of darkness within me only bristled at their words. Anger began to rattle the beast inside me as fragments of their hushed conversation filtered through the haze. Heat flooded my veins and my muscles quivered with the pent-up frustration I was trying to keep at bay.

"You know I'm standing right here," I snapped vehemently.

Stunned faces stared back at me, a mix of worry and concern written across each one. An overwhelming sense of shame washed over me. How could I be so cruel? They had just risked their lives to save me, and I'd repaid them with a scathing retort. My lip trembled, the anger beginning to subside. What was happening to me? Magic still pulsed beneath my skin, a steady reminder of the destruction I had caused and the power I could wield.

"We know, Braelyn," Verena whispered softly. "But we need some answers. How did you conjure magic like this?"

Shaking my head, I tried to find the words I needed to explain to my friends what had happened, but there were none. It was something I didn't fully understand myself, so how was I supposed to tell them how I'd managed to wield such power without effort or consequence? All magic required sacrifice. My head throbbed with the feeling of an oncoming headache—a pain I'd grown accustomed to when conjuring too much magic.

Verena's golden eyes watched me carefully, like I might burst into flames at any given moment.

I sighed, shifting my gaze to the ground to avoid seeing their expressions.

"I've felt the pull of dark magic ever since I first encountered the ash tree and it's been growing stronger over the last few weeks. The more anger and hatred I feel, the more it calls to me, urging me to use it. When I saw you all struggling to fight against Elias's men, I called out to it, knowing it was the only magic powerful enough to save you."

Verena let out a shaky breath and, finally, I turned my eyes to them. Theo rested heavily against Grey's side, his arm thrown over Grey's shoulder, his hand gripping the white fabric to keep himself upright. He didn't look at me, but down at his shoes. Grey had an arm around

Theo's waist, but he watched me carefully in that assessing way. Lastly, I turned my eyes up to Julien's. He still held me against his chest, but his face was stony.

"We should probably get moving in case anyone decides to return," Julien said flatly, pulling his arms free from my waist. I turned my gaze away from his intense stare as everyone started to head back to the safety of the trees.

I reached out a tentative hand—meaning to give Theo a light hug—but instead of letting me embrace him, he flinched away from my touch. His lips flattened into a thin line, his usually kind eyes glaring at my outstretched arms. There was a hardness in the way he watched me that had never been there before.

"Don't," was all he said before he motioned for Grey to follow the others.

Tears stung the backs of my eyes as a sharp pain pierced my already broken heart. A part of me had worried about how his trauma would affect him, and now it felt like my worst fears were true. He blamed me. I wrapped my arms around my waist, trying to hold the broken pieces of myself together. This moment should have been filled with joy and love at having Theo back, but now I only felt a gnawing dread. My friends were fearful of the magic I'd summoned to protect them and, honestly, I didn't blame them. As I watched Verena, Grey, and Theo retreat into the safety of the trees, I'd never felt so alone. I tightened my hold around my mid-section and cringed as a sharp pain radiated through my palm, making me pull away quickly. As I opened my hand, my stomach twisted. There, in the middle of my palm, was the consequence of my actions. A dark burn covered half of my hand, the swirling tendrils of shadow spreading like tiny rivers from the centre of the wound and out towards my fingers. It reminded of the bite Julien had obtained from the barghest the last time we were in these woods. Had I poisoned myself? Was that the consequence I was paying for calling on such dark magic? Was it the beginning of the darkness taking over my soul like Julien had warned me?

"Braelyn, are you coming?" Julien appeared between the opening of the trees, an unreadable expression lining his face.

Before he could say anything else, I clenched my hand shut, ignoring the pain as I walked into the shadows of the Ironwood. I was all too aware of the stare that followed.

Seventeen

Exhaustion pulled at our limbs, our bodies collapsing against the fallen pine trees once we finally made it back to the alcove. Verena conjured a small flame, the orange light accentuating the angry red marks entwining her arm. She relit the small fire from the night before, everyone sighing with contentment the moment its warm embrace caressed their skin. The heat from the flames instantly enveloped me in a blanket of heat, helping to ease the tension in my shoulders. I sat on a fallen log and rummaged through my satchel, producing the small bottle of healing elixir my mother had prepared for us. I tossed it to Verena, who gave me a small smile. After our efforts in the clearing, everyone needed some to help fight the effects of our magic use. Unstopping it, she squeezed three drops over her hands, then passed it around. Everyone placed a few drops over their fingers and arms, the angry, twisted veins receding with each minute that passed. My fingers toyed with the hem of my jacket as I searched the trees around us, waiting for Alpheus to return. He was supposed to meet us here after we'd rescued Theo, but there was still no sight of him. My mind conjured terrible images of him hurt and unable to make it back to us, but just as I was ready to go search for him, he limped into the alcove, his front left paw held aloft.

"*Alpheus,*" I thought, running over to assess to the damage.

"I'm fine, my friend, just a small burn."

Taking his front paw gently in my hands, I inspected the injury he'd obtained. It wasn't bad, but I was sure my mother's healing poultice would help speed up his recovery. Saying as much, I led him to the fire and lathered a generous amount of salve over his paw.

"Thank you," he said, his voice light. His almond eyes assessed my face closely, and I couldn't help but feel he was staring into the deepest parts of my soul.

"I know what it is that plagues you, my friend," Alpheus said gently.

"I don't know what's happening to me, Alpheus," I replied in my head.

My hands worried at the buttons of my coat as I tried to think of what to say next. Alpheus was an incredibly wise creature, but I doubted he would understand my feelings on the silent war being waged in the back of my mind. I doubted anyone could. For centuries, spirit witches had teetered on the brink of light and dark magic. In all my research, I was yet to come across texts describing a spirit witch who hadn't succumbed to the darkness. It was simply easier to give in.

"While I cannot say what it is that's happening to you, my friend, I can say it is amongst the darkness that light often shines the brightest. Do not turn away from your light when you need it the most." He turned his gaze to my friends, all of whom chatted quietly amongst themselves as they rested their weary muscles and recovered from their excessive magic use.

Theo and Julien sat beside each other, talking quietly as Grey busied himself with his rucksack. Seeing the two of them together helped lift my spirits. They had only just begun to mend their broken friendship when Theo was captured and I hoped Julien's role in his rescue would help ease some of the hurt Theo felt towards him. Julien gave Theo's shoulder a quick squeeze before making his way over to me, his eyes downcast.

"Your turn," Julien said as he took a seat next to me.

I let him take my hand as he squeezed a few drops of the healing elixir over the faint golden lines curling up my arms. His touch was soft, his calloused fingers gentle as he worked. When he took my right hand, I winced as the tips of his fingers brushed the burn on my palm. Julien's brows creased at my cry of pain and, letting out a deep sigh, I let him turn my hand over. His brows shot into his hairline as he stared down at my disfigured spirit rune. He still hadn't looked me in the eye.

"Braelyn." His voice was so full of angst, it pained me more than the burn did.

"It's okay," I replied softly. "It will heal once you use the elixir."

He placed three drops in the centre of my palm. I grimaced against the sharp sting radiating through my hand, but the elixir had already begun to work. The dark veins spreading to my fingers began to fade before the stinging stopped altogether. I offered Julien a small smile and he gifted me one in return, but it didn't reach his eyes. My heart clenched, but I let it go.

With everyone's wounds mended, we sat around the fire nibbling on some provisions Julien had thought to pack. Theo picked at a loaf of bread, barely touching the hard cheese, his appetite suppressed since his ordeal. Despite the worry that plagued my mind, I was happy he was safe, if not entirely okay. The longer I watched him, the more I began to see there was something different about him. His usually bright eyes seemed distant and cold, and there was a hardness to his posture that hadn't softened since our escape from the ash tree clearing.

"It's good to have you back, Theo," I said over the crackling flames, breaking the silence that had settled over our camp as everyone ate their fill.

Theo said nothing, but he glared at me with a pinched expression. Verena gave me a quick shrug, looking as confused as I felt. I'd known Theo had placed some blame on me for his capture, but I'd thought once we were back together in relative safety, his disdain towards me would clear up. Coming to sit beside him, I tentatively reached to place a hand on his arm, but before my fingers grazed his skin, he flew to his feet.

"What do you want me to say, Braelyn?" Theo's voice pierced the silence, his tone as hard as his gaze. "That it's so great to be back with everyone? That I'm so grateful it took weeks for someone to come and find me? That I needed someone to *save* me?! Do you know what I had to endure in the last two weeks?"

I recoiled from the sharpness lacing his words.

"Theo, I'm... I'm so—"

"What, Braelyn? You want to say you're sorry this happened to me?" Theo gestured to his swollen eye and split lip, then to the bruises staining his skin blue and purple. "If it wasn't for you, none of this would have happened to me."

I flinched at the harshness of his words, but it wasn't anything I hadn't already thought myself. Everyone had told me I wasn't to blame, but Theo *did* blame me. And he was right. None of this would be happening if it wasn't for my actions. Before I was able to utter another word, he turned his back on me and stomped into the thick-set trees. Grey gave me a reassuring smile before he ran after Theo, the darkness swallowing him.

My hands trembled as tears threatened to spill over my cheeks. I tried my best to blink them away, but it was no use. They fell hot and heavy over my face, leaving a burning trail on my chilled skin.

A warm hand slid into mine. "He'll come around, Braelyn. He's just been through hell and back. Give him time."

"He blames me, Julien." My voice came out no louder than a whisper. "And he's right. It is my fault. I should have rescued him sooner." I shook my head against the guilt building inside me.

"This isn't your fault," Verena said calmly from across the campfire. "Theo chose to push you aside—he chose to sacrifice himself to save you. Just give him time to remember that." She sat with her elbows resting on her knees, her hands held up against the fire.

I knew they were right, but it hurt me to see Theo so broken. To know that I was the cause of his pain made the anxiety in my chest twist like a dagger to my heart. I would give him all the time he needed to recover, especially if it meant he might one day forgive me.

Once we were all seated around the fire again, I held the crumpled piece of paper in my hand and explained what Maeve disclosed to me last night. How we couldn't go home. How Maeve said we needed to gather reinforcements because something dangerous was coming. I shared my theory on needing to form an alliance with the elves and dwarves and how this could be the only way to finally defeat Elias.

"So, what you're saying is that we need to mend a decade-long feud with the elves and dwarves to get them to help us defeat the very person that created that feud in the first place?" Verena looked at me as if I'd sprouted a second head. Her eyes shimmered in the firelight as she stared at me in astonishment.

"I know how difficult this must sound, but I trust Maeve. She wouldn't have told me to do something if she didn't believe we stood a chance of succeeding. And she gave me this, which is supposed to help." I held out the crumpled piece of paper.

Grey and Theo exchanged confused glances, before shuffling a little closer to the fire to get a better look at the parchment. Theo still hadn't spoken to me since our argument, but Grey had seemed to calm him down enough to re-join the group. I wanted nothing more than to sort out our differences, but Julien assured me time would help mend the wounds we couldn't see. All I could do was give Theo the space he need-ed to heal. Julien stood to my right with his arms crossed tightly over his chest. His face was concealed in shadow, but I knew his expression mirrored that of Theo and Grey: confused and cautious. Verena simply shook her head.

"How does this old piece of parchment help?" Theo's voice was light, but I could hear the slight strain in his tone.

"All I know is Maeve said it would help explain her instructions. I hav-en't had a chance to look at it since she gave it to me back in the dungeons."

I opened the paper and smoothed it out against my leg, trying to de-cipher the simple handwriting covering most of the aged parchment. My mind bristled at its familiarity, but it was the image at the bottom of the page that drew my attention. In the right-hand corner, a rough diagram had been sketched, but only the elements knew what it was. The only thing that stood out to me was a depiction of a stone. To my disappointment, most of the page was written in the language of old, something I wasn't well versed in yet. Mrs Boswell had tried to teach me a few phrases—saying it was necessary for the queen of Ellesmere to be knowledgeable in the languages of the kingdom—but I hadn't had enough practice to read an entire passage. Theo, on the other hand, had helped me decipher a passage from Althea's book on our first journey through the Ironwood.

"Can you read it, Theo?" I asked, a small sliver of hope making my voice quiver.

Before he could answer, Verena interrupted. "I know what it says, Brae."

She'd been sitting on the damp log next to me, clearly reading the passage over my shoulder. Hope swelled in my belly. If Verena could decipher the message, we would be one step closer to defeating Elias. Raising my eyebrows, I offered Verena a questioning gaze. When she didn't answer right away, I shuffled closer.

"Well?" I inquired. "What does it say?"

Taking a deep breath and letting it out slowly, she looked deep into the fire and spoke into its flames. "It talks of you, Braelyn, and how you will be the one to unite Ellesmere with..." Her voice trailed off, her eyes widening.

"With what?" I asked nervously.

She chewed the inside of her cheek, her eyes distant until she finally faced me.

"With a weapon that will make you the most powerful spirit witch to ever walk this earth."

The silence following Verena's comment was palpable, the air thick with fear and apprehension. Even the creatures who occupied the Ironwood seemed to have stopped making any of their nightly calls to one another. Swallowing hard, I looked around at my friends. Grey and Theo were bent over the parchment, their heads resting close together as they spoke quietly to each other, brows furrowed in concentration. Verena had discarded her seat by the fire and was now carving a path through the leaf litter, pacing back and forth. Lastly, I glanced over to Julien, noting the concern written on his face. His brow creased in worry as he continued staring into the fire with such intensity it made the flames spark wildly. Taking a deep steadying breath, I got to my feet—feeling too agitated to sit any longer—and stood by Julien's side. He neither moved nor acknowledged that I'd stepped closer to him. I could feel the warmth of his skin radiating through his woollen jacket and inched a little closer to feel the halo of his heat. Still, he said nothing.

The silence was overwhelming. Everyone seemed to be lost in their own thoughts and feelings about what we had just found out. Guilt twisted my stomach into knots. I hated that they had been dragged into this mess. I wished with everything I had that my friends didn't need to share in the burden. Deep down, though, I knew I couldn't do any of it alone. But if they wanted to leave, I wouldn't hold it against them.

I cleared my throat, speaking for the first time in what felt like hours. "I know this is a lot to take and that none of you agreed to help in solving Maeve's messages or journeying farther than the ash tree, so if you want to go back to the castle—"

"I'm coming with you," Julien said, cutting me off. "There's nothing left for me at the castle if you're out here."

"As am I," Verena said.

Grey looked towards Theo, whose expression was unreadable. "I can take you back to the castle if that's what you want," he whispered.

Theo glanced up at his words and looked between all of us. Finally, he released a long breath, his shoulders sagging before he rolled them back and sat a little straighter.

"No," he said, his voice icy. "I want to be there when Elias finds his end."

There were no words I could say that would help me express the admiration I felt towards the four people sitting in front of me.

"So, does anyone know what this all-powerful weapon could be?" Verena asked, fracturing the small sliver of happiness radiating through me.

Julien's jaw tightened at this comment, but I chose to ignore it. I knew he would hate what this meant for me—especially since my show of power in the clearing—but I couldn't ignore what I needed to do. Stopping Elias had always been my destiny and if finding and wielding a weapon of power was the only way to do this, I would. I would do anything to save Ellesmere and all those I cared about.

Grey was the first to speak. "There have been stories over the centuries about weapons said to have great magical power, but none come to mind that look like this." He pointed to the messy drawing in the corner of the page. "All the weapons I've heard of have been iron-made swords or axes. All of which, as you know, Braelyn, we can't wield."

"But Elias's men seem to have no problem using their magic when wearing iron-made armour, so there must be a way," I mused.

"There probably is, but however he does it, it's not done using any type of light magic. The whole thing reeks of dark magic."

Theo shuddered despite the blazing fire keeping us all warm. His eyes were distant and glassy as he seemed to drift back to his time spent amongst Elias's camp. So many emotions played across his face.

Coming to sit by Theo's side, I hesitated slightly before placing a soft hand on his trembling knee. He looked up at me, his blue eyes reflecting sadness and torment. His expression was almost my undoing. I knew I should be giving him space, but I wanted him to know just how sorry I was that he had been subjected to cruelty because of me.

"I'm so sorry for what you went through, Theo. I never wanted to put you in any danger." My chin trembled. I tried to keep my emotions in check, but it was harder than I'd expected. "If you ever need to talk about what happened, we are all here for you." Squeezing Theo's knee gently, I gave him a warm smile.

He smiled softly in return. It didn't reach his eyes or crinkle the scar on his cheek, but it was enough to fuse some of the broken pieces of my heart.

"I wouldn't even know where to begin. So much..." He wrung his hands together as if trying to warm them against the chill beginning to creep into the grove of trees.

"Why don't you tell them what you told me?" Grey said, his voice soft and soothing. "And if you struggle, I can fill in the rest." His hand traced soothing circles over Theo's back, coaxing the tension from his shoulders with gentle touches.

Theo nodded in agreement but kept his gaze downcast. "Well, after I was pulled through the portal, it brought us out to the clearing. Most of King Elias's men had fled and some were waiting for us by the ash tree. After a few hours, most of his loyal followers had managed to find their way back to him, but he was pretty angry that Sebastien and Victoria hadn't made it out of the castle."

Despite the seriousness of the situation Theo had been in, a small smile twinged the edge of my mouth. We'd managed to thwart some of Elias's plan.

"They kept a watchful eye on me, making sure my hands were manacled so I couldn't use any magic. That was until the iron cage was made. After that, they locked me in there for most of the time I was held captive."

"How did they manage to get a cage that big through the Ironwood?" Julien asked.

He'd left his post by the edge of the trees and finally came over to the fire, still opting to stand, obviously no longer concerned that something sinister was waiting for us.

Theo looked away into the flames as he spoke. "They didn't. Some of Elias's men were sent to the Ironwood Mountains to capture blacksmiths who worked in the mines. They brought them back to the clearing where he forced them to work on building the cage." Theo stopped for a moment to take a sip of water from Grey's waterskin. Wiping his mouth on the back of his sleeve, he continued, "Once they finished the cage, they asked to be taken back to the mountains, but King Elias refused. He said he couldn't have anyone knowing his location, so he... he killed them."

A stray tear fell down Theo's cheek. He brushed it away quickly, as if he didn't want anyone to see, but I was close enough to notice the wet streak on his skin.

"It's okay, Theo," Grey said gently. "You don't need to say anything else."

He shook his head. "No, there's one more thing I need to tell you."

I didn't want to pressure Theo into talking about his ordeal if it caused him too much pain, but from the sheer determination on his face, we couldn't have stopped him if we tried.

"What is it, Theo? What did you find out?" Julien asked, his voice hard but not unkind. He stood over the fire, his hands still crossed tightly over his chest.

Taking a deep breath, Theo turned his gaze away from the fire's flames and fixed his eyes on mine. They glowed such a magnificent blue in the light of the fire that I couldn't help but marvel at just how beautiful they were.

"King Elias intends to release Lilith from the Underworld on the next full moon of Samhain. That's in two weeks' time." When I opened my mouth to tell Theo we already knew this, he held a finger up. "I know you somehow know this already, but when you said to Elias that you and Victoria were the key to releasing Lilith, you were only partly right."

This time when I opened my mouth, Theo didn't stop me.

"What do you mean? In the vision I had, it was blood that opened the portal."

Theo nodded in agreement as he spoke. "Yes, but that's only part of it. Morrigan is the one who needs to speak the words to release Lilith from the Underworld, but the key that unlocks the door to letting her out is the death of a descendant and the death of a spirit witch."

Eighteen

My breath began to quicken. If I didn't get a handle on my emotions, my magic would spiral out of control. I closed my eyes and tried to block out everyone's voices. Counting to ten, I clenched my hands into fists with each inhale before relaxing them with each exhale. Slowly, my mind began to ease and my breathing became more relaxed. When I opened my eyes, everyone was still talking over each other, trying to get their opinions heard. It was only the pull at the back of my mind that alerted me of Alpheus's presence. He watched us closely, his dark eyes flicking between my friends and the Ironwood.

"They need to lower their voices," he warned. His stance was rigid. Alert. His ears twitched in every direction, trying to catch the sound of danger above the overbearing voices of my friends.

I rose, moving in the middle of my friends, their voices still fighting to be heard.

"We can't stay out here," Verena's voice trilled.

"Well, we can't go back to the castle. She'd be a lamb to the slaughter," Julien said.

I tried to speak up, but my words fell on deaf ears.

"We should continue with Maeve's instructions," Grey chipped in.

The anxiety churning in my stomach only moments ago quickly shifted to mounting frustration. Lightning laced through my fingers as I splayed my hands out, my exasperation turning to burning anger. Sparks erupted from my fingers, making the fire a deadly blue, sparking and spitting glowing embers into the air like tiny fireworks. Everyone's voices dimmed to silence.

"Thank you for finally including me in the conversation," I spat through clenched teeth. My hands were now balled in tight fists by my sides and my chest rose and fell rapidly.

"Braelyn," Verena began, "we didn't mean to—"

A low growl sounded in the darkness behind us.

I spun, staring into the shadows, trying to find the source of the sound. The anger I'd felt fizzled to unease at the thought of something watching us between the trees. I couldn't help but think of the barghest we'd come across the last time we'd been stuck here. Surely, it couldn't happen again? The odds were too ridiculous to even contemplate. As the silence lingered, the growling seemed to fade away into some other part of the Ironwood and I breathed a sigh of relief. My friends continued to watch me closely, as if preparing themselves for another fiery outburst, but the fierce anger I'd felt moments ago was gone.

Hanging my head in shame, I spoke quietly. "I'm sorry for lashing out, I just don't understand how this can be true."

"I don't know either, Brae, but I need you to believe me. I heard him tell his followers it had been written in this book—that to open the portal to the Underworld, only a direct descendant of Lilith and a true spirit witch could open the door or seal it."

My stomach gave a small jolt at Theo's mention of a book, but something else stirred at the back of my mind. I snatched the piece of parchment from beside Grey and studied the writing closely.

"What is it Braelyn?" Julien's voice sounded somewhere behind me, but I ignored him, too occupied with my thoughts.

Taking up my seat next to Julien again, I pulled Althea's journal from my satchel, riffling through the pages until the book fell open at the section where the paper had been torn out. I flattened the parchment Maeve had given me, smiling when the frayed edges didn't match up. The torn paper was slightly bigger than Althea's book and the writing was neater, written with a careful hand, not scribbled in haste. Could it be? I reached for my satchel, my fingers tingling with magic as I grabbed The Book of Lilith. In the days after finding it, I hadn't had time to study the dark witch's grimoire, but my intuition told me the page belonged here. I opened the tome and ran my thumb over the pages, flicking through until I found what I was looking for. My heart beat an erratic rhythm in my chest as I brought the torn parchment to rest perfectly beside the tear nestled amongst the open pages.

"By the elements," Verena said softly. "How did you know it belonged there?"

I stared up into the shocked faces of my friends, each one looking between me and the open book on my lap.

"When Maeve gave it to me, I'd first assumed it belonged in Althea's journal, because a few days ago, I found a page missing in the book. When we were reading it earlier, though, I realised the writing didn't match up." My fingers trembled as I ran them over the messy scrawl, my lips tipped up in a smile. "But I knew there was something familiar about it."

"How did Maeve steal a page from The Book of Lilith in the first place?" Grey asked.

"My father gave it to my mother when she fled Ellesmere seventeen years ago. I remember reading it in the apothecary one day. Maeve must have torn the page out before Elias found where they were hiding."

Images of the day I'd found The Book of Lilith came flooding back to me. It had been sitting on our bookshelf, nestled amongst the other books. If I'd had the gift of foresight, I would have tossed it into the fire and watched it burn.

"What I don't understand," Theo said, "is why Lilith would create a weapon to destroy herself?"

Julien scoffed at his words. I elbowed him in the side before shooting him a scowl. Thankfully, Theo was oblivious to Julien's reaction.

"She didn't create it to destroy herself, but to wield it. Her goal was always to be the most powerful witch in Ellesmere, so she created a weapon to become exactly that."

"So why is Elias trying to release her?" Verena asked, taking the book from my lap and flicking through its delicate pages. "If he wanted to be the most powerful ruler of Ellesmere, why would he want to release a witch more powerful than him?"

"Because he's been obsessed with Lilith since he was a boy." My mind sifted through conversations with Elias back at the castle. His obsession with The Book of Lilith and his determination to complete the circulum. From the beginning, I'd believed his actions were so he could prove he was divine and all powerful. But now...

"Everything he's done has been for her," I blurted out, the realisation finally dawning on me. "By creating the circulum, he thought he would be powerful enough to release Lilith. He was wrong. It's why he lured Victoria into his employ and why he tried to take my magic and pull me through the portal."

"So you would be weak enough to kill and release Lilith from the underworld," Julien concluded.

I nodded. "There would be no one strong enough left to challenge her."

Everyone was quiet for a moment, lost in their own thoughts of what this new information meant. Any small sliver of hope we'd had of returning to the castle had been quashed when the piece of parchment fit into The Book of Lilith. Maeve was right. We couldn't return to the castle without putting everyone in danger. The only option we had was to find allies. To try and mend a decade-long feud between witchkind and the elves and dwarves. How we would do this remained a mystery, but I owed it to everyone to try. I searched the faces of my friends. Verena stared into the dying flames of our small fire, her eyes illuminated a deep gold. Grey and Theo both held the same pinched expression, their lips thinned. Julien seemed to be the only one watching me, his dark eyes assessing my reaction.

"What's the plan, Brae?" Verena finally said.

"We leave at first light."

It was the small hours of the morning when I woke from a restless sleep. The moon was still high, and low hanging cloud clung to the canopy of the trees, making the air feel chilly. Eerie. The cool morning air caressed the exposed parts of my skin, causing a shiver to ripple down my spine. I wrapped my coat tighter around me and huddled into its warmth. Despite the thin bedroll I'd laid out, my neck was stiff. I massaged the muscles softly, trying to work out the kinks, but it was no use. With a huff, I sat up against the fallen log. Theo, Grey, Verena, and Alpheus were still fast asleep, so I pulled out The Book of Lilith, the leather cover soft and worn beneath my fingers. As I flicked through the delicate pages, they fell open on a sketch of the ash tree. The resemblance was uncanny. If I didn't know who Lilith was and what she was capable of, I probably would have marvelled at her talent for drawing, but I knew better. Incantations needed to be specific and detailed. One wrong word and you were at the mercy of the elements. I scanned the text, recognising words here and there, but there were several I was loathe to see. Trailing my finger over the looping letters, I stopped at the words confirming Theo's speculation. *Sanguis spiritus maga*. The blood of a spirit witch. My hands felt numb on the soft parchment. My eyes stared fixedly at the three words binding my fate to Victoria's. It wasn't that I hadn't believed Theo, but I'd searched in the hopes that he might have heard wrong. That the fate of my loved ones and Ellesmere rested not only in me, but in the one person who hated me more than anything. I'd come to terms with the situation last night, but it was a heavy burden. Uneasiness clung tightly to my heart, unyielding in its grasp. The last time I had a vision, Hazel told me what I'd witnessed was the outcome of my failures should I not defeat Elias. *Did my vision of Lilith mean the same thing? Was it a bad omen telling me that I would fail again? That no matter what I did, my destiny was to die so Lilith may live?*

A gentle rustle high above brought me out of my reverie. I searched the canopy for the source of the noise, but nothing showed itself. Just a whisper of the wind through the trees, it seemed.

"Braelyn, how long have you been awake?"

Julien stepped from between the pine trees, the collar of his coat turned up against the chill. He'd volunteered to take first watch.

"Only a few minutes," I replied quietly so as not to wake the others.

I was anxious to begin securing allies, but we'd been through a tiring ordeal yesterday and sleep was the oldest form of healing magic. We'd agreed the best place for us to start was the Ironwood Mountains. According to Verena, the dwarves would be easier to negotiate with because, like us, they had suffered severe casualties at the hands of King Elias. The elves, on the other hand, would take more convincing.

"Have you slept at all?" I asked, the building silence too much for me to take.

Julien brushed at a few leaves that had affixed themselves to his jacket before he ran a hand over his face and eased into a large stretch. The hem of his shirt lifted slightly to reveal the rigid sun-kissed skin of his stomach. A warm blush spread over my cheeks, but I couldn't look away. Something had shifted between us since our encounter with Elias and his followers—since my use of dark magic. He'd not mentioned it since we left the clearing, but from his short answers and narrowed glances in my direction, I knew it was something we needed to talk about.

"No, but we should get moving if we want to make it to the Iron-wood Mountains. It's a three day walk, and we'll need enough time to visit both the dwarves and elves before the first full moon of Samhain."

Julien held out a hand to help me to my feet. I took it, relishing in the small amount of contact and the feeling of his rough palm against mine. My brow furrowed as he quickly pulled his hand away, and I tried to decipher the plethora of feelings running through me.

"What's troubling you, Julien?" I asked softly, my voice wavering with the emotions wreaking havoc inside me.

He didn't look at me. "Nothing's wrong, Braelyn."

"You're lying. I know something's wrong because you've barely been able to look at me since we returned from the clearing."

He did look at me then, his jaw clenched and eyes blazing. He wrapped his fingers around my wrist and pulled me to the edge of the alcove, away from everyone's sleeping bodies. The chill of the air wrapped around me, making goosebumps rise over my skin.

"What's wrong, Braelyn, is mere hours ago I watched you conjure some of the most powerful magic I've ever seen, and you seem to think nothing of it," he replied through clenched teeth. "After everything I told you in Elias's study, you summoned a dark magic that will only grow stronger the more you use it."

He scrubbed his hand through his hair, making it stand on end. He still held my wrist, the fingers closed tightly around it making my bones scream in protest, but I ignored the pain. My eyes tightened on his stony expression, frustration flaring inside me.

"Don't tell me I don't think nothing of it, Julien." I pulled my wrist free of his grip and pointed a finger at my chest. "All I do is go to war with myself over the darkness plaguing my every waking thought. No one understands the consequences of this type of magic more than me, but I would wield it again and again if it meant you all survived."

My chin trembled, my chest heaving with each weighted breath. Julien stared at me, his jaw tense. I could feel the warm flush of embarrassment creep up my neck over my angered words, but I no longer cared. Taking one step forward, I closed the distance between us and stabbed a finger at his chest, the muscles barely flexing beneath my touch.

"You don't get to tell me what I think or feel, Julien Thorne, because I damn well know exactly who I am and what I want."

The weight I'd felt growing in my chest eased as Julien's dark eyes turned molten, reflecting the passion simmering deep in my heart. Gone was the stony expression he'd worn since returning from the ash tree. In its place was the face of the boy I'd come to care so deeply for. The deep flush over my cheeks burned against my chilled skin at that face. Beneath the hand I'd placed on his heart, Julien's chest flexed, his pulse beating in time with my own. My teeth tugged at my lower lip and Julien's gaze followed the movement. I tried to turn away to hide my growing desire, but his hand shot out, cupping my cheek gently and forcing me to face him. His brows softened as his hand found its way to the curve of my neck. He held my gaze for a few heart-fluttering moments before leaning forward, his lips so close to mine I longed to feel their touch.

"I would never dream of telling you what to feel, Braelyn, but I would rather die than know a world where your kindness and light no longer shines as brightly as it already does."

Julien took my hand in his, turning it over so my palm rested in the small space between us. The burn on my hand still ached, but the healing elixir had helped with the pain. Some of the ebony marks remained around the middle of my palm, but the pull of dark magic was growing weaker with the distance between us and the ash tree. Julien ran the pad of his thumb over my spirit rune before looking at my face once again.

"While you might do whatever it takes to save us, sweetheart, I will do all in my power to protect you."

With these words, the world seemed to fall away for a moment. My pulse raced and, from the playful smirk pulling at the corner of Julien's mouth, he could feel it. Something stirred in the pit of my stomach, an urgent longing that inched my feet closer to Julien's body. For weeks I'd wondered what it was that existed between us, and now it seemed I might have my answer. My breath hitched as Julien's hand once again found the nape of my neck, pulling me closer to him.

Grey, Theo, and Verena began to stir from their slumber. The soft swish of their blankets on the loose leaves was the only thing preventing me from pressing my lips to his in the urgent way I so desperately wanted to. Julien gifted me one of his dazzling smiles, his hands slowly running down my arms to settle on the curves of my hips.

"Next time, sweetheart."

Julien brushed his thumb tenderly over my lips, a light chuckle reverberating through him as he walked back to the campfire. My breath left my lungs in a shuddering wave, the alluring effect Julien had on me slowly ebbing away with each fall of his retreating footsteps. He had enamoured me, body and soul, and from the yearning in his eyes and the fast rhythm of his heart, I couldn't help but think he must feel the same.

My thoughts were broken only by the pull in the back of my mind, alerting me to Alpheus's approach.

"*It is time to go, my friend.*"

His tall antlers brushed my knees, his paw no longer troubling him thanks to my mother's healing elixir. Alpheus's injuries had mended much quicker than ours—a gift of being a creature with mysterious and mystical abilities.

"*The shadows are retreating,*" he added. "*Now is a good time to be on our way.*"

Throwing down a quick breakfast of soft sourdough bread and hard cheese, we stamped out the fire's dying embers and turned to face the looming trees ahead of us. They towered over the pine trees, intertwining with their neighbours and concealing most of the sky from view— caging us in like the monsters that lingered here. A shudder passed over me as I recalled the memories of the beasts we'd encountered on our last journey; the barghest, the gremlins, and the misty figures clinging to the shadows. The Ironwood only filled me with dread. Julien's hand slid into my own, spreading warmth up my arm. It helped ease the anxious beat of my heart, if only slightly.

"Out of the cauldron," Grey murmured in a shaky voice, "and into the flame."

"Do not forget the way you came," Theo continued.

"For the elements play a tricky game, in the Ironwood where all who enter, remain," Julien finished reciting the eerie poem.

I'd heard the children in the castle village singing it as they skirted the edges of the Ironwood. Many elderly witches and warlocks told tales of what happened to those who strayed from the path leading through the mystical forest. Even amongst young witches and warlocks, the Ironwood had a sinister reputation. Very few dared enter it without a protection charm or talisman.

My heart constricted as I looked between my friends. Each one was willing to put themselves in peril to help me. There would never be any words powerful enough to tell them just how grateful I was to have them here with me. Taking a deep, steadying breath, I glanced down to Alpheus, who waited patiently by my side. Our very own protection charm, and then some. Turning back to face the path before us, I straightened my spine and took a step forward. Then another. And another. I heard the shuffle of feet behind me as my friends followed, marching towards what I could only hope was the light at the end of the tunnel.

Nineteen

O n our second night, we set up camp just off the path to the Ironwood Mountains, but deep enough into the trees to provide protection. We'd made good headway over the last few days despite the plummeting temperature and deep weariness that clung to everyone like a heavy cloak. Theo sat huddled on the damp ground, his arms wrapped tightly around his knees as Verena continued to add more kindling to the growing pyre. Alpheus sat close to Theo's side. I'd asked him to stay with us on our journey to the dwarves, if only to help ease some of Theo's torment. Alpheus seemed to have a calming effect on those who were troubled in some way. He'd helped Julien through his pain with the barghest bite and had soothed my anxiety more times that I could count. I hoped having him close would ease Theo's suffering. Grey had already stretched out on his bedroll, his arm thrown lazily over his eyes. Theo had been relying on his help to trek through the uneven terrain, his body not quite strong enough to manage on his own. I tossed my satchel onto the damp mossy ground, collapsing in a tired heap next to Julien. Exhaustion pulled at my limbs, every movement of my arms feeling slow and sluggish. Julien chuckled beside me, his fingers toying with a small flame. It danced brightly in the growing darkness like a tiny fire sprite, flickering and glowing a beautiful orange red. With a gentle turn of his wrist, the flame engulfed the wooden pyre, casting an eerie glow around our small circle. I longed to use my own magic again. To feel the rush of air and water, the power of fire and the strength of my earth magic. Since the events in the clearing, everyone had thought it best if I refrained from conjuring any of the elements unless we were in dire need. It'd been so long since I had to resist the urge to wield my power that it felt almost like an itch I couldn't scratch. Magic rested just beneath the surface of my skin, but I was forbidden to use it.

"I'll take first watch," Julien announced to the group, not looking at me as he went to choose his post.

We hadn't spoken much since our last conversation, our days filled with little more than sleeping, eating, and navigating the path. Since our last intimate moment, fear of misinterpreting Julien's feelings had begun to gnaw at my insides.

Verena and Theo positioned their bedrolls around the fire, Verena yawning deeply and murmuring a quick goodnight. Theo's gaze lingered on my face and, for a second, I thought he might speak to me, but my hopes fell flat as he turned his back and pulled a light blanket about his shoulder. Our relationship still teetered on the brink of breaking. He hadn't said a word to me since the night we'd rescued him and, while I was happy to give him space to heal, each silent stare and unspoken word chipped away at the already fractured pieces of my heart. Letting out a long sigh, I positioned my bedroll on an angle, so Julien stayed in my direct line of sight. He'd turned up the collar of his jacket, arms folded against the chill as he stared into the night. I recalled the way those arms had held me close at the ball and the way his hands had rested lightly at my hips. It seemed silly to be thinking of such trivial things when the survival of Ellesmere rested on my shoulders, but it was a welcome distraction to all the death and destruction we'd encountered so far.

For a while I lay huddled on my bedroll, staring up at the dense canopy of trees and trying to find patterns amongst the branches. Every now and again my gaze would shift to Julien, making sure he was still there, but my eyelids soon grew heavy, my vision blurring. Grey's light snores lulled me into a sense of sleepiness and, closing my eyes, I welcomed the scratchy feeling of tiredness. I let the darkness envelop me and soon found myself drifting to sleep to the sounds of the crackling fire and an owl's gentle call. As my mind began to ease into the realms of sleep, I dreamed of the front garden of Hazel's cottage. The trees surrounding her house were coloured in magnificent shades of oranges, yellows, and reds, but the rest of the garden flourished as if spring had just begun. I could feel the life Hazel poured into her garden as I touched a jasmine bush. The soft, white flowers coating my fingertips in their subtle, sweet fragrance. A gentle smile tugged at the corner of my mouth. It was nice being back here.

"Well, it's about time you visited me, child." Hazels terse voice filtered down from the top step of the cottage, but a loving smile lit up her wrinkled face.

I started at the sound. This was a dream... how was it that Hazel could see me? Talk to me? Hazel made her way across the stone steps, her long green dress sweeping along the grass as she came to a stop at the end of her garden path. She watched me carefully, her pinched lips pulling up into a tiny smile. She reached out a wrinkled hand and brushed a leaf from my hair, the touch gentle and tender. This was real. It wasn't a dream.

"I'm sorry it took so long. I've been busy," I replied, closing the small distance between us, embracing my grandmother tightly. The time I'd spent with her upon my arrival to Ellesmere had been eventful to say the least, but it was a time I cherished. I'd missed her these last few weeks.

"So I hear, child. Maeve came to pay me a visit shortly after your decadent ball." She rose a thin brow at me. "I hear you're off looking for an all-powerful weapon?"

At the mention of 'weapon', my eyes widened.

"What do you know about it, Hazel? Please tell me. I don't know what to do." I shook my head as I stared down at my hands, the burn mark still visible in the centre of my spirit rune. Hazel took my hand in hers and ran the pad of her thumb over my palm. Like my mother's, Hazel's hands were rough and calloused from years spent grinding herbs. She placed a long, thin finger under my chin, tilting it up so I looked into her green eyes.

"Do not fret, child. You have all the answers in front of you. All you need to do is open your eyes. It begins with the bloodstone."

"What are you—" But I stopped myself, a dawning realisation hitting me and leaving me a little breathless. One of the sketches on the parchment Maeve gave me had been a stone.

Her voice turned soft. *"Invenire lapidem et ne timeas tenebras."*

I recognised the language of old, but its meaning was lost to me.

"You will be just fine, child," Hazel continued, placing a soft kiss on my forehead. "Stay true to who you are and you will never lose sight of the person you are destined to be Now, it is time for you to wake up, but remember, beware of the *iter montis*. It is not what it seems."

With a sharp pull at the base of my naval, my breath hitched in my throat. Jerking upright, I took in a shaky breath, frantically moving about my bed roll. No longer surrounded by Hazel's sweet-smelling garden, I was back on the damp ground, the spindly trees looming above me as if gawking at an animal in a cage. I was back in the Ironwood.

"Braelyn, are you all right?" Julien crouched by my side, his dark brows pulled tightly over his eyes. The concern on his face deepened the longer I didn't respond.

I smiled weakly, scrubbing a clammy hand over my face. "Yeah, I'm fine. I just..." My voice trailed off as I thought about my next words carefully. "Can witches teleport, by any chance?"

Julien's frown deepened. "Not that I know of, but there are some instances where charms can be placed on objects. They can act as a talisman if gifted by another, but that person would need to have an identical object. Why do you ask?"

My eyes shifted down to my clenched fist, a sharp pain lacing through my palm. I unclenched my hand, my eyes widening at discovering the wooden jackalope figurine grasped tightly in my fist. I didn't recall taking it out of my bag before I fell asleep. Hazel had given me the hand-carved figure before we left to rescue my mother, saying it was just in case we needed a good omen on our trip. It seemed there was more to the little wooden jackalope than expected.

"I think this is a talisman." I showed Julien the hand-carved figure. "I spoke with Hazel just now. She knew of the page Maeve had given me. She referred to the drawing on the parchment as a bloodstone."

Julien took the jackalope carving from my hand and studied it closely. His face gave nothing away, but I swore a hint of amazement shimmered in his dark eyes. Running a hand through his tousled hair, he breathed out a gentle sigh.

"If this is a talisman, your grandmother must have wanted to tell you something important, Braelyn. Did she say anything else?"

"She told me not to worry. That we had all the answers in front of us. She also said something in the language of old, but I didn't understand it." A small frown creased my brow as my mind sifted through Helene's lessons, trying to recall if I'd heard the words before, but I came up blank.

"What did she say?" Julien asked, a curious edge to his voice.

"Something along the lines of... *invenire lapid et ne timas tene*. Or something like that." I shrugged at his confused look.

"It's *invenire lapidem et ne timeas tenebras*. And I know what it means." Verena's voice made me jump. I hadn't realised she was awake.

She sat atop her coat with her legs folded underneath her. She wore nothing but her thin cotton shirt—her naturally warm blood leaving her cheeks rosy despite the chill in the air.

"Sorry. I didn't mean to startle you or to eavesdrop on your conversation, but I couldn't sleep." She came over to sit across from us, leaving her back to the fire. "The words translate to '*find the bloodstone and don't be afraid of the darkness*'. Does that make any sense to you, Brae?"

Dragging my bag closer to me, I pulled out The Book of Lilith and placed it on my lap. I flicked through the pages until I found the one Maeve had given me. It contained numerous passages written in the language of old, and the drawing of what I now knew to be the bloodstone stood out starkly on the page. But it was the sketch on the right-hand side that kept pulling my attention. I touched the delicate drawings, my head cocked to the side. There was something so familiar in the way the lines depicted a growing shadow—a solidified mass that moved over the page.

A flicker of fear ignited in the depths of my stomach.

"What is it, Brae?" Verena asked, her voice strained.

My fingers worried at the delicate pages. I knew the time would come when I needed to confess to the others what I had told Julien, but a part of me was concerned about what they would think of me. Would they be afraid? Concerned? Something shifted behind Verena. Grey appeared to have been jostled awake by our conversation. He sat with his hands clasped around his knees, eyes watching us from the dim glow of the fire's halo.

"It's about what happened at the clearing, isn't it?" Grey said, his voice hard, the muscles in his neck corded with anxiousness.

Theo was still sound asleep. His chest rose and fell softly as the rest of us spoke, and Grey brushed a piece of hair from his forehead before coming to sit next to me.

"Yes." I stared into their worried faces, knowing what I was about to say next would only be cause for more concern. "I think it's me. That somehow as a spirit witch, I can turn my use of dark magic into a weapon."

An array of emotions played out on each of their faces. Verena's golden eyes were like giant yellow suns filled with angst. Grey pulled his coin out of his pocket, flicking it over his deft fingers as he stared into the fire. Julien's arms remained folded across his chest as he paced in front of me, his eyes downcast.

"And what of the bloodstone?" Grey asked, still staring into the fire.

"Well, that's the thing," Julien said. "No witch or warlock knows where it is."

"It must be why Maeve told us to seek allies," I replied. "The dwarves mine for gems in the mountain, and if no witch or warlock knows where it is—"

"The dwarves must know," Verena gushed, nodding along as if trying to convince herself this was the truth.

My eyes danced over the pages of Lilith's book, trying to look for anything that we may have missed. I turned over the page. The parchment was almost completely blank, but the faintest glimmer of ink reflected in the firelight. Two sentences were scrawled at the top in the language of old. They looked to be written in light silver graphite ink. The handwriting didn't match Lilith's, which made me wonder if perhaps Maeve had written them in her haste to get to me before we left.

It didn't take long for Verena to translate.

"It says, 'they who acquire the stone shall possess the greatest power known throughout Ellesmere, for the ability to enhance one's magic will be imbued upon those who wield it.'"

Goosebumps prickled my skin. This had to be why Maeve removed the page before Elias had the chance to find it. It wasn't just the prophecy Elias had been interested in, but the information about the bloodstone as well. If he'd managed to get hold of it, there was no way I would stand a chance at defeating him. But now, with our knowledge of the bloodstone, we were one step ahead. If we could convince the dwarves to tell us of its whereabouts, I might just stand a chance of fulfilling the prophecy. My hands trembled slightly as I closed the book and placed it safely in my bag.

"Brae, are you okay?" Verena asked gently.

My shaky laugh seemed to echo around the small camp. "I'm fine. It's just, for so long I've worried about failing in my task and letting everyone down. That when the time came, I wouldn't be strong enough to actually defeat him. If we can find the bloodstone though? I can't fail." Relief washed over me, lifting a weight from my shoulders.

We sat in comfortable silence for a few moments, the wind whistling a quiet tune through the branches. The dying fire crackled softly and it was only the sharp snap of a branch that broke the easy calm and sent a cold shiver running down my spine. It was the second time the noise had sounded not far from where we rested. Something told me we were no longer alone. A low, menacing growl echoed through the darkness, sounding like it came from every direction. Julien and Verena stood behind me, arms held out wide by their sides, readying themselves for an attack we all knew was coming. Grey jostled Theo awake as another crack sounded from deep in the Ironwood. The trees groaned in unison as whatever moved in their shadows drew closer.

"In the name of the four elements, what is that noise?" Theo asked.

Both he and Grey had donned their coats and were now standing beside Verena, staring out into the never-ending lines of trees before us.

"I have no idea," I half whispered in response. "But whatever it is"—I swallowed the lump forming in my throat—"it sounds big."

Another growl rumbled through the darkness, making my hair stand on end. I squinted into the night, my eyes probing the darkness for what made the terrifying sound, but I could barely see the trunks of the deadened trees in front of us. Thick shadows hugged us from every direction and, despite the two sets of fiery hands beside me, Julien and Verena's flames did little to stop the encroaching shadows. They reached out to us like sinister fingers trying to latch on to any hope or light we produced. My heart hammered inside my chest as every instinct in my body told me to run, but my feet were rooted to the spot.

Everything went silent. Not a rustle of leaves or breath of wind could be heard. The faint rapid breathing of someone behind me sounded in time with my frantic heartbeat, but whose it was I couldn't say. Julien's fingers laced through mine as I took a wobbly step forward, my fire magic entwining with his own. We stepped towards the closest tree, our hands engulfed in flames. A deep rumble sounded right on cue. Swallowing hard, we lifted our hands towards the canopy of the trees. My arms trembled and Julien's grasp on my fingers tightened in response. As the light of our joined flames broke through the dense shadows, my breath hitched in the back of my throat. Nestled amongst the shadows was a bone-white ram's skull. Black eyes stared back at me with murderous intent, glistening in large eye sockets like obsidian jewels. Julien's body went rigid beside me, his muscles tense as he prepared for what came next. The creature snarled in our direction, its mouth creaking open to reveal razor sharp teeth. With every ounce of breath in me, I turned to the others and screamed.

"Run!"

Twenty

Monstrum barrelled through the trees behind us—growling and snarling as we pounded along the dirt pathway. Verena, Grey, and Theo were ahead of Julien and me, their terrified faces peeking over their shoulders every few seconds. Julien pulled me along next to him, our hands still clasped in a fiery grip, neither of us letting go out of fear of being separated. Together, we stood a chance at killing the beasts, but alone, we were dead. My feet thundered in time with my heart as I tried to focus on breathing. In and out. In and out. My chest burned with each inhalation, desperate to take in more oxygen. I needed to stop. We couldn't outrun these creatures—with each passing second their long limbs closed the distance between us. We needed a distraction. Something to deter the monstrum for a few seconds to give us time to prepare for an attack.

"Just say the word, my friend, and I'll provide it," Alpheus's voice sounded strongly in my mind. He was lost amongst the shadows, but I knew he was close.

"They'll tear you to shreds, Alpheus." I panicked at the thought of him facing down the two creatures snarling behind us. I tried searching for him, but the deeper we ran into the Ironwood, the harder it was becoming to determine friend from foe. The monstrum were so close, the ground shuddered beneath my feet, their growls growing louder as the thrill of the chase narrowed their predatory senses.

"Have faith, my friend."

Before I had the chance to reply, our tether snapped closed. Alpheus was done discussing the matter. Fear choked off my breath as something soft and rigid brushed against my legs. I came to an abrupt stop, my arm constricting painfully as Julien tried to pull me after him. I tugged on his hand to stop him, crying out to the others in the hopes they would hear me. They stopped a few strides ahead, eyes wide. Spinning back to Alpheus, I conjured a flame in my free hand while Julien still tightly held the other. For the longest second, nothing happened. It was like the Ironwood had frozen in time, the trees and woodland creatures waiting with bated breath. Then the earth shuddered beneath my feet. The ground rippled like it was going to open and swallow us whole, and a powerful force slammed into the monstrum, knocking them off their taloned feet. They hit the trees with a sickening crunch, their wooden limbs twisting into unnatural angles, but I knew better than to assume they were dead. Pulling my hand free from Julien's, I called out to my air magic. Long, sharp strings of lightning sparked menacingly between my fingers as the deadly creatures rose to their feet. Alpheus skittered to my side, sending leaves flying in all directions. Magic erupted behind me, everyone calling on their elements for protection. Verena's fire burned near my back before Grey conjured his water magic, sending a chill over my skin. The leaves around my feet parted as Theo's earth magic pulled at the vines on the forest floor. This was it. This was our only chance. The monstrum prowled in front of us like hungry animals assessing us for weakness. The gnarled branches that twisted around their legs creaked and groaned with each step, sending goosebumps spilling over my skin. Large obsidian eyes gleamed hungrily in the reflection of my flames, watching us. Waiting for the slightest break in our defence. The entire Ironwood stilled in anticipation as our lives hung in the balance.

"I'm done waiting," Julien said through clenched teeth. "It's either us or them and I'm sick of being chased by death."

Orange flames erupted from both his hands. A searing heat flooded the small path in front of us as tiny embers floated on the cool breeze. I took a tiny step back, the power of Julien's magic threatening to overwhelm me. With a flick of his hand, orange-red flames licked the undergrowth in an undulating wave. They snaked along the dried leaves and vines covering the floor, consuming everything in their path. Once it reached his target, Julien threw open his hands and my eyed widened as the fire consumed the monstrum in seconds. Flames engulfed the twisted, gnarled branches around its body, sending it up in a fiery inferno. The smell of burnt wood and brimstone billowed around the demonic creature, wafting up my nose and almost choking me. Julien's flame held true on its target, but despite his strength, his magic had no effect on the monster. Its long limbs swatted at the flames in angry arcs, but still the monstrum advanced. Sharp angry growls tore from its throat with each frenzied movement. Stepping back, Julien turned to me quickly. His dark brows knitted, the muscles in his neck straining against the tension in his clenched jaw. A knowing look passed between us, and my heart pounded in my ears. An almost deafening sound.

These creatures weren't of this world. They were demons created with dark magic and only severing their demonic heart would destroy them.

"Go for the heart," I shouted, praying to the elements my friends would hear me above the noise of battle.

Before I had the chance to unleash a deadly blow, they ran at us, bone jaws snapping in our direction. Their clawed hands reached out, craving a taste for blood. I called on the wind, pushing my hand forward to send a burst of air howling in their direction. The creatures were sent careening backwards, giving us a few seconds to regain our composure. The monstrum scrambled to their feet, launching forward to attack, relentless in their need to feast on our flesh. Running at us from both sides, they separated our group down the middle. Verena, Theo, and Grey battled against the first one. Their fire, water, and earth magic weaved around the monster, trying to stop it from tearing them apart. The second circled Julien and me with ravenous intent. Facing it head on, we watched the monster's obsidian eyes grow wide with rabid hunger. It paused for only a second before it threw the weight of its body in my direction. Julien tried to move in front of me, but the monstrum was too quick. It swung one long arm out and, with a sickening crunch, Julien was thrown backwards into the trees. His body went limp.

"Julien!" My scream burned in my throat as I tried desperately to get to his side, but I was trapped. The monstrum closed ranks around me, cutting me off from reaching him as it gripped the tops of my arms with taloned hands.

Pain radiated through me as one of its claws pierced my skin. Tears flooded my vision, a scream tearing through me as the pain became unbearable. Blood oozed from a deep gash along the top of one arm, warm and congealed, and the creature's mouth twisted into a sinister grin, its foul breath hot on my skin. The overpowering scent of decay wafted up my nose, making me gag against the horrid stench. I resisted the urge to vomit and tried desperately to free my hands, but it was no use.

To my left, Julien struggled to get to his feet, his arm gripping his midsection, a crimson stain seeping through his shirt. On my other side, the others were still trapped in a violent battle with the second monstrum. It lashed out at them, swiping clawed hands at anything that moved. Their magic was no match for a creature of such darkness. Struggling against the creature's tight grip, I tried to free myself once more, but it possessed a strength far greater than my own. In his desperation, Julien called out to it, taunting and goading it into tearing its deadly gaze away from me, but those obsidian eyes never strayed from my face. Its mouth twisted into a menacing grin, teeth close enough for me to see the sinewy pieces of flesh still trapped between its jaws—remnants of the last creature unfortunate enough to cross its path. Fear and anger twisted my stomach, but it was the urgent cries from my friends that was my undoing. Taking a deep breath, I pushed through the pain lancing through my arm and brought forward the darkness itching to come out. My hands tingled with the promise of magic as inky black marks swirled and coiled their way from my fingertips. The moment my magic connected with the creature's hands, it screeched, an agonising sound that threatened to burst my eardrums. The monstrum withdrew from my touch as if it was poison. Seizing the opportunity, I thrust my arm through the twisting branches of its chest and seized the large beating heart resting within its wooden cage. With a strength only adrenaline could provide, I yanked the heart free from its chest. A deafening screech pierced the air, making the hairs on the back of my neck prickle before it fell limp beside me, ichor staining the undergrowth like ink. Letting out a strangled breath, I collapsed amongst the leaf litter, trying to breathe in the fresh air before scrambling to my feet. Julien limped over to me, his eyes darting between me and the still warm organ clasped in my hand. I dropped it by my feet, turning to where my friends still faced the second monstrum. Verena's red hair clung to her brow, sweat dripping down the sides of her face. Theo's arm hung limply by his side, a long gash like my own spilling rivulets of blood over his shirt and jacket. He swayed from side to side, exhaustion rimming his eyes. He was far too weak for this. Grey's face was lined with grazes and scratches as he tried his hardest to dodge away from the creature's sharp talons.

Enough. My hands beckoned the magic forward as I called out to the darkness. Long, dark shadows poured from my fingertips, floating along the forest floor and undulating around our feet. The last monstrum stopped its assault and turned its attention to me. Cocking its head to the side, the creature's mouth creaked into a sinister grin displaying needle-like teeth dripping with blood. It watched my dark magic as if trying to decipher its next move, but after a moment of deliberation, it stalked forward.

Good, I thought. *Underestimate me.*

Its taloned hands clawed at the air in front of it, eyes locked with my own. I curled my fingers, willing the shadows around me to rise and merge together. When they were done, a sword made of pure shadow formed. Hardening my resolve, I gripped the shadow sword in both hands, unsure how to wield such a weapon. It didn't matter, though. I just needed to be close enough to pierce its heart.

"What are you waiting for?" I jeered, my voice coming out as sharp as the blade in my hands.

The monstrum bellowed its rage before launching towards me. My fingers trembled on the hilt, but as the creature closed the distance, I stabbed the blade forward with every ounce of strength I had left. It pierced through the monstrum's heart, the tip protruding from its back. My chest heaved with ragged breaths until my ribs felt like they'd break under the pressure. I narrowed my eyes at the monstrum's face, waiting for the moment its lifeforce left its body. It swayed for a few seconds, a low moan gurgling from its mouth, before toppling to the ground in a sickening crunch that reverberated through the Ironwood. A chill settled deep in my bones as I stared down at the demonic creatures lying dead at my feet, unable to shift my gaze from their twisted limbs and lifeless eyes. My arms felt like dead weights at my side, hanging limp as awareness began to wash over me. The soft caress of the wind against my heated cheeks, the feel of the hard ground beneath my boots. Hurried voices sounded, my friends' wide eyes and open mouths reflecting a shock that now made my muscles feel weak and flimsy. They looked between me and the monstrum, seeming like they didn't quite believe what they had witnessed. But, as the reality of what I'd done began to settle in, my legs trembled beneath me before eventually giving way. Exhaustion weighed me down and I was vaguely aware of Julien's arms wrapping around my waist just as darkness spotted my vision, the world around me blurring. I tried desperately to fight against the fatigue, but my body slumped against Julien's chest, his arms encircling me tighter. The last thing I saw before falling into unconsciousness was the open canopy above me and a lonesome crow cawing softly into the void.

Twenty-One

emories flittered across my closed eyelids like tiny fireflies, each one lighting up what had happened with the monstrum and the magic I'd conjured. How had it even been possible for me to conjure a weapon like that? In all my lessons with the elders, I'd never come across any witch or warlock being able to wield magic the way I had. My head ached the more I thought about it. With a resigned sigh, I slowly opened my eyes, my surroundings swimming like I was looking up at the world from underwater. As my eyes adjusted to the dim light, I glanced around the small chamber. Instead of the dark canopy of the Ironwood, a low stone roof hovered above me. A fire crackled warmly across the room, bathing my quarters in a comfortable warmth. Soft furs and pillows had been placed around my body—creature comforts I hadn't felt in days—but my mind whirred as my hands scrambled against the velvety pelts, trying to pull myself into a sitting position.

"Braelyn, you're okay. You're safe." The familiar voice instantly eased my anxiety. Julien's warm hands held my arms tenderly, his face hovering nearby, haloed by the firelight.

"Where are the others? Where are we?" I asked, concern making my pulse flutter.

Julien looked down at me, a warm, comforting smile lighting his face. "They're here too. They've been exploring the Ironwood Mountains."

My shoulders relaxed and I leaned back against the soft pillows, taking comfort in the familiarity of Julien's touch. My friends were safe and we'd made it to the dwarves. But, as I took in Julien's appearance, my throat grew thick at the multiple grazes lining his face and the dark circles rimming his eyes. Julien collapsed into a wing-backed armchair beside my bed, his hand clutching at his midsection as he let out a small grunt of pain.

"Your side," I whispered. "Are you okay?"

He chuckled softly. "I'm fine, sweetheart."

I could see the muscles straining in his neck each time he took a breath and the way his hand held his side like each movement was a struggle. I shook my head.

"You're lying."

Julien let out a frustrated sigh. He raked a hand through his hair, wincing as the movement jostled his injury. My jaw clenched, lips pressing together in a thin line.

"Show me, Julien."

"Braelyn." Julien's voice was terse, his eyes locked on mine as he urged me to let this go. But I couldn't, not until I knew he was truly all right.

"Show me," I said again, my voice strained.

A frustrated huff escaped his lips as he pushed himself up from the armchair. He shrugged off his coat, a deep frown etching its way between his brows as he tossed it onto the bed. Fiery red lines crisscrossed over his forearms, the deep red marks disappearing beneath his rolled-up sleeves. Untucking the hem of his shirt, he pulled it up to reveal the rigid muscles of his abdomen. My breath hitched as I stared at the hard lines of his stomach, but it was the long laceration and purple-black bruise blossoming over the right side of his ribs that made the colour drain from my face. He hadn't taken the healing elixir. Since my time in Ellesmere, I had endured my share of torment, but it was nothing compared to the agony of watching Julien suffer. The pain of seeing his injuries.

"I'm so sorry for what happened," I choked out.

Julien placed a finger under my chin, tilting my face back to his so our eyes met over the bed.

"None of this is your fault, sweetheart." The tenderness in his voice almost cleaved my chest in two.

"Yes, it is," I said a little louder. "All of it is my fault. Those creatures were sent after *me*. People I care about keep getting hurt because of *me*."

I wrapped my arms around my stomach, wincing when the movement jostled my right hand. A small white bandage had been secured around my palm, which pulsed in time with my heart, the pain lancing up my arm making the room spin. I tugged at the tied end of fabric but couldn't quite get it undone with one hand.

"Here, allow me," Julien replied, his face solemn.

He pulled at the knot, moving his hands away to allow me to unravel the last few lengths of cloth. Angry red welts littered the soft flesh of my hand, but they were nothing compared to the blackened and blistered sore that sat in the middle of my spirit rune. Ebony lines snaked over my hand like a slow releasing poison. Bile rose in the back of my throat as I turned my gaze back to Julien, my eyes brimming with tears.

"What happened to me?" I asked, my voice wavering with each word.

He stroked the back of my hand gently, his thumb tracing small, soothing circles on my chilled skin, but it did little to keep the panic at bay.

"Brae, the magic you used against the monstrum was something I'd never seen before. You solidified shadows and turned them into a sword."

I thought back on the battle and the way my magic had rippled and shifted into a weapon. I recalled the way the darkened hilt had felt in my hand, almost like we belonged together and were one and the same. How was that even possible?

Julien's eyes were downcast, staring at the burn mark on my palm.

"After you killed the monstrum, you collapsed. We tried to heal you with the healing elixir and gave you the convaluisset, thinking it would help with your exhaustion, but you didn't wake. You didn't heal." He rubbed a hand over his face. "So, I carried you to the Ironwood Mountains where you've been asleep for just on a day."

My eyes widened as I processed his words. "You carried me the rest of the way?"

Julien chuckled at the way my mouth fell open and how my gaze shifted to his arms. He'd left his jacket off, the sleeves of his shirt rolled up to his elbows. The tight muscles in his forearms tensed under my fixed stare, his fingers flexing where they rested on the soft pelts covering my bare legs.

"We weren't that far from the mountains already, but yes. It almost killed me to see you like that, Braelyn. I thought I'd lost you to the darkness."

"I'm sorry," I whispered. "I never wanted to scare you, but when I saw you on the ground—not knowing if you were alive or dead—something came over me. It was the same feeling I had back at the clearing. An overwhelming anger and fear for you and the others."

I held his gaze as I tried to explain how it felt when the darkness beckoned. When it called out to me with unwavering determination.

"When I looked over to see that the others were in trouble, it was like a wave of anger crushed me beneath its grasp, and all I could see was a solution. The shadows called out to me, and I seized them. The same thing happened in the clearing with King Elias and his guards."

Julien's gaze never left mine as he sat quietly, pondering my words. The intensity of his brown eyes pulled every secret from deep within as I continued to lay my heart's deepest secrets before him. It was like a gate had been opened. No matter how hard I tried to keep everything in, all the feelings I'd had over the last few days came tumbling from my mouth. Even if I wanted to stop it, I didn't think I could.

"The thing that scares me the most," I finished quietly, "is how much I like the power this magic gives me."

Sinking back into the soft pillows behind me, I pulled my gaze away from Julien's, focusing on the small circular window above his head. I wasn't sure I could handle the animosity I would see reflected at me. The truth was I no longer feared the dark magic. The consequences of wielding it still concerned me, but fear no longer held the darkness captive. Heat warmed my cheeks at my admission, but I no longer wanted to hide from Julien—or anyone else for that matter. As the spirit witch and Ellesmere's future queen, I needed to be strong. Who would ally with a fearful queen? How could I stop Elias if I feared the same magic needed to stop him? No matter how scared I was, I would do what needed to be done.

The seconds ticked over when Julien's fingers finally gripped my chin softly, pulling my gaze back to the internal fire blazing behind his beautiful eyes. Warmth deepened the flush on my cheeks, his touch lingering as soft as a feather, preventing me from turning away from him. There was no anger hardening his jaw or fear rimming his eyes, just a knowing smile that pulled at the corner of his mouth.

"Braelyn, it's okay to be scared. We all fear something." His eyes flickered with what I imagined was the thought of his own demons. "It's how we face it that truly matters. You wield this dark magic out of love, not power. It's what makes you different from the others."

I shuffled closer to him, his hand moving to my waist and pulling me forward a few inches so my legs grazed his beneath the heavy pelts. The room suddenly felt too warm. His hand found the curve of my neck, his touch gentle as he ran soothing strokes across my jaw. When I nibbled on my bottom lip, his eyes burned with a need I felt deep in my belly. His free hand curled around my waist, closing the few inches separating our bodies. A small gasp escaped my lips and that was his undoing. Julien pressed his lips to mine, soft and tender. My hands moved over the smooth lines of his chest, the warmth of his skin burning through the thin layer of his cotton shirt. Our kiss deepened and my breath hitched in my throat. Julien chuckled against my mouth, his hand running along my neck, feeling the jolt of my rising pulse. We eased out of our kiss, our chests rising and falling in rapid succession, our cheeks shaded a rosy pink.

"You will be the death of me, Julien Thorne," I whispered before pressing my lips to his, a little harder this time.

"Not if you kill me first," he breathed back.

A loud knock on the door startled us back to reality. I untangled myself from his embrace as Julien dropped his hand to the thick blanket—holding mine in a firm and reassuring grasp. Before I was able to gather my erratic thoughts, a stout dwarf bustled into the room, a thick fur shawl draped over her broad shoulders, making her seem a lot wider at the top. She wore a tunic of brilliant blue over a dark set of trousers, secured by a wide leather belt dotted with small pouches and pockets. Her fox-red hair was streaked with grey and secured in two long braids on either side of her round face. She bustled by the fireplace, dropping a few large logs onto the dying embers, stoking the fire eagerly with the iron poker. Turning on her heel, she faced the large bed, a cherry glow painting her cheeks. At seeing me sitting up amongst the bed covers, she beamed. The action lit up her entire face and, despite not knowing her, I couldn't help but give her a warm smile of my own—the motion causing my dry lips to crack.

"Miss Grey," she exclaimed. "How lovely to see you awake."

She hurried to the bedside, taking up my right arm and pinching my wrist between her plump fingers, her eye on a small watch hanging by her breast. Every now and again her lips would move, counting in time with my pulse. After a while, she placed my hand back on the bed, a smile tugging at her lips.

"Very good," she muttered to herself as she assessed the warmth of my forehead followed by the wound on my hand. "A nasty injury this one," she tutted. Her fingers poked and prodded the red skin around the burn.

Reaching to her belt, she opened one of the larger pouches and pulled out a small, round jar, its contents a rich green. The faint scent of chamomile filled the air when she opened the lid. She scooped some of the mixture onto her fingers and made to put it on my injured palm, but I pulled my hand away at the last second.

I winced at the sudden movement, cradling my injured hand to my chest.

"What is that?" I asked, unsure what the thick, green poultice would do.

Julien chuckled. "It's okay, Braelyn. This is Siv, she's a healer."

Siv smiled warmly down at me. "It's safe. This is a special healing poultice we make. It contains a rare nettle that only grows in the depths of the mountain."

"We tried using our tincture back in the Ironwood and it didn't do anything," Julien chimed in. "But this seems to be helping your palm heal." He nodded at the small pot Siv held.

"Okay," I replied, a little embarrassed I'd reacted so rashly. "I'm sorry, Siv. Please." I stuck out my injured hand and the kindly dwarf took it gently in her warm one.

"It's no trouble. After everything Mr Thorne has told me, you are right to be wary of strangers." She placed the poultice on my hand, which instantly soothed the pain. The thick, gritty texture felt rough on my skin, but the relief from the constant throbbing in my palm was intoxicating.

Turning the full extent of her moss-green gaze to me, she said, "You have no enemies here, Miss Grey. You're safe."

Still holding my injured hand in hers, she gave me a warm smile before placing it gently back on the soft fur covers. My throat grew thick with emotion, moved by how gracious and accepting the dwarves had been of our unexpected arrival.

"Thank you," I replied, my voice cracking.

"It's my pleasure, but I do come bearing tidings from King Vidar. He wishes to speak with you."

Siv moved towards a large baroque closet next to the bed. The dark panelling depicted beautiful images of bears, foxes, and deer, among other animals, and clearly had been carved by an expert hand.

"The king wishes to speak with me?" I replied, sitting up a little straighter in the bed. My eyes flicked to Julien, who shrugged, confirming this was the first he was hearing of it.

"Of course. You are a guest in his kingdom. He merely wishes to welcome you to our home." Siv closed the cupboard doors and placed a set of clothes next to the changing petition at the end of the small room. "Now, let's get you cleaned up and ready to meet the king."

Twenty-Two

The dwarves' home was unlike anything I'd seen before. Hundreds of tunnels had been dug into the mountain, twisting and turning before disappearing into deep, rocky crevices. It was an underground maze and Siv knew all the routes as though a map was imprinted in her mind.

I was grateful for the thick pants, long-sleeved tunic, and heavy fur-lined coat Siv had given me. As we walked through the numerous tunnels, cold air clung to the damp stones, sending chills over the exposed parts of my skin. I shoved my hands deeper into my pockets, walking closer to Julien to steal some of the warmth I knew would be radiating off him. He had opted to stay in his usual clothes, but it seemed someone had kindly washed them for him. His cotton shirt was now a pristine white and his dark trousers were free from dust and grime. At Siv's insistence, he'd also donned a fur-lined jacket, unable to bear the stern look on her face when trying to decline it. Whilst I'd washed and changed, Julien had allowed Siv to heal his wounds. She'd generously applied her healing poultice to his bruised ribs and he'd applied a few drops of the healing elixir to his hands, his arms now free of the angry red lines. I still watched him from the corner of my eye, though. Every now and again, his hand would hover over his torso, a grimace on his face. Siv had told me it would take a little longer for the poultice to work on such a large wound, but my pulse still jumped each time he winced. Siv had also been the one to heal Theo, Grey, and Verena. She'd confessed they had fared much better than Julien and me, with only a few superficial cuts and bruises. My mother's healing elixir had restored them to full health.

The tunnels were only wide enough for two people to walk abreast, so Siv led the way a few paces ahead. A heavy iron lantern grasped in her brawny hand illuminated the path. Small wooden doors dotted the rocky mountainside every few metres or so, their smooth surface a stark contrast to the rough walls around it.

"What's behind these doors?" I asked Siv, curiosity getting the better of me.

"Homes, of course," she said as if it was the simplest answer in the world. "Many of the dwarves in the Ironwood Mountains live amongst these tunnels with their families."

Julien's shoulders tensed. In the halo of Siv's lantern, I saw his gaze shift to each of the doors we passed, naturally sceptical of every person we met. We continued to wind through the damp tunnels at a slow pace, our footfalls on the packed rocky ground the only noise echoing through the empty passageways. Moss dotted the rocky walls and the stagnant smell of damp earth filled the air. It was like standing in the shade of the forest after a lengthy walk. Inhaling deeply, I breathed in the earthy scents of moss and damp soil. It was intoxicating.

Finally, the thin tunnel opened into one of the most magnificent sights I'd ever laid eyes on. My mouth dropped open in awe as I gazed around at the cavernous space before us. The rocky faces of the mountain appeared to have been chiselled and worked into gigantic stone columns which stood guard at the entrance to a bustling underground city. Warm light flickered in large iron bowls fixed to the walls, the face of the mountain never-ending. While its extravagance took my breath away, it was nothing compared to the sweeping valley that lay below. An enormous river carved its way between rocky banks, a bustling town emerging either side of the crystal-clear water. My eyes roamed every inch of the incredible underground city, drinking in as much of its beauty as I possibly could.

"It's a wonder to behold, isn't it?" Siv said, the pride in her voice making her chest swell. All I could do was nod in agreement.

I had no words for the sheer magnificence of this place. How something so grand could be hidden beneath the mountains astounded me. Siv led the way along the winding banks of the underground river. Clearer than any other body of water I'd seen, I was able to see all the way to the rocky bottom. Fish darted amongst the water weeds, their scales sparkling in the firelight cast by the large sconces lining the walls. As we ventured deeper into the city, signs of Mother Nature's presence became even more apparent. Creeping vines twisted their way around any visible structure, much like the moss that covered the walls and floors of the tunnels. It was a natural masterpiece and my earth magic bristled at the sights. Small shopfronts lined the mountain face. Warm, golden light filtered out through their windows, creating an inviting ambience as we walked past. Many of the dwarves smiled in our direction, while others muttered quiet words to their friends behind their hands. Julien shifted beside me. His hand hovered inches away from mine, fingers twitching every time someone walked too close.

"You're the talk of the mountains, Miss Grey," Siv explained as groups of dwarves parted for us to walk by, their eyes following us into the growing crowd.

Everyone wore similar clothing to Siv—long tunics over thick trousers, or corseted dresses that fell in waves of material from their waist. Whispers circled us and I sensed Julien's nerves fraying. His shoulders tensed at the attention we were garnering from the growing crowd.

Trust didn't come easy to Julien. It would take time for him to put his faith in anyone outside of our inner circle.

We rounded a small bend and the cavernous space opened to bright, warm sunlight filtering through a huge hole in the peak of the mountain.

"Welcome to Castle Elwood." Siv swept her arm out across the view, a bemused smile lighting her kind face as we gaped at the sight before us.

"See, Mr Thorne?" Siv said, elbowing Julien in the side and receiving a low grunt in response. "I told you that you were missing out on extravagance while you were pining away over Miss Grey's bedside."

He looked at her, his expression stony, but in the soft light cast over us, his cheeks were the slightest shade of pink.

"Yes, thank you, Siv," Julien replied flatly. "I can see that now."

Her wide smile made the skin around her eyes crinkle and I couldn't help but hide the grin that pulled at my lips. She simply waggled her eyebrows suggestively in response to Julien's retort.

Reaching out, I took Julien's hand in mine and squeezed it gently, not knowing how else to express my gratitude. He gifted me with a lopsided smile before releasing my hand and letting it fall between us.

"Your friends have been enjoying the hospitality of the dwarves very much since your arrival," Siv told us as she led us to the entrance of Castle Elwood.

At the mention of my friends, my heart lifted. "Can I see them?" I asked eagerly, increasing my pace so I was now in step with her.

She smiled kindly but shook her head, making her braids bounce. "Not yet. First, you must speak with the king. He doesn't like to be kept waiting. He's a kind ruler, but does not appreciate tardiness."

My shoulders slumped a little at Siv's answer, but I was eager to meet King Vidar and start securing us the alliances we needed to fulfil the prophecy.

The castle appeared grander now we stood before it. Two rocky pillars guarded the entrance. Taller than the trees of the Ironwood, they had been shaped into perfect cylinders, depicting thousands of carved images of dwarves wielding weapons and engaged in battle. They were a wonder to behold. Enormous stone steps cascaded down from the mouth of the castle and, standing upon the very last one stood a familiar face. Lorcan Lightbeard beamed down at us, his long white beard almost touching his belt.

"Braelyn Grey." He held his arms out wide in a welcoming gesture. "It is such a pleasure to see you again." He grasped my hands between his large rough ones, squeezing gently.

"And you, Lorcan. How did you manage to get back to the mountains so quickly? Was everyone all right? Did you happen to see my mother before you left?"

My questions came tumbling out of my mouth before I could stop them. Desperate for answers, I held my breath and awaited his reply. The sparkle glinting in his green eyes dimmed a little, his smile faltering as he looked at me.

"There were several casualties, but most managed to escape the creatures. Unfortunately, I didn't see your mother before my kin and I left the castle. As soon as the danger passed, we made haste for our home, our steeds carrying us swiftly back to the mountains." Lorcan placed a hand on my arm, his kind smile back in place. "I'm sure your mother is safe, my dear. She is a marvellous woman, capable and strong beyond reason."

I smiled appreciatively, grateful for Lorcan's reassurances, but it didn't do much to quell the worry churning in my stomach.

"Well, I'm glad you were able to make it home safe." The old dwarf beamed at my comment. "Are you here to take us to see the king?"

"That I am, my dear. That I am. Ever since my encounter with Elias, and after maintaining such a close friendship with your lovely mother, the king made me his personal advisor." Lorcan puffed his chest out proudly.

Secured on the left side of his green tunic was a beautiful pin which glinted in the light. It looked like a golden arrow pointing toward the heavens. A stunning yellow-brown stone had been fastened in the centre where the body of the arrow met the tip. Upon seeing me look at it, Lorcan reached up and touched the stone lightly.

"It's the warrior's pin. The arrow rune represents honour in battle, while the tiger's eye stone represents the warrior. You'll see that all dwarven warriors don amber-coloured armour—it is sacred and taken from the stone which offers us protection in battle."

"It is well deserved, Lorcan," I replied with a warm smile.

Lorcan inclined his head before gesturing with a sweeping arm for us to follow him. We stepped into a cavernous hall swathed in tapestries and carpets the same colour as the tiger's eye Lorcan wore pinned to his tunic. Small fires burned in large wall sconces, creating a blanket of warmth over the vast room. Dwarves milled about the hall, a few of them staring wide-eyed and open-mouthed as they hurried past. A broad-shouldered dwarf beamed at us as he walked past, carrying an array of weapons and spare armour. It looked awfully heavy, but he cradled everything in his arms as if it weighed no more than a pile of coats. He ventured towards a door across the other side of the room and disappeared down a dark corridor. A few others followed behind him, all carrying axes, swords and shields in their muscled arms. Weapons all forged deep within the mountain. Each dwarf tipped their head in greeting as they walked. One dwarf, with hair as dark as night and fastened at the base of his neck, gave me a dazzling smile, winking cheekily as he sauntered past us. My cheeks flushed a warm pink and I heard Julien mumble something unintelligible behind me. Lorcan chuckled happily as he watched them parade before us.

"You are somewhat of a heroine in our eyes."

My eyes grew wide at Lorcan's words and my cheeks deepened in colour. "What do you mean? I haven't done anything."

Lorcan chuckled again. It was a low and deep rumble that reverberated around the stone room. He turned his gaze to me, his forest-green eyes glistening like emeralds in the firelight. I could just make out his kind smile beneath his unruly beard.

"Do you know what dwarves value more than anything? More than gems, stones, and iron?"

I shook my head, unsure of where this conversation was headed. Until now, Lorcan had been the only dwarf I'd spoken to, and I was eager to learn more about their customs while visiting their home. I waited patiently for Lorcan to continue.

"We dwarves value honour and bravery above all else. When you rescued me from the depths of Elias's dungeons and fought valiantly against the cruel king to save your mother, you earned the respect of every dwarf under the Ironwood Mountain. In our eyes, you are a true heroine, worthy of the stories that have been told of you... even if you may not see it yourself." He raised a knowing eyebrow at me.

It was like he'd peered into the depths of my mind and extracted all my doubts. He was right, though. Despite going up against King Elias, defeating the monstrum, and trying to unite the people of Ellesmere, I didn't feel like a hero. No matter what people said, a small voice in the back of my head told me all I'd done is create more problems in need of solving. With the help of my friends, I may have rid Ellesmere Castle of King Elias's reign, but he still possessed a magic not his own and continued to hurt the people of Ellesmere without a single drop of remorse. And it was only going to get worse if I couldn't stop him before the next full moon of Samhain.

Sure, I had grown more confident in using my magic and more powerful than I ever believed I could be, but that didn't make me a hero. Heroes stopped the enemy and saved those they cared about. I let Elias escape and take my friend with him. How could the dwarves see me as a hero?

Lorcan came to stand beside me, his head just reaching the top of my shoulder. Leaning in close he whispered, "I know what battles you face within yourself, my dear, but you will soon know what others see in you. You just need to believe in your greatness."

I gave him a small smile, my stomach turning with uncertainty. I hoped he was right.

As we followed the white-haired dwarf, he took us through a series of long passages and curling stairways that had my head spinning by the time we reached a small landing. Lorcan wrapped his knuckles once on the dark wooden door before a booming voice shouted for us to enter. He held the door open, giving me a brief nod to enter. Julien made to follow, but Lorcan reached up and placed a large hand on his chest, forcing him back.

"What are you doing?" Julien growled.

"Only Miss Grey is permitted to enter the king's chamber, Mr Thorne."

Julien swiped at Lorcan's hand, trying to push through, but the old dwarf managed to hold him back.

"If you think I'm going to let Braelyn meet him alone, you're not as smart as I once thought." Julien's shoulders rippled, his eyes igniting with fire.

Lorcan stood firm. "As Siv has told you, Mr Thorne, Braelyn has no enemies here."

Julien opened his mouth, a retort ready on his tongue, but I stopped him with a gentle hand on his forearm.

"I'll be okay, Julien." I tried to put as much strength behind my words as I could muster. "You'll find me afterwards?" I asked, my eyes imploring.

With a resounding sigh, Julien raked a hand through his dishevelled hair, the action mussing his curls even more. His dark eyes locked onto my hazel ones.

"Always," Julien murmured before Lorcan relaxed his shoulders and moved him away from the closing door.

Swallowing hard, I cast one last glance over my shoulder at Julien. His lips were pressed into a hard, thin line, but he nodded once in encouragement before the door closed behind me with a low thud.

Twenty-Three

The room was decorated simply, with a large ornate rug and stone desk running along the far wall. Bathed in orange light, a dozen fiery sconces burned brightly around the walls, making the room feel uncomfortably warm. Sweat began to bead along my hairline, my hands growing clammy beneath the sleeves of my fur coat. Shadows flickered in the deep crevices of the room and I took a tentative step back, my magic eager to draw them close. Behind the desk, an elderly dwarf with light eyes stared fixedly at me as he seemed to soak up my appearance. His gaze travelled from my boot-clad feet and up towards my face, where, for the first time since I entered, our eyes met. They sparked with curiosity and, leaning back in his chair, he steepled his large, plump fingers beneath his chin. Standing behind him was a rather large dwarf with the same light blue eyes, and I recognised his face from the ball held at Ellesmere Castle. Had it only been four days since then? It seemed like a lifetime had passed. Both dwarves were dressed in the same leather vest and furs that Lorcan wore, but where the older one was a slim build, the younger dwarf behind him was mighty in size.

"Welcome, Braelyn Grey. I'm so glad to see you up. It has been a worrying time for your friends." Leaning forward, the older dwarf spread his arms out wide. "I am King Vidar." He inclined his head in my direction, his voice loud and strong.

I inclined my head in greeting. "Thank you for your warm welcome King Vidar. I'm feeling much better, in due thanks to your generous hospitality."

Vidar waved a large hand in dismissal. "Ah, no need to thank us, Miss Grey. We were happy to help the spirit witch whose tales of bravery have spread throughout Ellesmere."

My cheeks warmed at his words. So, Lorcan hadn't been exaggerating about the tales of my supposed mighty encounter with King Elias. Fiddling with the cuff of my coat, I tried to hold my smile, but my nerves got the better of me and it wavered slightly.

The young dwarf smirked at my discomfort.

"Lorcan told me of the valiant tales being told, but I'm sure they are nothing compared to yours King Vidar."

The dwarf king's booming laugh echoed around the room, rattling my bones. I let out a small breath, the unease I'd felt earlier beginning to dissipate.

"A modest and diplomatic answer. The Elders of Ellesmere have been teaching you well, I see."

He beamed at me, the expression making the deep wrinkles around his eyes more prominent. King Vidar seemed incredibly kind and accommodating but, while I was thankful for his hospitality, there were more pressing matters needing to be voiced. We didn't have long before Elias would attempt to summon Lilith from the Underworld and I didn't want to waste any more time. Clearing my throat, I took a small step toward the large desk, my clammy hands twitching in anticipation. The young dwarf took a step forward, his hand tightening around the hilt of the sword strapped around his waist. My eyes widened at his reaction, but the king dismissed him with a simple wave of his hand.

"I apologise for the overprotectiveness of my son, Miss Grey. He doesn't trust as easily as I do." King Vidar sat back in his chair, his plump fingers loosely clasped over his round mid-section. The dwarf prince rolled his eyes at his father before taking a step back.

"No apologies necessary, King Vidar. I'm just grateful for you taking me and my friends into your home."

The king eyed me carefully, a slow smile building across his lips. "It is our pleasure to host the spirit witch," he replied, rising from the seat behind his desk.

Unlike the one in Elias's study, the dwarf king appeared to be meticulous in his organisation. Loose pieces of parchment were stacked neatly in piles, and quills and inkpots were arranged in a straight line at the top of the baroque table. Rolls of parchment sat in a small tub by the corner of the large desk, the contents hidden and tightly secured by lengths of twine. King Vidar came to stand before me and leaned back on the edge of the desk, his hands resting lightly on either side.

"We are holding a great feast tonight in the banquet hall and I would very much like for you and your friends to join us as our guests of honour."

"My friends and I would be honoured, King Vidar." I inclined my head in thanks, but my hands shook slightly, not knowing how the next part of this conversation might go. It was now or never. "But there is something pressing I would like to speak with you about if you have the time to listen?"

Given the apprehension rolling in my belly, I was surprised with how confident my voice sounded. The room seemed to quieten as two sets of light eyes watched me with wary curiosity. The sconces behind the king's desk sparked menacingly, as if warning me to choose my words carefully. There was no knowing how King Vidar would receive my plea for help, and I couldn't risk him turning me down.

"And what is it you would like to speak to me about, Miss Grey?" Vidar crossed his legs at the ankles, his hands now folded lightly across his chest, which swelled with each deep breath he took.

"Well, the reason we journeyed to the Ironwood Mountains was to ask for your help. As you know, King Elias is threatening the livelihoods of all who dwell in Ellesmere. He plans to summon the dark witch Lilith from the Underworld, and we alone cannot stop him." Pausing, I watched the dwarf king closely, but his face was expressionless and gave nothing away. My palms tingled at my growing nervousness, magic bristling along the tips of my fingers. Squaring my shoulders, I spoke the words we had travelled this far to say.

"I ask for your allegiance in helping put a stop to King Elias and the cruelty he continues to bestow on us all."

To my surprise, it wasn't King Vidar that answered. It was the brawny dwarf standing behind him. He hadn't said a word since I'd entered the king's quarters, just merely rolled his eyes and huffed when I spoke. Now, it seemed, he could no longer hold his tongue.

"You come to us to ask for help?" He scoffed, his light eyes cold as he stared at me with contempt. "Surely the great spirit witch of Ellesmere requires no such assistance from the likes of us."

Like his father, the prince's voice was deep and husky, but it held none of the king's kindness. Only disdain. Narrowing my eyes in his direction, I returned his hateful gaze. He was rude and arrogant—someone I would never have aligned with back in Pryhollow. My magic bristled alongside my annoyance, but instead of retorting, I turned my gaze to Vidar, who had silenced his son with a simple wave of his hand.

"Riven, you should not be so rude to our guest. Please excuse my son, Miss Grey. He is only threatened by your power."

Riven scoffed at his father's comment, which made my lip quirk up an inch. This mighty dwarf warrior was threatened by me? I pressed my lips together to stifle my laughter.

Haloed against the dark window, the prince looked formidable as he rolled his shoulders and turned to his father.

"I am not threatened by her," he said, his voice hard, "But I don't think it wise to send our people to fight a war they cannot win."

"Well, Miss Grey. If we join your war, will we be on the winning side?" Vidar raised a questioning brow at me, his face carefully blank.

While I didn't have a definitive answer, I did have the prophecy to go off. It had said in uniting the people of Ellesmere, we would be able to defeat King Elias. I couldn't say how many people we would lose in the process. The prophecy's information only extended so far.

"The prophecy states that a spirit witch would unite the people of Ellesmere and defeat the cruel king. I can't predict the future, but I know we have a much better chance of stopping him if we stand together."

King Vidar nodded slowly, a small smile creeping across his weathered face. "Another diplomatic answer." He glanced up towards Riven, who stood rigidly behind him, his lips pinched in a scowl.

A silent exchange passed between father and son.

"Father—" Riven began, but King Vidar cut him off with a raised hand.

"At the feast tonight, I will put it to a vote. If my people are happy to follow you into battle, we will do so. If not..."

He didn't need to finish his sentence for me to understand what he meant. If the dwarves didn't join us, we would have to rely on the help of the elves alone and, if I was being completely honest with myself, I was worried about their allegiance. After the incident with Balor, they had kept their distance. Only a few representatives had attended the ball and they'd stayed silent for most of the evening, not venturing far from the corner of the room and only speaking a few words of elvish to each other. We needed the dwarves on our side if I were to fulfil my destiny. If I could secure their help, it might prove easier to convince the elves to join us.

"I understand, King Vidar," I replied calmly.

"Splendid," he said, clapping his large hands together. "We will have your belongings brought to a room in the castle. I'm sure you will find the lodgings to your liking."

"Thank you, that is most gracious."

With a small incline of his head, he dismissed me. Once my hand was on the door handle, I shot one quick glance over my shoulder at Riven. He whispered something in his father's ear before turning to me with a triumphant smirk on his face. My mouth flattened into a thin line. If he thought I would go down without a fight, he was sorely mistaken.

Lorcan waited for me outside the king's quarters and led me back down through the numerous tunnels and turrets of the castle. He chatted animatedly to me about the feast, but most of it went over my head, my mind too occupied with my conversation with the king. After a while, we reached the entrance hall and, after the stifling heat of King Vidar's study, I welcomed the cool breeze whistling through the castle's open foyer. With a tight hug, Lorcan bid me farewell and promised to find me at the feast later on.

Outside, I found Julien exactly where he said he would be. He leaned against a stone pillar at the bottom of the castle steps, hands tucked into his coat pockets. Theo, Verena, and Grey chatted happily beside him, their injuries appearing to be healing nicely. I silently thanked Siv for her kindness. It had been such a long time since I'd seen their faces free of concern. The tension that had plagued Theo since his rescue seemed to have eased slightly and the bruises around his eyes were almost non-existent. It lifted my spirits seeing my friends free from worry. Dashing down the front steps, I embraced them enthusiastically, feeling my own concerns dissipate.

"Brae, you're awake," Theo said, his smile crinkling the scar on his cheek.

His expression almost made me explode with happiness. It was the first time he'd spoken to me since his outburst in the Ironwood. I'd been so worried that our friendship wouldn't be the same—that he wouldn't be able to forgive me for the torment he'd endured—but as he wrapped a lanky arm around me, my worry began to subside.

"You're talking to me," I said, my voice a little shaky as he pulled away.

The others had moved, giving Theo and me the privacy we needed. They spoke in hushed whispers, but I knew they would be listening. Theo hung his head, his boot scuffing at the stone walkway. He seemed to unconsciously rub at his arm, his eyes unable to meet mine.

"I am."

A few silent seconds passed before he finally looked at me. His crystal eyes sparkled with unshed tears, the whites streaked with red.

"I'm sorry for the way I acted in the clearing, Brae. It wasn't your fault. I was scared and angry at myself, and I took it out on you. I hope you can forgive me." He wiped his nose on the back of his hand, stifling a sniffle. "If we went back in time, I would make the same decision because..." His bottom lip trembled, his voice wavering with remorse. "Because you're my best friend and I love you."

Tears fell silently over my cheeks as I pulled Theo close, wrapping my arms around his slim frame. He was still so thin, my fingers able to feel every rib. A part of me would always blame myself for what happened to him, but hearing he forgave me was enough to mend some of the sorrow. We eased out of our embrace, both our cheeks damp. As I brushed away a lingering tear streaking Theo's face, he smiled. The smile I'd dreamed of. The same smile that pulled at his scar and crinkled the freckles across his nose.

My face lit up. "There is nothing to forgive, Theo. I love you, too."

He let out a shaky laugh before giving my shoulder a playful nudge. It seemed we would be all right. The others inched back over, their faces split with smiles of their own.

"It's good to have you back, Brae," Grey said, giving my shoulder a squeeze.

Verena beamed at our exchange, her golden eyes sparkling with tears.

"What did the king want to speak to you about, Braelyn?" Julien's voice punctured the small bubble of happiness I'd wrapped myself in.

He examined my face closely, his dark brows furrowed as he stood closer to me. I relayed my conversation to the group. A few of the dwarves milling about the castle steps threw curious glances in our direction, but the noise of the bustling streets below prevented anyone from over-hearing our conversation.

"Do you think the dwarves will help?" Theo whispered, his eyes shift-ing nervously.

"The dwarves are some of the greatest warriors in Ellesmere," Grey chipped in. "Surely they wouldn't shy away from a battle worthy of the name?"

Verena paced back and forth, her hand stroking her chin in quiet con-templation.

I looked between everyone. "Well, it all depends if I can convince them of an assured victory. If not..." I didn't bother finishing my sen-tence. From my friends' furrowed brows and pinched lips, they under-stood the gravity of the situation.

"So, what are we going to do?" Verena finally asked, her voice low.

Letting out a long sigh, I said, "We try to show them that the future queen of Ellesmere is their best option for a better future." Gnawing nervously at the inside of my cheek, I continued, "And that I am the brave warrior they believe me to be."

Julien shrugged his shoulders. "Well, shouldn't be too difficult. From their reactions this morning, they already seem to adore you."

I couldn't help but notice the edge to his tone. His gaze was down-cast, his face tilted away from me. Something told me his blunt re-sponse had been because of the actions of the winking dark-haired dwarf from earlier. *Was he jealous?* Julien had admitted how protec-tive he felt toward me, but in all the weeks we'd known each other and all the time spent together, I had never seen him have a jealous streak. We'd grown closer while planning Theo's rescue, but aside from a few fleeting kisses and lingering touches, our relationship remained a mystery. With each passing day, my feelings for Julien only increased, growing stronger with each shared moment. At times, I wondered where these emotions would lead me; if there was something more beneath the hand holding and warm embraces, or if it was only our shared traumas that entwined our hearts together. In many ways, Ju-lien was still a closed book. His strong, dangerous demeanour always shifted back into place the moment the emotions between us became too intense or too real.

Verena, Grey, and Theo moved uncomfortably on the spot, their eyes darting between Julien and me, trying to figure out what caused the shift between us.

"Well," Julien said again, his voice firm, "your admirers await." He swept a hand over the busy street below.

Magic bristled beneath my skin at his behaviour. If something was bothering him, why didn't he just tell me? I stalked passed him, shaking my head as we descended the stairs. I didn't bother to see if he followed.

Twenty-Four

We spent the rest of the day along the bustling main street of the Ironwood Mountains, talking to the patrons and enjoying the hospitable company of the many dwarves who went out of their way to greet us. Their cheery and kind nature was infectious and, after a while, I soon forgot about Julien's jealous words and just enjoyed myself. The town was not unlike the one in the Ironwood Village. Shopfronts were set deep into the steep mountainside, tiny bells tinkling each time someone walked through the door. Bakeries filled the air with sweet-scented pastries, while gems glistened in the front window of a shop that looked like a witch's apothecary. Opposite the shopfronts, dwarves of all ages wandered between wooden carts stocked with food and other goods. We walked by a delicious-smelling cart that housed some of the largest potatoes I'd ever seen. Split down the middle, they were topped with a variety of different gravies and cheeses, the smell making my stomach rumble loudly. Theo drooled over the plump potatoes, his eyes wide with delight. The dwarf manning the cart seemed to take a liking to him and, with a small laugh, gifted him one to eat. Another cart boasted beautiful silver jewellery which hung from wooden shelving in all shapes and sizes. Long necklaces swung gently in the breeze, while thick silver bands inscribed with different runes sat nestled amongst pillows of silk.

"For the spirit witch," said a beautiful young dwarf as she draped a bright silver chain over my head. Her blonde hair fell in loose waves around her face, the front two strands pulled back in thick braids clasped with a silver pin.

"Thank you," I said. "It's wonderful."

I smiled fondly down at the beautiful jewel hanging from the intricately woven metal, noting the warrior's stone glinting in the light.

The farther we walked through the markets, the busier the stalls became. Crystals sparkled like diamonds refracting the sun as cart after cart overflowed with multitudes of different coloured stones. Many of the stall owners tried to catch our attention, but one elderly dwarf women caught my wrist in her hand and pulled me to her cart. I shrugged at Julien's narrowed eyes and allowed her to show me some of her most precious crystals. She was a little taller than the other dwarves and her long dark hair was flecked with grey.

"Mined from this very mountain," she told me proudly as she held out the largest moonstone I'd ever laid eyes on.

She eyed my reaction, but I couldn't help but notice the way her gaze flicked to my right hand. I dismissed it, not thinking anything of it until something occurred to me as I eyed the many different stones within the small boxes lining her cart. This dwarf was clearly knowledgeable on the stones she possessed, and I wondered if she might be able to help us with the whereabouts of the bloodstone. I said as much to my friends, who all appeared sceptical.

"Brae, it might be too risky," Verena whispered. "Maybe we should wait and consult the king tonight at the feast."

Julien nodded his agreement. "I think Verena's right, Braelyn. What if the wrong dwarf overhears us?"

"We might not get the chance tonight, but we could find some answers here and use that knowledge to our advantage."

Julien and Verena looked between themselves, an unspoken conversation passing between them. Theo was still scoffing down his potato beside Grey. Both were too engrossed in watching a dwarf throw a battle axe at a wooden plank to even overhear our conversation. I let out a frustrated sigh. I understood their apprehension—we could hinder our alliance with the dwarves if someone ratted us out for asking about one of their most prized possessions—but I wasn't going to let this opportunity pass by. Moving over to the cart, I smiled sweetly at the elderly dwarf and pulled out the crumpled piece of paper from my pocket, showing her the drawing.

"Do you know where we might be able to find a stone like this?" I pointed down at the drawing of the bloodstone. My hand shook a little as I eagerly waited for her to reply. If she knew where the stone was, we would be one step closer to our goal.

She gazed at the paper for a long time, her eyes darting all over the page as if trying to commit it to memory. When she finally looked up at me again, her eyes were full of astonishment, her face ashen. Staring between me and the page, she blinked rapidly, like she was trying to believe it was real.

"How did you find this?" she asked quietly.

"A very dear friend gave it to me. She told me it was very important." I shifted uneasily on my feet, but it was now or never. "Have you seen this stone before?"

A knowing glint flickered in the dwarf's grey eyes and a smile lightened her wrinkled face. I waited patiently, my palms growing slick with sweat the longer I waited for her reply. Grey and Theo finally re-joined us, glancing between the elderly dwarf and me. They turned to the others, who simply shrugged in response. After a few more moments passed, the dwarf seemed to decide on something, her grey eyes bright.

"Come with me," she said.

Turning on her heel, she folded down the sides of her cart and fastened them with a lock. She took a step closer to me, reaching out a shaking hand and grasping mine with unexpected strength. Turning my hand over, she brushed a soft thumb over my spirit rune. Now that it was no longer riddled with dark magic, it stood out dark on my skin. A perfect circle. With a quick nod of her head, she took hold of my wrist and pulled me towards a narrow bridge running across the river.

I glanced back to my friends, their confused stares following us before they gave chase, catching up in a few strides. Our mystery lady weaved through the flowing river of dwarves with the ease of someone who'd lived here for a long time. My eyes never strayed from her flyaway hair and pink shawl in the off chance we might lose her amongst the streaming crowds.

"What's your name?" I asked, a little out of breath.

"Runa," she said over her shoulder, not stopping.

She led us over the small bridge which arched like a waning crescent moon over the river below. It creaked a little under our weight, but delivered us safely on the other side where it was quieter. Fewer people crammed onto the street, and the warmth of the fiery sconces didn't quite reach this far across the river. A few small shopfronts were visible amongst the shadows, their rickety wooden signs displaying each owner's goods. As we walked to the end of the street, a burly dwarf with a red, unkempt beard exited a shop, bringing with him the acrid smell of hot iron and coal. Through the soot-stained windows, I could just make out the large forge burning brightly as a dwarf fuelled its flame. Another store was home to fleshy chunks of meat. The overwhelming stench of blood flooded the street as a dwarf wearing a white apron, now stained with dark blotches, hoisted a large piece of meat onto an iron hook. The sight made my stomach roll a little. We approached the third and final shop and, stepping over the threshold, the excited hum of the dwarves shopping in the town square died down. The hushed whispers of the ale house sounded almost non-existent compared to the din outside. A large fire crackled in the fireplace on one of the far walls, warming the small tavern to a comfortable temperature. Tobacco smoke floated on the roof like a formidable dark cloud, the acrid stench making me cough more than once. Runa inclined her head to the maid behind the bar, who gestured towards a table to the left. A lone hooded figure sat hunched at the table, their face hidden beneath the dark cloak.

"Over here," Runa said, leading us towards the figure's table.

"Runa, who is that?" My pulse raced as we neared the unknown person, but I didn't need to wait long for an answer.

As we neared the table, the mysterious figure pulled down their hood.

The breath caught in my throat. Maeve's kind face stared back at me and, for a second, my legs felt frozen to the spot. Then I was rushing forward and flinging my arms around her neck. My hands trembled as I pulled away from her, a small sob escaping my lips. I didn't think I would ever see her again.

"How did you...What are you...?" I fumbled, unable to form the right words.

Maeve smiled as she squeezed my cheek. Something she'd done since I was a child.

"Runa is an old friend. When you fled the castle, I sent word to her asking her to keep an eye out for you and, when she found you, to bring you here."

Maeve turned to Runa then and placed a delicate hand on her shoulder, inclining her head in thanks. Runa simply placed a hand over her heart, an unspoken bond between old friends. Maeve gestured for us to sit, but as Runa turned to leave, I embraced her warmly.

"Thank you, Runa, for everything." I glanced back at Maeve, making sure she was still there and not just a figment of my imagination.

"You are welcome, *heltinne lys morke*." She turned to leave, but I caught the top of her arm gently before she could disappear.

"What does that mean? *Heltinne lys morke*." A puzzled look crept over my face, but Runa simply chuckled.

Reaching up a bejewelled hand, she cupped my cheek gently. "It is dwarfish for heroine of the light and dark."

My eyes widened at her translation. Panic began to climb my throat, making my breaths come in shallow gasps. Unfazed by my growing unease, she smiled warmly and patted my cheek.

"I have been around for a long while, Braelyn, and while I may not possess the type of magic you are able to wield, the crystals have given me the power to read others—to see the type of person they truly are. While you may possess a magic of darkness, you are not the enemy." She removed her hand from my cheek, the skin cool where her warm hand had been. "You are who they say, Braelyn. Once you accept this, you will be unstoppable."

Bowing her head, Runa turned on her heel and exited through the door we'd come through, not looking back.

"Braelyn," Julien called. He waved me over to them, his eyes darting between me and Runa's retreating form.

Suddenly feeling very warm, I shrugged off my coat and draped it over the back of a very rickety looking chair, then took a seat between Julien and Theo. Maeve sat across from me and slid forward, grasping my hands between hers just like she had done the morning of my induction ceremony.

"Maeve, what are you doing here?" I whispered with a half-smile.

A barmaid dressed in a smock dress revealing a little too much of her bust slid a pitcher of ale over to us before giving Maeve a sidelong glance. She disappeared briefly behind the bar again, soon returning with six wooden cups. Maeve poured us each a drink, the amber liquid sloshing as she drank deeply. I took a tentative sip of the sour-smelling liquid, but to my surprise, it tasted quite nice. Creamy woody notes danced along my tongue as I took another long sip, draining the cup.

Julien eyed Maeve carefully, his ale left untouched in front of him. Grey and Theo seemed to have already finished theirs and were looking to signal a barkeep to get them another, but Maeve shook her head.

"Go easy, lads, there will be plenty more at the feast tonight and you'll want to have your wits about you when trying to convince the dwarves to ally with you."

Grey and Theo slumped back in their seats, pushing their cups to the edge of the table where a stout-looking dwarf came and scooped them into a large barrel. He smiled down at Maeve, displaying a few missing teeth before hobbling through a dingy looking corridor. I looked back at Maeve, but she was already watching me, a quizzical look in her eyes.

"So, are you going to tell us why you're here?" Julien's voice was not unkind, but it held a note of weariness towards Maeve that made my hands clench in annoyance. She wasn't the enemy.

Maeve sat back in her chair, the wood creaking with the movement. She looked a lot older than the last time I'd seen her. As she brushed a wrinkled hand over her face, I noticed the dark circles rimming her eyes and the tangled mess of grey hair that, somehow, seemed greyer.

"The elders were livid after you left the castle, Brae. They questioned everyone close to you, trying to find out where you had fled to. When no one could give up your whereabouts, Aramis volunteered to lead a search party."

My brow creased. Of all the elders, Aramis was the one I had little to do with. Aside from his support regarding my vision, he'd barely uttered a word to me.

"Why him?" I asked.

"Your mother and I said the same thing. We agreed one of us should find and make sure you were safe, but with the elders watching your mother, she couldn't leave the castle."

"She's okay though?" I asked urgently.

Maeve nodded, easing my mind. "Yes, she's fine, pet." She gave me a reassuring smile, but it didn't reach her eyes. There was something else she wasn't telling us.

Verena pushed her ale towards Maeve, some of the liquid sloshing onto the already sticky table. "You seem to need it more than me," she said at Maeve's raised brow.

Maeve drained the cup, wiping her mouth with the sleeve of her shirt.

"Confirming my safety isn't the only reason you came, is it?"

"No, pet." She turned a wary glance towards each of my friends before looking my way again, her hands worrying at the frayed edges of her cloak. "It's about the page I gave you back at the castle."

"It's okay, I told them about it," I replied nonchalantly and pulled the page out of my pocket. "We know about the bloodstone and the power it possesses."

Julien shot me a dark look out of the corner of his eye and I saw the faint orange glow of his hands as he quickly stuffed them back under the table. He kept scrutinising Maeve's face, which only served to irritate me further.

"You've deciphered a lot more than I expected," she said, looking around at all of us, her eyebrows raised in amazement. "Do you know where it is?"

Silence fell over our group. It was the only piece of the puzzle we hadn't been able to solve yet. We knew it must be somewhere in the Ironwood Mountains, but we were relying on our alliance with the dwarves to be able to reveal its location. Even that plan teetered on the edge of a knife.

"I remember you," Julien said suddenly, straightening. He watched Maeve with wary apprehension. "You used to visit my mother's apothecary with the Wise Witch Althea."

My mouth hung open in surprise at Julien's revelation and I was glad to see that everyone else wore similar expressions to my own.

Julien continued, "I couldn't recall who you were when you met us in the dungeons but it's coming back to me now."

"Wait, what was Althea's surname?" I blurted.

Maeve answered my question.

"It was Pearson." Her hands clenched together as she grew unusually quiet for a moment. She released a long breath, and a few tears streaked down her cheeks. She smiled at Julien, who sat rigid in his chair. "I'm surprised you remember that, Mr Thorne. You were only a small boy when your mother called for Althea's help."

"So, who is she to you?" Julien asked.

Maeve gave him a rueful smile. "She was my grandmother."

Digging around in the folds of her cloak, she pulled out a small piece of parchment. The paper was thin and worn around the edges, and the ink seemed to seep through to the opposite side. With gentle fingers, she unfolded the paper carefully, all of us waiting in excitement.

The ale house had grown considerably louder since our arrival. A group of drunken dwarves sung deep ballads in their addled state, their voices high-pitched and eyes glassy. Maeve threw a wary glance over our heads to make sure no one was watching, but everyone was too far gone to even notice our presence.

She placed the page in the middle of the table. After reading Althea's book for weeks, I recognised the handwriting immediately. The messy scrawl covered the page haphazardly—words scribbled out and replaced with new ones.

"This is the missing page from Althea's journal," I whispered, trying to read the text upside down. "I've wondered for weeks who had taken it. Why? And why not give it to me in the dungeons?"

I finally glanced at Maeve, a small twinge of annoyance flaring inside me. This vital piece of information could have saved us all the guesswork of deciphering the message in The Book of Lilith.

"I know what you're thinking, Braelyn, but I couldn't give you both pieces. One speaks of the bloodstones power, and this one"—she tapped the parchment still on the table—"reveals its location."

Her voice was barely audible over the drunken shouts of the dwarves at the bar, but she pushed the piece of parchment across the table, her hand trembling.

My mouth felt dry and my stomach twisted itself in knots. Maeve had just given us the final puzzle piece. The text was written in the language of old. Much of it didn't make sense to me, but I managed to decipher 'mountain', 'dwarf', and 'secret'.

"It says the bloodstone is hidden deep within the heart of the mountain," Maeve explained as she moved a long finger over the line. "It speaks of only the dwarf king knowing its whereabouts and, for anyone to obtain it, they must prove themselves worthy."

The dwarves' voices grew louder the more they drank, but I barely heard them. The alehouse had grown uncomfortably warm and sweat trickled down my back.

"How is it Althea knew all of this?" I asked her, tapping the fragile bit of parchment and raising a brow. "Surely the prophecy didn't reveal the stone's whereabouts?"

Maeve cleared her throat softly. "Before the Royal War, the elves, dwarves, and witches lived together peacefully. There was no divide—we were simply just Ellesmere, a land of greatness and magic. Just before the war began, Althea's visions started. I would often hear her telling Hazel of *seeing* a child so powerful, none could compare."

Maeve stopped speaking as two dwarves sauntered past our table. They looked down at us, their eyes glazed over with drink. They inclined their heads in our direction, wobbly smiles revealing blackened and missing teeth. They mumbled something towards me before breaking out in raucous laughter, their shoulders shaking with amusement. They eventually moved past, their broad backs bent as they tried to walk in a straight line towards the door.

"Dwarves," Julien muttered, scowling in their direction. He watched them push through the exit before turning back to our group, his scowl still in place.

"Hazel told me about Althea coming to her," I said to Maeve, recalling the day I learned of the prophecy. It seemed like such a long time ago now.

"Yes, they were quite close, Hazel and Althea. It's how your mother and I became friends. We spent a lot of time at Hazel's cottage in those last few weeks before the war." Maeve's eyes grew distant, like she was recalling all the memories she had created at my grandmother's cottage. It wasn't hard for me to picture her in Hazel's garden with my mother, their smiling young faces crinkled in laughter as they ran amongst the tall pine trees.

Maeve continued. "As tensions with the royal family grew, Althea's visions became stronger. She could see a darkness growing in Elias, so she warned your father, who kept a close eye on him. When she *saw* the bloodstone, she ventured to the Ironwood Mountains. Althea had many friends amongst the elves and dwarves and hoped they would be able to shed light on the meaning of her vision. She knew the stone was a powerful relic in need of protecting. She warned the dwarves of the possibility of it being sought after, but they assured her it was well hidden."

"How did she find out about only the worthy being able to wield it?" Verena asked sceptically. It was the first time she'd spoken since offering Maeve her ale.

"Runa told her," Maeve replied simply. "Rumours spread of the Wise Witch coming to warn the dwarves of their bloodstone. Runa heard them and told Althea of the properties the bloodstone possessed—healing qualities, strength, and stamina. Being well-versed in crystal magic, she explained how the alchemy of the bloodstone worked."

"How did Lilith find out about it then?" Theo asked. "She wrote about it in her grimoire, and if the bloodstone is one of their most secret relics, why would the dwarves tell her about it?"

It was an intriguing question, but I already knew the answer.

"She didn't ask them," I replied before Maeve could respond. "She used the Lilithium Mortiferum to torture it out of them."

I recalled the beautiful purple flower we'd come across in the middle of the Ironwood—the same one used to torture witches and warlocks who'd stood against the king. My eyes darted to Julien, who stiffened beside me. His hands clenched into tight fists at the mention of the deadly plant he'd helped King Elias obtain.

"It was a fate worse than death," Maeve said solemnly. "When your father gave The Book of Lilith to your mother, she told me about the darkness it contained. In that moment, I knew you were the child the prophecy spoke about. Althea confirmed as much to me when she told me I needed to protect you both. When your mother said she was leaving Ellesmere to protect their unborn child, Althea tore this page from her book and made me swear I would keep it safe until the time was right."

"Why not tell me this back at the castle?"

"Because I needed to explain this to you, pet. Obtaining the bloodstone isn't as simple as asking King Vidar to give it to you."

"I don't care," I said quietly but determinedly. "Obtaining the bloodstone is the only way to fulfil the prophecy and ensure no one else suffers at the hands of Elias's cruelty."

My cheeks were flushed from the heat emanating around the ale house and my muscles tightened with resolve. Magic tingled beneath my skin, a few sparks igniting at my fingertips with my growing emotions. Maeve placed a cool hand over mine, the calm flow of her magic bristling against her palm and easing the tension in my body.

180

"I have every faith in you, pet, but are you going to share with me why Runa referred to you as the heroine of light and darkness?"

For a brief moment, everything fell away and it was just Maeve and me surrounded by a frenzy of veiled voices. My heart felt like it slowed to a stop before it began to beat rapidly behind my ribcage.

"How did you hear...?" My voice trailed off at the look Maeve gave me. A mix of apprehension and curiosity tightened the lines of her usually relaxed face.

"Not unlike these dwarves around us, Runa's voice carries across rooms, Braelyn. Now, what did she mean?"

I glanced from Maeve to my friends. My stomach clenched at the thought of having to divulge my secrets about the dark magic blossoming like poison ivy beneath my skin. It had been hard enough confessing my need to use it to my friends, but looking into the face of one of my most beloved family members, it seemed almost impossible. My mouth opened and closed in soundless motions, unable to find the words to explain to Maeve what Runa had told me. Julien reached for my hand beneath the table and gave it a reassuring squeeze, giving me the strength I needed. The words came out fast, pouring from my mouth as if I had no control over them. Maeve sat quietly, her hands folded on the table as she listened intently to every word. When I finally fell silent, the pressure in my chest immediately eased. After a moment of silence, I took a deep breath and admitted what I'd been thinking ever since the darkness had come forth in the clearing.

"I don't know how to stop it from happening," I whispered, my voice cracking with emotion. "It scares me, but what frightens me more is how much I like the power it gives me. When I wield it, I'm no longer afraid."

Only Maeve looked in my direction, and I worried my admission had been too much for the others to handle.

"Do you know why spirit wielders eventually give in to the darkness, Braelyn?" Maeve's voice was soft, but it held the steely resolve it usually did when she wanted me to pay attention. "It's because they crave power more than anything. It consumes them, festering like an open wound until they know nothing else. You need not be afraid, pet, because unlike other spirit wielders, what you crave most is peace for those you care about. You may possess the power of dark magic, but your light shines far greater, Braelyn."

Maeve's words washed over me like a healing elixir, cleansing the last bit of fear inside me. There were no words I could say that would truly convey how grateful I was to have her here.

"And what about you lot?" She looked around at Verena, Grey, Theo, and Julien. "Will you stand by her while she faces the cruel king? Protect her as she wishes to protect you all?" Maeve levelled them each with a calculating look, her voice strong and steady.

Theo nodded quickly. His eyes never strayed from Maeve's face as he spoke. "I will help her no matter what."

Verena nodded. "I will stand by your side, Braelyn."

"Until the end," Grey said, placing a hand over his heart.

Lastly, she turned her questioning gaze to Julien, but his dark eyes never left my face as he spoke. "I'll protect her until my last breath. Always."

Tears stung behind my eyes, their words making my heart race as the love I felt for the people sitting here threatened to consume me.

Maeve smiled broadly between us. "You have a bond that will serve you well for all that is to come." Picking up my hand, she placed it in the middle of the table and gestured for everyone to do the same. My friends placed their hands on top of mine and Maeve squeezed them gently. "Never lose sight of what is truly important in this world. No matter the darkness looming before us, together we are strong."

With a weary sigh, she eased to her feet and waited expectantly for us to do the same. We each gave one last glance at our linked hands on the table and stood simultaneously, following Maeve out of the ale house. Once out in the frigid air, she turned to face us.

"At the feast tonight, you'll need to highlight how much is at stake. The dwarves need to join this fight, Braelyn, otherwise we won't have the strength to overpower King Elias."

Giving her a curt nod, I squared my shoulders and followed her back to the castle where the feast would be held. All the while, I thought about how I would secure the bloodstone and the implications of what would happen should I fail.

Twenty-Five

Dusk cloaked the mountains in a beautiful array of colours. The window in my bed chamber looked over the town, the streets growing quieter as the small sliver of sky became bathed in oranges, pinks, and deep purples. The air had long since lost any warmth and a shiver passed over me as a gust of cool wind caressed my cheek. Samhain had reached the mountains and soon we would need to journey to the elves' home to convince them of our plan.

So much had changed in one day, but for tonight I needed to remain focused on securing an alliance with some of the proudest occupants of Ellesmere.

I turned away from the window, rubbing my hands against my arms to ease the chill settling in my bones and glimpsed myself in the tall mirror. Siv had kindly found me a dress to wear for the evening and, despite my last minute change, it made me feel quite beautiful. It was cut from heavy emerald velvet, the sleeves long and bell-shaped, with a sweeping neckline that left nothing to the imagination. The skirts fell loosely from my hips and a thick leather corset had been tied about my torso, pulling in tightly at my waist to accentuate my curves. Siv had brushed out my hair, which now fell in dark waves over my shoulders.

A light knock pulled my attention away from the mirror before Julien stepped through the door. His broad shoulders filled the small door frame and, ducking his head, he stepped over the threshold. Clad in his usual black trousers, he'd donned a dark V-neck tunic that revealed the deep line of his bronzed chest. His black leather coat was trimmed with gold detailing and hugged the muscles of his arms tightly. I drank in his appearance, marvelling at just how handsome he was. He ran a hand through his dark curls and finally looked in my direction, his eyes growing wide.

I was suddenly too aware of how snugly the leather corset hugged my curves, making everything more prominent. His dark eyes drank them in before settling on my face.

"You look beautiful, Braelyn." His voice was deep, alluring.

My cheeks flushed warmly at his compliment. He didn't move towards me, instead opting to stand in the doorway, hands stuffed into the pockets of his coat. My heart fluttered like the soft beat of a butterfly's wings, my fingers tingling with the longing I felt to reach out and touch him. Something had shifted between us since this morning and I couldn't wait another second before finding out what.

"Have I done something to upset you?" I asked, my voice clear despite the hammering of my heart. "You've barely looked at me all day."

Julien ran a hand through his hair again, the movement mussing his dark curls. "We don't have time for this, Braelyn. King Vidar is waiting for you."

I crossed my arms over my chest, standing my ground. Whatever had been going on between me and Julien needed to be mended.

"I don't give a damn," I said, my voice rising. "Tell me!"

Julien turned and slammed the door, anger bristling along his rigid shoulders. He faced me again, his dark eyes burning. I took a tentative step back, but continued to glare in his direction. His tough act didn't scare me.

"You want to know what it is, Braelyn? It's you!" He stabbed a finger in my direction. "Ever since the ball, I haven't been able to stop thinking about you. Every time I'm near you, my entire body feels like you've set me on fire. I can think of nothing else but your face, your eyes, the curves of your body. It's maddening."

My chest heaved, my mouth unable to mutter the words dancing on the tip of my tongue. Julien paced back and forth in front of my door, his hands clenched in fiery fists.

"To watch those dwarves look at you the way they did made me want to burn the world around them," he continued. "Watching you face near death nearly cleaved my heart in two. To know the only person who understands me could have been ripped away at any moment threatened to cut off every ounce air. Braelyn, for so long I believed my biggest fear were the shadows and the darkness, but now, my only fear is losing you."

Crossing the room, he grasped my wrist and pulled me flush against his body. My breath hitched in my throat as my hands came to rest on his chest, the muscles beneath tensing at my touch. The warmth of his body washed over me, sending a fresh wave of heat over my cheeks.

"For so long I've tried to deny my feelings for you, not believing that I deserved you, not believing I was strong enough to face a world where you no longer existed." He ran the backs of his fingers along my cheek-bone, my body trembling with desire. "You've enchanted me, Braelyn, and I don't have the strength to stop myself from containing it any longer."

"Then don't," I whispered, leaning forward so my lips were inches from his.

His hand gripped the back of my neck, his fingers curling in my hair. Those deep, dark eyes burned before he pressed his lips to mine, the intensity of his emotions making me gasp. Our kiss deepened as my hands roamed slowly over the hard planes of his chest, feeling every rigid muscle beneath my fingertips. My entire body ached to be closer to him, my hands finding their way around his neck and pulling him closer. Our kiss was urgent and pleading, pulling every feeling we'd held for each other to the surface. For weeks I had craved his touch and the feel of his lips against mine. Now the moment was here, I never wanted it to end.

Sliding my hands down Julien's arms, I grasped at his shoulders, making him groan low in his throat. The sound made a spark of pleasure shudder over my body. He pushed me against the wall, his hands sweeping down my waist to rest on my hips. I sucked in a breath, relishing in the feel of the cool stone on my flaming skin. I could feel his urgency in the way his lips parted, the way his hand slipped down my leg and squeezed my thigh. Every inch of my skin felt electric beneath his touch, each gentle stroke making me sigh against his mouth. It was maddening in the best possible way.

Our kisses slowed, tasting the sweet sighs that passed between us. Julien's cheeks were flushed a beautiful rosy hue, his eyes like melted honey as he brushed a thumb slowly over my swollen lower lip. He let another kiss simmer between us before brushing a loose curl away from my face, his warm finger lingering a few seconds before he ran his knuckles along my jawline and under my chin. With one finger, he tilted my head up and, lowering his, he took my bottom lip between his teeth, tugging gently.

It was my undoing.

My fingers curled in the lapels of his jacket, pulling him closer until it seemed not even the air in the room could separate us. My breath quickened as Julien leant forward, his hands resting against the wall, caging me in. My heart fluttered against my ribs, his heady scent of smoke and fire filling my nose. A deep flush blossomed over my chest, making Julien chuckle against my lips, his hand moving to stroke the sharp contours of my collarbone.

A sharp rap on the door broke the blissful silence and, without waiting for an answer, Siv bustled into the room, her boots scraping along the rocky floor. Julien took a large step away from me, running a hand through his tousled hair. He shot me a small, lopsided smile and my heart ached at the sight of it.

"Miss Grey, King Vidar and the dwarves await your arrival."

She flittered about the room, picking up a long emerald cloak and fastening it to the shoulders of my dress. She circled me, looking me up and down before nodding in approval, satisfied my appearance was appropriate. She shot Julien a wary glance, her eyes narrowing as she looked between the two of us. The curls she'd tamed were now a tangled mess, my lips and cheeks flushed a deep pink. Julien toyed with the lapels of his jacket, smoothing out the creases I'd made, but there was no mistaking the small smirk tugging at the corner of his mouth.

I tried to hide my small smile as I brushed my fingers over my face, but Siv let out a long breath and shook her head, the action making her fox-red braids bounce about her face.

"If you two are quite done, shall we make our way to the feast?"

She didn't wait for our answer. Siv turned on her heel and strode through the door, mumbling something about the tardiness of witches and warlocks. Julien and I continued to stare at each other, neither of us ready to leave the private confines of the room.

Eventually, he turned his gaze away and held out a hand for me to take. My heart slowly returned to its normal pace as I placed my hand gently on top of his, smiling as his fingers curled around my own. Our heated moment had passed, but the feelings we shared still lingered in the air.

I was eager to know what they meant.

Twenty-Six

The rooms King Vidar had provided us were only a short distance from the great hall and, with Siv leading the way through the dark corridors, we arrived quickly. Standing between the tall arched doors, I stared at the magnificent room and the large host of dwarves descending upon the castle. It was almost time for the feast to begin and now we were here, I couldn't help but feel nervous. So much was riding on this gathering.

My fingers fiddled with the laces on my corset, the stupid thing suddenly feeling too tight. I longed for Alpheus's calming abilities, but as a creature of superstition, it was best he remain hidden.

Theo, Grey, and Verena hadn't arrived yet. Siv muttered she would find them, then left Julien and I alone at the entrance to the hall. He wrapped a warm arm around my waist, pulling me to his side, then ran a soft hand down my sleeve. With gentle hands, he relaxed my fingers, winding his between my own.

"Are you ready?" he whispered in my ear, his breath tickling the hairs on my neck and sending a pleasant shiver over my skin.

His brown hair fell in loose curls over his forehead and a light stubble covered the lower half of his face. Those brown eyes burned like melted honey in the flickering firelight as he searched my face for my answer. He was so incredibly handsome.

"As ready as I'll ever be," I replied, rolling my shoulders to ease the strain.

Julien gifted me one of his lopsided smiles. It seemed his admission back in my room had broken the tension between us. Even in times of turmoil, he had so much strength. It was one attribute I admired most about him. He always believed me to be brave and strong and worthy of the immense power flowing in my veins. It may have taken me some time, but after our conversation with Maeve, I was finally starting to see what everyone else saw in me. All I needed to do now was learn to control my dark magic. As chaotic and dangerous as it was, I longed to tame it.

↞↞↞↞

As we passed through the doors of the great hall, hundreds of excited voices filled the air. They spoke in rushed voices as they shuffled through the wide double doors—eager to get to the feast. Like the rest of the Ironwood Mountains, the vast space was magnificent. Carved from the mountain like the rest of the town, it boasted high stone ceilings and beautiful archways covered in crystals. A large wooden chandelier hung in the centre of the room, catching the eye of many who entered. Its beautifully carved arms were a dark red, while the pans holding the candles were welded from iron as dark as night. It was a masterpiece.

We wove through the growing crowd and up to the head table where King Vidar sat waiting for us. Long benches adorned with copper serving trays ran the length of the room and delicious smells of roasted meats and baked potatoes wafted up from beneath the lids, making my stomach grumble loudly.

I took the seat beside King Vidar, who inclined his head in greeting before turning to his son, who sat to his left. The dwarf prince was immaculately dressed in a loose dark shirt and leather armour, his light brown hair pulled back from his face in thick braids ending in iron clasps. He threw a sideways glance in my direction, his eyes distant and cold as he cracked his knuckles. No doubt a show of intimidation.

Shaking my head, I turned my attention back to Julien, who watched Riven and me closely. The muscles in his shoulders were taut, his hands gripping the arms of the chair. Our earlier conversation flashed through my mind and, placing a soothing hand on his arm, I felt the stiffness beneath my fingers relax slightly.

"I don't trust him," Julien whispered to me, inclining his head in Riven's direction. "He's threatened by your power. I can see it in his eyes and the way he looks at you."

"You don't trust anyone," I replied with a small smile. Julien simply glared at me. "Well, we can add him to the list of people in Ellesmere who are threatened by my magic."

A flicker of red caught my eye and I beamed as Verena and the others came to sit beside us at the table. She wore a brilliant silver dress of similar make to my own, her fiery hair piled atop her head in a messy top knot. She was radiant, catching the eyes of many dwarven warriors sitting below us.

Theo and Grey were both dressed in attire like Julien's, but wore their warlock armour over their dark shirts. They walked into the hall side by side, their shoulders brushing together as they sat beside Verena. I smiled at the look of adoration that passed over Theo's face as Grey brushed his fingers over the sleeve of his tunic.

The remaining guests took their seats as King Vidar rose, commanding silence with his large hands. A hush fell over the room, anticipation rippling through the crowd as they stared up at me, quiet whispers spreading like wildfire from one dwarf to the next.

"Welcome, my friends. Tonight is a very special feast. We are joined by Braelyn Grey, spirit witch and future queen of Ellesmere." A loud applause sounded around the cavernous room. King Vidar held his hands out once again, silencing the crowd. "We welcome our new friends and look forward to more discussions, but for now, let us eat."

Once the servers pulled the covers off the dishes, my mouth immediately began to salivate. Glistening, juicy meat steamed on a platter in front of me, spreading the aroma of rosemary and wine around the room. Crunchy potatoes and succulent vegetables sat in bowls along the table and, without another word, I began piling food onto my plate, not realising just how famished I was.

My stomach growled in agreement. As I bit into the soft meat, flavours unlike anything I'd tasted danced along my tongue. The food at the Forest Festival had been good, but this was indescribable.

As everyone ate their fair share, the chatter in the room increased. Ale was passed around in large tankards and I watched as Maeve and Lorcan chatted animatedly at the table below us. It was a merry affair, but despite the delicious food and taste of ale, my stomach still rolled as the minutes ticked past. My nerves were getting the better of me. Soon King Vidar would announce the reason for my visit and I would need to show the dwarves I was worth following.

As if reading my thoughts, the king stood up and wiped his mouth on a napkin, addressing the crowd once more.

"Fellow dwarves, there is much we need to discuss before this night—and the ale—gets away from us."

A few dwarves in the crowd cheered merrily. I suspected they'd already had more than their fair share. King Vidar's deep laugh echoed around the room as he took a long swig from his own tankard and continued.

"As you all know, the warlock king has threatened Ellesmere for near on two decades. Long have we waited for the chance to stand against him." Valiant shouts burst from the mouths of many as they beat their tankards against the wooden tables. "Well, we now have that chance."

Whispers slowly unfurled around the room as everyone began to speculate on King Vidar's words, but they didn't need to wait for long.

"The spirit witch is our chance, my friends. It has been prophesied that Braelyn Grey holds the ability to defeat the cruel king and restore Ellesmere to its former glory." The room erupted into a wave of cheers and shouts, but King Vidar raised his voice to speak over them. "Yes, this is the greatest of news. But, my friends, she cannot do this alone."

The dwarf king turned to me and nodded once. Here was my chance.

Taking a deep breath, I squared my shoulders and mustered every ounce of courage I could find in myself.

"King Vidar is right. I am the only one who can stop King Elias, but I cannot defeat his army of monsters alone. Dwarves are some of the mightiest and bravest of warriors, and I ask you to fight alongside me, so we may put a stop to the cruel king once and for all."

Agreeable shouts bounced through the hall, but there were a few whose worried expressions stood out amongst the sea of faces staring up at me. It was their faces that stuck with me because, despite their bravery, our enemies were monsters not of this world. They were terrifying. And while bravery was a powerful feeling, fear could be overwhelming.

"You speak of this battle as if it is an easy win, little spirit witch, but I know of the otherworldly demons the cruel king has created. Word has reached us of these so-called monstrum and they will stop at nothing to kill and maim anything that stands in their path."

Riven's voice carried around the room, plunging it into silence. It dripped with agitation and, as his eyes finally rested on mine, they held not only anger, but concern for his people. At that moment, I realised he didn't care that I was powerful, he only cared if my power was strong enough to protect his kin. This was something we had in common.

"If we don't stop King Elias, his power will allow him to retake the throne. Ellesmere will crumble, and his monsters will come for the mountains. But there is hope. I know how to kill them and have done so before. And I promise, I will do all I can to protect you."

Riven scoffed. "And how do you plan to protect us, spirit witch? You are only one witch and, while you might be powerful, you tire like any other."

Strong murmurs of agreement began to filter through the crowd, many of the dwarves nodding along with Riven's words. He was their prince—his voice commanded people to listen. He was strong and mighty and, if he had trepidations about our alliance, it wouldn't be long before others followed suit. They were losing faith in me.

I glanced to Maeve, whose steely expression confirmed what I needed to do.

"It's true," I said loudly. "I tire like any other, but not if I had the bloodstone."

Riven glared at me, eyes narrowed to slits. King Vidar sputtered into his tankard, choking on the sip he'd just taken. The dwarves bellowed at my statement, a few of their angry retorts reaching me at the head table.

"How dare she—"

"That's our sacred stone—"

"She might be the spirit witch, but she's got some nerve."

"So that's your agenda, witch," Riven gritted out between clenched teeth. "To try and win us over so you can take the bloodstone for yourself."

I shook my head. "That's not my plan at all, but with the bloodstone, I will not weaken. I can conjure magic without consequence, which will give me the strength needed to defeat King Elias. That's what you all want, isn't it?" I said to the crowd, my voice as hard as the stone walls around me. "To finally be rid of the cruel king? The prophecy might speak of King Elias needing to die by my hand, but this war will only be won if we unite. If we stand together once more as the proud people of Ellesmere, fighting side by side. As one, our magic and might will prevail. Together, we will defeat King Elias."

"My child, it is all good and well for you to wish for the bloodstone, but you need to show you are worthy to wield it," Lorcan said, his green eyes shining brightly in the firelight.

"I will show you I am worthy," I said, raising my chin.

"Then I challenge you, spirit witch," Riven said loudly, "to a one-on-one battle. If you show your worthiness, you may hold the bloodstone in battle and we will fight alongside you. Fail, and you leave here empty-handed."

Julien stiffened beside me as the crowd cheered for their most valuable warrior. The weight of everyone's gaze pressed down on me, waiting for my response. From the corner of my eye, I could see my friends' faces. Their worried expressions did little to ease the nerves fluttering in my stomach, but I didn't have a choice. We needed the dwarves, and I needed the bloodstone.

"Braelyn," Julien whispered. His voice was full of angst, but I couldn't back down.

"I accept your challenge, Riven."

"Good. At dawn tomorrow, we fight."

The dwarves hollered at Riven's words, marking the end of the formalities. The warriors poured ale for any dwarf in proximity and, soon enough, they were all deep within their cups, singing ballads of their great warrior prince. King Vidar bade us goodnight, gesturing to Lorcan to follow him before they disappeared through a side door.

Maeve joined us at the table. "Do not worry, pet. All will be fine." She placed a comforting hand on my shoulder.

"You can't know that," I whispered back.

She smiled lovingly at me. "You needn't be afraid. You possess a great power. Harness it, and you will prove to be more than worthy." Her cheeks were flushed and her eyes glassy from the ale, but she spoke passionately. "Now, best you all be off to bed."

We walked back to our rooms in silence as the sounds of celebration followed us through the hallways. The soft sigh of the wind whispered through the halls and soothed some of my nerves.

To my left, Theo opened and closed his mouth as if wanting to say something, but thought better of it. I was glad he kept it to himself. I didn't know if I had it in me to discuss what I needed to do in the morning. Eventually, Theo, Grey, and Verena said goodnight before splitting off from myself and Julien—who had been unusually quiet on our trip back.

I pushed open the door to my chamber and he followed me inside before locking the bolt behind him. My heart beat a fast rhythm in my chest as those brooding dark eyes watched me carefully. Removing the cloak attached to my dress, I draped it over the end of the bed, collapsing against the soft furs with a resounding sigh.

"You don't have to do this, Braelyn." He spoke quietly, his voice so heavy with emotion it almost shattered me.

"I have no choice, Julien. We need the dwarves on our side and I need the power of the bloodstone. It's the only way I can beat him."

Tears stung my eyes and threatened to spill over my cheeks, but I blinked them back, not wanting Julien to see just how much this decision affected me. He came to rest beside me and took my face in both hands, running a rough thumb over my cheekbone.

"You always have a choice, Braelyn," he whispered back.

"I know, but the choice for me is life or death, Julien. And I refuse to let others die just because I'm afraid."

He studied me carefully, as if hoping he could convince me otherwise, but he wouldn't. After Maeve's comforting words, Runa's revelation, and Lorcan's encouragement, I was ready to embrace the dark side of my magic and welcome it as part of who I was. The nerves rolling in my belly were nothing compared to the resolve in my heart. I was ready to put my fear behind me.

"And what if you get hurt? Braelyn, you may think I'm strong, but when it comes to you..." He let out a shaky breath and sat up, his face downturned. "You are my biggest weakness."

I lifted myself up, sitting beside him as I took his hand in mine. Since we'd met, there had been few occasions when he'd shown this sort of vulnerability with me. The first time was in the Ironwood after our encounter with the Lilithium Mortiferum and the second was after Theo had been pulled through the portal, but this was different. In those instances, he still had an air of strength to him, a fierce drive to protect me no matter the cost. Today, his emotions had been stripped, peeling back the tough outer shell and laying bare his sole desire to keep me safe.

Leaning towards him, I brought my hand up to his cheek, the rough stubble casting a light shadow over his jaw. He rested his palm on mine, his thumb stroking my hand.

"If I am your weakness, Julien, you are my strength. You have shown me what it means to be strong and fearless."

I placed a soft kiss against his lips and he responded, gently moving in a calm rhythm with my own. Moving my hand over his heart, I counted the beat—*one, two, three*—smiling against his lips when my touch made his pulse jump. Our kiss deepened and my face warmed with the desire blossoming like a flower in the pit of my stomach. His hand slid to the curve of my neck, and my skin tingled beneath his fingers.

"You have bewitched me, Braelyn. Body and soul." His brown eyes blazed warmly as he searched my face, looking for permission.

"And you have stolen my heart," I whispered back.

Julien pulled me into his lap, closing the last few inches between us. My head rested on his shoulder, my arms wrapped tightly around his broad back. He cradled me against him, our bodies fitting together perfectly.

"Promise me you'll be careful tomorrow."

I leaned back and stared into his face. His thick brows were pulled low over his dark eyes, the muscles in his jaw tight.

"Always," I promised.

Twenty-Seven

After Julien left my room, I snuggled into the comfy blankets, trying to let sleep pull me under. I tossed and turned for hours before letting out a frustrated sigh and shoving back the heavy fur blanket. Goosebumps prickled over my bare arms, so I draped one of the fur blankets around my shoulders and padded over to the window. My feet moved silently over to the thick rug, my toes curling into the soft fabric. I looked up to the cavernous opening in the top of the mountain, the sky still a perfect smudge of darkness.

So deep in the mountain, it was hard to guess how far away dawn was, but trying to sleep was a pointless endeavour. I pulled the blanket tighter around me, my mind too preoccupied to rest.

Today's battle must go in my favour—the fate of Ellesmere depended on it. Upon leaving the castle to begin our journey, I'd always been in two minds about my queendom, not truly knowing if it was a path I wanted to walk along. But being in the Ironwood Mountains with King Vidar and his kin had given me a new sense of self belief. That perhaps, despite the whispers that flittered through Ellesmere Castle, I was worthy of the title.

So, if my mind wouldn't allow me rest, the least I could do was give myself a fighting chance to win. I shrugged on my white cotton shirt and stuffed my legs into my trousers. My clothes smelt slightly fragrant and were softer than I remembered. Siv had clearly taken it upon herself to do our laundry. She had been so welcoming since the moment we'd arrived.

I frowned, the thought of leaving a little too hard to bear. Wrapping the belt around my waist, I took my time lacing up the leather chest armour, making sure it felt secure before taking a deep steadying breath, feeling more at ease than I expected. Whether it was because I had finally come to terms with the darker side of my magic or pure determination in showing Riven I wasn't a power-hungry witch queen, I didn't know. One thing was for certain, I was going to show the rude dwarf prince exactly what I was made of.

I retraced our steps from last night, following the long hallways Siv took us through on our way to the great hall. The castle was dark and quiet, the shadows seeping into every corner. Instead of shying away from them, I welcomed their presence. They rippled at my outstretched fingers, sliding through them like satin. I turned a corner and passed the grand entrance, making my way to the door we'd seen the dwarf warriors go through with their stacks of weapons. My thin shirt and armour did little to keep the chill out while I walked, and I wrapped my arms around my mid-section, cursing myself for leaving my fur-lined coat on my bed.

With a quiet snap of my fingers, I conjured a small flame in the palm of my hand. It encased me in its warm glow, making me shudder with contentment. The light illuminated the space around me, spreading warmth through my frozen bones.

As I descended into the cavernous foyer, a flicker of movement amongst the deep blue shadows caught my eye. Grey sat with his back towards me, gazing out the open doors at the quiet town nestled below the castle. When I took a seat beside him, he barely flinched at my approach. Not wanting to disturb the serenity, I looked towards the mountaintop. The sky was still cloaked in deep blue twilight, the crater large enough for me to see some of the stars still winking away. It couldn't be long until dawn was upon us.

"You're up early," he said finally, breaking the silence. "I didn't expect to see you until the battle was ready to begin."

"I couldn't sleep. My magic feels like I've had one too many cups of coffee."

Grey nodded, his smile understanding. "It's normal to feel this before a fight. Add the element of magic and it feels even worse." He flipped the small silver coin over his long, elegant fingers, the silver glinting brightly as it caught the flicker of my flame.

"I've seen you with that coin since Julien returned from the village," I said, dipping my head towards his hands. "Does it mean something special?"

Grey chuckled softly, smiling down at the smooth face of his treasure. "It's actually not a coin." He handed me the small silver piece and I held it between my thumb and pointer finger, my eyes narrowed as I turned it over so the face caught the light. It was a smooth silver disk with a symbol carved deep into the metal—it looked like a lopsided letter F.

"It's called a denarium," Grey explained at the blank look on my face. "It's a dwarf rune representing wealth or luck. My father purchased it from a band of travelling dwarves before he died. He'd told me it was going to make our lives better and change our luck. He was clearly mistaken."

Grey's lips pulled down, his face solemn. No longer holding his token, his hands tugged at the hem of his coat.

Grey had told me a little about his family. His father had died fighting in the Royal War, leaving Grey to help mend his mother's broken heart. He'd assisted her in running their merchant store until the promise of more coin brought him to the castle to help me.

"Why do you carry it if it brings you sadness?" I asked, handing him back the denarium. He held it in the palm of his hand before closing his fingers around it.

"It doesn't bring me sorrow," he explained. "It reminds me that only I have the power to change what happens to me. It's part of the reason why I took up the elders' offer of training you." He gave me a small smile. "No matter what the prophecy says, you have the power to choose your destiny."

In the few short weeks Grey had been at the castle, we'd grown close. We had comforted each other when Theo's loss grew too much to bear on our own and he'd pushed the limits of my magic and offered me advice when I had no one else to turn to. His words settled over me, soothing my nerves. I was grateful for his guidance and friendship.

"Thank you," I said.

My shoulders dropped from around my ears as I gave Grey's hand a comforting squeeze. His thin lips curved into a smile.

"Defeating King Elias might be your destiny, Brae, but you control your dark magic, not the other way around. Don't be afraid of it."

The slightest shades of pink and orange were peaking over the sides of the crater, light slowly filtering down into the mountain. Magic prickled beneath my skin and I flexed my fingers to ease the nerves making my hands tremble.

Grey wrapped a comforting arm around my shoulders. Unlike Julien's broad, warm chest, Grey's was cool and bony, made of sharp edges and sinewy muscle. His embrace comforted me, nonetheless.

"Thank you for helping ease my anxiety," I said.

"What are friends for?" he replied as he pushed himself up and dusted off his trousers.

He held out his hand and pulled me to my feet. Taking one last deep, steadying breath, I followed him towards the door leading to the training arena, each step bringing me closer to what might be one of the most important fights of my life.

≺≺≺≺•

My battle against Prince Riven would take place not long from now. Grey and I wandered past the armoury where six or more dwarf soldiers were already sparring against each other, their fighting skills impeccable. They brandished their swords and shields without fear and I swallowed hard at hearing the sturdy blows of iron against wooden shields.

We followed a long, winding path down to a giant stone structure in what felt like the very depths of the Ironwood Mountains. It loomed over us, dark and imposing and I couldn't help but shiver against the cold clinging to its surface. A large archway led through to the arena and, stepping beneath it, my magic began to tingle at my fingertips, itching to be conjured.

Loud voices filtered down the path towards us as we neared the entrance to the arena. As I stepped into the cool light, my eyes went wide, shock halting my steps and freezing me in place. My gaze shifted skyward, my fingers idly rubbing at my spirit rune as anxiety slowly tightened my chest. Despite the early hour, almost every seat was taken.

Hundreds, if not thousands, of dwarves stared down at me, their shouts and jeers bouncing off the rocky walls. Grey gave the top of my arm a reassuring squeeze.

"You've got this, Brae."

"I thought I would at least have time to practise," I said around the lump in my throat. I ran a hand over the back of my neck, my muscles tensing with each shout from above.

Grey shook his head. "I heard some of the dwarf warriors say last night that a fight like this needs to be spontaneous. It prevents either opponent from having time to better themselves over the other. It makes the fight fair."

My eyes travelled across the sea of bellowing dwarves, where they locked onto the faces of my friends. They stared back at me from the very first row, their faces stony and serious. Julien jumped over the low barricade with ease and wrapped me in a tight hug, but this time, his usual comforting touch did little to sooth my nerves.

"How are you feeling, Brae?" Theo's voice wavered with worry as his long arms snaked around me in a bone crushing hug.

The whites of his eyes glistened in the firelight as he stared at the dwarves jostling each other in the stands. Every so often he'd flinch at the noise and I wondered if the loud jeering reminded him of his time as a prisoner. But the look was gone as quickly as it came, his eyes softening as he turned back to me.

"I'm okay," I replied, shooting a grateful smile in Grey's direction.

And I was.

Even though my heart fluttered nervously in my chest, speaking with Grey had secured the belief in myself that had slowly been growing since we'd arrived at the Ironwood Mountains. I was capable of greatness.

"I can do this. We need the dwarves on our side and I'm going to make sure that happens." My voice didn't waver and I hoped my steely resolve would help ease the worry creasing their brows.

"Brae, you need to be on your guard," Verena said, her voice calmer than Theo's had been. "Riven is a great warrior. The dwarves have said he wields a sword better than anyone in their clan, but that he always steps with his right foot before making a move."

I wondered how Verena had come to know such information, but from the adoring looks she received at the feast, I believed her flirtatious nature had something to do with it.

Grey nodded in agreement. "He's strong, Brae, but it means his agility isn't as good. Make sure you move quickly and never lose focus."

Julien was the only one who remained quiet. He watched my face and inclined his head to the side, gesturing he wanted to speak to me alone. We stepped just out of earshot, but close enough that I could see the quick glances pass between the others.

"I'm sorry about last night, Braelyn. I should have been encouraging, but instead I let my fear get the better of me. I know you can do this." Julien's voice was firm, but a soft smirk tipped up the corner of his mouth as he took my hand in his. I returned his smile and gave his hand a reassuring squeeze. "Your bravery is admirable, sweetheart, but if anything happens to you, just know…" He leant closer to me, his mouth brushing against my ear. My fingers twitched and, with a quick movement, I ran them up his exposed forearm, smiling as my touch sent goosebumps trailing over his skin. "I will burn this place to the ground."

My body stilled as Julien pulled away from me, the fire in his eyes blazing with ravenous hunger, and I had no trouble believing his words.

An uproar from the dwarves made me spin around. Riven had entered the arena, a sword strapped tightly at his waist and two small battle axes secured to his back. He was dressed in battle armour and looked ever the mighty warrior. A leather vest covered his broad chest, making him formidable. The hair around his face had been pulled back in two long, thick braids while the rest of his dark hair trailed down his back.

Seeing Riven draped in iron-made weapons made me feel utterly naked standing in a battle arena with no physical weapon of my own. I'd never fought against anyone wielding an iron blade, but my magic was as deadly as any sword or axe.

With one last look at my friends, Maeve's face stood out against the rest. She sat beside Runa, her eyes watching me closely but unlike the others her expression revealed nothing but pride. I held on to that as I moved towards the centre of the arena where King Vidar stood proudly by his son's side. Shouts from the crowd continued to flood my ears, but I tried my best to ignore them, keeping my chin held high. King Vidar smiled broadly at me as I approached, while Riven simply sniggered.

"Where are your weapons, witch? You don't honestly think you can defeat me in a battle with solely your magic?" He laughed uproariously, his large eyes stripping me bare as he took in my feeble armour.

Despite the nervous ache in my belly, I scoffed at his words. "You'll be choking on your taunts when we're done, Prince Riven."

King Vidar roared with laughter and clapped his son on the back just as Riven took a step forward, but his father put a large hand on his chest.

"She has the might of a dwarf, my son. I feel you may have finally met your match."

"We shall see," Riven growled.

He unsheathed his sword and the metal clinked menacingly against the scabbard, sounding like a cutler sharpening their blades. Riven took a few steps back, his eyes never leaving mine. I mimicked his movements, stepping back to put as much distance between us as possible. I didn't know his battle strategy but, if he rushed me, the distance would allow me plenty of time to conjure my magic before he was able to impale me on the end of his sword. Before we could begin, King Vidar raised his hands and the crowd grew silent.

"Witches, warlocks, and my fellow dwarves"—his eyes twinkled as they shifted over to where my friends and Maeve sat on the edge of their seats—"the time has come to see if the brave spirit witch is worthy of our precious bloodstone."

A wave of jeers hit me almost as hard as a sword, the dwarves bellowing their feelings down towards me. So much for thinking me a hero. I flinched at the chorus of laughter, but flicking my hair over my shoulder, my spine stiffened with resolve. I was ready.

King Vidar raised his hands once again and the crowd lapsed back into an eerie silence.

"Both warriors will fight until first blood. Only then will the bloodstone tell us if Braelyn Grey is a worthy carrier of the stone's power. Are our warriors ready?"

Prince Riven bounced on the balls of his feet, sending small puffs of dirt and dust swirling into the air. He swung his sword in a circular motion, cutting through air with a loud swoosh. My stomach hardened. He was trying to intimidate me, but I wouldn't let that happen.

I inhaled a calming breath, the action soothing the nerves curling in my belly. A sense of ease washed over me like the calm before a heavy storm. With a quick snap of my fingers, blue sparks ignited around me. The dwarves closest to me gasped and shuffled back from the stone balustrades, their eyes bulging at the lightning lacing through my fingers.

Others were pressed up against the barriers, trying to get a better look at the magic now emanating from my fingers. To my satisfaction, Riven took a tentative step back, but his face remained stoic.

"Okay, warriors," King Vidar announced. "Take up your weapons and let the battle begin."

His voice was immediately drowned out by the screams of the spectators.

For a few moments, no one moved. We stood our ground, eyes locked on each other, trying to assess the other's weaknesses. Riven stepped out first, but his movements were cautious. He advanced, his shoulder forward and sword held near his face in a hard grip. With one foot in front of the other, he stalked me. My hands tingled with the promise of magic and, no matter how much noise echoed around the stadium, my eyes never strayed from his face.

Riven manoeuvred me around the large arena. If he stepped left, I moved right. The minutes ticked by and still neither of us attacked. My heart thundered in my ears, adrenaline urging me to do something before I lost the edge of surprise. Calling on the elements, I summoned my air magic again. The cool morning breeze increased its intensity, picking up small particles of dirt and dust and creating a mini tornado between me and Riven. Shouts of awe and surprise rained down around me, but I ignored them—heeding Grey's warning to maintain my concentration. I pulled my hands out wide, growing the tornado. It swallowed everything in its path, including the dwarf prince. He spun around, his sword still held aloft, both hands securely on the hilt as he watched my magic curl around him. If it fazed him, he never let on. Riven squared his shoulders and narrowed his eyes before he darted through the gusts of wind with ease. We had regained our original starting points, but he was closer to me now.

This time, the prince didn't hesitate. He moved quickly, both hands grasping the hilt of his sword. Heat rushed over my skin as I called out to my magic once again, sending balls of fire raining down around him. Riven pivoted left, my flames hitting a stone balustrade. He dodged left again, the second one extinguished before it had the chance to hit the crowd. This time he advanced with caution, swinging his sword, the hilt turning over in his large hand as the blade cut through the air. Swearing to myself, I conjured more fire magic, a line of flames rising dangerously in front of him. Riven's eyes blazed as he stared at me over the growing inferno. How was I going to draw first blood if I could barely avoid my blood being spilled first? My fire magic bought me a few seconds reprieve before he threw himself over the flames, his body arching over the blaze. He landed in a perfect crouch, his sword thrust before him, the tip reflecting my magic with a gold spark. The dwarves of the Ironwood Mountain bellowed at his bravery and even I had to admit he had courage. It would take more than a few flames to beat the warrior prince. Riven stood up, a smirk pulling at the corner of his mouth. His eyes stared at me down the length of his blade.

"Face it, witch. You're not strong enough to beat me."

My lips pinched together in a thin line. The cockiness in his voice sent a wave of heat over my face, matching the flames still flickering in my hand.

Riven laughed. He was taunting me, trying to get me to lash out.

I would give him what he wanted, but he wouldn't be met with the power of just any witch. I was the spirit witch, and I was done playing games.

"I'm stronger than you think," I said through gritted teeth.

It was all I needed to get under his skin. He was a great warrior, but I easily riled him.

He lunged, the tip of his sword missing me by mere inches and slicing through the air. My heart hammered against my rib cage. It was a close call, but Riven was near enough now that I knew he wouldn't stop until he drew blood. My fingers tingled like static as the shadowy tendrils of dark magic called out to me. I barely had a moment to catch my breath before Prince Riven was in front of me once more. He thrust his sword up and I jolted out of the way as it arced past my chest, the tip of the blade skimming the leather. Spinning around to face the warrior prince once again, I finally had a moment to conjure the dark magic clawing to get out. Smoky tendrils fell from my fingers, spilling along the rocky floor like an obsidian waterfall.

Riven kept his composure, his sword at the ready as he advanced to strike the final bloody blow. All around us, dwarves screamed, their words muffled as I focused. Riven pointed his sword at my face and I stared down the sharp iron blade, eyes narrowed in his direction. A satisfied smirk tipped up the corner of his mouth.

The prince thought he'd won. He moved to lunge forward, his blade ready to taste blood, when my eyes flicked to his feet. Remembering what Verena had said, I retreated as Riven thrusted, his blade slicing the air where I'd been standing. I mimicked his movements and the shadows around me solidified into a sword of my own. It met his iron blade in a thunderous clash of metal and magic. Gold sparks burst like a firework as the two magical weapons came together. The blow of Riven's sword reverberated through me, a sharp intake of breath catching in my throat as I flexed my fingers to try and ease the sharp pain lancing through them. Sweat dripped down my brow, but I didn't dare shift a hand. Exhaustion pulled at my muscles, slowing my movements and making my arms feel heavy by my sides.

Riven looked like he'd barely broken a sweat. He was too strong and I was on the losing side. A heaviness settled in the pit of my stomach as doubt clouded my judgement. Maybe I wasn't as strong as I believed? Perhaps I didn't deserve the power the bloodstone contained?

As my mind and body began to tire, Riven struck out with the tip of blade. At the last moment, I stumbled back, trying to maintain my footing, but the strength of his strike sent me off balance. I fell against the hard floor, the impact rattling my bones. Stars exploded in my vision and, despite the pain that cut through my palms, I scrambled against the stones, pushing myself to my feet. Swaying from side to side, I tried conjuring my dark magic once again, but the dizziness clouding my mind was too thick.

As Riven lifted his sword to end the battle, I called on my earth magic in desperation. Long, serpent-like vines slid along the ground, wrapping around his feet and holding him in a vicelike grip. Riven growled in frustration, his lips pulled back in a snarl. He reached behind him, pulling free one of the battle axes affixed to his armour and hacking at the vines with almighty strength. He cut through the thick wood with one fell swoop, but it was all the time I needed to regain my composure.

My palms still stung and my head ached, but I called out to the shadows and they answered in full. Darkness swirled around me, but I was no longer afraid. My fingers curled into my palms, beckoning the shadows closer as they shifted along the arena floor. Loud gasps and panicked cries filtered down from the spectators above, but I ignored them, narrowing my focus on Riven.

The prince had broken free of my earthly restraints and converged on me. Chest thrust out and elbows wide, he glared at me.

He was ready to end this, and so was I.

Waiting until he was so close I could smell the tangy stench of sweat on his skin, I let my magic loose. Thick vines shot from my hand like an arrow being released from a bow. Riven's sword cut through the air, but with a flick of my hand, he was ensnared in a tangle of creeping plants, his sword arm held aloft. The dwarf prince snarled like a wild animal, his teeth bared in my direction. It took all my concentration to keep the restraints in place as he thrashed. Exhaustion pulled at my muscles making my limbs feel like lead. As powerful as I was, the consequences of my magic weighed me down.

With all the energy I had left, I reached my hand out to the shadows, summoning a small ebony dagger. With a quick flick of my wrist, the vines ensnaring Riven's sword hand began to unravel and, just as Riven broke free of my restraints, lunging forward with his battle axe, my eyes dropped to his feet. As the mighty dwarf warrior took a step to strike his winning blow, I ducked beneath his blade and swiped the dagger across his thigh, spilling the blood I needed to end the battle.

Twenty-Eight

The arena fell into deadly silence. Prince Riven stood in front of me, his eyes darting between me and the bloody cut on his thigh in disbelief.

My magic was now a gentle tingle beneath my skin, but my right palm was a mess. Angry red burn marks snaked over my hand, disfiguring my spirit rune as a consequence for summoning dark magic once again.

After a moment, I realised a growing buzz had filled the air. As I looked into the faces lining the arena, hundreds of loud shouts filtered down to me, praising me of my bravery.

"So powerful—"

"Incredible magic. Did you see—"

"Braelyn, Braelyn, Braelyn."

All of it fell away when I spotted my friends' beaming faces. Verena and Theo stood side by side, their faces split in a smile. Grey's eyes shone with pride, his hands clapping with the rest of the crowd. Maeve stared at me, her eyes glistening and her cheeks streaked with tears. Lastly, my eyes turned to Julien. He wore my favourite lopsided smile, the dimple in his cheek flashing as he winked at me. Before I was able to rush over to them, Prince Riven grasped the top of my arm, startling me. Sweat rimmed his hairline, but I was surprised to see his expression was soft. His shoulders and arms hung loosely by his sides, their usual tension gone.

"You fought bravely today," he said, slowly releasing a deep breath. "I apologise for my rudeness when we first met, but many people have come to the dwarves for an alliance. Most do it for their own greed. I needed to make sure you were not like them."

Gone was the rude, uptight prince I'd first met. In his place was a warrior who seemed almost as kind as his father. He cared deeply for his people and I had to wonder if the people he spoke of were perhaps King Elias or Lilith. If this was true, I understood why he needed to be sure of my intentions.

"Thank you, Prince Riven. You didn't fight too bad yourself."

He chuckled deeply, his shoulders lifting. Being kind suited him more than being surly and impolite. From the corner of my eye, I could see King Vidar walking over to us, his chest puffed out proudly.

"Time to see if you are indeed worthy of the bloodstone, witch." Riven smiled playfully before turning his attention to his father.

I returned his smile and looked towards King Vidar, who now stood in front of Riven and me, his face splitting into a broad smile.

"Well done, Miss Grey. Well done. You have proven yourself a brave warrior, but will the bloodstone deem you worthy of wielding its power?"

The elation I'd felt only moments before seemed to shrink with each passing second, the nerves rolling in my belly making my hands feel clammy. I scrubbed them on the front of my pants, biting at the inside of my cheek as my wounded palm screamed with pain. I'd won the battle against Prince Riven and secured our alliance with the dwarves, but I still needed the bloodstone to truly defeat King Elias. Without it, my magic would weaken. Elias would only siphon more magic, and no one would be left to stop him. At least with the power of the bloodstone, that couldn't happen.

Lorcan stepped into the arena, holding a small rectangular box between his large hands. Not a single sound could be heard throughout the crowd—even the wind seemed to be holding its breath.

Lorcan stopped before King Vidar and handed him the small wooden box, his green eyes sparkling with pride as looked at me. He patted the warrior's pin secured to his chest before stepping aside and taking his place behind his king.

Closing the few steps between us, King Vidar held his hand out to me, the delicate wooden box perched perfectly on his large palm. With the other hand, he gently pulled open the lid.

I sucked in a quick breath, my eyes widening at the bloodstone sitting on a cushion of deep red velvet. No bigger than a silver coin, the stone's colour was a beautiful blend of jade green and earthy reds interspersed with tiny spots of pearly whites and obsidian, making it look like a speckled hen's egg.

The king cleared his throat, drawing my attention to his face.

"Braelyn Grey, to assess your worthiness, we will need a drop of your blood." He held a tiny silver pin between his fingers and, with a movement so quick I barely saw it, he pierced the tip of my pointer finger. A single drop of blood seeped to the surface. "Hold out your rune hand."

I did as he asked. King Vidar curled his fingers around my wrist, pulling my arm towards him. He plucked the stone from its box and placed it in the middle of my palm. The wound on my hand burned as the stone's cool surface touched the raw skin over my spirit rune. I bit down on my lip, the metallic taste of fresh blood coating my tongue as I tried to breathe through the pain. As he gripped my finger between his thumb and pointer finger, holding it over the bloodstone, I watched a single drop of blood fall onto it.

"What happens now?" I asked King Vidar, uncomfortable with standing here while everyone gawked down at me.

"Now, we wait," he replied simply. "It won't take long for the bloodstone to decide."

I glanced at all the eyes focused on me and King Vidar, their gaze narrowed into slits as everyone stared at the stone balanced on the palm of my hand. The seconds ticked by, but nothing seemed to happen. My fingers twitched nervously as I watched the stone with such intensity, I thought it would crack under the pressure of my gaze.

I'd failed.

Despite everything we'd been through, I wasn't worthy of the bloodstone's power. I shot an anxious glance back to my friends, my teeth worrying at my lip, but their expressions were blank. The air around us grew thick with apprehension when slowly, the skin of my palm began to warm. Magic sputtered in my veins, reacting to the power the bloodstone possessed. The small, speckled stone felt scalding beneath my touch, the swirls of greens and reds now a brilliant, gleaming gold. Loud murmurs rippled through the crowd as the glow grew to an almost blinding light, exploding around me in a shower of glittering sparks.

Magic surged through my veins. A small gasp reverberated through my chest as the intensity of the stone's power swelled beneath my heated skin. Golden tendrils danced around me like mist on a cool early morning. They weaved about each other, creating stunning patterns that looked like the woven threads of a tapestry. I reached towards them, my fingers trembling with the apprehension gnawing deep in my belly. As my fingers brushed against the golden mist, it stilled, hovering in the air for a few fleeting seconds—frozen like golden streams of sunlight—before they wrapped themselves around my right hand, shimmering like a golden tattoo. My mouth fell open as magic seeped into my skin, crisscrossing over my arm and leaving a distinct pattern. Gold lines twisted over my hand, sprouting tiny leaves as the bloodstone connected with my earth magic. Golden flames ignited over my hand next, entwining with the gentle flowing contours of my water magic. Lastly, faint, wispy lines curled through the other three elements as my air magic fluttered softly beneath my skin. Once the mist settled, the gold markings of earth, air, fire, and water, fully imprinted on my skin.

For a few seconds, the air was still. Every set of eyes was trained on me as an uproarious shout made me jump. The cheers and applause were so loud, I swore they would be heard back at Ellesmere Castle. Riven came to my side and clapped me on the back as a broad smile lit up his dirt-smeared face.

"It will be an honour to fight alongside you, Braelyn Grey, the last true spirit witch of Ellesmere."

I didn't know what to say. Blood pounded in my ears, my voice unable to form the words my mind urged me to say. I simply nodded once and returned his smile.

King Vidar was the next person to approach me and he laughed heartily as he took the bloodstone from my hand, placing it gently back in the intricate box for safekeeping.

"I had a feeling the bloodstone would take a liking to you, Miss Grey. You have earnt the respect and alliance of the dwarves of the Ironwood Mountain. When the time comes, we will follow you into battle." He placed a tender hand on my shoulder, squeezing gently in reassurance. "You are always welcome here."

My throat grew thick with emotion as I stared into his kind face. He'd believed in me even before I had proven myself in battle. He cared deeply for his people, but also for all who lived in Ellesmere, just like I did. I was grateful for his hospitality and friendship.

"Thank you, King Vidar."

"Think nothing of it." Removing his hand from my shoulder, he clapped them together—the sound ringing loudly through the arena. "But now the formalities are over, we celebrate. Clean yourself up and meet us at the front steps of the castle. A festival shall be held in your honour."

"Oh, that's not necessary," I replied meekly, waving a dismissive hand. "And besides, we really should make our way to Silvae."

King Vidar waved his hands frantically. "Nonsense. You've had a tiring morning and will feel much better once you are well rested and back on the road."

There was no point in arguing with him. Sighing softly, I nodded in agreement. "Okay, but we really must be on our way before first light."

"And so you shall be," King Vidar replied.

The walk back through the twisting corridors of the castle was long and tedious. After my conversation with King Vidar, I was finally reunited with my friends, who pulled me into tight hugs the moment I saw them. Julien wove his fingers between mine and refused to let go of my hand until he saw me safely back to my room. I didn't mind it though. His hand was a warm comfort and his presence was an anchor preventing me from being swept into the sea of jovial dwarves as we manoeuvred our way through hallways.

Everyone wanted to stop and congratulate me on my outstanding win over their chief warrior. While I appreciated their words, all I wanted was to bathe and have a few moments to myself to process what had happened and what was to come next.

Theo, Grey, and Verena had all stayed back at the castle, their moods significantly improved now the pressure of securing our alliance with the dwarves was off. We'd agreed to meet at the stairs of Castle Elwood once I'd cleaned myself up.

Back in my bedchamber, Siv had drawn me a hot bath. The smell of cedar and sandalwood wafted from behind the changing screen, coaxing me to the side of the stone bathtub.

Removing my dirt-covered clothes, I stepped into the water and rev-elled in its warmth, sighing as the tension in my tender muscles washed away with each deep inhalation. As my body relaxed, my mind sifted through the morning's events. Magic still bristled against my skin, but coupled with the power of the bloodstone, it felt almost euphoric. When the stone's magic had combined with my own everything inten-sified—the fire burning in my blood, the calm waters flowing beneath my skin... even the airy fog that clouded my mind now curled around my heart with the strength of the mighty vines I conjured from the essence of the earth. But, so too did the darkness. It unfurled inside my chest like a blossoming night flower, eager to be called upon.

Its shadowy fingers reached out, beckoning me to wield it. I lifted my hand from the steaming water, rubbing the tips of my fingers togeth-er, feeling the knowing tingle spark beneath my touch. My eyes shifted to my spirit rune. The pain in my palm had dulled to a low ache, the bloodstone's power healing every ailment that weakened my body. It was blissfully overwhelming, and every fibre in my body longed to sum-mon the magic flowing easily beneath my skin.

With the help of the bloodstone, I was strong enough to finally bring Elias to his untimely end. All parts of the prophecy were beginning to align, my destiny growing closer by the day, but despite the battle I knew we faced, I no longer feared the path ahead.

I sunk low beneath the steaming water, a small smile tugging at my mouth.

"I hope you haven't fallen asleep in there." The sound of Julien's amused voice filtered over the changing screen.

My mouth quirked up again and, with one last deep inhalation of the water's sweet woody scent, I stepped out of the tub, water sloshing onto the floor as I wrapped myself in a warm towel. Siv had draped a wool dress over a chair in the corner, its dark browns and greys a stark contrast to the emerald dress from last night. I changed quickly and ran a brush through my tangled waves. The woollen dress was a little snug around my waist, but it would do for one night.

Julien lounged on the heavy furs draped over my bed, his feet crossed at the ankles. He leaned back on one elbow, a small fireball hovering above his upturned palm. Tiny flames danced along his fingers, the light catching the honeyed tones in his hair. Upon seeing me emerge from behind the screen, his fingers curled into a fist, snuffing out his magic with ease. His eyes found mine, a lazy smile curving the corners of his mouth. He swung his legs over the side of the bed in a movement far too elegant for someone his size and waggled a finger in my direction. I met him at the edge of the bed—even sitting down he was almost taller than me—our faces the same height for once. His arms curled around my waist, pulling me between his knees.

"Let's not go to the festival. We can stay here, just the two of us," he said wistfully.

I chuckled lightly. "They would notice we weren't there, then someone would be sent to find us anyway. We might as well go for a little while."

I ran my hand through his dark curls before trailing my fingers softly down the side of his face to rest under his chin. My heart beat hard against my ribs as my fingers drifted over the curve of his neck. I moved them lower, tracing the rigid lines of his chest as a low moan reverberated through him.

Julien's eyes raked over every inch of my body before they settled on my face, a burning desire flickering in their dark depths. My hands came up to cup his face as I pressed my lips softly to his. His arms tightened around me, pulling me flush against him as our kiss deepened further. His hands moved to settle on the small of my back before circling around me once more, crushing me to his chest. Our breaths quickened as our lips moved together, urgent and pleading. My skin felt feverish beneath his touch, the room suddenly feeling too warm.

My lips parted in a small sigh before Julien's claimed mine again.

In this moment, I knew I loved him with every fibre of my being. I moved my hands to the edge of his collar, touching the soft skin at the base of his throat as he moaned softly. Smiling against his lips, I went to move my hand lower to undo the button of his shirt, but his hand grasped mine tenderly, preventing me from moving any further. My brow furrowed as quiet tendrils of anxiety began to wrap around my heart. Seeing the troubled look on my face, Julien tilted his head and kissed me—softly this time, all urgency now gone.

"It's not that I don't want to, sweetheart, it's just..." He trailed off, running a hand through his already dishevelled dark hair. "I just want it to be perfect." He tucked a stray curl behind my ear, brushing his fingers against my cheek. "And like you said, someone will come looking for us soon if we don't make our way down to the festival."

His eyes searched my face, looking for any hurt he might have caused, but there was none. I knew he was right. It was just, for the first time in a long time, everything seemed to be settling into place. For once, I'd let myself be lost in my own selfishness. We still had a long road ahead and honestly, any alone time I was able to have with Julien was enough.

"I understand," I said, stroking the back of his neck. "Sometimes I just wish my life was normal. Not one that requires me to save the world and stop evil from wreaking havoc on literally everything I care about." I let out a dramatic sigh, falling back against the soft furs.

Julien chuckled. "You were never born to be a normal witch, Braelyn. Your soul burns so brightly, you were always going to stand out." He took both my hands, pulling me back into a sitting position before placing a light kiss on my forehead. He stood up and held out his hand. "Come on. Let's go have some fun for once."

I smiled and, taking his hand, I let him lead me towards the festivities.

⨠⨠⨠⨠⸰

If I thought the festivals in the Ironwood Village were grand, they were nothing compared to what lay before me now. Hundreds of dwarves flitted and danced along the winding river as deep soulful music echoed around the rocky walls. A trio of dwarf men blew on giant horns at least three times as tall as them. They beat on drums attached to their chests as two beautiful dwarf women with deep onyx hair sang ballads in the dwarfish tongue. Tables ran as far as my eyes could see, filled with smoking meats, roasted vegetables, and warm, crispy bread, the decadent scents making my mouth water and my stomach grumble loudly. Snatching up a piece of bread, I bit into the crunchy crust and moaned in delight as the bread's soft filling warmed my stomach. Huge casks of ale lined the steps of the castle and, to my surprise, this is where we found Theo, Grey, and Verena. Already a few tankards ahead of us, they laughed heartily, all of them dancing merrily to the booming music. Grey was the first to spot us, his eyes heavy with drink as he stumbled over.

"Brae, Julien, you're here." He dragged out the last word, his breath smelling strongly of ale.

I hid a smile as he pulled me towards Theo and Verena, whose glassy eyes struggled to focus. I shot a wide-eyed look back to Julien, who smirked playfully. They embraced us clumsily before handing us our own tankards. The ale sloshed over the side, dampening my skirts, but there was nothing that could spoil this mood. Grey raised his glass, and Theo cleared his throat loudly.

"I'd like to, um, propose a toast. T-to Brae and her marv–marvelous performance in the battle." Theo stammered over his words, before producing a wide grin. "To Brae!"

The dwarves around us—who also appeared to be well into their cups—followed suit, shouting into the night air. Before long, it seemed every dwarf in the vicinity chimed in.

As the din died down, we spent the next few hours laughing and drinking the woody ale. Maeve joined us a short while later, her smiling face a welcome sight.

"You fought bravely today, pet," she shouted to be heard over the merriment. "Your father would be proud."

My chest swelled at her compliment. "Thank you, Maeve. We really couldn't have done this without you."

She shook her head. "I did nothing, Braelyn. This"—she waved her arm around at the swarms of dwarves enjoying the festivities—"was all your doing. One day, you will make a great queen." She pulled me into her embrace, hugging me tightly. "I wanted to say goodbye. I'm heading back to Ellesmere Castle tonight."

I pulled away from her, a deep frown creasing my brow.

She held up a hand, touching my face lightly before pulling on her coat. "I'll be fine."

"Travel safe," I replied, my eyes prickling.

And with one last look back at me, she disappeared into the crowd.

With casks of ale that never seemed to empty and the upbeat ballads echoing down the steps, the festivities lasted well into the night. Even after my teary goodbye to Maeve, I felt at ease. I twirled around the dance floor, my arms spread wide as the music picked up its pace.

Julien watched me from the stairs, his shirt sleeves rolled up as he drank deeply from his tankard. His dark eyes burned brightly as he met me on the dance floor, pulling me close so our bodies were only inches apart. Julien pressed his lips to mine, the movement soft and swift.

Verena clapped from her seat atop one of the large ale barrels, her beautiful fiery hair flowing over her shoulders. Theo and Grey joined us next, their hands entwined as they danced around us in circles. Throwing my head back in giddy happiness, I soaked up the feeling, knowing my shoulders would feel heavier come morning, when the remainder of our journey would begin.

Twenty-Nine

J ulien and I waited for Theo, Grey, and Verena at the entrance
to Castle Elwood, the first light of dawn only just bright
enough to light the sky above. My eyes were scratchy and sore
with tiredness, but despite the early hour, I was eager to get back
to the Ironwood—a sentiment I'd never expected—and continue
our journey. Julien and I had retired earlier than our companions and, as they trudged over to us, I knew we'd made the right
decision. Theo's and Grey's eyes were rimmed red, their clothes
dishevelled as they shuffled up the stairs one by one. Verena's
hair was pulled into an untidy topknot, her gaze glassy as she
rubbed at her temples, eyes fluttering closed for a few seconds at
a time. Julien shook his head, an amused smirk spreading across
his face.

"Good morning," I said when they stopped in front of us. Not
bothering to hide my smile, I let out a small laugh.

"It most certainly is not," Verena grumbled. "I've had some of the
best elvish wine in Ellesmere, but it's nothing compared to whatever
they put in that ale. My head is throbbing."

She continued to massage her temples, leaning against the stone
pillar and inhaling deeply before letting her breath out slowly. Theo
and Grey didn't seem to be any better.

At that moment, King Vidar descended the stone stairs, bellowing a loud greeting to us. I watched in amused silence, swallowing back my laughter as Theo and Grey grimaced against the noise.

"I came to see you all off," King Vidar continued in his jovial voice. "It has been an absolute pleasure having you all here, and I hope all goes well with the elves in Silvae."

He pulled everyone into a rough hug, Theo wincing as he slapped a meaty hand on his back. King Vidar embraced me last, his kind eyes creasing at the corners as he smiled at me.

"We'll be ready for your call, Miss Grey." He patted my arm before stepping aside and letting Lorcan and Riven say their goodbyes.

Lorcan wrapped his arms around my shoulders and held me for a little longer than the others. My chin trembled as tears prickled behind my eyes. It was a bittersweet farewell, knowing the next time we would see each other it would be on the battlefield. Giving me one last tight squeeze, I felt his breath against my ear.

"Beware of the road to Silvae. Sinister things lurk within the shadows of those woods."

My shoulders stiffened at his words, a small frown creasing my brow. What sinister things could he be speaking of? He stepped out of my embrace, his lips pinched into a thin line as he stared at me with a fierce intensity. I tried my best to give him a reassuring smile.

"We'll be careful," I promised.

He nodded once, his long white beard shifting with the movement. "Until we see each other again, Braelyn."

Riven stepped forward, his hands clasped firmly behind his back. I inclined my head in his direction, and he chuckled deeply, a smile lighting his face.

"I have something for you," he said, bringing his hands out in front of him.

Balanced on his palm was a small silver dagger. The blade was short and narrow, no longer than my hand, and the hilt was engraved with golden filigree. Whoever had forged the delicate weapon had taken extreme care in its creation.

"It's beautiful. Thank you, Riven." I returned his smile, taking the small dagger.

"Everyone should have a secret weapon to protect themselves. You especially, spirit witch." His eyes glinted mischievously as he bowed in farewell and returned to his father's side.

I placed the dagger in the top of my boot before taking a small step back, staring into the faces of my allies and friends. A heaviness seeped into my muscles, pressing down on my chest like a sack of stones. Although it had been chiselled from rock, the Ironwood Mountains were warm and homely and it was now another place I so desperately needed to protect. Tears stung my eyes, threatening to spill over, but I smiled through my sadness, knowing it wasn't goodbye forever. I would do all in my power to protect them against King Elias. I just hoped it was enough.

⁕⁕⁕⁕⁕

We exited through the mouth of the mountains, the large archway opening into the Ironwood and bathing us in warm, golden sunlight. The smell of pine and fresh air overwhelmed my senses and I breathed in the beautiful earthy scents, savouring the feel of the crisp morning breeze on my face.

While the Ironwood Mountains were wonderful, everything seemed a little less intense so deep beneath the ground. The breeze was soft, the smells subtler. Out here, it felt as if I was experiencing the world for the first time. My senses were heightened, my fingers bristling with the silent song of magic. Even Theo, Grey, and Verena's spirits seemed to lift as we stepped onto the leaf-strewn path. Witches and warlocks, it seemed, weren't meant to live beneath rock and stone, but amongst the elements where we thrived in all our vulnerability and strength.

With the sun at our backs, we walked in silence, each of us absorbed in our thoughts. I turned my gaze to the trees lining one side of the path, their thick overhanging branches filled with green foliage, the ash tree's deadly magic unable to reach this far north. A cool wind whispered through the leaves, the gentle hum lulling me into a quiet calm.

As I settled into the silence, a loud rustling sounded deep in the woods, shifting my gaze. The trees were too dense for me to see very far, but I got the feeling we were being watched. My hands turned clammy, the hairs on the nape of my neck prickling as my eyes played tricks on me, making me believe I'd seen movements in the shadows and the curves of the tree branches. I narrowed my gaze, searching the dense tree line for whatever sinister creature Lorcan had warned me about.

Could we not just have one day where we weren't running for our lives?

Another noise echoed through the trees, closer this time. With a quick snap of my fingers, the air turned frigid. A quiver of sharp needle-like icicles hovered above my upturned palm, their points trained on the woods. The others were on their guard too. Julien and Verena held fireballs in both hands, the flaming spheres sending a wave of heat over my back. Grey and Theo flanked me, their eyes trained on the shadows between the trees, arms held wide at their sides, waiting for my command.

The muscles in my shoulders began to tense the longer we waited for our chance to strike. Just as I was set to release my first barrage of magic, Alpheus hopped from the shadows, his antlers scraping the trees as he tried to manoeuvre through the thickly packed trunks. It had been days since we'd last seen him and a smile lit my face as he stopped before us. Kneeling, I threw my arms around his neck, burying my face in his soft caramel fur.

"*I've missed you, Alpheus,*" I said silently, trying to put as much feeling into my thought as possible.

The jackalope bristled beneath my fingers. I could almost hear his soft, lilting laughter, a light and airy sound in my mind.

"*I've missed you too, my friend. But we must keep moving.*"

Pulling away, I looked into his deep almond eyes. Gone was the mystical twinkle that once lingered in their depths. Instead, all I could see was concern. My mouth went dry and I placed a gentle hand between his russet antlers.

"*Tell me everything, Alpheus.*"

He inclined his head. "*I shall, but not here. There is a cave a ways along the path. We will be safe there.*"

The cave was a fair walk. Once we arrived, dusk cloaked the sky in perfect pastels, the sun disappearing behind the peaks of the mountains. Everyone was exhausted from our time with the dwarves and agreed that a restful sleep would be better in the safety of the cave. The inside was damp and smelt of mildew, but it would suffice.

Julien and Grey built a small pyre and, with a quick click of Verena's long fingers, a glowing fire crackled to life. Everyone took up their place by it, warming their hands and setting up their bed rolls for the night. Crossing my legs tightly underneath me, I warmed my icy hands at the fire's edge, my mind preoccupied with whatever information Alpheus might have collected. Julien settled behind me, his legs resting on either side of my own. He pulled me to his chest, and I shuddered with contentment as the warmth of his body eased the deep chill permeating over my skin.

Verena had taken a seat beside us, her arms thrown back behind her. She stared intently into the fire, her golden eyes narrowed in quiet contemplation. She'd grown rather quiet since Alpheus's return, and I wondered if her mind turned with the same questions plaguing my own.

Alpheus looked at me, his eyes twinkling like little golden suns in the firelight.

"There is much disruption happening within the Ironwood. The trees whisper of terrible things happening around the ash tree clearing. Dark and dangerous magic is growing throughout the trees, attracting the grimmest creatures."

My eyes widened at this knowledge. I didn't need to imagine what havoc Elias was creating at the ash tree—we'd witnessed it in the decay spreading through the trees surrounding the clearing and the creation of his monsters.

We were running out of time and needed to reach Silvae. If we waited any longer, there was no telling what other dark and harrowing creatures Elias would summon to his side.

I conveyed Alpheus's message to everyone, their faces reflecting my own feelings. The air was thick with concern and fear for our loved ones in Ellesmere Castle and beyond.

"Does Alpheus know what creatures this magic is attracting?" Julien asked.

I couldn't see his face, but his muscles stiffened beneath my back. I asked Alpheus as much and the response I received made my blood run cold. My magic hummed beneath my skin, my fingers tingling in response to the fear settling over me like a chilling cloak.

"Creatures who should not be a part of this world. Barghests and pixies have crawled from their holes to join him. And the creatures he created have multiplied as well as the cruel king's followers. They have grown in numbers. He will soon have enough force to attack."

Relaying Alpheus's words to my friends, they stared at me with wide eyes and dark expressions. We'd lost crucial time whilst under the mountains and my main concern now was not getting to the elves in time to secure our last alliance. I wished I was able to control the visions I'd had before—to be able to conjure them like my spirit magic to see if we would indeed succeed.

"We should get moving now then." Theo's concerned voice pierced the silence. "If we don't know how much time we have, we should make headway while we can."

"Don't be daft, Theo," Julien replied, his brow furrowed. "To venture into the Ironwood at night wouldn't be wise. We need to wait until first light."

Grey squeezed Theo's arm reassuringly and nodded in agreement with Julien. Theo let out a low sigh, but nothing more was said on the idea. Slowly, everyone settled in, pulling blankets out of the rucksacks the dwarves had so kindly given us. They'd packed us some bread, cheese, and meat for our journey to Silvae and, after nibbling on some our rations, I lay back on the soft, worn blanket beside Julien.

While my body was exhausted, my mind wouldn't turn off. The more I imagined the chaos occurring at the ash tree clearing, the more my stomach rolled in an anxious reply. What would happen to my friends and family if we didn't succeed in stopping Elias? It was a thought that came to me as often as breathing, but tonight I couldn't face the answer. Rolling into Julien's arms, I pressed my face into the curve between his neck and shoulder—inhaling his sharp scent of smoke and fire, letting it soothe the nervous ache growing in the pit of my stomach.

Before long, my eyes grew heavy, the soft sound of Julien's breathing lulling me into a dreamless, dark sleep.

Thirty

I stared at the rocky ceiling above me, still too tired to coax my aching muscles to move. Everyone's slow, easy breaths filled the cave with a gentle hum, so it seemed I was the first to wake.

Last night's conversations sent a tremor rolling down my spine, the gravity of Alpheus's words weighing heavy on my shoulders as my mind conjured everyone's reaction to what he'd seen amongst the Ironwood. So much was riding on us convincing the elves to join the fight.

Hundreds of situations and outcomes flittered through my mind as I tried to find a solution to our problems. We couldn't allow Elias to garner any more followers. Even with the dwarves' alliance we would be lucky to gather enough soldiers to make the battle a fair fight. If I was going to succeed in fulfilling the prophecy, we would need a strategy that would secure our forces and lead us to victory.

Maybe it would be better for us to split up? To send Theo, Grey, Verena, and Julien on to Silvae to warn the elves of the oncoming darkness. I could meet King Elias head on before he had the chance to destroy more of Ellesmere.

I sighed, immediately scrapping the idea. One witch against an army of Elias's deadly creatures and his band of followers? He'd kill me the first chance he got, siphon my magic, and drain me to summon his dark queen from the depths of the underworld. A martyr for all of Ellesmere to remember.

Julien's embrace suddenly felt too hot. I turned my head slightly, taking in his face relaxed in sleep. It was enough to ease the anxiety rolling in my stomach a little. This was the most relaxed I'd seen him in weeks, his eyelids quivering as if lost in some magical world only he had the joy of seeing. His face was smooth, free of the usual frown that created a permanent crease between his eyes. Wrapped tightly in his arms, it amazed me how—without even trying—he managed to calm the storm inside me. Even in sleep, he held on tight, arms draped over my waist as if I might blow away in the wind.

My gaze trailed over his broad chest to the soft hollow beneath his throat, then down to the fingers splayed softly over my hip. I smiled when my heart rate spiked.

How cliche, I thought.

After all these years of hearing about love-struck heroines from centuries past, I was finally experiencing it myself. Wrapped in a loving embrace and with my friends around me, I could almost picture what my life may have looked like if the prophecy had never been written. I thought the image would make me sad, but instead, it brought me peace. If Althea had never written the prophecy, this moment may never have come to pass. I may have stayed in Pryhollow, never venturing to Ellesmere and meeting my friends, Hazel, or Alpheus.

Despite the challenges ahead, I couldn't help but wonder what would come afterwards. What my life might look like once the prophecy had been fulfilled and Ellesmere was once again a kingdom of peace. Would Julien stand by my side as I ascended the throne? Would Theo's memories within the castle walls be too much for him to stay? Would Verena and Grey go back to their previous lives, no longer required to help the spirit witch master her magic?

I let my gaze settle on Julien's face, his dark lashes fanning delicately across his bronzed cheekbones. Whatever the outcome, I would be forever grateful to the elements for bringing me to Ellesmere and for gifting me with the most wonderful group of friends.

"You know, it's strange to watch someone while they're sleeping," Julien mumbled against my hair, his voice thick with sleep. A small smile pulled at the corner of his mouth.

Opening his eyes slowly, I was pulled into their dark depths, lost forever in the fire that reflected at me. There was no turning back. My heart belonged to him.

"You just looked so peaceful. It's been a long time since I've seen you so at ease." I placed a tentative hand on his chest, smiling as his pulse quickened beneath my soft touch.

Julien brushed the tip of his finger over my lips, his hand lingering lightly on my cheek before he brought it back down to rest at the curve of my hip.

"What's going on, sweetheart? I can tell something's troubling you." He shifted beside me, propping himself up on one elbow, his body angled towards mine. A deep frown began to furrow his brow the longer he watched my face, trying to work out what was running through my mind.

"It's nothing," I whispered back, gifting him with a sweet smile to ease his concern.

It's not that I wanted to keep my thoughts a secret. They were fleeting things, brought on when my mind struggled to rest in the early hours of the morning, or when the weight of the prophecy felt too heavy to bear. These thoughts helped ease the tension and gave me hope there was something more to come after all of this was over.

Julien ran a finger down my jaw, his finger coming to rest beneath my chin, tilting it ever so slightly so our eyes were locked over the small space between us. His light touch warmed my cheeks, and my body shifted slightly beneath the blanket.

"I'm glad," he whispered. "You deserve some peace."

I smiled against Julien's outstretched arm. For the first time in a long time, I was truly at peace. And, while a part of me was ready to achieve my destiny, a small part wanted to remain here, locked in this moment of pure bliss.

Grey's light snoring filtered through the cave, his eyes still relaxed in a deep sleep. Theo was curled up on the bed roll beside him, his hand resting beside Grey's, their fingers almost touching. Had they drifted to sleep with their hands entwined? My heart swelled at the thought. Both Theo and Grey deserved some happiness after all they'd endured.

Verena's face was turned away from the fire and, although she lay quite still, the slow rise and fall of her shoulder made me believe she was still asleep.

"We should probably get moving," I said finally.

The darkness outside was beginning to wane, the soft light of dawn teasing the edges of the cave's opening. With so many eyes and ears lingering in the Ironwood, leaving just before dawn may work in our favour.

Julien yawned, stretching out his muscles before moving into a sitting position, his forearms resting on his knees.

"Well then, let's be on our way."

Silvae lay to the east of the mountains, nestled amongst the outer edge of the Ironwood. Our journey to the elves would be relatively easy, at least until we reached them. Elves were some of the oldest magical beings in Ellesmere, their knowledge and wit rivalling that of the elders. They were strong-minded and fickle beings, relying heavily on astrology and nature to guide them. They'd suffered severe casualties in the Great War and had kept a wary distance from witches and warlocks since. To secure an alliance with the elves would prove a greater feat than my battle against Prince Riven.

The scenery along the path made for a picturesque journey. Wispy grass moved delicately on either side of the road, the scent of jasmine and wildflowers carrying on the breeze from somewhere within the tree line. My mind was immediately transported back to Hazel's garden and I smiled sadly, rubbing my fist against my chest to try and soothe the ache that blossomed beneath my ribs each time I thought of my grandmother. I missed her desperately.

Attempting to distract myself, I turned to Theo, hoping he'd be able to take my mind off the agonising thoughts plaguing my mind. He seemed to be having one of his better days, when the trauma from his capture wasn't weighing on his shoulders. His features were smooth and his eyes bright. I looped my arm into the crook of his elbow, nudging him playfully to summon his smile. Theo stared down at me, his ocean blue eyes crinkling at the sides as he covered my hand with his and gave it a small squeeze. Before I had the chance to speak, a movement in the trees beside us pulled my gaze away, a fixed look of concentration settling over my face. The shadows were still too deep for me to see anything. As I turned my attention back to the path, Julien's dark eyes watched me carefully.

"What's wrong?" he asked, his usual frown back in place.

"I don't know. I thought I heard—"

Pressing a hand over my mouth, Julien twisted to stare at the trees, his eyes narrowed on the spaces between the tall pines. A faint rustling echoed around us, too loud to be caused by the gentle wind raising the hairs on the back of my neck.

"What is it?" Verena whispered, her hands alight.

"I can't see through the shadows," Grey replied, taking a small step towards the noise.

"Grey, don't." Theo's voice dripped with worry, his hand clinging to Grey's coat.

Julien conjured his fire magic, both hands instantly engulfed in flames as he stared beyond Grey. I pulled the dagger from my boot, holding it out in front of me as I scanned the clearing, trying to locate the source of the noise. Julien's keen eye had settled on a twisted patch of trees to our right. The tangled mess of branches and thorn bushes were only a short distance from the path. If we ran, we could probably get ahead of whatever creature lurked beyond.

Before I had the chance to voice my plan, the noise suddenly stopped. I took a tiny step forward, my knuckles white around the hilt of the dagger, but before I could move any farther, a pair of round yellow eyes stared at me from between the leaves of a juniper bush.

Thirty-One

My heart pounded against my ribs as the familiar eyes darted between myself and Julien. We couldn't see who they belonged to, but if my suspicions were correct, I didn't need to see in order to find out.

"Grugo, is that you?"

The reply came quickly and quietly in my mind, but as I listened to the gremlin's voice, an unsettling feeling sent my blood running cold. Something was wrong.

"Yes, it be Grugo."

As the small creature ventured out of his hiding place amongst the bushes, my hand flew to my mouth, helping me hide the quiver of my lip. His long limbs were covered in cuts and grazes and, from the slight limp in his left leg, he appeared to be sporting more serious injuries. I placed the dagger back in my boot, rushing over to kneel beside the small gremlin, smiling softly. His large yellow eyes darted in every direction, wary of every shift in the shadows.

"It's okay," I told him. *"You're safe now. What happened to you, Grugo?"*

Julien knelt next to me, his flames extinguished, and Theo and Grey stood on either side of us, not letting their guard down as they surveyed the area. Verena dug around in her backpack, pulling out and discarding items until she found what she was looking for. She handed me the jar filled with the healing poultice.

I unscrewed the lid, the scent of rosemary filling the air around us. In the wispy grass, Grugo could barely see over the tops of the long stems, so, coaxing him from the shadows, I applied the gooey poultice to some of the more sinister cuts on his head and arms.

"*We not be safe*," he managed to get out, wrapping his spindly fingers around my wrist and trying to pull me along the path.

I frowned at him, my hands fluttering around his shoulders, trying to get him to remain still long enough for me to apply the salve.

"*What do you mean we aren't safe?*"

Before he could answer, a loud shout punctured the air. Dozens of witches and warlocks descended upon us like flies to a dying carcass. My mind reeled as more than twenty of Elias's guards rushed forward.

Julien was on his feet in a matter of seconds, his hands blazing with a fire so intense it licked at his forearms. He stood in front of me, his body angled so I was concealed behind his towering frame. Theo slunk back, his face turning ashen, no doubt the memories from his imprisonment surging to the surface. Grey and Verena held their ground, hands held protectively in front of Theo, who continued to tremble behind them.

I called out to my magic, lightning sparking brightly against the looming shadows as it curled around my arm, flickering with murderous intent. My hands trembled slightly at the number of guards standing at the ready. There were far too many for us to take on our own and fear clawed at my throat, threatening to choke me.

"How the hell did they find us?" Julien's voice dripped with disdain.

My mind reached out silently to Grugo, relaying his question.

"*It be the gremlins. They choose the cruel king over the witches.*" Grugo hovered behind my legs, peering out to the witches and warlocks hell-bent on seeing King Elias's commands through.

"*Why?*" I asked, trying to understand the gremlins' reasoning for siding with him.

"*He promised them treasures. Magic items they try to steal. But not Grugo. Grugo come as soon as he heard talk of this. Come to warn you, I did.*"

Placing a soft hand on his head, I gave him a reassuring pat, hoping he knew just how much this meant to me. He'd given us somewhat of a fighting chance. I relayed Grugo's words back to Julien, who swore under his breath.

Elias's guards began to converge, their hands raised in a flurry of flames, ice, and lightning. His earth wielders manipulated the soil beneath our feet, the ground shifting and threatening to swallow us whole. I scanned the crowd, searching for the one person with the power to change my fate.

"Looking for me, Miss Grey?"

Even though I was expecting him, my blood ran cold as Elias's voice rang loudly through the trees. Stepping out from behind two burly guards, he grinned menacingly at me. He wore a simple ebony tunic over a dark pair of trousers embroidered with an emblem I'd never seen before. He appeared paler than the last time I'd seen him—courtesy of spending the last few weeks hidden amongst the Ironwood, no doubt. The trees creaked above him, the branches bowing under the weight of hundreds of gremlins, their large yellow eyes glaring towards where Grugo still stood hidden behind my legs.

"Has your voice abandoned you, Braelyn? Or is that shock I see on your face?"

My nostrils flared, anger burning inside me. I narrowed my eyes and rolled my shoulders, trying to calm the beast rearing to be released. I needed to bide my time.

"I'm shocked it took you so long to find us, seeing as you have the whole Ironwood bowing to your will," I replied through clenched teeth, my hands curling into fists.

Elias smiled, shrugging. "It was only a matter of time before I finally found you. Better still, with an array of magic ripe for the taking."

His hungry onyx eyes darted between my friends before settling on me, the silver-tipped circulum glinting in the firelight of Sebastien's fiery hands.

Julien growled low in his throat as he stared between his brother and Elias, his flames igniting into a frenzy of blue fire—the deadliest kind.

"Touch her, and I will relish in watching you burn." Julien's voice was venomous. His eyes lit with the deadly inferno burning brightly around his clenched fists. I didn't know if he was talking to his brother or the king.

Elias's cold, cruel laugh echoed through the trees. "Very valiant of you, Mr Thorne, but I'm afraid there's no escaping me this time."

A low growl sounded behind him, and my stomach hardened. Two large barghests emerged from between the trees, their black fur rippling with each menacing step forward, blood-red eyes trained on our position.

Grugo cowered beside me as the death dogs stalked towards us, their jowls pulled back in a snarl. We were surrounded. Guards flanked us on either side, the steep mountainside behind us.

Running was out of the question. If the guards didn't get us, the barghests would hunt us down in seconds, their long, batlike ears perfect for tracking prey. The only way we were getting out of this was with a fight, and by the elements I would make them feel my wrath. I was sick of hiding. If I was going to die, I might as well take a few of Elias's men with me.

My hands blazed with fury, but it did little to deter the barghests from stalking toward us, teeth dripping with drool and lethal poison.

"There is no escaping your fate, Braelyn," Elias said with a smirk. "Come with me now and I'll let your loved ones live."

With the click of his fingers, an icy orb appeared mid-air. Bile rose in my throat as I saw Ellesmere Castle in its depths, surrounded by dozens of monstrum. Small squares of light flickered amongst the castle's exterior, and my mind immediately thought about how many people resided inside the walls. It would be a blood bath.

I couldn't let that happen. I glanced quickly at Julien, his eyes filled with a fear I knew was in my own.

"Braelyn." Julien's voice quivered on my name.

The sheer emotion in his voice almost brought me to my knees. He knew I would do anything in my power to protect those I loved, and there were so many of them in Ellesmere castle. Smiling sadly, I took his hand in mine, squeezing tightly. There was no way out of this now. The only way for me to protect everyone was to go with Elias to the clearing and try to prevent him from unleashing Lilith from the Underworld.

I pressed my lips to Julien's, savouring the feel of them against mine, the way he held my face between his warm hands as he deepened our kiss. Tears streaked my cheeks at the thought of this being the last time I would ever be close to him. Julien rested his forehead on mine as we pulled apart. My heart felt as if it was going to be ripped in two.

"I will find you," Julien promised.

"Take care of them," I whispered, breaking away from his embrace.

Theo stepped forward. "You can't do this, Brae. He'll kill you. I won't let you go."

He surged forward, his long legs closing the distance between us in seconds. He reached out a hand, his fingers brushing the sleeve of my coat, but Julien wrapped his arms around Theo's torso, preventing him from following me into the fray. Theo fought against Julien's grasp, his hands scrabbling. King Elias gazed between us with an overly bright smile and, instantly, I wanted to tear him apart. I hated him with every ounce of my being.

"See, Miss Grey, isn't it easier to simply comply?" Elias raised a dark brow at me, his hands clasped lightly behind his back.

With one foot in front of the other, I stepped into the fine grass and met him with a steely gaze.

I smiled coldy. "I will never let you win, Elias. I swear the last thing you see before you die will be my face." My voice was flat and cold as fire engulfed my forearms in a dangerous blaze.

Elias had the decency to look shocked, eyes widening to the point of bulging before his face twisted, his nostrils flared and teeth bared. I didn't wait for him to respond. The bloodstone's power seemed to unfurl inside me, spreading through my veins like a growing wildfire. My magic ignited in a show of brilliant gold, flashing behind my eyes.

I sent a wave of fire barrelling towards him, guards hurling themselves from the path of my flames. Elias darted to the side, the edge of his dark tunic catching alight as he barely escaped my wrath.

A tall, wiry guard rushed towards me, her hands pulled out wide, ready to summon her element, but I was too quick. The overhanging branches groaned as I pulled them forward, reaching out with long, deadly fingers. They encircled her waist, hauling her into the depths of the Ironwood, her screams dying out.

A handful of guards surged towards my friends. Julien and Verena burned like the sun, their hands a bright mix of fire and smoke. Theo cowered behind Grey, his eyes bulging as he looked between each of the guards before his gaze drifted to Elias. The terror in his face made my heart constrict. As the guards screamed and rushed forward, I thrust out my hand, air gushing forward and sending them careening back into the woods. Elias's face tilted to the side as he watched, his shoulders perking up as I conjured more magic.

My hands curled into fists, calling forth the darkness lashing at the edges of my vision, the shadows between the trees unfurling like a thick black cloak. Just as my magic reached its peak, Elias whispered something in Sebastien's ear and, in a matter of seconds, guards swarmed me from every direction. I brought my hands together, readying myself to release the wrath of my darkness when a force slammed into my side, knocking me to the ground, my bones shuddering at the impact. Julien hurled himself at his brother, whose hand gripped a small dagger raised in my direction. Bile surged up the back of my throat as my fingers clawed at my boot, the dagger Riven had gifted me no longer there. They collided, hands aflame, Sebastien's hand raised and my dagger sparking in the light of Julien's blaze. I scrambled against the dirt, pushing myself to my feet, summoning yet more magic when Grey shouted my name. A witch not much older than me slammed a set of iron shackles around my wrists, the metal burning my skin, their magical properties disarming my spirit magic.

Elias's guards rushed forward, disarming my friends with shackles of their own. Julien was only a short distance away, trying to overthrow his brother. I struggled against the shackles, trying to conjure my magic. A small golden spark ignited along the tips of my fingers, but not enough to do any harm.

"Julien." I screamed his name as I watched him defend himself against the vengefulness of his older brother.

Julien's hands were ablaze, but even from where I stood, I could see the fatigue warring with his magic. Streaks of red snaked up his forearms as his magic ate away at him.

Elias stood to the side, his face and neck flushed with the pleasure of watching his traitor be disarmed by the only family he had left. Elias had taken everything from Julien and he would watch as Julien's love would be the thing to take him from me.

"End this, but don't kill him yet," King Elias said with a quick wave of his hand. His dark eyes flicked over to where I struggled to get to Julien. "He might prove useful."

Julien managed to land a punch to Sebastien's jaw, his brother spitting blood into the dirt before Sebastien snaked his arm around Julien's throat, cutting off the air supply. Julien clawed at Sebastien's hold, trying desperately to free himself. His gaze darted to mine and my heart cracked at the fevered look of desperation washing over his face. Sebastien raised my dagger, the tip glinting in the cool sunlight as his eyes found mine. The same eyes as his brother's, but where Julien stared at me with love and light, Sebastien's gleamed with malice, a cruel smirk curling over his face as he tormented me with the one thing that could break me. Sebastien thrust the dagger towards his brother and I screamed at him until my throat was hoarse. At the last moment, he twisted the blade between his fingers and brought the pommel down hard against the back of Julien's head.

I emptied the contents of my stomach into the grass. Julien's body lay limp in the dirt, blood trickling from a gash on his head. With a strength I never knew I possessed, I threw myself against Elias. We tumbled to the ground, locked in a deadly embrace. Despite the surprise of my attack, Elias recovered quickly and, with a quick flick of his hand, I was blasted off him as a torrent of air hit me square in the chest. Landing on my back, I scrambled to get up, but a pair of guards rushed forward, hurling me to my feet by the tops of my arms. My body felt limp beneath their grip, the iron shackles clanking loudly as despair begun to numb my extremities. A sour taste coated my tongue as the gravity of our situation settled over me, making my head spin. Elias had righted himself, but I could see the faint cracks in his usual stoic facade.

"My patience is growing thin, Braelyn. I thought there might have been some mutual understanding between us, given we're family, but I can see you are beyond saving."

My spine stiffened as he stepped closer and reached out a hand, the sun glinting off the circulum. He gripped my chin between his long fingers as it bit into my skin. Warm blood trickled down my cheek, but I refused to react.

"I will happily kill you once you have fulfilled your purpose, and I will make your traitorous lover watch as my monsters tear you limb from limb."

Elias tilted my face to where two burly guards dragged Julien's limp body through the grass. A second group of guards pulled Verena, Grey, and Theo to their feet, hands clasped firmly in iron shackles before them. I pulled against Elias's grip, trying to get to Julien's body. The sharp tip of the circulum pressed deeper into my flesh, but my mind didn't register the pain. He must have grown tired of my feeble attempts to break free of his grip, as he let out a bored sigh and roughly pushed my face away from him. Scrambling towards Julien, I knelt next to him. To my relief, his chest moved silently, but the gash on his head still bled little rivers down his face.

"How touching," Elias crooned behind me. "Now, get up. We have much to do."

A pair of cool hands pulled me to my feet, pushing me in the direction of the Ironwood. I craned my head behind me to see a warlock who was wide as he was tall scooping Julien's body up from the ground. The guard assigned to my capture pushed me forward and I stumbled against the force of his touch. I managed to right myself before we were thrust back into the depths of the Ironwood, hurled towards the place that would secure my destiny.

Thirty-Two

We'd been walking for hours when we finally entered the ash tree clearing. My legs burned, the muscles screaming in protest as the warlock behind me pushed me through the last spindly trees. My spine stiffened as I once again laid eyes on the tree that started it all. My hands were slick with sweat, the iron shackles doing little to quell the surge of magic stirring beneath my skin. Its chaos surged against the surface, lashing against the iron.

The ash tree loomed ahead of us, its monstrous branches reaching out and beckoning me closer. The last time we'd been in this place, I'd unleashed a deadly magic on any who dared come close. It was stronger now, the power of the bloodstone only heightening the darkness inside me.

Despite what happened here, King Elias's followers had grown as Alpheus had said, and my stomach dropped upon looking at the sheer number of them. The jackalope had managed to escape unseen into the woods before anyone saw him and I hoped he was someplace safe—perhaps even seeking help from our allies.

"See what awaits your friends, Braelyn, should you not cooperate." King Elias stood at my side, his face a mixture of pride and excitement as he stared around the clearing.

Anger burned through me like a deadly flame. He would see every witch and warlock killed in order to get what he wanted.

"You're going to pay for this, Elias," I said between clenched teeth, wishing more than anything my hands weren't bound.

"Such brave words from the spirit witch," he crooned. "Pity you won't get the chance to save any of them."

"Why are you doing this?" I spat, tugging against the guard's hold. "You wanted to be the most powerful warlock in all of Ellesmere, but Lilith is twice as powerful as you'll ever be. Releasing her won't get you what you want."

Elias stopped in his tracks, the barghests by his sides growling low and menacing in my direction. Teeth gnashing towards me, their foul-smelling drool pooled at their feet as I strained against my binds. The guard's grip on my arm tightened, his knuckles turning white the longer we stood before the monsters.

Elias's eyes narrowed into slits.

"How do you think Lilith will reward me when I am the one to release her from her purgatory? She does not wish to concern herself with ruling a kingdom. She needs to be released to rid this wretched place of the atrocious ancestors who burned her at the stake all those years ago. She will reign hellfire down upon them all and, as King of Ellesmere, I will aid her." He looked me up and down, his eyes cold, nose wrinkling in disgust. "Get her out of my sight."

He sauntered off, the barghests close to his side. With the death dogs out of sight, the guard regained his composure and hauled me away, his grip tight on my upper arm. As he pushed me by the ash tree, I tried reaching out to the magic within it, but with the iron shackles still secured tightly around my wrists, its magic lay dormant.

"Keep walking, spirit witch," the warlock spat venomously.

I tried digging my heels into the dirt, but he jerked me forward with a low growl.

"Keep your hands off her."

Julien's angry voice sounded somewhere behind me, but the guard's grip was too tight on my arm, preventing me from spinning to find him. He'd roused not long after we'd entered this area of the Ironwood, his muffled groans easing the worry buried in my heart. A loud thump sounded to my left and, without having to look, I knew Sebastien had hit him again. There was no love lost between the brothers, their hatred towards each other evident in their fevered glares and clenched jaws.

I pulled against the guard's firm hold, but this only made him tighten his grip. As Elias's minions pulled us across the clearing, every face we passed turned in our direction. Many scowled at us as we walked by, but some—the viler ones, it seemed—spat vicious words and snide remarks, their angry voices following us until we reached the iron cage.

The tangy stench of metal was overwhelming, mixing with the stink of hundreds of unwashed soldiers. Bile rose in my throat, my eyes frantically turning to Theo, who stilled beside me, his face pallid. A witch standing by the heavy door pulled out a collection of silver keys set on a large ring. The lock's teeth clicked back from the mechanism, the hinges squeaking in protest as she pulled open the door just wide enough to let the guards push us through. Theo thrashed against his captor, the tendons in his long neck bulging as he clawed at her face. The witch hissed in his direction, but her unsavoury words were lost amongst Theo's loud sobs. His shoulders shook uncontrollably, his feet digging into the muddy ground as he used every ounce of strength he had left to stop her advancements. Grey tried to soothe him, murmuring calming words in his ear, but Theo's eyes were frantic, his chin trembling the closer he got to the cage.

With the help of a rather large, muscled warlock, the witch thrust Theo's shaking body through the door, her snarl rivalling that of the barghest. She swiped at a long scratch tracking down her cheek, blood smearing over her small face. Once the rest of us filed into our iron prison, the witch with the keys slammed the heavy door closed with a menacing thud, the sound rattling my bones.

"Your hands," the witch barked, her fingers tightening around the silver ring, the keys clinking softly together.

With a quick, confused glance at Julien, I placed my hands beside the bars. The witch located one of the smaller keys and, with a quick click, the shackles fell away from my wrists. The iron had burnt red rings into my flesh and I rubbed my fingers gingerly over my raw skin. She proceeded to remove everyone's shackles before turning on her heel and stalking towards the centre of the clearing, not uttering another word to us.

"Why would they remove our shackles?" Verena asked, rotating her wrists.

She looked at Julien, but he was too busy pacing the confines of the cage to answer her, not that there was much room to move. He crossed the width of it in four strides.

"They don't need us to be shackled with this much iron around us," I replied, my hands clasped around the cool metal bars, eyes roving over the clearing.

Most of Elias's minions patrolled the tree line. Evenly spaced, they stared into the shadows, eyes trained for the slightest movement. Some were posted by the entrance to Elias's tent, standing like formidable sentinels, their bodies never moving. The rest hovered around the ash tree, sparring with magic or stuffing their faces as they laughed and jeered around open campfires.

My hands tightened around the bars. How could so many witches and warlocks be so blind to the wrongdoings of their so-called king? A small ripple of lightning laced through my fingers, and I frowned against the faint blue tinge of my fingers. I turned my back on the clearing, staring down at my spirit rune and recalling the last time I'd come face-to-face with dwarfish iron steel. It was in the dungeons of Ellesmere Castle when I'd been desperate to find my mother. I'd tried to conjure a flame in the hopes of locating her, but my magic had been rendered useless with so much iron in the room. My hands had been voided of magic, but now, something had changed. Whether it was my proximity to the ash tree or the bloodstone's mystical properties, my hands tingled with the tell-tale sign of magic and, like a lit flame, hope ignited within me.

Julien came to a halt beside me. He pulled my hands towards him, rubbing a gentle thumb over the raw skin around my wrists. The bloodstone's healing properties were working their magic, the red marks already beginning to fade.

"How are we going to get out of here?" Grey whispered.

I winced at the dark bruise blossoming under his left eye. On our journey to the clearing, he had copped an elbow to the face when he'd tried to help Theo to his feet after he'd stumbled.

The temperature had dipped since the morning and, shivering against the chill of the wind, I was grateful for my fur-lined coat. Breathing into my cupped hands, I thrust them into my pockets, trying to keep the heat in when my fingers brushed over something hard in the bottom. I pulled the solid object from my pocket, frowning as I stared down at the wooden jackalope figure.

"I think I may have an idea," I said quietly, a small smile warming my chilled face.

My quickly-hatched plan was a gamble, but if Julien was right and Hazel did in fact hold the other talisman, we might be able to alert her of our situation and get her to send word to the castle. If we could pull this off, we still stood a chance of winning this fight.

Thirty-Three

We observed our surroundings for hours. Time seemed to move differently around the ash tree. With its wide, dense canopy, there was no telling what hour of the day it could be. I'd tried to keep track on our journey here, but the moment we'd entered the clearing, all matter of time was lost to me.

By the third guard change, the temperature had plummeted. Even with our thick fur coats, goosebumps pimpled my skin and my teeth chattered noisily, my jaw aching as we tried our best to keep each other warm.

"Will you stop that incessant tooth rattling?!" said the witch on guard. "You're driving me crazy!"

Her hair was in a tight bun atop her head, making her face look rounder. Her dark green eyes glared down at me from between the iron bars and she let out a frustrated huff before turning back towards the comings and goings of the other guards, her hands tucked tightly beneath her armpits as she tried to keep warm. Julien pulled his arm tighter around me, but even his naturally warm temperature did little to ease the chill rattling my bones.

"When do you think you'll be ready to test out your theory?" he whispered.

His mouth was so close to my ear, it tickled the fine hairs on my neck, sending a fresh wave of goosebumps over my skin.

"Soon. I would prefer to wait until there are fewer guards milling around, though."

My first thought had been to try and pick the lock on the cage, but it was a useless plan. Elias had confiscated our belongings upon reaching the clearing and it was only a matter of time before he riffled through my satchel and came across both Althea's journal and The Book of Lilith. With the two missing pages tucked between the others, he'd soon find out about the bloodstone, rendering everything we'd done up until now pointless. So, rather than continue to wait like lambs to slaughter, we'd decided to test if my assumptions about my magic were right. If I could use the talisman to reach Hazel, I might be able to summon enough magic to get us out of here.

Biting at my nails, my eyes shifted from one end of the clearing to the other, trying to assess the quickest escape route should my plan work. The iron cage was situated on the opposite side to the path leading back to Ellesmere Castle and there were too many guards around for us to make an escape across the clearing. If we did manage to breakout of our iron prison, we would need to run directly into the labyrinth of the Ironwood.

I turned my gaze back to the female guard. She bounced from one foot to the other, trying to keep warm, but on closer inspection, she appeared to be conjuring her magic. Tiny icicles formed in mid-air as she moved her hands in front of her. A pang of jealousy materialised in the pit of my stomach. I envied her. The few times I'd been unable to use my magic had left me feeling uncomfortable, like a part of me was missing. Julien noticed my distracted stare and leaning forward, turned to face the guard.

"It's an awful feeling knowing you have magic running through your veins, but aren't able to conjure anything." He sat forward, arms resting on his knees, a sad smile on his face.

Verena, Grey, and Theo perked up at Julien's comment, each of them huddled deep in their coats. It was the first time Theo had shown any interest since we were thrown into the cage. He'd withdrawn into himself, his eyes glassy and distant, his arms wrapped tightly around his legs.

"You speak as if you know from experience," Grey said, the tip of his nose red from the cold.

Julien's lips pinched into a thin line, but he nodded once.

"What happened?" I asked, my voice soothing.

Julien had always been very secretive about his past, only ever telling me fractured bits and pieces when he had no other choice. All I knew were the whispers people still spoke about him and I was eager to understand more about his life before I came to Ellesmere. The little snippets he'd told me over the last few weeks had led me to believe that all the rumours about him were exaggerations from petty gossips, desperate to have someone to blame.

"You don't need to hold everything so close to your chest, Julien," Theo said. "Maybe it's time you learned to trust we are looking out for you."

His voice wasn't unkind, but there was still a wariness there, the memories of their previous feud perhaps still too raw for Theo to completely forgive him.

"You can talk to us," I said, my eyes never leaving Julien's face.

He stared down at his hands, not looking at anyone as he spoke. "It was my mother," he whispered. "She was King Elias's first victim in testing out the circulum. She volunteered to have her magic siphoned because she and my father believed in the lies Elias spread." He focused on his rune, the small triangle standing out stark against his calloused palm. "They believed it was a privilege to help him gain enough power to rid Ellesmere of those who didn't deserve it. Little by little, he took her fire magic until she was left with nothing."

Finally, after a minute's silence, he looked up, but there was nothing but pain in his eyes and his hands were now clenched into fists.

I tried to take one to comfort him and help ease the anguish tightening his jaw, but he flinched away from me. I tried to think nothing of it as I shoved my hands beneath my arms, but his reaction cut deep, making my stomach feel hollow.

"That's why I'd seen Althea and Maeve before," he continued. "After my mother had the last of her magic siphoned, she turned sickly. Her eyes were always empty, void of any emotion. Althea would come with draughts and potions to try and bring back her magic, but her attempts were futile. My mother died not long after."

"I'm so sorry, Julien," I said, my voice shaky. "He will pay for what he did."

Everyone stayed quiet, not knowing what to say. Julien shuffled to the opposite corner, feigning tiredness, but deep down I knew it had caused him great pain to share so much heartache with us all.

Rubbing my fingertips together, I tried to pull on the invisible string connecting me with my magic, coaxing it from the shadows as I had done so many times before. Julien's story of his mother was fresh in my mind and it scared me to think about what it would be like to no longer have magic—to spend so many years of your life able to tap into the magic of the elements, only to have it ripped away.

My magic was a part of me as much as my heart or lungs. To no longer be able to feel that would be like losing a piece of myself. Sparks sputtered along my fingertips, easing the anxiety eating away at me. If my plan was going to work, I needed to try a lot harder.

"Well, well, well, what do we have here?"

The familiar leering voice sent a cold chill down my spine. Victoria's icy blue eyes looked down her nose at the five of us huddled together. Her blonde hair was pulled back into a long ponytail, making the sharp edges of her cheekbones stand out in the warm light of the lanterns dotted around the clearing.

"How the tables have turned, Braelyn." Victoria's voice was hard and sharp. The hatred she felt towards me oozed from her very being, but it couldn't hide the glint of happiness that shone in her eyes at seeing us locked up.

"Victoria, you look as spiteful as ever," Julien shot back, his voice laced with malice.

"Oh, Julien, how I've missed your handsome face." She made to stroke his cheek, but he flinched away from her fingers. She pouted in feigned sadness. "It's a pity you chose the wrong side of history. We could have made an unstoppable team."

Julien growled low in his throat, which only made Victoria's smile broaden in glee. She seemed to be enjoying getting under Julien's skin. I, on the other hand, couldn't stand her presence any longer. There was a reason she was here and I was going to find out why.

"What do you want, Victoria? If you've come to gloat, just get on with it!"

My patience was wearing thin, and I didn't have time for her vindictive games.

"Oh, Braelyn. I could, but where's the fun in that?" She laughed softly. "There is a reason for my visit, though, aside from wanting to see you behind bars. King Elias will be calling on you soon to complete the ritual. He wanted you to be at your strongest, so I come bearing a gift."

It was then I noticed the small linen bag draped over her shoulder. She opened it and pulled out a few apples, a hunk of cheese, and a loaf of bread. My stomach rolled hungrily as Victoria dangled the food just outside our grasp. It had been hours since we last ate anything. I wanted nothing more than to taste the sweetness of the red apples, but my pride was more powerful than any hunger.

"If you wish for us to beg for the food, Victoria, you're sorely mistaken." My stomach gave another loud grumble, betraying my pride, and Victoria's smile grew to a beaming grin. If she wasn't such a horrible person, she really would be quite pretty.

"Oh, I don't know. If I waited long enough, I'm sure you'd cave. Unfortunately, I haven't the time nor the patience. I need to get ready to play my part in this."

Victoria tossed the food through the bars, the bag landing on the cage floor in front of us. No one moved to touch it. Tossing her ponytail over her shoulder, she made to leave, but my curiosity got the better of me.

"You know it's going to take more than a single drop of blood to wake Lilith," I blurted. "How can you be okay to sacrifice your life for the cruel ideations of an awful king?"

Victoria stopped in her tracks, turning to face me as she stalked back to the bars.

"Because I believe in the greater cause, Braelyn! Because once Lilith has risen, she will have the power to bring me back more powerful than before."

Hunger flashed in Victoria's crystal eyes, but beneath her need for power, there was something else. A twinge of fear, perhaps, or a need to belong somewhere or to someone. If the light flickering in the lanterns had been any dimmer, I might have missed it, but it was there. No matter how much she yearned for power stronger than her air magic allowed, she feared the path before her. And, despite everything she had done to me, I pitied her.

"You don't need to do this, Victoria. You can be powerful just as you are. You only need to search inside your heart to find that strength."

Victoria sniggered. "That's rich coming from the spirit witch. The one who has so many people to rely upon, the one who holds more power than she knows what to do with. How the elements deemed you worthy enough to wield such magic is laughable, but none of it will matter once Lilith has returned."

My heart thundered in my chest. No matter what I said, Victoria would never listen. Her heart was set on being the king's martyr. I disliked her, but it still hurt to know the girl standing in front of me truly believed what she was doing was for the greater good. That, with Lilith resurrected, she would finally have a family.

I reached out to take her hand—to try and show her she wasn't alone. Her eyes softened slightly as my fingers brushed the top of her hand, but at the last moment, she flinched away from me.

I let out a long sigh. For a moment, I thought my words had finally broken through her cold exterior.

"Elias will never let you live, Victoria." My voice was soft, pleading. "All he cares about is summoning Lilith for his own cruel gains. The moment you have served your purpose, you'll be forgotten."

Julien placed a warm, reassuring hand on my shoulder. He knew as well as I that my words would have little sway with her. But I had to try.

Victoria stared through the bars with such fierce intensity, I could almost feel my skin burn. For a moment, I believed my words might have gotten through and she might abandon sacrificing herself for a doomed cause, but it was nothing but a moment of weakness on her part. Squaring her shoulders, she tossed her white-blonde hair over her shoulder, smirking down at us with the air of a haughty princess who always got her way.

"Your words are wasted, Braelyn. I will help summon Lilith from the depths of the Underworld, and then I'll watch as you and your precious Ellesmere is remade!"

My heart sank into the pit of my stomach.

Victoria turned on her heel and, without a backward glance, stalked away into the growing mass of guards who had begun to congregate in front of the ash tree. I might have despised Victoria, but I had wanted to believe there was some good in her. Perhaps I was wrong. She appeared rotten to the core. Drunk on the promise of power.

"You tried, sweetheart."

"I know," I replied, my voice weak.

Julien's words did little to comfort me. Time was running out.

Thirty-Four

"It's time," I whispered to everyone.

We sat huddled together in one corner of the cage, our backs to the ash tree.

"What do you need us to do?" Julien whispered.

I dug around in my coat pocket, my fingers grazing the smooth surface of the wooden jackalope. Even in the warmth of my pocket, it was still cool against my palm.

The plan I'd concocted sounded perfect enough in my head, but whether it worked was another story. With the talisman in my palms, I could speak with Hazel, who could then alert the dwarves and everyone at Ellesmere Castle. With this much iron subduing my magic, though, I had no idea if it would work.

Wrapping my fingers around the smooth surface of the wooden figure, I took a few deep breaths, letting go of all my apprehension with each exhale. Julien's broad back shielded me from the prying eyes of the guards in front of us and, with Theo and Grey flanking me, Verena kept an eye on the activity in the clearing. From afar it would seem like we were huddled together to keep warm. With one last deep breath, I closed my eyes and shut out the world. I had no idea how to activate the talisman's magic, but I hoped the elements were on our side and would guide me.

As I rolled the small figure around my fingers, I tried to empty my mind as Hazel had taught me. I let go of everything besides my magic, but I could feel the iron taking its hold each time I beckoned my power closer. It was like being trapped in both a literal and imaginative iron prison. A frustrated breath escaped my lips and I threw open my eyes, finding Grey frowning down at me.

"It's not working," I muttered quietly.

My arms felt as if they had been carved from stone. After shaking them out, I took a few more steadying breaths before trying again.

"Keep your eyes open, Braelyn. You need to embrace your surroundings and let yourself feel everything. You're a spirit witch and your magic thrives off your emotions. Feel the pain, the sadness, the happiness. Let it all in."

As I stared into Grey's eyes, I knew deep down he was right, but a part of me—the part that craved the chaos and darkness—still scared me a little. To unleash all my emotions in the presence of the ash tree could be deadly, especially now I harnessed the power of the bloodstone.

Nodding once, I shook out the tension lacing the muscles in my shoulders and firmly grasped the wooden jackalope. Focusing my gaze just above Grey's head, I cleared my mind, letting my thoughts float away like a leaf on the breeze. My gaze softened and my breath came in long, even bursts. It was a strange, yet wonderful feeling.

Darkness tinged my vision, blurring around the edges and making the world appear soft. Slowly closing my eyes, I counted to three before opening them again. A warm flush spread over my skin, soothing the chill in my bones.

I smiled around at Hazel's small cottage. Nothing had changed. The two wingback chairs sat before the large hearth, a fire blazing and crackling in the grate. Glass clinked together and the rustle of herbs reached my ears as Hazel busied herself in her small kitchen.

"Tea will be ready shortly, child. Take a seat."

Swallowing the lump in my throat, I replied, "I can't stay long, Hazel. Things are bad. We need your help."

She turned to face me, her terse expression softening at the worry on my face. "There is always time for tea. Rest for a moment, child."

With a resigned sigh, I collapsed in the chair closest to the door. I sank into the soft cushions, my muscles relaxing as the warmth from the fire eased the tension in my neck. As the seconds ticked by, I began to feel the fear leech from my body.

Hazel placed the tea tray in between us and poured the steaming liquid into two floral china cups. The calming scents of lavender and chamomile made me sigh with contentment. Hazel handed me a cup and I drank deeply, relishing in the feel of the steaming liquid sliding down my throat and warming my insides. The magic of the talisman seemed to transport my soul to Hazel, who held the other charm. However this type of witchcraft worked, everything felt incredibly real.

"Now, where are you, child?" Hazel asked. She drank deeply from her cup before setting it down on the tray again.

"We're at the ash tree clearing in the middle of the Ironwood. Elias plans to sacrifice Victoria and me to release Lilith from the Underworld. We're trapped in an iron cage and I have no idea what to do, Hazel. I thought I had more time!" The words poured out of me like word vomit. Once I started, I couldn't stop. "We thought we had until the first waning moon of Samhain, but it seems we were wrong."

Hazel stared at me for a moment, her nostrils flared and her mouth a tight line. She reached up to the small pendant she wore around her neck, twisting it gently in her long fingers. The room was quiet, the only sounds the light crackle of the fire and gentle groans of the wooden cottage. Picking up her cup once more, she drained the remainder of her tea and returned the cup to the saucer with a small clink. Her eyes shifted slightly to my clasped hands and, in the flickering light, her mouth twitched ever so slightly, but I was almost sure it was the flicker of a smile.

"It's okay, child. Everything will work out. I'll send word to the elders of your whereabouts. I trust the dwarves will also act on the news?"

"Yes, they will," I replied with a smile, my heart feeling lighter.

"Very good. You've done well." Hazel gifted me a rare smile. She took up my runed hand and turned it over, drinking in the shimmering gold patterns running up and down my arm. "This is your ticket out of the cage. Call forth your spirit magic and be the witch you were born to be." She patted my hand gently before placing it back on my lap.

"Until we meet again," I said.

Hazel let out a loud laugh, her face transforming to look like my mother's. It suited her. "Let us hope so, child. There is still much for you to learn. Now go. I'll do my part. It's time for you to do yours."

Heat flooded up my arm, blinding in its intensity. I glanced once more at Hazel, who nodded once, then cool air rushed over my face. My eyes adjusted to the darkness around me and a steady hand on my shoulder pulled me back to the light. Theo's scarred face hovered in front of mine, his brows drawn down in a worried frown.

"Brae," he whispered, but I barely heard him.

Pulling my hand from my pocket, I stared down at the jackalope figure which sat perfectly in the centre of my upturned palm. My spirit rune pulsed around it like the still-beating heart I'd pulled from the monstrum's chest. Running a hand over my spirit rune, I recalled my first magic lesson with Hazel. She'd told me to call on my magic, which had seemed to break through that last barrier.

I would need to call on it again.

"Spiritus," I whispered.

With one last beat, a shock of pain ran up my arm, making me gasp. I doubled over, shoving my fist into my mouth to stop the scream threatening to tear me apart. It was *excruciating*, like someone was sticking a white-hot fire poker into my veins. A small cry escaped my lips and Julien made to come to my side but, putting a hand out, I stopped him. We couldn't alert the guards.

The salty, metallic taste of blood washed over my tongue and I knew my teeth had bitten through the skin on my hand. Tears pooled at the corners of my eyes as the pain grew to a dizzying crescendo. Just when I thought it would never end, the pain released its fiery hold on me, easing my body back into the cool abyss of nothingness.

"By the elements, Braelyn," Julien said softly. "Look at your spirit rune."

I opened my eyes and glanced down at my palm. My spirit rune glowed the same gold as the rest of the fine lines on my arm.

"It has to be the magic from the bloodstone," I replied, flexing and curling my fingers, my spirit rune glittering brightly with the movement.

"There's only one way to be sure," Grey said, his eyes trained on my upturned palm, his knowledge of magic burning brightly in their hazel depths.

Julien released my hand and instantly, the knowing tingle of magic consumed me. Only this time, its intensity was overwhelming.

"Whoa," I gasped out. "I understand why the dwarves don't want anyone getting their hands on the bloodstone. This power is unlike anything I've ever felt."

Julien's answering grin was all the response I needed and I gifted him with a wide smile. He wrapped me in his arms, crushing me to his chest. Breaking apart, I pulled my coat sleeve down, trying to hide as much of the gold lines as I possibly could. The plan was in motion. Now, all we had to do was execute the next step perfectly and not get caught.

We each knew the part we would play in our escape. Verena would be the lookout, watching the guards' movements to make sure none were alerted to our escape plan. Grey and Theo would distract any guards that happened to come our way. And then there was Julien; the slightest misstep could cause him to remain trapped in our iron prison, but he assured me everything would be fine.

We waited patiently as the next guard relieved the witch with the tight bun. To my surprise, it was someone we knew. The guard's bushy blond beard covered most of his face and he stood almost a head taller than Julien. My heart sank into the pit of my stomach.

Blight's beady blue eyes shone like frozen sapphires. Of all the guards in Elias's regiment to be posted here the hour we planned to escape, it had to be him.

"It makes me so happy to see the two of youse stuck behind these bars," Blight said, his smile revealing a mouth full of missing and rotten teeth.

Julien leaned against the back wall of the cage, his arms crossed tightly in front of his broad chest. "Well, I can't say I feel the same way, Blight, but it beats the dungeons at Ellesmere Castle. Oh, wait, isn't that where your friend Zuko is being held?"

A fiery glint flickered behind Julien's dark eyes and I smirked at the look on Blight's face. In a matter of seconds, Julien had managed to get under his skin.

Maybe this wouldn't be as hard as I'd thought.

Anger rippled off the bear-like guard in waves, his hands trembling as he brought them up to point a stubby finger in Julien's direction.

"You jus' wait, Julien. You'll get what's comin' to ya! And I hope to Lilith I'm the one to land the final blow." Spittle flew from his mouth as he emphasised the last word, but rather than repulse him, it only broadened Julien's playful grin.

"Oh, come on, Blight. We both know I'm a much better fire warlock than you'll ever be." Julien pushed off the iron bars with little effort and sauntered over to where Blight stood, red-faced and fuming.

His hands glowed a soft red and I knew he would be trying to summon every ounce of his fire magic to show Julien just who was more powerful.

Glancing over my shoulder, I looked to Verena, who gave me a reassuring thumbs up. Their argument hadn't alerted any additional onlookers. The elements were on our side. The remainder of Elias's guards seemed more concerned with stuffing their faces than the brawl about to break out here. I tried to locate Elias, but he was nowhere to be seen, most likely tucked away in the confines of his tent. Still, my gut told me to be wary. He had a knack for showing up unwanted.

"Watch ya tongue, Julien. We can't kill ya yet, but there's nothin' to say I can't punish you and ya little spirit witch before that." A malicious smile spread over Blight's grimy face. I had no doubt he was imagining every terrible thing he could do to cause Julien pain.

Julien leaned in so close to Blight's face, their noses were only inches apart. I began to summon my magic, readying myself to play my part in our escape. Behind me, Grey and Theo shifted their weight, the cage creaking beneath their feet. Verena moved a few paces closer to me, readying herself to dart from the cage on my command.

"What are you waiting for?" Julien said through clenched teeth. "I'm right here."

Blight's hands brimmed with the fire Julien was unable to conjure, the iron cage preventing him from using it. Julien grabbed Blight's jacket by the lapels and smashed his head against the side of the bar. Eyes widening in surprise, Blight swayed for a second before his head fell limply forward. A small trickle of blood oozed from his hairline as Julien held him against the bars, making it look like Blight was simply leaning against the cage.

"Do it now, Braelyn," Julien barked at me.

Tearing my gaze away from them, I called out to my spirit magic. After hours of feeling only a trickle, it didn't take long for it to react to my call. My fingers tingled violently as I welcomed the electric feeling through my veins. The air around the clearing turned misty as thick plumes of white fog rolled like waves through the close-knit trees around the clearing, enveloping everything in their path. For an instant, the clearing went silent. Not even the sounds of night creatures could be heard as all eyes turned to the mysterious mist billowing in and covering everything in a thick blanket of cloud. It was the perfect cover. Shouts rang out, the soldiers' voices clear but their sight obscured by the thickening smog.

"Get to the spirit witch," someone called to my left.

"Which way do we go?!"

A smile tugged at the corner of my mouth as I listened to the confusion raining down around me, guards trying to pick their way through the misty veil surrounding us. Stepping towards the door, I placed my hand over the lock and let lightning lace through my fingers. Electricity cracked loudly around us, the currents fracturing around my hand burning white-hot as it struck the lock, the iron groaning in heated protest as I continued to push all my magic into its foundations. I felt the mechanism crack like splintered wood beneath my touch, my air magic obliterating the lock in a flash of blinding light. My body sagged against the bars, a shaky laugh parting my lips as I fell through the door, everyone hot on my heels.

My hands brimmed with the promise of more magic as the bloodstone's power continued to heat my veins. Even after such extensive magic use, I didn't feel drained. There were no menacing golden veins creeping up my arms, leeching the magic from my soul.

No wonder the dwarves kept the bloodstone concealed from prying eyes. In the wrong hands, this type of magic would be catastrophic.

My air magic still provided us with the protection we needed to escape to the cage unseen and, with one last glance behind me, I took Julien's hand in my own and pulled him towards the Ironwood's dark embrace.

Thirty-Five

Once we were out of the clearing, the sounds of shouting slowly faded.

I let the tether to my air magic dissolve until it was like a long-forgotten memory. With my hand still clutched in Julien's, he pulled me through the dense trees, neither of us wanting to stop until we put as much distance between us and the chaos unfolding behind us. Verena, Grey, and Theo's loud footfalls sounded behind me, sticking close to our backs. My leg muscles burned as we pushed on, my chest aching with the need for air and rest. But we couldn't stop, we needed to put as much distance between us and Elias.

"Brae!" Verena's voice sounded from behind me. "We need to stop. Theo can't—" Her voice trailed off to ragged gasps.

I slowed my pace, Julien reluctantly coming to a halt by a fallen tree. His chest rose and fell in quick bursts as he doubled over, hands on his knees. The others pulled up short beside us, their faces red and eyes bright. I turned to Theo, whose face burned a deep wine colour. His hollowed chest rose and fell rapidly as he tried desperately to suck in air. My eyes softened at the pained look he gave me.

"Brae, I'm... sorry, but I...I can't."

I placed a hand on his shoulder, squeezing gently. "It's okay, Theo, we can rest for a second."

I tried to sound sure, but my voice wavered and Theo's shoulders slackened as he heard my uncertainty.

The fact was, we shouldn't be resting. We needed more distance between us and the clearing, but I couldn't run my friends ragged. Their bodies were already fatigued, their arms covered in the twisting marks of their magic use. Sagging against the rough bark, I gulped down the cool, fresh air and tried to get my bearings. We'd been so focused on putting as much distance between King Elias's guards, I had no idea how far from the clearing we were or how close we'd be to Ellesmere Castle. If Hazel had managed to get word to the elders and the dwarves, we would need to bide our time until they reached us.

Darkness closed in on all sides and, tilting my head to the canopy of the trees, I could only just make out the silver of the moon. Whether it was late evening or early morning, I couldn't tell. After a few moments of rest, my heart began to resume its usual rhythm and I welcomed the chill over my sweat-slicked skin.

"Do you know how far we are from the clearing?" I asked Julien, my voice sounding too loud against the silence of the Ironwood.

Standing up straight, Julien took in our surroundings. He spun on the spot, looking like the needle of a compass trying to pinpoint north. Raking a hand through his dark curls, he let out a frustrated sigh, sending my stomach plummeting.

"I was so focused on trying to put as much distance between us and the clearing that I wasn't keeping track of which way I was going. This bloody forest all looks the same."

He turned to us and swore beneath his breath. My heart was finally beginning to beat at a normal rhythm, but with the look of frustration on Julien's face, it began to quicken.

"Are we lost?" Theo asked, his voice surprisingly calm given our situation.

Julien came and sat beside me on a fallen log, his head in his hands. After a moment's hesitation, he turned his beautiful brown eyes on me. I didn't need him to speak the answer aloud. His eyes said everything I knew he didn't want to.

Jumping to my feet, I paced in front of him, my hands worrying at the hem of my coat. The temperature in the air was icy, making my teeth chatter. I tried to figure out a way out of my mess.

Why had I thought it a good idea to run aimlessly into the Ironwood?

"Could I be of some assistance?" Alpheus's voice sounded lightly in my head, my eyebrows shooting up as he appeared between two trees. Yeah, the elements were definitely on our side.

Alpheus led us over the quickest path through the Ironwood. It wasn't an easy hike by any means, but we ran as far and as fast as the terrain would allow, only stopping when necessary. Vines tipped with thorns clung to our clothes, nicking our faces as we passed under low hanging branches. Twisted tree roots threatened to trip us every few steps, but after a while we managed to find our way back to the path.

Everyone rested for a few seconds to catch their breath and soothe their aching muscles, but something was gnawing at the back of my mind.

Why hadn't Elias found us yet?

He controlled these woods now—had boasted how he commanded the creatures and monsters here—so what was stopping him?

"Which way is the castle?" Verena pressed, her face as bright as her hair.

She leant against a towering oak tree, her back pressed against the bark as she lifted each foot, trying to relieve the pressure in her feet. Alpheus looked up and down the length of the path, his almond eyes watching cautiously for any danger. My teeth worried at my bottom lip, the incessant gnawing in the back of my mind growing more persistent.

"I don't think we should go to the castle." Julien's voice punctured the silence, pulling my gaze to where he stood beside Verena, studying my face closely. "You're thinking the same thing, aren't you, Braelyn?" He cocked his eyebrow.

"What are you talking about?" Grey chimed in before I could reply. "Of course we have to go to the castle."

He looked between Julien and me, his mouth agape.

"I think we'd be walking into a trap if we go to the castle," I replied earnestly. Verena stared at me, her eyes so wide they were like tiny golden suns, glistening in the moonlight.

"Brae, the castle is the only place we can be safe." Theo's voice was strained.

He sat amongst the damp leaf litter, his frail body hunched over his knees. He'd receded back into his shell after his second ordeal in the clearing, his eyes flat and empty.

"Have none of you noticed that nothing has come after us since we escaped the clearing? We've had no monstrum attempt to kill us, no barghest hunting us down. Why? Because Elias knows our first instinct would be to get to the castle. All he would need to do is bide his time and wait for us to walk straight into his hands."

I rubbed a hand over the back of my neck, my friends' faces all reflecting the same pinched expression, their unease at my words evident as they glanced between each other. The only one who seemed confident in my thought process was Julien.

"Brae," Verena said, "I don't—"

"I know it's a long shot, but what other reason would Elias have to not send one of his monsters after us? He knows we'll come to him."

"So where do we go then?" Grey questioned, pushing the sleeves of his shirt up. "We can't go to the Ironwood Village."

His frown deepened. I knew he was concerned for his mother and Gillie, with their home in the village not far from the castle.

I shook my head. "We go to Hazel."

We approached Hazel's cottage from the dirt pathway, Theo shooting wary glances at every shift of the shadows or rustle amongst the underbrush. Julien kept scowling as Theo knocked shoulders with him each time a noise startled him.

I had to admit, after spending so much time trying to remain hidden, it felt oddly unsettling being out in the open. The soft moonlight cast an eerie glow over the cosy cottage, the chill in the air biting at my cheeks and sending a cold shiver cascading down the length of my spine. The moon sat high in the sky, which put the time at around midnight by my guess—the perfect time for sinister tidings. It was a superstition many of the older residents residing at Ellesmere Castle shared. All would safely lock themselves away before the moon reached its peak, their charms hanging by the door to protect them.

As I eyed Hazel's home, my brow furrowed and I wrapped my arms around my mid-section to try and quell the rolling in my stomach. The lantern hanging by her door was doused, its usual orange glow casting a heavy shadow over the porch. Every window was dark, not a single candle flickering within.

I ascended the porch stairs and peered through the front window. Everything was as it should be, but from the looks of the empty hearth, it appeared Hazel hadn't been home in days. My frown deepened as I turned back to the woods surrounding the cottage, the churning in my stomach hardening into a feeling of dread. The wind had stilled, the leaves motionless.

"Something's wrong," I whispered, my hands trembling in apprehension of what had brought the woods to a deathly quiet.

"This can't be good," Verena replied.

The muscles in Julian's arms tensed, his hands clenching into tight fists, readying himself for an attack. My skin bristled with magic, my head turning in every direction, trying to find the source of the silence. Theo shifted his weight from one foot to the other, his hands held out in front of him. But, even in the moon's faint light, I was able to make out the soft shivers that rolled over his shoulders. Grey's posture was stiff, his eyes narrowed toward the darkness in front of him.

The seconds ticked by slowly and I watched the darkness cautiously. Then, I heard it: the shift in the undergrowth followed by a deep growl echoing through the night. The creaking and groaning of twisted limbs sent a chill right down to my bones. I stared between my friends' faces, their eyes widening.

We all knew what was coming for us.

Thirty-Six

King Elias stepped out of the shadows, flanked by a dozen monstrum, their long, gnarled limbs creaking with each menacing step. A group of guards hovered behind him, their hands already alight with magic as dozens of witches and warlocks encircled us. Julien's fingers twitched, the warmth of his flames washing over my side.

No. They weren't supposed to find us here. I'd been certain Elias would track my whereabouts to the castle, knowing I would want to ensure everyone's safety.

Elias's smile twisted into a smirk of pure elation the longer he stared at the stunned expression on my face.

"How?" was all I managed to breathe out.

"It was simple really," Elias replied with a shrug. "We think the same, you and I." He took a step forward, his hands clasped loosely behind his back as he paced in front of me, his eyes never leaving mine. "You see, I did go to the castle in the hopes my trap had lured you there. It would have been much easier if you did, but something told me you were smarter than that, Braelyn. If our roles were reversed, I would have done the same thing, so, I thought of all the places you'd think to hide from me. Many came to mind, but then I recalled the first time we met. It was at the Forest Festival, which you attended with your grandmother. Thus, here we are." He waved a hand, gesturing to the woods around us.

"I'm nothing like you," I hissed.

My hands sparked with rage. Hate was such an overwhelming feeling and had been an emotion my mother told me not to take lightly. She would often say how hatred could consume a person and addle their mind until they could no longer feel anything besides the hate and anger. I'd always believed there was nothing anyone could do that would make me feel such things, but standing here in this very moment, I understood. My chest rose and fell quickly with each heated breath. King Elias simply chuckled at my response, which only made my blood burn even hotter.

"Are you sure, Braelyn? I seek the promise of power and, as I understand it, so do you. Or is the bloodstone not the reason you ventured to the Ironwood Mountains?"

My blood ran cold, chilling me to my very core. So, he had found The Book of Lilith and Althea's Journal amongst my belongings.

"Everyone in this world, Miss Grey, is after something. Whether it be magic, love, peace, or power, if you find out what motivates them, you can almost guarantee they will follow the person who can give them what they want." He continued to pace in front of us, bits of dirt and leaf litter flicking up each time he shifted. "Take the gremlins, for instance, who seek magical objects. Once I have fulfilled my duty, the people of Ellesmere will no longer need such things, so I offered the gremlins these items in exchange for their service."

"In other words, you have others do your dirty work for you," Julien said.

Elias's head snapped to Julien, his face contorting into a look of pure loathing. In the blink of an eye, Elias closed the distance between us in a few long strides and wrapped his hand around Julien's throat. The sharp tip of the circulum hovered above Julien's sternum, the hum of the magic used to forge it, buzzing through the air like the heavy beat of a bee's wings. Julien grit his teeth as a calculating smile tipped up Elias's mouth. I raised my hands, electricity and fire sparking, but the cool kiss of steel against my skin put a quick stop to the onslaught of my magic. In my peripherals, I could just make out Sebastien's dark curls and the hand holding my gifted dagger to my throat.

Elias pulled the circulum away an inch, a long, thin line of red pulling from the centre of Julien's chest. Julien bellowed at the pain I knew would be wracking his body, the all too familiar sensation making my knees go weak. He was siphoning his magic.

"If you want the traitor to live, Braelyn, I wouldn't summon any more magic if I were you." Elias's dark eyes flicked over to me, nothing but cruelty and malice within their depths.

The feelings in my heart waged an internal war with the thoughts in my head, but I knew magic was no use to me now.

"Brae, don't," Julien managed to grit out between clenched teeth, his hands fisting in his dark curls as if trying to squeeze out the pain the circulum caused him.

It didn't matter if I was stronger than every witch and warlock in Ellesmere. Elias had found my weakness and wouldn't bat an eyelid to use it against me. Lowering my hands, I let my magic recede, my eyes never leaving Julien's face. As the last of my magic disappeared, Elias released Julien from his hold, pushing him aside like dirty linen. His knees buckled as the intake of oxygen rushed into his lungs and, taking a deep, ragged breath, he glared at Elias's retreating form.

"By the elements, I will kill you." His voice dripped with such intense hatred, I flinched at the harshness of his words.

Elias simply smiled, undeterred by Julien's comment. "There seems to be a lot of that sentiment going around these days, Mr Thorne, but I am yet to find anyone worthy enough to defeat me. So, please, give it your best shot."

Julien let out a low animal-like growl, but he made no move towards the king. He, as well as I, knew he was in no state to fulfil his promise. Sebastien retracted his blade, coming around to stand beside Elias.

"Now, tell me where the bloodstone is," Elias said smoothly.

My heart slammed against my rib cage as I stared back at him, trying to keep my face as expressionless as his own. The bloodstone's magic swirled heavily in my runed palm.

"I don't know where it is," I replied simply.

A malicious laugh oozed from Elias's lips. "Like your father, you're a terrible liar, Miss Grey. *Tell* me where it is."

My palms were slick with sweat and I could feel the weight of everyone's gaze glued to my face, watching and waiting. I squared my shoulders and narrowed my eyes on the shadows behind Elias, my fingers curling into fists as I slowly summoned them forward.

Elias raised a perfect dark brow. "I'm waiting, Braelyn."

His eyes flicked over my face, waiting for the moment the chink in my armour cracked open wide enough to reveal the truth. But I wouldn't break. The bloodstone was coveted—an important relic belonging to the dwarves of the Ironwood Mountains. I would rather endure every ounce of pain before I handed over information of its whereabouts to anyone, let alone Elias. With the bloodstone and the circulum, he'd be unstoppable.

"I'm growing impatient, Miss Grey. Hand over whatever magical object you have obtained, or I will pry it from your cold, dead fingers." His voice dripped with hatred. "Either way, I will have it."

Sweat trickled down my face and placing my hands behind my back, I smiled sweetly at him, my face a mask of indifference. "As I told you before, I don't have anything."

If looks could kill, I would have been struck down where I stood. But I didn't wait for Elias to react. Extending my hands, I coaxed the shadows forward, electricity crackling within the eye of my storm. With one quick push of my hands, the shadows surged forward, sending the guards barrelling for the trees. The stories of my last assault were clearly fresh in their minds.

A few warlocks closest to us tried to fight against me, but the sheer force of my air magic sent them spiralling through the air. Julien gripped my wrist and pulled me towards the path leading into the Ironwood Village. A blonde-haired witch ran towards us, her hands lashing out as ice-tipped arrows flew towards us. As we ducked out of the way, Julien flicked his wrist, sending a fireball careening into the witch's chest. Her knees buckled as she screamed.

Catching Theo's wrist as we ran, we created a chain of linked hands, none of us wanting to be separated. Still maintaining my air magic, I threw a quick glance over my shoulder, wanting to see the look of frustration on Elias's face as we made our second escape in mere hours. Instead, a small sneer darkened his features. The colour drained from my face, sending a rush of icy terror down my spine. This wasn't over.

He raised his hands almost exactly as I had and immediately, a force stronger than anything I'd ever felt pushed against the walls of my magic. Julien must have felt the pressure settle around us as he pulled up a few paces short of the tree line—his chunky black boots skidding in the thick, leafy underbrush.

"What's happening, Braelyn," Julien asked, his voice shaky with worry.

"It's Elias," I replied, my voice raspy. "He's drawing on my magic somehow."

I clutched a hand to my chest, feeling like the air was being sucked from my lungs in a way that would only result in one ending. Death. My ribs constricted beneath the pressure, and I grit my teeth against the pain.

"Braelyn, he's bound himself to you using blood magic," Verena said hurriedly. "I can see the sigil on his hand."

I looked to Elias, searching for the marking Verena spoke of. After a few frantic seconds, I found it on his palm: Three perfect, overlapping circles drawn in blood.

"I don't..."

Realisation dawned on me and, reaching a shaking hand up to my neck, my fingers came away slick with blood. Too caught up in my concern for Julien's life, I hadn't realised Sebastien's blade had pierced my skin. Despite the fear rolling in my belly like a waking beast, anger surged its way forward, hot and heavy in its pursuit to control me. My breaths came in ragged gasps, sweat dripping over my forehead as I gritted my teeth against Elias's control.

His mood shifted from sheer delight to growing irritation.

Clenching my hands into tight fists, I tried taking a shaky step forward, but it was no use. Elias had turned my own power against me. With the power of the bloodstone coursing through my veins, it was too much. I needed to break the bond he'd created.

As if he could read my mind, Julien made a break for Elias, sprinting in the direction of the cruel king, his hands ignited in white-hot flames. Before he'd managed a few metres, Elias thrust his hand out to the side, bending my earth magic to his will.

Thick, sweeping vines shot from the depths of the Ironwood, wrapping around Julien's torso in a tight grip. I cried out to Elias to let him go, but he simply smirked down at me as he sauntered to where I'd collapsed to the ground. Tears streaked my dusty face and my chest screamed in silent pain. Little by little, my lungs fought to steal as much air as they could, but it was useless.

Elias tilted my chin up with the tip of the circulum so our eyes met. My vision blurred as I tried to stop the tears from cascading down my cheeks. I didn't want to give him the satisfaction of seeing me cry.

"You would do better to hide the things that make you vulnerable, Braelyn," Elias said, his voice dripping with condescension. "It also seems you've gained more power since your little visit to the dwarves." Snatching my runed hand up in his, he inspected the golden marks on my arm, his eyes narrowed and lips pinched. "I'll ask you again. Where. Is. It?"

I gritted my teeth together so hard they might crack.

"By the elements," I rasped, "I will be the last face you see before you die."

A small smirk pulled at the corners of his mouth as he bent towards me—the tip of the circulum never leaving my throat. His mouth was so close to my ear, I could hear his breath. The hairs on the back of my neck prickled at his closeness.

"I look forward to it," he whispered before pulling a dagger from his belt and bringing it down hard on the side of my head.

The last thing I saw was the spinning greens and browns of the forest before everything went black.

Thirty-Seven

The smell of decayed leaves and damp soil tickled my nose as I came to. My head ached with each inhalation as, miserably, I opened my eyes. After having them closed for the elements knew how long, my vision was blurry and each spark of light sent sharp pains ricocheting through my temples.

I pushed through it, squinting against the growing flickers of light in search of Julien and my friends. I scanned every witch and warlock's face amid the large gathering until, finally, I found him.

Julien's limp body was tied to the thick trunk of a tree only a few metres from me. His head hung forward, chin resting on his broad chest. I frantically tried to get to him, my boots scrambling against the damp dirt but, like Julien, I'd been restrained. A thick rope wrapped tightly around my waist, holding me firmly against the rough bark. Unlike Julien, my hands had been secured behind my back with thick, heavy shackles. It seemed Elias was taking no chances this time.

I studied Julien's limp form and could just make out the slow rise and fall of his chest. He was alive. Sagging back against the tree, I let myself relax for a moment. My vision still blurred around the edges, but searching my surroundings, I found the other faces I desperately needed to see.

My relief was short lived as my stomach lurched.

Verena, Grey, and Theo were back in the iron cage we'd just escaped from, each with a new set of injuries. So, Elias had brought us back to the clearing to finish what he'd started.

Blood trickled down the side of my face, the gash on my head burning each time the wind shifted. The bloodstone's magic clearly didn't have any effect on wounds not caused by magic.

My heart beat a fast rhythm in my chest, my mind turning over how much longer it would take for our reinforcements to arrive—if I could wait that long for their help. My fingers tapped nervously against the cool iron shackles. Iron was no longer an issue for me with the power of the bloodstone, but there was no way I could escape with the growing number of Elias's followers. Barghests stalked the ground in front of me while hundreds of eyes flicked back and forth between me and their task at hand. It would be a pointless endeavour and we would die before making it a few steps. It was better to bide my time, assuming I had enough left.

With nothing to do other than wait, I sat back against the rough bark and studied my surroundings. Julien and I had been tethered to the trees directly in front of the ash tree, the hole in the middle giving me the perfect view of Elias's quarters. The front of the tent had been tied open and, in the very minimal light, I could just make out three shadowed forms bent over a table in the middle of the dark space. It had to be where Elias and Victoria were preparing for the ritual.

Fires had been lit at varying intervals throughout the trees, lighting the clearing and the small path carved between the looming trees. A path we had walked on only a week ago. With this much light illuminating the clearing, the dwarves and guards of Ellesmere Castle wouldn't be able to miss us.

"Ah, you're finally awake." King Elias smiled at me as he stalked over with his hands folded softly in front of his mid-section—the circulum still fastened securely to his pointer finger. "I was beginning to worry."

"I highly doubt that," I replied.

He chuckled lightly before crouching before me, his face half-concealed in shadow.

How fitting considering the army of shadows he intends to unleash on the world.

"You're exactly like your father. He, too, had the same fighting spirit."

The mention of my father hit me like an arrow to the heart. My mind flashed with imagined scenarios of his last few moments in life. Had he been held prisoner like me, shackled and bound so he couldn't fight back? Or had his brother simply disposed of him like one does an empty ink pot?

It didn't matter now. Elias had slain him in cold blood and even though I'd never had the chance to know my father, I knew he would have gone down fighting for those he loved. I would avenge him. Blood roared in my ears as I stared into the smug face of the only living relative on my father's side.

"Then you know I'll stop at nothing to finish what he couldn't."

"That might be true, Miss Grey, but not unlike your father, the love you have for others makes you weak." Standing at his full height again, he beckoned to two guards standing amongst the trees behind me. "And, like your father, it will be your downfall."

A guard no older than I crouched beside me, her jet-black hair falling over her eyes. She refused to look at me as her hands tugged at the rope around my waist. The natural fibres of the thick jute caught instantly from her fire magic, burning like kindling. After a few seconds, the rope slackened around my waist and I let out a sigh of relief as the blood started to circulate through my arms, sending pins and needles running down my fingers. My relief was quickly forgotten as a second guard pulled me to my feet. His dirty dark hair curled around his ears, shielding most of his features from view, but it did little to hide the sneer that twisted the bottom half of his face into a look of pure hatred.

"Move, qui deceptor." He shoved me forward with glee. "I must say, it gives me great joy to see you and my spineless brother here. How the tables have turned, Braelyn."

My name sounded odd on his lips. Like his brother, Sebastien's voice was deep and smooth. The only difference was the cold tone lacing his words. The two boys were so alike, but in all the ways that mattered, they were different.

"He's your better in every regard," I said, trying to twist my arm out of his heated grip.

Sebastien's fingers only tightened in response. A bitter laugh escaped his lips, sending goosebumps trailing over the back of my neck.

"Believe what you want," he replied. "Soon he'll be wishing he chose the right side."

Sebastien pushed me forward, no longer interested in conversing, but his grip remained tight as we crossed the clearing. After sitting for so long against the jagged bark of the tree, my back ached and my legs stumbled over the giant tree roots intertwined over the forest floor. Sebastien swore under his breath as he pulled me to my feet more than once, pushing me towards the tent. Elias walked a few paces in front of us, his hands clasped delicately behind his back. He looked more like a man out for a leisurely stroll rather than a tyrant king marching me to my death.

My hands trembled in their shackles, the tell-tale tingling growing beneath my skin the closer I was pushed towards the ash tree. I could feel the cold snap of ice trickle down my spine as my water magic surged to the surface. Electricity prickled at my fingertips, my air and water magic merging in a whirlwind. Taking a deep steadying breath, I tried to calm the storm brewing inside me, knowing this wasn't the time to unleash it. As we neared the base of the gigantic tree, I craned my neck sideways, trying to get a last glimpse of Julien, but he had disappeared into the sea of witches and warlocks who crowded behind their leader.

⟨⟨⟨⟨⟨

After all the stories my mother had told me about great battles long ago, nothing could have prepared me for the sights I looked upon now. Hundreds of Elias's followers gathered along the edge of the ash tree clearing, their magic ignited in displays of orange flames, white-blue ice and deadly lightning. Earth wielders conjured their magic from the depths of the Ironwood, where serpent-like vines crawled across the leafy ground to stand beside them like great wooden sentinels. My stomach rolled, an overwhelming feeling of dread squeezing my chest. More than fifty monstrum stood behind them in the darkness of the trees, their bony heads turned in my direction. Hundreds of obsidian eyes watched my every movement, their gnarled wooden arms poised to strike with deadly force. Swallowing hard, I turned my gaze to the towering tree before me, where I could just make out the worried expressions of my friends through the gaping hole in the middle of its trunk.

Sebastien pushed me forward one last time before blending back into the shadows amongst the rest of Elias's guards. I frantically searched the trees lining the clearing, hoping to find the familiar faces of the castle guards, Maeve, or my mother, but from this far away the shadows oozed out of every crack and crevice, cloaking the space between the trees in darkness.

Fear had once again begun to uncoil in my stomach. No matter how hard I tried to push it aside, it dug its claws in deep. My heart raced as I tried to free my hands from the iron shackles, but the more I tugged against the cool metal, the more my wrists burned in protest.

"It's no use, Braelyn. You won't find a way to escape me this time." Elias's calm, crisp voice washed over me, sending a new wave of chills down my spine. "However, if you hand over the bloodstone, I might consider letting you live."

His greedy eyes never left my own. He watched me with rapt attention as if his entire plan centred around the answer I provided. His back was turned against the wall of his followers and not a line of worry crossed his porcelain face.

Squaring my shoulders, I narrowed my eyes at him, trying to put as much hatred in my words as I could muster. "I would rather die."

A small chuckle escaped him.

"Oh, how predictable you are, Miss Grey. But, if I'm being honest, I'm glad you're not giving up. It will make my next move so much more fun."

He snapped his fingers and hurried movements broke out to the right of us. I turned my head, a gap no wider than a metre splitting the line of Elias's guards. From between the tight line of witches and warlocks came a sight that turned my stomach to lead. Blight walked towards us, a cruel smile disfiguring his face as he dragged Julien along behind him, his wrists clapped in irons. My hands trembled behind me, making my own shackles clatter loudly. My nostrils flared as I spun to face Elias once again, a cruel smile spread across his face.

Blight roughly deposited Julien at his king's feet. Julien's knees hit the ground with a sickening thud that made my legs go weak. After a second, he lifted himself from the ground, so he was once again at eye level with the king.

"Julien, so lovely you could finally join us." Elias swept his arm out. "I've been looking forward to this encounter."

Whatever Elias had in store for us, I knew it couldn't be good. I tried to inch my way over to Julien's side, but despite my minuscule steps,

Elias's eyes barely looked in my direction before he stuck out his hand and my movements were halted. The rush of air slamming down on me almost sent me reeling backwards. Steadying myself, I pushed my shoulder against Elias's onslaught of magic, but it was no use. An invisible wall kept me from taking another step forward.

A thick blanket of silence fell over the clearing as every set of eyes watched Elias with rapt attention. His followers smirked, their eyes hungry for their king to dispose of the obstacle in their way. From the direction of the iron cage, terrified shouts drifted on the wind.

Verena, Theo, and Grey fought against the iron bars separating them from Julien and me. Everyone knew what the king was capable of, but no one knew what his next move would be. Elias let his hand drop to his side and I felt the low whoosh of his air magic being pulled away, like a weight had been lifted from my body—the wall no longer holding me back. I made a move towards Julien, but the low creak and groan of wooden limbs stopped me in my tracks.

"Take one more step, Miss Grey, and my monstrum will tear you apart. While I might need your blood, you don't need to be alive for me to get it."

Elias stood beside Julien, that small smile transforming into a malicious grin.

"You might think you know my weakness," I hissed, "but I know yours too. If your monsters kill me, you'll never have the bloodstone."

A low growl reached my ears. If I hadn't been watching Elias closely, I would have sworn it came from the monstrum. Satisfaction swelled inside me as I watched his thoughts tick away behind those obsidian eyes.

He now paced in front of Julien, dressed in his usual black trousers, a blood-red tunic with gold filigree falling to his knees. He looked ever the royal ruler with his black cape draped heavily over his shoulder. Continuing to pace, Elias turned his gaze in my direction. His previous anger had dissipated, a small smile lifting the corner of his mouth.

"While you might be right in your assumptions, Miss Grey, I believe what I'm about to do next will quickly change your mind about withholding information from me."

He reached into his billowing cape, pulling out a dagger. It looked no longer than the length of my hand, but I knew a weapon didn't need to be large to cause damage. My blood boiled beneath my skin, anger flooding my face and making my cheeks burn.

"Touch him and I will have you beg for your life," I shouted, lunging towards them.

Elias stood behind Julien, his hand resting lightly on his shoulder. "Well then, I'm going to tell you one more time, Miss Grey. Hand over the bloodstone."

My palms were slick with sweat and my shoulders ached from having my hands secured behind my back for a lengthy period. Elias tightened his grip on Julien's shoulder as he waited for me to decide.

My mind raced. He'd figured out how my magic had grown more powerful—had spotted the signs on my arm, but his belief I held the magical relic was proof he hadn't read Althea's journal. I sifted through my options. I couldn't hand over the information about the bloodstone. The dwarves had warned me of the repercussions should it land in the wrong hands. But if I didn't... Julien would suffer, which I couldn't allow either. I loved him with every fibre of my being and there was no reality in which I could lose him.

I shifted my gaze to Julien's face, his dark eyes watching me closely. He gave me a small, lopsided smile—the one that sent my stomach fluttering—and from this gesture, I knew he understood the war raging inside me. The battle of my head versus my heart.

With the smallest of movements, he moved his head from side to side. My heart almost shattered. Tears stung my eyes and my chest felt like it was going to crush me under the weight of what I was about to do.

With one last look at Julien's face, I turned my attention to Elias. His grip on Julien's shoulder turned his knuckles white, his dark eyes shining with an eagerness I'd never witnessed before now. The weight of every pair of eyes threatened to crush me beneath their heavy gaze as silence filled the air. Even the strong winds of Samhain had stilled in anticipation of my words. Taking a deep breath in through my nose, I let it out slowly as I readied myself for what I was about to do.

"For the last time, I don't know where it is."

To my surprise, my voice came out stronger than I expected. It shattered the silence that had settled around us and sent a wave of voices crashing down on me. King Elias bared his teeth, his lips curling back and twisting his features. The resemblance to one of his monsters was uncanny.

"Have it your way then, Miss Grey."

And in one swift movement, he plunged the dagger deep into Julien's chest.

Thirty-Eight

"**N**o!" I screamed gutturally as Elias twisted the dagger into the hard muscles just below his shoulder. Julien never made a sound as the tip of Elias's dagger pierced his flesh. He swayed on the spot, blood blossoming over his white shirt.

Tears spilled over my cheeks. Relief over Julien's survival flooded through me and my shaking legs finally gave out from under me. My knees hit the ground with a sickening crunch, the sharp crack making me grit my teeth against the pain.

Elias laughed manically as he watched the turmoil spread across my face.

"Did you really think I would kill the only thing that will make you break?" he said through gritted teeth. "We're just getting started, Braelyn. The longer you deny me, the more he will suffer!" He shouted the last word at me with such force I shrank back slightly.

He pulled the dagger from Julien's chest, blood dripping from the tip. Julien groaned as Elias grabbed him by the hair, jerking his head back. His usual calculating demeanour had turned manic in his desperation to have the bloodstone. Elias placed the tip of the dagger over Julien's heart, his eyes wild.

"Shall we go again?" His fingers moved to Julien's shoulder, his fingers pressing down on the gash above his heart, but Julien did nothing but grit his teeth against the pain, his beautiful dark eyes never leaving mine.

For the first time since meeting my uncle, I saw the monster capable of slaughtering his family for the power he thought he deserved. I couldn't tell him of the bloodstone's location, but by withholding it from him I was dooming Julien to pain and death. Fear clawed at my insides. I hated this. I was playing with fire and, if I wasn't careful, I risked losing everything I cared about in a matter of seconds. My hands trembled with anger and magic, the iron shackles rattling behind my back. I summoned my elements, letting them unfurl deep in my belly. The darkness answered my call, awoken by the fresh wave of hatred roaring in my ears. My fingers curled into fists, my skin straining against my knuckles. I couldn't let Julien suffer for my mistakes. It was my fault we were in this situation and I would die before I let Elias torture him further.

A pull in the back of my mind sent my stomach into a flutter as I searched for the connection that would be our saving grace.

"*We are close, my friend.*"

Alpheus's voice gave me the last bit of strength I needed. Elias watched me closely, eyes narrowed, the muscles in his neck straining against his skin as he leaned toward me, dagger still pressed against Julien's heart.

"Fine," I said to him. "I'll tell you."

Elias's eyes widened momentarily, the whites a stark contrast to the black irises staring at me with rapt attention. His fingers loosened on Julien's shoulder, but still, he didn't let him go. Julien was his leverage, and he wouldn't give that up so easily.

"I'm waiting."

My gaze shifted to where Verena, Grey, and Theo were pressed up against the cage, gripping the iron bars tightly, their expressions a mix of confusion and concern. I wished I could ease their minds, but all I could do was give them a small nod and hope they trusted me enough to believe everything would be okay. The seconds ticked by and Elias's fingers curled into fists before he threw Julien to the ground and stormed in my direction. His impatience far outweighed the leverage he held in his hand. He closed the distance between us in three long strides, his nostrils flared and eyes wild as his cloak billowed out behind him.

"Stay away from her!" Julien yelled as he tried and failed to rise, scrambling against the dirt and blood at his feet.

Elias's lips pulled back from his teeth, a guttural roar tearing free from his chest.

"Tell me where it is!" he shouted, spittle flying from his mouth.

He was unhinged, utterly mad from his craving for power.

Shouts and jeers rang out around us, but before I could comprehend what was being said, Elias backhanded me across the cheek. He hit me with such strength, my head whipped to the side, making every bone in my neck crack against the force of his blow. Witches and warlocks cheered at his display of violence, their taunts a hollow drone, lost amongst the ringing in my right ear. Magic swelled in my chest, my veins alight with fire as my fingers itched to call on the power of the bloodstone. As the ringing in my ears began to subside, a few fractured, angry words from my friends sounded, but I only heard one voice.

"We are here, my friend."

My cheek burned white-hot, my skin tingling as the sensation slowly returned to the right side of my face. Tears blossomed in my eyes not from pain, but anger. Elias looked at me with a triumphant smile. He'd clearly believed he'd broken the last of my strength—and he almost had—but a new sense of courage burned brightly in my veins. I would use every ounce of it to prevent the cruel king from hurting anyone else.

Soldiers from Ellesmere Castle and dwarves from the Ironwood Mountains surged into the clearing, their war cries drowning out the shouts of Elias's guards. Led by the elders, the magic of the witches and warlocks illuminated the clearing in brilliant shades of orange, green, and blue. In the front lines, my mother, Maeve, and Hazel stood defiantly, their expressions pinched with worry as they stood shoulder to shoulder, hands linked together. I stared into the faces of the three women who had raised me, cared for me, and loved me—who had taught me to be strong and resilient. With their shoulders thrown back and their chins raised, they looked fierce and proud in their leather armour and my chest swelled to be part of an ancestral line of such powerful woman.

The dwarves flanked them on either side, their iron-made weapons held at the ready. King Vidar and Prince Riven looked formidable at the head of their company, each of them brandishing a sword and axe.

I squared my shoulders and lifted my chin at Elias. "For my father and Ellesmere," I screamed, magic spilling from my fingers.

The dwarves bellowed, their battle cries echoing around the clearing as they surged forward, weapons raised and ready for blood. My mother rushed to Julien's side, her hands fluttering to a small pouch secured to her waist. She pulled back his shirt, her steady hands working on mending the deep puncture wound in his shoulder.

The elders commanded our reinforcements to advance, every witch and warlock summoning their magic with full force. My hands erupted in an inferno of magic as all the power I'd been holding back finally burst free. Blue flames took over every fibre of my body, burning with such fierce intensity, the air around me glowed a brilliant sapphire. The iron shackles around my wrists squealed in protest, but they were no match for the heat of my flame and snapped apart with a satisfying *clink*. The once cool metal now burned like hot vambraces around my wrists, protecting my arms in an armour made of fire. King Elias watched me with round eyes as the battle broke out around us, Ellesmere soldiers advancing on his minions, their fire raining down around them. All around the clearing, witches, warlocks, and dwarves clashed together. A line of dwarves swung their swords in sweeping arcs, their blades finding flesh as their forward ranks advanced.

"No!" Elias screamed and, for the first time since our encounter at Ellesmere castle, I saw fear in his eyes.

The fear that someone could be more powerful than he so desperately dreamed to be. It only lasted a moment before he regained his composure, the cruel mask once again back in place. My blood thrummed with the promise of magic and I relished in the feeling as I let my magic build beneath my skin.

The sky turned ashen as thick storm clouds formed above us, blanketing the clearing in an eerie darkness. Lightning flickered amongst them like the forked tongue of an invisible serpent, tasting the air for prey. Golden strands of magic crisscrossed over my forearms, catching Elias's attention.

"You think you're the only one with great power?" Elias shouted over the growing wind.

With a sickening smile, he held up his hand and the monstrum surged forward, having finally received the command from their master. They descended into the chaos, talons extended, teeth gnashing at the air. The dwarven host quickly shifted, raising their shields around them just as the monstrum collided, swiping at the protective wall they created. Behind them, witches and warlocks conjured their flames, balls of fire curving through the air to ignite the creatures' twisted limbs.

My magic pulled me towards Elias like we were the opposite ends of a magnet. The need to end the battle overwhelmed all my senses. His hands swirled around him, calling on his most potent element. The air throughout the clearing grew thick and, thrusting out a hand, it summoned me forward. Thick branches shot from the shadows, banding around me and securing my arms by my sides. The rough bark scraped against my skin, heat burning over me as Elias reached for me, the tip of the circulum glinting menacingly.

Not this time.

Rumbles of thunder echoed around the clearing before a resounding boom shook the earth. Lightning struck the ground at Elias's feet, missing him by inches. Raising his hand to shield his face, the magic he summoned began to falter, falling away as he stumbled back, collapsing against a mound of kindling. The branches entangling me were now motionless around my feet. The arm of his tunic was in tatters, black burns feathering over his pale skin where the lightning had made contact. Power flowed through me, entwining with each angry breath I took.

"What's your plan, Braelyn?" Elias snarled.

I stood over him, the reflection of the ash tree bright in his beady black eyes. Even as he stared up at me, they glittered with malicious power.

"My plan has never changed. I will kill you."

He chuckled. "I would like to see you try."

The edges of the kindling began to ignite, my fingers curling into a fist as I summoned a deadly flame. Despite his position, Elias still wore an expression of haughty derision which made my hands shake. Drawing on the power of the bloodstone, I conjured as much strength as I could muster before I raised my arm and punched him in the face.

Thirty-Nine

My fist collided with Elias's nose in a sickening crunch—his head snapping back against the kindling burning around him. My knuckles ached, the skin reddening as I opened and closed my fingers. With one hand clutched to his face, he struggled to right himself. Ellesmere guards swarmed around me, their protection preventing Elias's minions from reaching me or him. Just like his dark witch, I would watch him burn, but first he would suffer. He would feel the same torment he had inflicted on so many others.

Dozens of Elias's followers fought against Ellesmere's soldiers, but our numbers were strong. I held my palm to the sky, flames lining my fingers while the fire continued to blaze around Elias.

"I told you my face was the last thing you'd see before I killed you," I said in a scathing tone.

A frenzy of shouts and magic flowed in the background, but I blocked them out. In this moment, it was just me and Elias. As each of my fingers closed, the fire inched closer, deadly and destructive.

Elias watched me through slitted eyes and, lifting his hand, called upon his magic once again. He flicked his wrist and a torrent of air hit me in the chest, knocking me back. The force of it made me gasp, but there was no real strength behind it. He was beginning to weaken and with no one near enough to siphon their magic, he was vulnerable.

The guards around me stood their ground but they, too, grew weaker the longer they tried to protect me. Elias stood on the pyre, his legs weak, but I knew not to underestimate him. I ran toward him just as a low growl made the shadows around the clearing tremor. My feet froze, recognising the sound. Dozens of barghests stalked from the depths of the Ironwood, moving like a formidable shadow. Hackles raised, they launched at the guards surrounding us, sharp teeth snapping at their flesh. Screams pierced the air, making my blood turn cold.

Elias fell from the pyre, a smug smirk the last thing I saw.

I darted forward, scrambling over the blood-soaked ground as a warm hand encircled my wrist. Julien pulled me to his side, a set of serrated teeth closing around the space I'd been standing in only seconds before. The bhargest whirled around, crimson eyes focused in our direction. It ran a tongue over its jagged teeth, tasting the air as bloody drool dripped over its clawed paws. Fear tightened my muscles, the memories of the bhargest's lethal venom rendering my feet useless. The creature launched towards us, its oily black fur glistening against Julien's flame, but it didn't get far. The bhargest collapsed with an intense howl before falling still, an icy shaft embedded in its side.

Grey stood a metre away from us, his hand held out, ice crystals calcifying along his fingers. Theo and Verena stood beside him, their faces streaked with blood and dirt.

"How?" was all I managed to breath out before I spotted Victoria lingering behind them, the keys swinging from her outstretched hand.

Eyebrows raised, I shook my head, not quite believing what had happened. It seemed all my desperate pleas to get through to her had finally shattered the icy wall she hid behind. She nodded in my direction, a small smile quirking up the corner of her thin lips.

I ran to my friends and we embraced one another tightly, our arms refusing to yield as we held each other as if letting go may physically break us. When we finally tore apart, I searched for Victoria but she had disappeared into the chaos of the battle.

Verena whirled.

"Where's Elias?"

"When the bhargests attacked he got away, but there's only one place he'll be. I need to get to the ash tree."

Everyone nodded, keen to end the bloodshed.

Bodies of witches, warlocks, and dwarves alike littered the battlefield, their open eyes unseeing. So many lives had been lost in Elias's pursuit for power and attempts to summon Lilith, but also because of what the prophecy had foretold. For weeks Elias had gotten the better of us—gotten the better of me—but not tonight. On this day, he would meet his end. Theo smiled at me, his scar puckering as he took up my hand. I looked at the handful of people who'd suffered and endured countless dangers beside me and a thought struck me.

"It's time to use my so-called weakness to my advantage."

The corner of Julien's lip quirked up in a lopsided smile. "Now we're talking."

"Elias would never suspect I'd ask you all to help. He knows my love for you is far too great to put you in harm's way."

Grey nodded. "It's perfect. We can wait in the shadows until the time's right."

"Yes," Theo replied, "but Elias also knows Julien would never leave Brae's side. He needs to accompany her to the ash tree."

Julien rolled up his shirt sleeves, the muscles in his forearms straining as he cracked his knuckles. Red marks corded the skin, his magic use sapping at his energy.

"It would be my pleasure." He gave me a wink.

I shook my head, but I couldn't help the small blush that heated my cheeks. Everyone knew their role. Verena and Grey retreated to the edge of the clearing, but as Theo turned to leave, he looked back at Julien, his eyes hardening with an icy resolve.

"Take care of our girl," he said.

"Always," Julien replied.

Theo followed the others and disappeared into the shadows bordering the ash tree.

As we fought our way across the battlefield, fire wielders continued to light up the sky with balls and rivers of blue flame. Three monstrum broke through the dwarves' defensive line and a group of witches entwined their hands, combining their magic to send a raging wildfire barrelling through the creatures. King Vidar advanced, thrusting his sword through the heart of the first monstrum. As the creature's pained squeals fell silent, he pivoted and stabbed his sword towards the second one, his blade finding its mark with a sharp crack. Lorcan fought bravely by his king's side, his broad sword plunging into a barghest's hide, disposing of the creature in seconds. The people of Ellesmere retaliated with strength and vigour. A couple of fire warlocks conjured a canopy of flames, stopping the deadly ice arrows from finding their target, the ice melting to a fine mist against the heat. Air wielders tried their hardest to push back the onslaught of vines sweeping along the ground, their strength unbearable as they curled around anyone in their path. A warlock bellowed as we ran, his screams choked off as thorn-tipped vine punctured his throat, blood gurgling from his lips.

Julien and I dodged a few of the smaller icy daggers falling around the clearing, but as we sidestepped a fire warlock, a tree was torn from the ground and hurtled towards us with lightning speed. Thrusting my arm up, I conjured my air magic and, with a quick swipe of my hand, the blackened tree changed direction. It took out two monstrum and a few bhargests as it flew.

Two down, dozens more to go.

Flames ignited behind me as Julien sent a stream of fire in the direction of the monstrum closest to us. Like kindling, its body ignited, the smell of burning wood filling my nostrils and burning my throat, but the creature continued to advance.

They weren't going down without a fight.

I flicked my wrist, wrapping lightning around the barghest in front of me. It struggled against my electric binds, its teeth gnashing at the fine blue strands, whining as the power in my magic became too much to contend with. My hand clenched into a fist and the bolts stabbing through the barghest's thick hide stilled its heart.

Another monstrum to my left charged at us, its claws outstretched and ready to tear us apart. I reached out to the low hanging brambles, their thorns sharp and deadly. They shot through the air, coiling around the monstrum's torso and squeezing it tight until the creature shattered in an explosion of splintered wood.

Next to me, Julien fought against three of the creatures, their twisted wooden bodies seared black. Julien's hands ignited with his deadly blue flame, eyes narrowed at the closest demonic creature. It advanced towards him, mouth contorted in a malicious grin, needle-like teeth flashing menacingly. As the creature grew closer, Julien plunged his fiery hand between the twisted branches of its ribs, his fingers grasping its blackened heart. A guttural roar echoed through the Ironwood as he pulled the organ from its chest.

Monstrum and bhargest descended on us with fierce determination, but I threw my hands wide, calling forth the darkness as it swept over the remaining monstrum, consuming every inch of its gnarled body. The barghests' agonised snarls filled the air as their serrated teeth tried to find flesh where there was none. The monstrum clawed at the shadows wrapping around its body before I clenched my hand together and it crumpled to the ground, its cries silent.

"We need to move," Julien shouted.

Prince Riven led a group of warriors forward, shields held protectively in front of them as they advanced towards the ash tree. They fought against Elias's followers, swords and axes slashing at their flesh. Riven sported a deepening black eye, the skin swelling beneath the purple-blue bruise.

Chunks of the ash tree were missing from its trunk and King Elias's followers were now climbing the gnarled branches to gain an advantage over those below. Monstrum continued to pour from the depths of the Ironwood, their sharp growls echoing through the air. A few metres away, some of Elias's crones spotted us and charged in our direction, their eyes bright and their hands flaring with magic. With a quick flick of my hand, a gust of wind sent them soaring across the battlefield where they collided with another group of Elias's guards.

The people of Ellesmere fought hard, but they were no match for Elias's monsters. A group of gremlins slashed their taloned hands towards Helene and Aramis. It was the first time I'd seen the elders since they had arrived at the clearing.

Aramis sent a ragged line of flames streaming over the undergrowth, his eyes trained on the devilish creatures. They hissed at the magic billowing before them and scurried back to avoid being burnt.

Helene wrapped the group of gremlins in a length of vine before she turned to fight Elias's guards.

Magic rained down everywhere, the booming crash of boulders finding their targets making the ground tremble beneath our feet. Magdalena and Silas fought back-to-back, their air and water magic circling around them. I spotted my mother not far from the ash tree, her hands fluttering over a fallen Ellesmere guard. She tried to apply salve to the deep gash along their arm, all the while blasting back gremlins with the deft movements of her hands. Maeve shadowed her, protecting her from any attacks as she fought off a duo of witches.

I took a step forward, but my ankles were caught in the tight grip of earth magic.

The warlock snickered. "We've got you now, spirit witch."

I struggled against his hold, each movement only encasing me further. With the snap of my fingers, flames erupted along the looping vines and engulfed them instantly. The earth warlock cried out in pain, recoiling from the heat of my fire magic. The vines around my feet fell in burnt cinders to the ground and, without a second glance at the warlock, Julien gripped my hand and pulled me to where Elias stood at the base of the ash tree, his dark cloak billowing out behind him as he watched the chaos unfold before his eyes.

Sebastien flanked his left side. The dutiful guard protected his king's exposed side, his hands folded in front of him. To my surprise, Victoria watched the battle unfold where she stood on Elias's right. Her iron-clad hands tugged at her long hair, sweat beading her hairline. A dark bruise blossomed over her pale cheekbone, her eyes glistening as she spotted me amongst the swarming crowds. Nausea rolled in the pit of my stomach. Elias must have found out about her efforts to help the others escape. There was only one way I could save her, save everyone from further torment.

Julien took my hand in his and gave it a reassuring squeeze. "Are you ready to fulfil your destiny and end this?"

I watched Elias relish in the destruction his minions and monsters caused. Witch, warlock, dwarf and monster, all caught in his web of chaos while he watched from the sidelines. Magic flared in my chest, mixing with a rage that blossomed like a spring flower in my heart. Turning back to Julien, I squared my shoulders.

"It's time to kill a king," I said, before walking head on into the prophecy.

Fourty

E yes narrowed, I closed the last few metres between me and my enemy, my chest heaving in quick succession. It took him a moment to see us, but when his eyes settled on my face, an unkind smile curved over his lips.

"Braelyn, what kept you?" Elias asked. "I was beginning to wonder how long I would have to wait before you came to find me."

The look of glee turned to a bemused smile. He took a few steps forward, hands clasped behind his back. Sebastien's attention was focused solely on his brother, his stiff posture identical to Julien's.

"Wouldn't it have been easier for you to come find me?" I spat back. "Imprisoning me seems to be a favourite pastime of yours." He threw his head back and laughed, which sounded strange coming from him. "I'm glad I humour you," I replied blankly.

"You are so like your mother. Incredibly headstrong, driven by your love for others, and yet, I see so much of your father in you."

"Don't you dare talk about my father as if you ever loved him!" My lips curling over my gritted teeth. Magic tingled at the tips of my fingers, sending sparks of lightning flickering over my hand.

Elias snickered. "There it is. His stubbornness and hot temper. Don't get me wrong, your father was a kind and gentle soul, but get him fired up and he would erupt like a hot-tempered fire warlock."

I took a step forward, my hands clenched in tight fists by my sides. My air magic cracked with fierce intensity the closer I got to the cruel king. Victoria flinched, but Sebastien only snickered.

"Braelyn," Julien said. "Careful." Warning laced his voice, but I refused to listen.

I knew Elias was goading me and attempting to get under my skin, but I didn't care. I was tired of listening to his conniving words and watching him destroy everything that mattered to me.

The power of the bloodstone pulsed through me, sending golden strands of magic cascading up my arms. Flames unfurled in my right hand, their heat licking up my forearm.

I summoned the shadows, which slithered from the Ironwood, curling together with the fire magic and igniting my arms into flaming black wings. Victoria stumbled backwards, her hands thrown out as the trunk of the ash tree caught her fall. I smiled in satisfaction as Elias's eyes widened and his lip curled back in a snarl.

"You will fulfil your purpose, Braelyn. And before you take your final breath, the last thing you see will be the wraiths who will wreak havoc through Ellesmere."

The air around us shifted as he raised his hand. Elias bared his teeth like a wild animal as the air pulled from my lungs. Julien coughed and gasped for breath beside me, his eyes bulging and bloodshot. Focusing all my attention on the magic ensnaring us, I pulled it in towards me. Slowly, my breaths returned to normal, giving me the edge I needed.

Bringing my hands together, I quickly drew them apart as icicles formed around my curled fingers, each one larger and sharper than the last. They hovered above my hand, waiting for my command. With a simple twitch of my wrist, the icy arrows shot towards their target. They embedded in Elias's wrist with expert precision.

He grunted in pain and dropped his hand, his air magic receding. Julien coughed and spluttered as he gulped down the cool night air, no longer suffocated by the thick blanket Elias's air magic had cast over us.

"Are you okay?" I asked as Julien slowly recovered.

I cupped his cheek, which was warm beneath my touch. He stirred beneath my fingers, his groans like music to my ears, if only for a moment.

Blight stepped from the hole in the ash tree, flanked by two hulking barghests. They stalked towards us, their black fur rippling with each menacing growl.

I took a slow step back, my shoulder bumping into something warm and solid. Julien took up a protective stance in front of me, his body shielding mine from the barghests' deadly bites and the spiteful attacks we knew Blight was capable of. Julien shifted only slightly, his body still angled in the bhargests' direction.

My gaze never strayed from Elias's face. In the depths of his dark eyes, I saw nothing but hatred and cruelty. Victoria stood beside him now, her blonde hair cascading down her back in a long sheet. Staring at her feet, she held her stomach like she was trying to keep herself from falling apart, but after a second, her eyes found mine, tears glistening in their icy depths. My heart ached for the poor girl who'd fallen into Elias's trap. She'd believed the lies that had slipped from his serpentine mouth, only to realise too late.

But I could still save her.

"What are you going to do, Braelyn? You know the power of a barghest bite."

Behind us, the battle had begun to slow. So many bodies littered the ground it was hard to tell which side had suffered more casualties. Every witch, warlock, and dwarf now watched the events unfolding beneath the tree that started it all. After the loud clashes and shouts of battle, the clearing seemed eerily quiet now. The wind and low growls of the barghests' were the only sounds floating on the air.

"You have no other options, Braelyn," Elias said, a victorious glint flashing in his eyes. He stroked the barghest's fur, but the creature never moved as it watched me. Its blood-red eyes glinted in the erupting firelight and Julien's hand tightened around my runed palm, his fingers gripping mine with such force the bones in my hand ached.

"Lilith will rise again." Elias's eyes flicked to Sebastien. "Bring her to me."

He stepped forward, hands blazing, but before he could take another step, flames carved a path through the underbrush with deadly speed. Julien strode forward, his hands held out, controlling the blaze separating Sebastien and me. The brothers glared at each other through the thick columns of smoke, their muscles rigid and eyes burning with

286

fierce hatred. Julien's fire still burned brightly between us and Sebastien, but he advanced on Julien with one thing in mind.

Elias shot a string of icy daggers in my direction, but with a quick swipe of my hand, they changed course and lodged into a tree trunk with a deep *thwack*. He flicked his wrist and a group of monstrum stalked towards us, their talons extended and pointed teeth bared.

Summoning his water magic, Grey raised his hands high above his head and a wall of thick ice shot into the air, cutting off their assault. The monstrum stopped in their tracks, but it only took a second before they hacked at the frozen wall with talons sharper than any dagger. Grey gritted his teeth against the creatures' onslaught but held his ground.

Lightning cracked around my fingers as it twisted through the flames blazing up my arms. My hands swirled in front me, fire and lightning glowing through the billowing smoke. Through the inferno, I watched Verena surge forward, balls of fire beating against any guard or monster that got too close. The noises of battle floated on the air, the clash of claws against shields sounding as the dwarves reformed their defensive line. Elias's followers converged on the residents of Ellesmere, their magic shooting at them in a steady rhythm, but they fought against the onslaught, shielded by the dwarves' first line of defence.

I took a step forward and Elias mimicked my movements, each of us needing something from the other. Magic rolled in my hands before I sent a barrage of electric fire in Elias's direction, each blaze arching through the air and missing my target as the barghests took the brunt of my attack.

Elias sneered, his chest rising and falling as his breaths became ragged. Thin, silvery lines snaked over his forearms, blending with the tree-like lesions covering his biceps.

This close to the ash tree, the call of the darkness was so strong my breath caught in the back of my throat. The dark tendrils of magic seemed to pull me closer to the bark, as if devouring me from the inside, begging me to wield them.

"You can feel it, can't you?" Elias crooned. "The darkness."

He stalked in front of me like one of his barghests, fingers coiled, teeth bared in a vicious snarl.

The icy wall Grey had erected shattered like glass, the shards impaling Elias's followers, their cries not even earning a glance from their so-called king. Grey swayed where he stood, exhaustion finally pulling him to his knees. Theo took a protective step in front of him, his magic flourishing as branches tore through the air like arrows, imbedding into the monstrums' chests. I stepped towards Elias, my eyes narrowed into slits as I stared at his cold, cruel face. My shadows billowed forward with each twitch of my fingers.

"I told you I would be here when darkness overtook you." Elias glared in my direction, his eyes so wide I could see the whites rimming his dark irises.

Victoria's shackles clinked as she tried to move back, but Elias's hand whipped out to grip her arm. Julien's flames flickered menacingly in the air, growing larger with each surge of magic. Sebastien stepped through the billowing flames, his hands ablaze with magic of his own. He advanced towards his brother, fire and blade in hand. Sebastien lashed out with the dagger, his flaming hand darting out to get a firm grip on Julien's wrist. He pivoted away from Sebastien's attack, fire rippling over his forearms, accentuating the deep red lines that burned into his skin. Julien stepped towards his brother and landed a blow to Sebastien's jaw. Eyes blazing, Julien gripped his brother's throat, the muscles in Sebastien's neck straining as Julien overpowered him. Sebastien may have been older, but Julien's heart pulsed with pure vengeance. Sebastien's grip on his dagger weakened and, as he grappled at his brother's hand, Julien pried the dagger from his fingers before sinking the blade deep into Sebastien's heart.

Lifting my chin, I flexed my fingers by my sides and watched as the shadows twisted around me, golden sparks bursting amid their darkness.

"It can't overtake me, Elias, because I've welcomed it with open arms."

Elias seethed, his pale skin turning a mottled pink. He cracked his neck from side to side, jabbing a long finger in my direction, the tip of the circulum curling like a talon.

"You will die by my hand, Braelyn. The ritual will be complete and Lilith will rise."

Reaching into the breast of his tunic, he produced the small dagger he'd used against Julien. The blade was stained a deep crimson and still crusted with his blood.

A loud rush sounded in my ears as Elias stepped closer to me. Magic surged within me, dark and angry as I watched my uncle smile with glee.

For a moment, the world stilled. Nothing existed except Elias, Victoria, and me. The cries of battle fell away, dimming with each step, the silence unnatural after the roar of combat.

An anguished cry escaped Victoria's lips, my skin prickling at the sound. But there was no time for me to comfort her or tell her she would survive, because in an instant, Elias plunged his dagger deep through her belly.

Fourty-One

Victoria's eyes widened with surprise before they flicked down to the dagger protruding from her torso. Blood dampened her light blue tunic, spreading like a dark stain across her midsection. Her elegant fingers clawed at Elias's hand, her nails biting into his skin as she desperately tried to free herself. The air around us stilled, holding its breath as if waiting for the ritual to begin.

After a few agonising seconds, Elias pulled the dagger from her stomach and watched as Victoria's face slackened before she collapsed against the roots of the ash tree. His guttural roar punctured the silence of the clearing, his eyes wild as his gaze settled on the dagger Julien had planted in Sebastien's chest.

Julien's face was ashen, his eyes staring blankly at his brother's wavering body. Sebastien slumped forward, blood dripping from between his lips as he mouthed something to Julien. Elias held his palms towards the sky, the strength of the wind biting against my skin. The trees moaned in protest, dead leaves skittering along the ground as Elias summoned his most potent element.

"You will never beat me alone, Braelyn," Elias shouted.

My boots shifted through the blood and mud covering the forest floor and I dug my heels into the ground, feeling the pull of my earth magic holding me in place.

"She's not alone," Theo said strongly from behind me.

Stepping forward, my friends took their places beside me. Despite the exhaustion lining their faces, Verena's hands were alight with magic the colour of her fiery hair. Theo stood tall, his arms held wide to his side, the earth's magic crawling over his hands.

"You think you've won, Braelyn," Elias seethed, his eyes wild with rage.

He threw his dagger at me, the blade flying from his hand, turning over and over in the air, the tip aimed directly for my heart.

My eyes widened. A cold sense of fear washed over my body, freezing my feet in place. Time slowed as the dagger inched closer to my chest. I brought my hands up, ready to flinch out of the way just as a blur of caramel fur darted in front of me.

Alpheus fell to the ground, his body unmoving.

I dropped to my knees, my hands fluttering around the dagger in the jackalope's side. His small brown eyes watched me closely from where he lay atop the leaf litter.

"*My friend, are you hurt?*" he asked, voice weak.

Tears filled my eyes. "*I'm okay, but please, save your energy. We need to get you to a healer.*"

My eyes roamed the clearing for my mother, whose medicinal pouch would have something to help him. Blood trickled from where the dagger still lay lodged in his side, staining his beautiful caramel fur a deep red. My heart ached with a pain I never knew possible until today.

My hands brushed the soft fur between his antlers. "*Please don't leave me,*" I whispered. "*What will I do without you?*"

"*You will go on because this world needs your love. Dark times lie ahead and no matter the darkness that fills you, you will forever be the light in this world.*"

Tears streamed down my cheeks. I screamed for my mother, who shoved against the witches and warlocks blocking her way, the desperation clear on her face.

"*I'll always be with you, my friend,*" Alpheus said, his voice faint.

His almond eyes sparkled one last time before his breaths stopped—his body going still. A small sob wracked my chest before an anguished scream tore from somewhere deep inside me. The sounds of the battle grew dim as I sat in the deep sorrow that pulled me towards the darkness. My hands trembled as I pulled Alpheus's limp body onto my lap and buried my tear-stained face in the soft fur of his neck. Too much had been lost today and I didn't know how much more I could take.

My nails bit into the flesh of my hand as a wave of anger unlike anything I'd ever felt ripped through me. Pulling the dagger from Alpheus's side and carefully resting his body on the ground, I shot to my feet, eyes locked on Elias. Legs planted wide, he stood by the hole in the ash tree, nostrils flared.

"Pity about your little jackalope friend. Maybe now you'll see love for what it truly is... a weakness. How many more of your friends need to die for you to see that strength comes from the power one possesses?"

As if trying to prove a point, he summoned his magic and the air around the clearing whipped up into a gale-force wind. Fire brimmed his hands before unleashing and licking the underbrush to circle around us.

"Love might be my weakness, but it is also my greatest strength. It's what drives me, sustains me, and you will never understand because you are incapable of feeling anything other than envy and jealousy."

Elias's lips curled into a smirk. "Well, let us see how far your strength gets you."

Lunging forward, he closed the distance between us in a few angry strides.

I ducked out of the way as an identical dagger swiped at the air where my head had been mere moments ago. Elias slashed in ravenous fury as he tried to obtain a single drop of my blood. Vines slithered towards me, attempting to wrap me in their tight embrace.

Flames bloomed in my hand and I sent a line of fire over the space between us. Elias's earth magic recoiled from the flames before a burst of water extinguished them. I backed away just as my boot caught on something and sent me sprawling against the ground. Lorcan lay in a heap, blood trickling from a wound on his head. Bile tasted like acid at the back of my throat. With my attention elsewhere, Elias thrust the dagger downwards and a sharp pain radiated through my upper arm. I felt the warm trickle of blood coat my shirt, my chest constricting at what had just happened. Elias held the bloodied knife in front of me, dangling it just out of reach.

"You have lost, Braelyn," Elias said with a smirk, backing up towards the hole in the middle of the ash tree, my blood dripping into the dirt at his feet.

"Not yet," Theo shouted.

Vines shot like spears from the shadows of the Ironwood, entangling their way around Elias's wrists and throat, stopping him where he stood. Theo stepped out of the darkness as dense, sticky mud oozed around Elias's legs, holding him in place. Theo winked at me and a beaming smile split my face. He moved his hands in large flourishes and more vines snaked along the ground like giant serpents in search of prey.

Elias roared and struggled against his restraints. Theo stepped forward, a vein throbbing in his neck as he glared at the warlock responsible for his torture. His fingers retracted like claws and thorns burst from the vines wrapped around Elias's arms, sinking deep into his flesh. Elias grunted, each slice of his skin bringing a snarl to his thin lips. He tried to summon his magic, but the silvery marks feathering over his neck told me he was no longer strong enough. Verena walked up beside him, a pair of shackles hanging limply by her legs.

Elias locked eyes with me and I couldn't help but give him a satisfied smile.

Grey secured the iron around Elias's wrists and, with one last show of strength, Theo clenched his hand into a fist, smiling as the thorns sunk deeper. A vein pulsed in the side of Elias's neck, a hiss spitting from his lips.

My hands tingled violently as I reached out a beckoning hand towards not only the darkness but the light. I called on my spirit magic and she answered with fervour. The shadows around the Ironwood moved like weightless waves against the ground as each one answered the call of my magic. Combined with the power of the bloodstone, my spirit magic burst from my hand in a shower of golden light. It snaked through the shadows in a blinding display representing both sides of who I was. It was then I recalled what Alpheus had said once before.

"*It is amongst the darkness that light often shines the brightest.*"

A small smile touched my lips. In the darkest of moments, I had found who I really was. Despite all my attempts of trying to be a normal elemental witch, I'd finally embraced the fact that I wasn't.

Elias hesitated as the darkness around him twisted and curled into an army of shadow figures. The creatures stood at attention behind me as if waiting for my next command. Their golden eyes glowed like tiny suns in the darkness.

Somewhere to my left, one of King Elias's guards yelled out as they rushed towards my shadow army, their attention drifting from the battle at hand to the one about to erupt. The corner of my mouth pulled up in a malicious grin as I clenched my fists by my side.

"Impetum." The word came out as nothing more than a whisper, but my shadow monsters heard. *Attack.*

Swift like the shadows they were made from, they descended on Elias's men, their ebony forms colliding with the flesh of his minions as screams rained down around me. The creatures slashed at the guards, tearing limbs and sinking razor-sharp teeth into the necks of anyone I directed them towards.

Standing at the base of the ash tree, I watched as the shadowed figures dismembered each of Elias's followers. Many tried desperately to use their magic to destroy the creatures, but it had no effect, simply running through the shadow monsters and dissipating into nothing. A handful managed to escape the creatures' grasp, but the people of Ellesmere and the dwarves of the Ironwood Mountains were there to dispose of the remaining guards. As the shadows consumed the last of Elias's followers, they swarmed around me, sensing there was only one danger left. The remaining bhargest and monstrum leered at the golden-eyed creatures, talons and teeth at the ready.

"Consummare eos," I yelled to the shadows. *Finish them.*

For a moment, the shadows stilled around the clearing, frozen in time. Then, with the flick of my wrist, they slithered over the demonic creatures, consuming and chasing them into the darkest parts of the Ironwood.

Elias looked around the clearing, staring coldly at his dead army.

"You've failed, Elias," I said to him.

The people of Ellesmere crowded behind me, eyes turned to the disgraced king of the Ironwood. Magic still flickered about their fingers, everyone too nervous to let it dissipate.

They were right to be wary. The smirk pulling up the corner of Elias's mouth made my stomach feel like it was tied in hundreds of knots.

Stepping forward, I summoned a shimmering dagger in the palm of my hand.

"It's not over until I say, Miss Grey."

From between the twisting trunk of the ash tree, Morrigan stepped forward, muttering under her breath.

Fourty-Two

The blood drained from my face as Morrigan knelt by the ash tree, her hands pressed into the dirt where mine and Victoria's blood now seeped into the roots. It ran like tiny rivers towards the bark of the tree, reaching into the darkness within.

Elias laughed maniacally as dark, wispy shadows began to seep from between the trunks of the ash tree, the bark splintering as Morrigan called forth the nightmares from the underworld. Time stood still as everyone stared with wide eyes at the chaos unfolding before our eyes.

Coming to my senses, I gripped the golden dagger in my hands for what I hoped would be the last time, and charged forward, closing the small distance between us. The Kingdom of Ellesmere rallied behind me and surged forward, magic erupting in a display of brilliant intensity. My mother reached Morrigan before anyone else and, grabbing her by the back of her hair, she yanked the Wise Witch away from the ash tree. Morrigan clawed at the air, pulling against my mother's hold on her as she tried desperately to maintain her touch on the tree. The fissures in the bark began to close, the darkness spewing from them choked off.

Elias glared around, his nostrils flaring as he watched his world crash around him. With one last show of effort, he tried to call to his magic, but with the weight of iron about his wrists, he was rendered useless. The heels of his boot collided with a curving tree root and he tumbled backwards, hands scrambling at the dirt for the dagger he'd dropped earlier.

He wouldn't find it.

In his desperation to free himself from his shackles he hadn't seen Verena kick it away. Morrigan now battled against Maeve and my mother, their magics merging together to rain down icy daggers towards her. Morrigan managed to hold them off, still murmuring under her breath until the sharpened tip of a branch was thrust through her chest. Hazel glared at the Wise Witch's wide eyes, her bloodless skin turning ashen. She fell to the ground in a heap, her lifeblood seeping through her tightly knitted hands.

I switched my gaze back to Elias, finding him staring up at me. For the first time since our encounter at the Forest Festival over a month ago, genuine fear contorted his body. Elias ran his tongue over his dried lips, his shoulders stiffening as I stared down at him. Julien and Grey looped their hands under his shoulders and hauled him to his feet. Elias's gaze dropped to my hand, my fingers clenched tightly around a dagger made of light and shadow. The tendons in Elias's neck strained, his hands trembling as I stepped forward, the tip of my otherworldly blade pressed over his heart.

"Long live the king of nothing," I whispered before stabbing the blade into his chest.

Elias swayed on the spot, his eyes blinking rapidly. He cast one last glance behind him before I removed the blade, the tip soaked with warm, sticky blood.

Eventually, his knees gave out and he crumpled to the ground, eyes still locked onto the ash tree, even in death.

My hand hung limp by my side, the gilded shadows evaporating as I stared down at the warlock responsible for so much destruction.

My legs grew weak and, no longer able to support the weight of my body, they gave out under me. A sob tore through my chest, my lungs burning with the fevered cries tumbling from my mouth.

Julien and Theo came to my side, their faces hovering in front of me. Theo pulled me to him, his lanky arms wrapping around me, tightening as each sob threatened to tear me apart. I was vaguely aware of Julien shouting over his shoulder to someone, but I couldn't hear the sound over the pounding in my ears. Slowly, the pain and shock of the last few weeks began to ease and I closed my eyes, breathing in the soothing scent of lavender and rosemary.

A sense of peace settled over me, warming my skin and, despite the pain aching in my heart, I smiled. Eventually, my eyes fluttered open and the world came into brilliant focus. My mother sat before me, her arms gripping my hands tightly. I didn't know when Theo had taken his leave, but for now I was grateful for my mother's embrace. Her hazel eyes, so like mine, were brimmed with tears, each one falling silently down her cheeks. She let out a breathy laugh before pulling me to her chest.

Witches and warlocks bustled around me, some checking the fallen to see if any might still be alive. The dwarves gathered by the side of the ash tree, their faces solemn as they stood over their fallen comrades.

The metallic stench of blood washed over everything. I could taste it in the back of my throat, smell it in the air. My hands were sticky with it. I wiped my palms on the legs of my pants and, with Julien's help, I pushed to my feet. I walked around the clearing with Julien close by my side and a mixture of smiles and tear-stained faces staring back at me.

A group of elderly witches and warlocks sat together, their hands clasped over two witches who hadn't made it. Their soft cries made my heart ache. All around me, witches, warlocks and dwarves were in mourning. We may have defeated Elias and won this battle, but we had lost so much more.

"Miss Grey." King Vidar's kind voice pulled my attention from the grieving group.

He appeared mostly unharmed. A few cuts along his brow and scorch marks to his coat were the only signs he'd been in a battle.

"King Vidar, I'm so happy you're in one piece. Are the dwarves okay?" My voice echoed my worry. Glancing towards the opposite end of the clearing, I witnessed the dwarves laying out their dead, making sure their weapons were held firmly in their hands so they could reach Himmel—the place where deceased warriors reigned from above. Lorcan lay amongst the fallen, his forest-green eyes closed against the brightening sky. Tears tracked down my cheeks as a small sob wracked my body, threatening to tear me apart. My grief was too much to bear.

King Vidar followed my gaze, his shoulders drooping slightly. "We lost many great warriors today, but they will be honoured at the doors of Himmel." He bowed his head, and Julien and I followed suit. I hoped they would be welcomed to the halls of their fathers with open arms.

"You fought valiantly, Miss Grey," King Vidar said, his eyes watching me try to keep my emotions at bay. "You are always welcome in the Ironwood Mountains and should you ever need us, we will come."

With one last reassuring squeeze of my arm, he turned on his heel and strode back to where Riven watched us from the head of his kin. His armour was blood-spattered, and dirt covered most of his face, but he smiled kindly, inclining his head in my direction. Returning his smile, I watched them cradle their loved ones before they made their preparations to leave the ash tree clearing and return to their mountain.

"Are you okay?" Julien asked, his hand resting lightly on the small of my back.

"I don't know yet," I replied earnestly, silence wrapping around us once again.

We continued around the clearing, stopping by Victoria's body where my mother checked her wounds. She was beyond saving. I knelt by her side, resting my hand over hers as I stared into the face of the witch who was no longer my enemy. Victoria's belief in herself had finally won out in the end, and despite all the torment I'd been subject to by her hand, I shed a tear for the girl I couldn't save.

"I forgive you," I whispered. "And I hope you finally find your family."

Blood seeped into the centre of the ash tree, its magic now seemingly dormant. Aramis knelt by Morrigan's side, his face turned to the ash tree as he and Helene checked the void between the roots. Dozens of small cracks in the branches were the only evidence of the near catastrophic event.

"Brae," Theo said from behind me.

A set of lanky arms wrapped around my shoulders and I beamed at the faces of my friends. Theo's face transformed into a brilliant grin, the scar on his cheek puckering. His crystal eyes swam with tears as he pulled me to him once again, his arms trembling with each soft sob. I rubbed a gentle hand on his back, letting my own tears cascade down my cheeks. Verena and Grey stood a little way back, watching our reunion with soft smiles. Once Theo finally released me from his arms, I dashed over to them both and buried my face in their shoulders. They chuckled in unison. For the first time since finding out about the prophecy, my heart felt light, like the worst was finally behind us.

Elias still lay at the base of the ash tree, his eyes staring at the place where he'd thought his luck would change. Stepping towards him, I pulled the circulum from his finger and placed it safely in my pocket, unsure what would become of it. And without a backward glance, I retreated to the path that would lead me home.

Epilogue

T hree days had passed since the battle at the clearing and life was slowly beginning to return to a new kind of normal. Funerals were held in the sacred garden for the countless number of witches and warlocks lost in the battle. Dressed in our black finery, the kingdom watched tearfully as our brave elemental wielders were cocooned beneath the twisting bark of the giant yew tree. A silver coin was placed beneath their fingers to pay the gatekeeper to reach Altera Vita. A witch or warlock's next life. Despite their traitorous crimes, Victoria, Sebastien and Elias were placed beneath the tree, too. The elders were too superstitious to leave their bodies amongst the Ironwood, so it would be up to the gatekeeper to accept them into their next life or condemn them to the Underworld. Perhaps Elias would even be reunited with Lilith as he so desperately wanted.

Julien, Theo, Grey, Verena and I had a small ceremony in one of the gardens to honour Alpheus's brave sacrifice. My heart still ached at his loss, my mind often reaching out to hear his lilting voice before remembering what happened. We placed him beneath a beautiful white rose bush overlooking the sprawling gardens. A place we all could visit often.

As the Samhain Festival drew closer, signalling the end of autumn and the beginning of the winter solstice, the elders had deemed me ready to be crowned queen of Ellesmere. Despite their frustration at my disobeying their orders to rescue Theo, they had seen the bravery I'd displayed at the ash tree clearing.

Since returning to the castle, I'd attended all my lessons with increased interest. So long as I continued to learn everything to know about my newfound ability to wield both dark and light magic—as well as the bloodstone's continued effect—the elders believed it was my time to take the throne.

To my delight, Maeve had opted to stay in Ellesmere to help prepare me for my crowning day. My mother was overjoyed by her plans to make Ellesmere her permanent home once again, but instead of remaining in the castle with the rest of us, Maeve insisted on staying with Hazel—wanting to learn more about becoming a Wise Witch.

My mother had become increasingly over-protective since our return to the castle, but despite her constantly hovering about, it was nice having her close by.

Verena and Grey would stay at the castle as my magic advisors, while Theo had decided to help my mother in the apothecary. She'd taken him under her wing and, by her accounts, he was proving to be an extremely talented healer.

Since returning from the clearing, not unlike my mother, Julien never strayed far from my side. We spent our days out in the gardens, strolling through the fields hand in hand and enjoying the last of the long days. With the arrival of Samhain, the days would grow shorter and even colder, bringing with them the lead up to my ascension.

One blistery day, Julien and I sat at the edge of the training area, steaming cups of apple cider clutched between our hands. We stared out at the hills below, our legs covered by a large woollen blanket Mrs Boswell had knitted for me. My mind drifted to the battle at the ash tree, recalling different memories I had tried desperately to forget. Since returning to Ellesmere, my dreams were constantly plagued with nightmares of the monsters in the Ironwood. My waking mind would sift through the events of the battle, believing that we'd missed something crucial and that Lilith had, in fact, been resurrected. I confessed my fears to Helene, who had told me it was normal to feel this way, but as time passed, I would heal. And the nightmares I faced at the end of each day would become nothing but fleeting memories.

"Is there something on your mind, sweetheart?" Julien's voice pierced my thoughts, bringing me back to the present.

Turning away from the scenic view, I tried to give him a reassuring smile, but his dark eyes saw right through my lie. I let a small sigh escape my chilled lips before revealing what I'd been thinking about.

"I understand," he whispered back. "Each night I close my eyes and Sebastien's face stares at me from the darkness. He taunts me still, even in death."

The wool was soft beneath my fingers, and placing my mug on the ground beside me, I laced them through Julien's, relishing in the warmth his hand provided. I recalled the look on his face the moment he pierced Sebastien's heart. Despite the hatred that fuelled their relationship, Julien had suffered greatly since the loss of his brother.

"What did he say to you?" I asked quietly. "I saw him murmur something in your ear when he fell."

Julien let out a deep sigh, his gaze turning back to the rolling hills below us. Snow dotted the mountains beyond as the leafless branches of the oak trees creaked in the cool wind. I watched his lips curve up in a sad smile, but his eyes remained distant.

He said, "*Pro sanguine et gloria*. In the language of old it means for blood and glory. It was something my father used to tell us as children." He shook his head, his eyes downcast. "Even before death he believed in my family's ridiculous values."

I shuffled closer to him, my leg brushing his as I placed a gentle hand on his cheek, turning his face towards me. Those dark eyes finally met mine and in them I saw nothing but sorrow for the family he despised, but mourned nonetheless.

"What are you going to do now?" I asked, my hand coming to rest in my lap.

I watched his face carefully, but he gave nothing away. I didn't know what I would do if he chose to no longer remain at the castle. Julien's home was in the Ironwood Village. He had his apothecary to run and with Theo back home, he was no longer bound to remain by my side. A deep chuckle reverberated through his chest, and I couldn't help but smile at the sound. It was intoxicating.

"I don't know," he replied. "For so long I've thought of nothing else but Theo's rescue and Elias's demise." He ran a hand through his hair before his gaze settled on my face, a lopsided smile pulling up the corner of his mouth. "I suppose I should stay here for the time being as I believe there's a new queen to be crowned."

Julien leant forward and placed a soft kiss on my forehead. He wrapped an arm around my shoulders, pulling me to his side as I nestled in close, my heart swelling at his decision.

The days ticked by and, laying amongst the soft sheets of my bed one night, I watched the last full moon of Samhain inch its way higher into the sky. The same day Lilith was said to be summoned from the Underworld.

Before leaving the clearing, the elders had inspected the blood magic tied to the ash tree. It appeared when Hazel had slain Morrigan, her summoning spell hadn't been completed. But, erring on the side of caution, they had warded the tree with a rune of protection.

Despite their numerous reassurances, unease still quivered in my stomach. With sleep eluding me, I sat up against my pillows and pulled Althea's journal from the drawer beside my bed. When the elders learned of The Book of Lilith, they had taken it upon themselves to lock it—along with the circulum—in the castle archives. A room only each of them held a key to.

They'd told me it would be the safest place until they decided what would be done with the magical relics. I focused back on Althea's book and turned through the pages, my fingers prickling with magic. I read the text slowly, hoping the flowing words would bring about the sleep I so desperately needed.

Just as my eyes grew heavy with exhaustion, something dark flickered by the open window. Sitting up straight, I stared at the place the shadow had been, waiting for whatever lingered in the darkness to come crawling out. There was nothing.

A trick of the light, perhaps.

But my eyes still combed the darkness, no longer tired. I pulled at the cotton sheet, twisting it over in my fingers. My heart hammered in my chest and, with a quick intake of breath, I clicked my fingers together, summoning a flame. As the warm tendrils of my fire magic reached the edges of the room, a tall figure stepped from the lingering shadows. Fear froze the scream building in my throat. With my hand still held aloft, the flame illuminated the blood-red sigil drawn on the woman's forehead.

The witch's eye.

Lilith cocked her head to the side, her ruby eyes locked onto mine. She leaned forward, her face contorted into a cruel smile as the world around me seemed to freeze.

"You failed, Braelyn. The queen of darkness has risen."

Acknowledgements

As I sit here trying to write this acknowledgment, there are no words strong enough to say just how grateful I am to the many amazing people who have supported me over the last eighteen months. I have been inspired, encouraged, guided and sustained by so many incredible souls that the tears are rolling down my cheeks as I write this.

To my readers, thank you! Without your love, devotion and excitement for Braelyn and the world of Ellesmere, The King of the Ironwood would never have been possible. You are the driving force behind my words, and I hope you know just how much your support means to me. Without you, this story would cease to exist, so from the bottom of my heart, thank you for loving my books as much as I do.

To my incredible beta readers, Shannon and Steph, thank you for your invaluable feedback. Without you, I couldn't have gotten The King of the Ironwood to a final draft. Your guidance and encouraging words helped push me through writer's block and imposter syndrome and gave me the courage to finish my book.

To my amazing editor Chloe Hodge, you are my saving grace. Thank you for all the writing sprints and advice, wise words of encouragement, and friendship. I couldn't have done this without you.

To all the people who made this book as beautiful as it is: Tess Pollard, Sara Oliver and Susanna Kanto. Your design skills are impeccable, and I will be forever grateful for your beautiful art, which has transformed my manuscript into something made of pure magic.

About the Author

Born in Sydney, Kirsty grew up writing from a young age. Ever the dreamer, she was forever writing creative short stories and could always be found with her nose in a book. Always day-dreaming about one day writing a book of her own, she fulfilled her publishing dream with her debut novel The Witch of Ellesmere.

Still living in Sydney with her husband and mini-lop bunny, Winston, she is a lover of tea, books, and all things magical. When not writing, Kirsty can be found sipping on copious amounts of tea and snuggled up with a good book. If the weather is nice, you may also find her outside in the garden tending to her many plant babies.

www.ingramcontent.com/pod-product-compliance
Lightning Source LLC
Chambersburg PA
CBHW030530120726
47904CB00005B/1703

* 9 7 8 0 6 4 5 1 6 7 8 1 8 *